ALSO BY B. CELESTE

Underneath the Sycamore Tree

Lindon U
Dare You to Hate Me
Beg You to Trust Me

BEG YOU TO TRUST ME

B CELESTE

Bloom books

Sourcebooks and the colophon are registered trademarks of
Sourcebooks. Bloom Books is a trademark of Sourcebooks.

Published by Bloom Books, an imprint of Sourcebooks
P.O. Box 4410, Naperville, Illinois 60567-4410
(630) 961-3900
sourcebooks.com

Originally self-published in 2022 by B. Celeste.

Cataloging-in-Publication Data is on file with the Library of Congress.

Printed and bound in the United States of America.
VP 10 9 8 7 6 5 4 3 2

To my real life "Olive" for saving my freshman year of college. Love you, Frupple.

PLAYLIST

"Bad Liar"—Imagine Dragons

"Delicate"—Taylor Swift

"Breakaway"—Kelly Clarkson

"Just a Kiss"—Lady Antebellum

"Heavy"—Linkin Park ft. Kiiara

"Come Over"—Sam Smith

"Mercy"—Brett Young

"Praying"—Kesha

"Skyscraper"—Demi Lovato

"Look at Her Now"—Selena Gomez

TRIGGER WARNING

This book deals with bullying, harassment, and heavy topics such as assault on college campus.

Chapter One

SKYLAR

BAD DECISIONS TASTE LIKE rum, coke, and something metallic. A taste that reminds me of the time my older sisters dared me to see how many quarters I could fit into my mouth at once.

With fluttering eyelids and heavy limbs, I come to with a dry mouth and cloudy head, finding it hard to move in the soft sheets covering my chilled body. Sheets that don't feel as soft as the expensive, certified-organic cotton threads covering the twin mattress in my room.

The bed under my leaden limbs feels too lumpy, nothing like the thick, foam pad covering the school-supplied mattress on my raised frame.

One of my sticky eyelids peels open in confusion, vision blurry but able to take in the unfamiliar setup of the room. It's bigger and colder than the double I share with my freshman roommate Rebecca, and the furniture is nothing like the stuff I have.

It takes a few seconds, but I quickly realize the reality

of the situation. Bolting upright, I careen to the side when dizziness slams into me. The black sheet falls down my body, exposing the untied, wrinkled purple wrap shirt I borrowed from my friend Aliyah that's exposing the peach bra I'd slipped on underneath. I suck in a sharp breath when my eyes go to the empty spot beside me, then slowly to the side, where I see what's thrown onto the carpet.

Time stops.

Panic seeps into my rib cage.

I lift the sheet and shakily lower it once I see the naked skin it's covering, then glance back at the black leggings and panties in the middle of the floor. They're the only things I'd worn that were mine. The shirt, shoes, and new pushup bra were all from the girls I befriended who insisted I needed to dress up for the party they were dragging me to.

You'll have fun.

We won't let you out of our sight.

My recollection of the events beyond letting them play with my stubborn, black-dyed hair and telling me what makeup would look best on my tan skin is fuzzy.

Too fuzzy to put together how I got in a room I don't recognize with my pants off.

Doing a quick scan to double-check that I'm alone, I toss my legs over the side of the bed and wince at the ache between them. I bolt toward my clothing, worried someone will bust in. Tugging the panties up my legs, I stop when I glance down and see the small smears of blood on the insides of my thighs.

I stare.

Not breathing.

Not blinking.

Thud, thud, thud. The drumming between my head and

2

heart is in sync, demanding my attention as I stare at the red smattering my skin.

A moment or two later, I force myself to finish getting dressed with shaky hands.

Pressing an ear against the wooden door to see if I hear anyone outside it, I quietly turn the knob and creep out of the room with my borrowed black heels tucked in my hands and my heart lodged in the back of my throat.

I cringe at each creak of the floorboards under my bare feet as I tiptoe down the narrow hallway toward the wooden staircase. I don't know what time it is because my phone is dead, but the sun is out and blinding me, making the headache throbbing inside my temples ten times worse.

As I creep down the steps and toward the front door, I notice that there's no remnants of a party left. No plastic cups lying around, no food on the carpet, no weird boozy smells that I vaguely remember from the night before. The bits I do recall consist of a packed house that made me feel claustrophobic, loud music that made it impossible to hear what my friends were saying as I followed them into the mass of bodies, and the scent of cheap beer.

I'm almost to the door when I freeze midstep after hearing, "Who the hell are you?"

My body locks up from the deep voice behind me. I don't recognize it, not that that says much. I'm not familiar with most men around here, since my small circle of peers is made up of my roommate Rebecca and a few other girls—Deanna and Aliyah—I met during orientation a month before.

Footsteps come from somewhere else, stopping close by. A second voice, less deep and more amused, says, "Huh. I thought everyone did their walks of shame already. Sorry, big man."

I make myself look over my shoulder, but I don't know why. I'm met with two different faces. One boyish and clearly amused, if the mischievous glint in his blue eyes is any indication, and the other full of...nothing. No emotion. Nothing readable. The shorter of the two—though not by much—grins at me before scoping out my body in a once-over that makes me want to make a break for it.

If I were smart, I wouldn't let them stare and leer. The shorter one cocks his head until his messy blond hair flops over his forehead and lips kick up. He elbows his friend, who looks massive and far less enthused by my presence in comparison.

Both are built like athletes. Strong. Broad. Like they could take down another person their size or larger if they wanted to. Deanna said the party was at the football house.

We won't let you out of our sight is what Dee promised me.

How did I get separated from them?

"We didn't know anyone else was here," the taller, stoic-looking one tells me. His lips press into a firm line as he watches me, eyes narrowing. Accusatory.

I'm uncomfortable.

Hungover.

Confused.

It doesn't take much to figure out what exactly happened last night, and it makes me feel itchy. Dirty. My mouth feels dry as cotton, and I just want to go back to the dorms and take a long, hot shower.

We won't let you out of our sight.

But where are they now?

I swallow, stuttering through the nerves rising up my throat. "I–I..."

Unable to form proper words, I shake my head and dart

toward the door. I don't know where I'm going since it was dark out when we drove here, but I don't stop or look back either.

I walk fast, following the sidewalk and feeling the hot sun heating the pavement and burning my feet. I only get a few feet away before having to stop and empty the contents of my stomach into a bush.

When I stand up, I blink a few times to ward off the tears glazing my eyes, brush off my mouth with the back of my hand, and accept what happened last night.

I, Skylar Vivian Allen, lost my virginity at a party I didn't even want to go to. To a man I don't know. In a house I don't know.

Where my friends left me.

Freshman year at Lindon University is *not* off to a good start.

Chapter Two

SKYLAR

Three weeks later

THE WATER POOLING IN the bathroom sink is dark purple and giving me a headache from the strong smell invading my nostrils.

"You should have let a professional do this," Rebecca, or Becca as she prefers being called, grumbles, picking up the cheap box dye I got from the corner store down the street from campus when she, Dee, and I went for a walk yesterday.

I met Becca on the incoming freshmen Facebook page for Lindon U. It was a group meant to help us make introductions and friends, and I'd boldly asked after a few conversations if the volunteer firefighter studying to be a doctor wanted to room together. I'd thought at the time it'd be better than random selection, but clearly I was wrong.

She puts it back down on the wet countertop. "Now the whole suite smells."

I hadn't thought about that when I started applying it. The five other girls who live here, mostly upperclassmen, have been gone since this morning, including Becca until ten minutes ago when she walked in and started gagging.

"Sorry," I say under the running water, squeezing out my thick strands of hair and examining my palm to see how much dye is left.

She mumbles something under her breath before grabbing one of my towels and setting it beside me by the sink. "I thought you were going back to blond."

She and Dee had been too busy flirting with the boy behind the counter at the store to notice what he was ringing up for me.

I try talking as the dirty water runs down my face, some of it making me sputter as it gets in my mouth when I answer her. "I decided on this instead."

This is supposed to be Coca-Cola brown since the black in my hair started fading to a mahogany purple a couple weeks ago. Becca had commented on my roots more than once and suggested on finding a salon in Bridgeport to take care of it, but I hadn't decided on what color to do next.

And deciding things, no matter how mundane, has become important to me.

After all, every choice you make is what makes you who you are as a person. And it's not just the decisions you're making that shape you but the consequences that come with them.

In my short time at Lindon, I've made a handful of choices that I can't take back. Ones that I have no other option but to live with or else I'd end up letting them consume me—drowning me in murky water like the dyed liquid inches from my face.

This color choice will set me further apart from the blond bombshells I left behind in California. Even if I can't live in my sisters' shadows from the other side of the country, I still feel the need to prove I'm my own person.

All the children of Brenda and Thomas Allen are beautiful. Me included, I guess. All-American. Blond hair, blue eyes, and tan skin. Except all my sisters have blond hair that's a little lighter than mine, blue eyes slightly darker, and bodies a tiny bit leaner. I was a late bloomer, not getting the C-cup breasts that ran in the family until seventeen, and I didn't have a growth spurt to the five seven I am now until later that year.

Thankfully, the baby fat on my face evened out and my body became way more proportional. I've never been embarrassed to buy a size ten when I'm shopping. Not fitting that mold always made me stand out. Especially since I started dyeing my hair and wearing clothes that hugged my curvy figure.

Becca hasn't helped make the transition from California to New York any easier with her unsolicited advice and suggestions on how I should live my life here. Even after I gave her the cold shoulder for ditching me at the football house, she still has something to say about what I do or don't do or how I dress or what I eat.

She thinks I'm too quiet.

Too clingy.

Too introverted.

I went from constantly feeling judged over what I did at home to feeling it tenfold here because of the girl I room with.

Not once did she bother asking me about the party. Instead, she brushed me off like I was ridiculous for bringing it up in the first place.

After realizing that the anger bubbling deep in my veins would get me nowhere, I forced myself to let it go.

For now.

Another decision I made for myself.

The thing is, you think you're ready to handle your life when you turn eighteen. You get to choose what happens after being passed your diploma.

High school never prepares you for reality though. It never gets you ready for the repercussions of the domino effect that will inevitably take place.

And there will always be one.

No matter the scale.

That night at the party was mine.

Because I didn't say no.

But I can't remember if I said yes either...

~

I scan the Latte Lounge for the group of girls I was supposed to meet ten minutes ago. Class ran over thanks to my eccentric professor who enjoys ripping apart Jane Austen a little too much. The new coffee establishment on campus is the farthest building across from where I've spent the last hour.

Thankfully, Lindon U isn't a large campus. The residential dormitories, dining hall, and student center are on one side of the only road that cuts through campus, and the academic buildings, library, and coffee shop are on the other. All the buildings are older and rustic, and there's pretty, spacious landscape and newly updated paved walkways that make my home away from home for the next nine months seem cozy.

I don't see the girls who insisted on coming here and trying the low-calorie fruit smoothies since they're determined not to gain the freshman fifteen. I may have been worried after the horror stories told to us at orientation, but

I don't obsess over cutting carbs or using the campus gym almost every day like they do. I'd only gone with them a few times before realizing that walking around campus is good enough for me, especially since I seem to chase after them so much.

I'm about to grab my phone when I see a bright orange backpack resting on one of the tables in the far corner. I know it's covered in *Supernatural* and *Doctor Who* pins. It was the neon color and choice of decor that made me walk up to the owner and say hi after our first Intro to Communication class.

"Hey," I greet Olive Henderson, another communications major.

The day we exchanged names, I'd been prepared to say, "Yes, Skylar is a boy's name" until she told me, "I'm Olive, like what they put in vodka martinis, which my parents obviously drank too much of before deciding on my name."

I liked her instantly after that.

"Hey, Sky," she says, smiling with her signature pink lips. She's a makeup connoisseur and always wearing something no matter where we are. Usually something contoured to perfection with bright lipstick and eyeshadow. I thought I was decent at my makeup skills until meeting her, but she's already shown me way more in my time here than my three older sisters have over the course of my life.

"Have you seen Becca and the others?" I do another scan of the bodies, not sure if I'm disappointed or relieved they left already.

Olive brushes some of her light-brown hair, chopped in a cute, stylish short bob, behind her ear. When I was thirteen, I'd asked Mom if I could cut my hair in a similar style, but she'd nearly had a heart attack, telling me my hair was my "best feature" and I couldn't cut it above my shoulders because I didn't have the face for it. It wasn't like any of the Allen women were ugly, whatever standard that was measured by, but I definitely fit the tomboy aesthetic more than my siblings, and I think it worried Mom for the sake of the image she wanted me to fit.

"They left, like, five minutes ago," Olive tells me, her green eyes sympathetic. Anyone who's around me and Becca can sense the tension. It's the elephant in the room that we both seem to ignore. "I'm not sure where they went. They all got a nasty-looking green smoothie before leaving."

Something resembling relief lightens the tightness in my chest as I glance at the door. Everyone I know says their roommate is their first friend at college, which is the only reason I keep holding on to hope that Becca and I can at least try to get along. But with every passing day comes a new challenge, and I keep wondering why I bother.

Fidgeting for a second as I look over my shoulder at the people waiting in front of the register, I pull out the chair across from Olive and drop into it. "Can I ask for a favor?"

My voice is sheepish, but it doesn't change the way her smile goes right to her sea-green eyes that I'm slightly envious of. Not only does she have a kick-ass personality, great taste in television shows and makeup, but she's uniquely herself. Strong-willed. Confident. Out of our small friend group here, we're the curvier girls with a love of swear words, daring hair choices, and sugar. "Of course, girl."

Nibbling the inside of my cheek, I wring my hands in my lap and let loose a quiet sigh. "I was wondering if you could drive me to the health clinic over in Bridgeport. You're the only person I know with a car, so I figured I'd see if you were free. But if you're not, I can look at the bus schedule and figure out when to go."

"I'll totally take you! Are you okay?" Her eyes scan over my face. "You do look a little pale. Did you catch that bug going around? My mom keeps texting me every day, reminding me to wash my hands and sanitize."

Shifting in my seat, I lift a shoulder and try not thinking of the discomfort I've been feeling in areas I know aren't normal. I don't want to tell her that though. "I just don't... feel too hot. And the campus clinic probably can't give out any prescriptions if I need some, so I thought it'd be better to go right to the clinic instead."

She nods. "Good thinking. When do you want to go? I'm free all afternoon. My last class starts in twenty minutes and ends at three."

"You really don't mind?"

Her head shakes. "You'd know if I minded. Trust me."

I can't help but smile, even though I'm dreading what's to come. I've been putting it off for a week now, but it's time. Long overdue, based on my many late-night Google searches once I'm bathed in blackness and there's nothing but Becca's even breathing coming from across our room.

"You're the best." I let out a heavy breath and sink into my chair. "So how have classes been?"

We spend the next ten minutes venting about professors, homework, and other students until we have to part ways. It isn't until I'm walking back to my dorm after making plans with Olive on where and when to meet that I let the possibility of what I'll be told sink in.

Maybe Mom was right. I shouldn't have turned down my full ride to Penn State or any of the Ivy League schools I was accepted to. Because then I wouldn't be in this situation, sweating through my shirt and feeling like I'm going to vomit.

When I walk into the dorm room, I instantly find Becca scowling from where she's perched on the bed.

"Tyler came by *again*," she informs me, pushing the laptop from where it's perched on her lap. I can tell she's irritated by the boy I met in class, not that I understand why. He's nice enough, even if he's a little clingy. "This is the third time he's dropped in. It's getting annoying, Skylar. This is my space too."

She doesn't explain why she didn't wait up for me at the lounge as she grabs her smoothie from her desk and takes a long sip like she's rubbing it in.

Then again, I don't ask her the reason.

Our "friendship" seems to be strictly need-to-know.

And maybe I shouldn't be okay with that, but I'm learning to be. Because at some point, the things bubbling deep inside me will boil over, and I have a feeling Becca will be the first casualty if my sanity isn't.

"I'll deal with it," I tell her.

She grumbles something about me and guys, making my skin crawl with faraway memories.

I don't let myself think about them for too long.

Chapter Three

SKYLAR

My entire body is on fire as the nurse takes my vitals and then sits behind the computer attached to the wall and begins asking me questions.

"When was the date of your last period?"

I squirm on the cushioned table, listening to the paper crinkle under my butt. "Um, two weeks ago. I don't remember the exact date."

The dark-haired woman presses her lips together before glancing at the calendar on the wall and typing something in.

"So what brings you in today?"

This is where the words get jammed in my mouth, twisting around my tongue and trying to slide back down my throat. "Er…" Sweat dots my forehead as the woman looks from the computer screen to me, her plucked eyebrows drawn up. My hands clasp together tightly in my lap until my knuckles turn white. "I—I think I may have a UTI…or something." The last part is choked.

"Or something?" she repeats, voice monotone as one of those eyebrows arches higher on her forehead.

I swallow past the huge lump of embarrassment in my throat. "I've had UTIs before. This doesn't feel like that. It's different."

Deep down—deep, *deep* down—I know what it is. I know it isn't a UTI. I know that the symptoms are similar but nothing like what I've been experiencing for the past week.

The nurse types something in the computer and asks, "Are you sexually active?"

"No!" The high-pitched tone of my voice makes even me cringe as I pinch my eyes closed and feel the heat creep up the back of my neck and settle in my cheeks. "I mean, I wouldn't call myself *active*. It was one time. Once. That's all."

God, this is humiliating.

"Did you use protection?" is her next question as her nimble fingers fly across the keyboard.

I blink. "I'm on birth control."

"Birth control doesn't prevent you from catching STDs though. Did your partner use a condom?"

It's hard to breathe.

Deep breath in, deep breath out.

In, out. Repeat.

Those meditation classes my sister Serena made me take with her a few times back in Cali paid off. It's a solid ten seconds before my eyes trail down to the floor. "I don't know."

Not even the clicking keyboard greets me, which is the only reason I look back up. The nurse is studying me, eyes narrow as she takes me in. I don't know what she's thinking and probably don't want to.

Eventually, she continues her questioning. "Can you list your symptoms, please?"

The *please* surprises me, even if it's not delivered in the soft comfort I need right now. But I do as she asks, flinching as I list the burning, pain, and discharge. All the dirty, ugly details that make me feel…ashamed.

Guilty.

Tainted.

Ever since I noticed something was wrong, I tried patching together the night of the party. I vaguely remember following someone upstairs and feeling hands on my body and lips on mine once a door clicked closed behind us. I remember liking the way he kissed and the way he traced my curves like he was worshipping them. But everything that came after? Nothing.

I've searched for the two-letter word I could've said to avoid being here right now.

No.

But I come up blank every single time.

Once the woman collects everything she needs, she opens a cabinet and passes me a paper-thin green gown. "The doctor is going to want to do a physical examination. Before you change into the gown, head across the hall and pee into this cup"—she passes me a plastic cup with an orange lid and some sort of sticker with information on the front—"so we can collect a urine sample. Put it on the back of the toilet and I'll grab it. Once you're changed, gown open in the back, Dr. Patterson will do an examination, collect some labs, and you'll be set to go."

She says it so quickly, so routinely, that I can't help but wonder how many times she's gone through this. Lindon's campus clinic lists this one as its main recommended clinic to see outside the university, which means everyone who works here probably gets an earful from the students who come seeking help.

Forty-five minutes later, I'm back in my favorite baggy destroyed jeans that are getting loose around the waist and my new college sweatshirt that matches the one Becca bought with the school's red dragon stitched across the front, and I'm walking out of the room with a prescription in my hand.

A prescription for antibiotics that will help get rid of the problem.

The problem seemed quickly detectable, according to the white-haired doctor with a far kinder smile than her nurse. She was 99 percent positive it was chlamydia based on my symptoms and examination. I was supposed to get official confirmation via a phone call in a matter of days when the labs came in, but she didn't want me to wait to start treatment. And as if the diagnosis wasn't bad enough, I got the safe sex talk and was told that I'd need to talk to anyone I was sexually active with to let them know I'd tested positive.

And that causes even more problems.

Obvious problems.

Ones that I didn't voice to the doctor, who was being comforting instead of judgmental. If I told her I didn't remember who I had sex with, that I wouldn't be able tell him this vital information, she might have changed her tune. Maybe even looked at me with the same unimpressed gaze her employee did. So I kept my lips shut and simply nodded.

It isn't until Olive and I walk out to where her car is parked that she asks, "Are you okay?"

I hold back my tears as we climb in the car and buckle our seat belts before plastering a fake smile on my face like I was trained to do growing up.

Save face, Skylar, Mom would tell me.

"Yeah." I don't recognize my hoarse voice as my leg starts bouncing with anxiety.

My phone goes off in my hand, causing my eyes to go down to the screen.

Tyler: You free tonight?

I ignore the text, feeling only slightly bad for the boy with pretty brown skin and prettier gemlike greenish-blue eyes. We met in class weeks ago, hung out a few times to go over homework together, and text on occasion.

He flirts with me like he flirts with everyone—it's second nature to him. So I never take it to heart when he finds a way to brush our hands or legs together when we're sitting beside each other or when he comments on how pretty he thinks my outfits look on me.

He's a guy.

A guy who I'm positive didn't sleep with me, because something tells me if he did, he wouldn't be that interested in charming me into taking my pants off a second time. I may not be experienced, but I know his type. Love them and leave them, as my sisters would say.

Stay away from those ones, Sienna would tell me, making Serena—her twin—laugh, since we all know Sienna never follows her own advice.

Olive drives us to the closest pharmacy so I can get my medicine, then looks at me when she stops at a red light. John Mayer croons softly from her speakers as she studies my tense face, glances down at the white plastic bag of random things I bought while waiting for my prescription to be filled, and taps her fingers against the steering wheel.

"You know what always makes me feel better?" she asks chipperly, gratefully ignoring the internal meltdown I'm having as my eyes glaze with oncoming tears. "McDonald's."

That's how we find ourselves bringing back two bags of greasy food to campus. Food that my parents would probably scold me for indulging in if they knew.

Then again, it'd be the last thing on their minds if they knew why my friend was trying to cheer me up in the first place.

I just hope they never find out.

Eventually, I text Tyler back.

Me: No

Chapter Four

SKYLAR

My FAMILY COMES FROM new money, which is why all my siblings were able to get into the colleges they wanted without any financial burden. Unlike my sisters, who chose various prestigious schools like Stanford and Yale, I chose Lindon U, a school clear across the country from my entire family and the pretentious people they surround themselves with. I don't know what my parents were like before their bank account was heavily padded thanks to Dad's business-savvy investments, but the people I grew up with cared way too deeply about appearance. It was all about the looks— how big the house was, how we dressed, and how we acted in public. That life has never been for me.

Still, my parents tried to do everything to get me to change my mind about coming here for college. They accepted my decision and paid for it in full despite their hesitation though. I had to promise to be on my best behavior, which had made me roll my eyes. I'm not the child who got too many parking tickets and ended up getting my car towed and impounded or the one who got so drunk that I was arrested for public indecency.

But I *am* the one who went to my first ever college party, drank when my roommate kept putting cups of gross, warm alcohol in my hand, and then woke up alone in a strange room without my pants on and a sexually transmitted disease.

The things my sisters did only required a little extra ass-kissing and a lot more batted lashes before my father was wrapped around their fingers again. If he ever found out what I did, he probably wouldn't be able to look me in the eye. I can barely look at my reflection without staring at my lips and wondering whose I let touch them or studying my body and trying to pinpoint the second I'd made up my mind about who I let touch it that night.

"Dude." The sound of my roommate's voice stirs me from the textbook I've been staring at absentmindedly for the past who knows how long. I've read the same paragraph at least four times without soaking up any of the information, so I close it and turn to Becca as she eyes me in exasperation. "What's your deal?"

My deal. It's sort of an amusing question in a sad way. *My deal* is that my roommate and I have nothing in common. She's six feet tall with fiery red hair and a killer confident attitude that I've respected from the start. She owns her height and her body and her life like I haven't been able to manage so far. She came here on a full ride to study biology and wants to move on to medical school after she gets her bachelor's. From day one, she's known what she wants and plans on doing everything in her power to achieve her goals.

It was my choice to tag along to the party at the football house, hoping she'd like me better, just like it was my decision to go to a second party with them a week later. I refused to let my first experience scare me away from having a social life and fitting in. I'd wanted to impress my new friends.

But I'd lasted only ten minutes before the constant brushing of bodies against mine had me bolting from the cramped house.

Tyler had found me ditching and walked me back to my dorm, convincing me to watch a movie with him since my suite was empty. Becca had found us asleep on the couch in the common room and told me I needed to let her know when guys were sleeping over, as if she'd found us in some sort of compromising position.

"You're doing it again," she says, running a brush through her hair. She converted her desk into a makeshift makeup table, even bringing her own mirror to perch on the top of it. She and Olive bonded a few times over the brands of makeup displayed there, but they lost me after talking about the best application techniques.

I stand up and stretch my stiff muscles before sitting on the edge of my bed. We tried matching our room in a purple-and-teal color scheme, though my stuff was definitely pricier thanks to the catalog Mom made me pick things from. I'll admit, my bed is ten times more comfortable than Becca's. The first week of school, we watched *Once Upon a Time* together on her twin mattress after she found out I'd never seen it. While I normally didn't care about material things with a higher price tag, I was glad Mom was insistent on the memory foam pad and bedding set, because I slept like a baby most nights.

At least until the football party.

Now, Becca gives me more flak than ever because I annoy her with my restlessness. Once, she told me to sleep on the couch that we share with the other girls. The suite we have is nice, split into four different rooms plus a bathroom, and on the first floor near the main doors, laundry room, and vending machines. But it's also loud, crowded, and usually uncomfortable for me when everybody is here. I've never made friends very easily, and the other girls intimidate me more than my roommate does. They remind me of my sisters and their friends, all confident women who love watching reality TV at night and gossiping about guys.

Once upon a time, I would have chipped in on the guy conversation, but I haven't been able to talk about anyone in that capacity since I wandered back on campus the morning that I woke up in that room. They've asked about Tyler since he's been around, but I never change my answer. *He's in one of my classes and we hang out.*

Becca always rolls her eyes at that, obviously not seeing the distance I put between Tyler and I even when we are around each other. Gone are the days of flirty touches. No matter if we're in our room, the library, or somewhere else, I always find a way to put something between us so he doesn't see the way my body locks up.

The morning I'd walked back to campus from the football house, a few of my suitemates got one look of me closing the suite door and congratulated me on my first walk of shame like I should wear it like a medal.

I'd simply grabbed a fresh pair of clothes as quietly as possible, because Becca was still sleeping, and took a forty-minute shower that consisted of me trying to keep my sobs quiet until the water ran cold.

It hasn't been easy keeping the events of that night at bay, but Becca hasn't exactly made me feel like I could talk to her about it. And the more time passes, the less I want to speak on it anyway. The night after the party, I lashed out at her for telling me the details of her latest boy obsession. I didn't care about how cute he was or how many times he looked at her during their class. And I definitely didn't want to hear about her intention of hooking up with him.

She called me a bitch.

I flipped her off.

The tension between us grew.

Hefting a sigh and forcing myself to forget about all that for now, I ask, "Do you want to go to Huden Dining Hall with me for dinner?"

She pauses from applying eyeliner in the mirror to look at me. "I was planning on going into town with the girls to grab something to eat at the diner. Dee mentioned the bakery across the street being pretty good too, so we might stop there." Her focus goes back to her makeup, carefully applying the black liner under her lashes before sighing. "Did you want to come with us?"

It's an afterthought, a pity invite that makes my lips twitch into a frown, but I find myself taking it anyway. Mostly because I know Olive went home for the weekend to see her mom and, technically, I became friends with Dee and Aliyah first. I'd met them both at orientation in the group we were all put in together. It was Becca who decided she wanted to be their friend too and took up most of their time with plans that she stopped inviting me to a while ago.

But despite the rocky start we've had, any company is better than sulking on my own. That's when anxiety tightens itself around every organ until it squeezes me half to death.

When we all meet up at Birdseye Diner, I fall into conversation with the girls where I can but find myself tuning out and glancing out the large window that faces Main Street when they start talking about some band I don't recognize.

All the buildings are similar to the ones on campus—brick, old, but renovated to attract students with their modern interiors. Lindon U is basically built in the center of the town of Lindon. It's one big community. In a way, its small size and easily walkable location are what drew me to the campus in the first place. It feels homier than my parents' house in Beverly Hills.

My attention is quickly drawn to a group of guys walking down the sidewalk opposite the diner. They're all tall, big, and loud. A few of them are laughing; one is shoving another until he almost gets pushed into the road, where a car honks as it passes them and gets a few more laughs from the men built like mountains.

I lock up when I notice the one toward the back. He's nudging the person next to him, and looks…familiar? The feeling doesn't settle right in my stomach, and I have to force myself to look back at the girls so I don't investigate it.

"Didn't think you'd be the type to drool over the jocks," Becca muses, her smile smug as she notices the same group disappearing into a building with a Bea's Bakery sign hanging above the door. "But I guess I shouldn't be shocked since you were having a *really* good time at their party."

Every muscle of mine freezes, ice slowly coating my bones as I meet my roommate's dark-brown eyes. One of her eyebrows is quirked up in a challenging way, the same side of her lips tilting up like she knows exactly what happened that night.

But she doesn't know.

Not really.

Because neither do I.

My nostrils flare as I meet her gaze straight on. "I don't know what you're talking about," I tell her with false bravado.

Aliyah looks around me and frowns at the glass, missing the stare down between me and the ringleader of our little group. "I missed them! Where'd they go?"

"Bakery," Dee says, pointing at the building in question. "We should stop there after we're done. I hear their coffee is really good and they make their baked goods fresh every morning."

That *does* sound good, but I don't know how I feel about going in there if *they're* all inside. I could make an excuse. Say I need to head back because I've got plans. Tell them I'm not feeling well. But considering I've used that excuse at least three other times in the past two weeks, I don't think they'd buy it. It was hard enough hiding the antibiotics and taking them at a time Becca wasn't around to witness my humiliation. She'd ask questions if she knew I asked Olive to take me to the clinic, and she'd pry until she knew what I was taking and what it was for.

And the truth is, I didn't trust her with that information.

My attempt at deterring them is weak at best, but I still try. "I thought you wanted to watch your carbs? Going there would derail all the progress you've made at the gym."

They all look at me, my roommate's eyes narrowing. My statement isn't meant in offense, but it seems that's how they all take it.

"We're definitely going," Becca decides, to spite me if nothing else. I've poked the bear, so I have no doubt she's going to hold it against me if her attitude in the past is a clue.

Once our food gets delivered, I doctor up my fried fish sandwich with the sauce it comes with on the side and use one of the fries to scoop up the rest of it from the small plastic dish.

"Do you know how many calories all that is?" my roommate asks, singling me out even though the other girls have similar dishes in front of them.

I pause with the glass Heinz bottle floating over my fries. "Um…no?"

She rolls her eyes. "A lot, especially considering you inhaled home fries for breakfast this morning and barely even touched the eggs on your plate."

The girls remain silent, but I see the tiniest wince from Aliyah.

I feel the telltale sign of a blush forming as I try not letting her words get to me. Mom makes comments about my food habits too, and so does Sienna, who's been trying to get more modeling gigs in Los Angeles for the past few years. Those two and Serena are always about the newest trending diet, while I've always indulged in food with actual taste.

I lift a limp shoulder, knowing nothing I say will affect her like her constant jabs do me.

I don't know what to do when we leave the diner and start heading to the curb to cross the street. For some reason, I follow them despite seeing the mass of large bodies still inside the bakery and the awkward silence that took over our dinner.

I hesitate at the bakery door, only walking in because a young couple behind me is trying to get inside with a polite "excuse us." It's loud with laughter and conversation, and I notice a blue-haired girl behind the counter with a younger girl who can't be more then fifteen or sixteen.

The bakery is quaint. It smells like French vanilla and sugar, two things that make my mouth water, and all the tables are already taken by mostly college students, some on laptops, some with friends talking while they dig into their food and drinks. I lock up when I hear, "Get it, girl," followed by bellowed laughter from the group of guys in the back. When I turn, I see them looking at some girl trying to out-chug the boy across from her.

Turning back to face the menu, I try ignoring the noise behind me. I'm glancing up at the menu written in chalk on the wall behind the counter when the girls start ordering.

"Are you getting something or not?" Becca asks, eyeing me when I don't move toward the barista.

After I pick something random and stumble through the ordering process, I feel heat prickle the back of my neck when the girls giggle over my fumbled words. The blue-haired girl takes notice, giving a cold, narrowed look at them that my roommate doesn't seem to appreciate.

The girls are all huddled off to the side, Becca making eyes at the group of guys while Aliyah giggles over something my roommate says. I could join them and figure out which guy they're scoping out, but I don't. I pull out my phone while I wait for my order and scroll through the group messages I've ignored all day.

Serenity: Sky, Mom says you're not coming to the banquet.
Serena: Yeah, Serenity keeps bugging us about why you're not coming. Put her out of her misery so she'll leave us alone
Serenity: You talk to Skylar more than I do, that's why I asked if you knew!
Sienna: That's because you only want to talk about work, the foundation, and whatever Tony is planning for you two. Nobody wants to hear about that all the time

Serenity: I see nothing wrong with that
Serenity: So are you coming, Skylar?
Serena: She has school, pushy
Serenity: The banquet is on a weekend. She can
easily book a flight and be back before Monday.
I used to do it all the time

That's as far as I get before rolling my eyes and clicking off my phone. Serenity always expects us to come to her foundation banquets that consist of snooty people with deep pockets. I don't remember what she's raising money for this time, but it has to do with something involving the law office that she's a new junior partner at.

I groan louder than I mean to, thinking about how much my family is going to harass me leading up to the event. The likelihood of me getting out of it is slim.

"There are rules against being in bad moods at Bea's," a voice that definitely doesn't belong to any of my friends says. My eyes snap up to the tall, burly body standing in front of me, blocking what's left of the sunlight streaming through the large storefront windows.

Long legs covered in dark denim.

Lean waist covered in a white tee.

Broad shoulders stretching the material.

A goofy grin spread on a boyish yet masculine face.

Blond hair that's long in the front, toppling over his forehead, and shorter on the sides.

I've seen him before at the football house. The guy who saw me after I walked downstairs, who teased me unknowingly.

He's smiling down at me, stunning blue eyes shining until he gets a look at my panicked expression. His lips slip into a frown and his matching blond brows pinch. "You okay?"

My fight-or-flight response kicks in when the anxiety starts choking me, and I don't even think about the stuff I ordered and paid for or the girls I followed inside before my feet jerk me around the stranger and toward the door.

For a second time, the blond with a flirty smile and playful eyes sees me run away.

And suddenly, I'm struck by a memory I didn't remember before.

A hard body dancing behind me to a popular song. Big hands encasing my legging-clad hips, kneading, wandering upward. Soft lips on my neck that made me shiver. Words whispered into my ear that are still muted in my mind. Something hard pressing against my lower back.

I vaguely remember looking up at my dance partner and seeing...

Blond hair.

From behind me, I hear, "Wait! Where are you—"

But the door closes behind me before I can hear him finish his sentence, and I'm 99 percent positive I break a record for how fast I can get from Main Street back to my dorm room.

Safe.

Blond hair.

Blond hair.

Blond hair.

"You're safe," I whisper to myself, curling up on my bed in a fetal position. "You're safe."

Chapter Five

DANNY

I STARE AT THE door in confusion while the guys all hoot and holler at my epic failure.

"I've never seen someone run away from you that quickly before," one of my teammates bellows, wiping a tear from under his eye as I approach the table again.

Dropping back into my seat, I twist to glance at the door again and shake my head.

"That chick ran faster than our QB at the last game," another one of the guys calls out.

More snickers from the peanut gallery.

Someone pats me on the back. "Must not be a football fan."

Definitely not a jersey chaser.

Too skittish.

Her friends, though, are a different story. I've felt them staring since they got here, all giggling and trying to act casual as they scope us out from the counter. It gets annoying after a while, which is why I liked that the pretty but timid brunette with long dark locks and tight jeans hugging her ass was off to the side, not paying us any mind.

"Shut it," I grumble to the dicks as they keep hounding me.

I'll admit, it's been a while since I tried charming a girl, but I barely even laid on my moves before she bolted like a track star after the starting gun went off. She looked familiar, probably someone I saw at a party or maybe shared a class with at some point, but I couldn't pinpoint a time or place.

Unlike a lot of the girls who surround the football team, she didn't have makeup caked on her face or show off a lot of skin. The sweatshirt she had on was too big, leaving me wondering what exactly was underneath. I'm an ass man, but I can appreciate a nice chest when I see one.

Getting turned down in front of the idiots happily narrating the rejection like we didn't all just witness it means everyone will know about it by tomorrow morning. My teammates gossip worse than most of the girls I know, and that includes Grandma Meadow, who reads every tabloid known to man and sends me updates on celebrities I couldn't care less about. But I indulge her on her need to stay in the know and always respond to her texts about what's new in Hollywood and the happenings in her friend group. And there's some shit I really don't want to know, including the sexual practices of people Grandma's age.

I swear the woman tells me these things just to see me blush.

"Is Aiden coming?" I find myself asking, hoping they'll let the subject change.

Caleb, a running back for the Lindon Dragons, snorts. "It's Sunday. What do you think?"

Both of our eyes go to the chick with colored hair

32

behind the counter that our tight end always watches a little too closely. Aiden Griffith hasn't shown interest in many women since transferring here from Wilson Reed University. Honestly, there was a bet between a few of the guys about whether he batted for the other team. But as soon as he saw the girl currently calling out a few orders and passing bags and cups to customers, I knew that wasn't the case.

"He didn't come here this morning," Caleb adds, sipping his coffee and cocking his head at the employee. He knows her through his girlfriend, Raine or some shit like that.

One of the second-string players chips into the conversation. "He was talking to Wallace. Guess Coach heard some shit and Griffith decided to pull him aside."

Internally, I groan. Ricky Wallace is a grade A douche who's after our captain's position as quarterback. He's a damn good player with a shitty as fuck attitude. "Was it about the party? Griff wasn't even supposed to be back for another few hours. He never would have known."

Aiden chewed us all out after finding out we'd had a party at the house, then made us clean up the entire place until it was spotless before the sun was fully up. Most of us were hungover as hell. You would think *he* was the captain after hearing him bark orders. I'm surprised he didn't make us scrub the damn floors with our toothbrushes and make us run laps after until we vomited our guts out.

"Well, if Coach found out about the party, I doubt it would've been just Wallace he wanted to talk to, even if he was the one being a douche the whole night. Maybe Coach finally got sick of his holier-than-thou bullshit and gave him a warning."

Coach? I make a face at the name and shake my head. I respect Coach Pearce. He trains us hard, pushes us harder, and gives us hell if we fuck up on the field. It's justified. But the only one he really gives a damn about is Aiden. Fathers him to death while training him for the NFL. The rest of us he couldn't give a crap about beyond following policy, protocol, and the playbook, because nobody mirrors the same talent our star tight end has. Coach wants to train winners, not wannabes.

I'm one of the best damn wide receivers Lindon has seen in years, but that hasn't been good enough for Coach. It's not my ego saying that either. It's the stats. ESPN mentioned me once or twice when they were reviewing game reels during one of their shows.

It's stiff competition out there though. I may be one of the best this university has seen, but there are men ten times better than me out in the league who are still drafted as third, fourth, and fifth picks. I may be fast, but I'm not good enough for the people who make the decisions. There's always someone faster, better.

I'm man enough to admit it.

I have other plans anyway, other goals in life that go beyond the turf. But until I get my marketing degree, I'll live my damn life, enjoy the game, and kick ass until the real world kicks in. I may have come from old money, but I have every intention of making my own and starting from the bottom up until I get where I want to be in life.

Caleb opens his empty coffee cup and throws his balled-up food wrapper inside. "Either way, I think it's going to take a lot more than one conversation with Aiden to straighten out Wallace."

He's not wrong. "Maybe we're underestimating Griff though. The dude has that look that makes you swallow your words pretty damn quickly."

A few of the guys snicker, one of them saying, "Probably all that pent-up frustration. I don't think he ever gets laid."

Also true, but if he keeps coming to Bea's Bakery as much as he is and hitting up the pretty girl behind the counter, maybe that'll change. Hopefully for all of us, since it'd get him to stop chewing us out over stupid shit.

Like *one* little party. He's strict against us throwing bashes at the house, but we have the space. We're always careful not to let anyone go down to the basement where he sleeps, so I don't see what his problem is. We've never had the cops called or gotten any complaints, and everyone leaves happy.

More than happy.

Before any of us can say anything, an order is called a few times with nobody grabbing it. I turn to look around and realize it's probably for the brunette I chased away. One of her friends has the same idea, because she walks over to take the bag. "That's my roommate's stuff. I'll bring it back."

I'm not sure why I do it, but I get up and jog over to her and the other girls as they're walking toward the door. "Wait up a sec."

They all pause, the tallest one with bright hair turning to me with a flirty smile instantly plastered on her face.

"You're DJ, right? One of the football players? I've seen the games." Her eyes roam over me with a knowing look on her face. Between her height and hungry eyes, it's pretty clear she's a man-eater.

"Thanks for the support. Hey, I wanted to ask about your friend."

Her face twists, the flirty expression turning into a scowl. "I don't know if I'd exactly call her that. This is, like, the third time she's ditched us." Her eyes go to the other two girls, both looking anywhere but at the ringleader of their little clique. A lot of people think college is different from high school, but sometimes it's a second, pricier version with the same types of mean girls. It's a popularity contest, one you don't know you're in until you surround yourself with the wrong kind of people.

The chick standing in front of me looking like she might have balls bigger than mine is one of them.

Ignoring her quip, I gesture toward the door. I don't care if I get flak from the guys. "I just wanted to make sure she was okay."

Her eyebrows go up. "You're worried about her? She's fine. She doesn't do well with social interactions without copious amounts of alcohol." That gets a couple small giggles from her friends, making the redhead grin. "You obviously don't remember that. I think you may have had more to drink than her, which is pretty impressive."

"What are you talking about?"

"The party at your house. She didn't come home until later the next morning, so I assumed she stayed over. She always has some sort of guy around, so I assumed you were one of them she has on speed dial."

Oh shit.

That's where I remember her from. She's the black-haired girl who left hours after Aiden grilled all of us until we cleaned the place. When he stopped her at the door, I swore the girl was going to piss herself. Not that I blame her. Aiden is a big guy. Bigger in height, muscle, and broodiness. I'd probably be scared shitless too if I were approached by him.

She looked different then. Different hair. Paler, I guess. Her clothes were tighter and a little haphazard, and she was rocking the just-had-sex look.

Huh.

Maybe I pegged her wrong if what her friend says is true. The small sneer on the redhead's face doesn't sit well with me, telling me there's more to the story than she's letting on, but I'm not sure I want to learn it. I'm not one to compete with other guys for a girl's attention. Even one as pretty as the brunette.

"Good to know," I murmur, clear disappointment in my tone.

Her laugh cuts through my pity party. "You're not missing much, trust me. But if you're looking for someone who knows how to have fun..."

The invitation is wide open, but I don't take it despite her best efforts.

"Rain check," I tell her, offering a wink and smooth smile. It'll never happen, but unlike her, I don't like making people feel like shit about themselves regardless of what they do with their time and body. For somebody so willing to offer me hers, she's judgmental about her roommate's antics. I back up, shoving my hands into my jeans, and add, "Hope your roommate is all good."

Even though I probably dodged a bullet as I sit back down with the guys, who are discussing our next away game, I can't help but feel a little irritated. At what, I don't know.

The heavy feeling lingers in the pit of my stomach the rest of the night.

~

Practice was brutal. Coach was in a shit mood for some reason, and my muscles are screaming at me in retaliation despite taking the longest, hottest shower known to man after we were dismissed to the locker room. If I had time, I would've soaked in an ice bath. Hell, I should have just skipped my last class to take some extra healing time. That way, Coach won't be in an even worse mood tomorrow when he sees how stiff I am.

But the three-hour film class only happens once every Wednesday night, and the young, thirtysomething professor—from NYU as he so humbly announced the first day—made it clear that he didn't tolerate anyone skipping even one class. He excused one absence with some sort of note, but after that, he deducted points from our final grades. And even though Coach could have easily gotten me out of this class thanks to our team's winning streak as of late, I didn't feel like granting the douche who teaches it the satisfaction. He made it clear he didn't like me, or any jocks, early on and wouldn't let us off the hook because we won the school trophies for their case.

Clearly, the dude had his head stuffed in one too many toilets by athletes in his day.

When I finally arrive at Fitzelle and drag my sorry ass to the theater that, thankfully, is on the first floor, I don't bother taking the many sets of steps down to my usual seat up front but rather drop into the one closest to the doors in the last row. No way are my legs going to take me back up the small incline to leave when the time comes. And I don't feel like being death-glared at by Mr. NYU if I fall asleep, which is a high probability. I look forward to this class, especially knowing we're watching *The Big Lebowski* tonight, but already know I don't have the energy to keep my eyes open past the first forty-five minutes, which consist of him lecturing on film techniques.

I almost don't notice that there's somebody else a few

seats down from me until something heavy thuds against the cement floor in between the rows of layered seating. My eyes move toward the girl whose light eyes look bugged out as soon as they meet mine.

The brunette from the bakery.

What are the odds?

"Didn't know you were in this class," I remark, suddenly a little more awake.

She only stares, her blue eyes humorously cartoonlike as she gapes at me.

"What's your name?" I ask, studying her curiously as more people fill the room. It shouldn't surprise me that I haven't noticed her until now. The seat she's in seems strategically picked, probably the one she's been in since the first day. I'm usually one of the first people here and always head toward the second row in the front where me and a few buddies of mine chill.

Still, my new seat neighbor remains silent, but that doesn't stop me. "I'm DJ. Sorry about the other day. Didn't mean to freak you out at Bea's."

Her fingers grip the armrests until they turn white, and I wonder if she's going to try running. Except she can't. Not easily, anyway, since I'm right in her way. Unless she vaults over the chair, which would be epic to see.

"You mute or something?" Ma would smack me upside the head if she heard me ask anyone that. We have a neighbor who is deaf, Craig. I was six when I asked him why he always made weird signs with his hands instead of just talking, and I think my mother about murdered me. Thankfully, Craig didn't seem to mind. He and Ma are still friends, and he even plays card games with Grandma Meadow once in a while.

I sigh when she gives me nothing except that deer in the

headlights look. Even freaked, she's still cute in a girl-next-door kind of way, doe-eyed and soft-faced.

"Listen, I didn't mean to wig you out at the bakery. I just wanted to say hi. Introduce myself. You know, properly, since we didn't at the football house."

Her face drains of color.

"I'll admit, I was going to give you my number," I continue, probably hopelessly, "but I don't do the double-dipping thing. It's not my style. Told myself a long time ago that I was done with that shit. So..."

Once the words are out, I realize what a douchebag I sound like. Christ, I used to have manners. She didn't need to know that I wasn't going to dip my wick in something one of my teammates already did. If I were smart, I would have let that go unsaid, but now I sound like motherfucking Wallace.

I groan internally and swipe a hand down my face when she sputters out, "Wh-what?"

So she does talk. "That was a dick thing to say. Sorry. You're acting all weird on me and it sort of just came out. My ma says I need to work on my filter. Most people who know me say that, actually." I offer a limp, apologetic shrug. "I don't mean anything bad by it, by the way. We've all been there. Party hookups, I mean. I definitely had my fair share over the past couple of years. And back in Boston where I'm from? Yeah, pretty sure Ma was worried I'd knock someone up."

Casual hookups stopped appealing to me a long time ago, so I stopped participating in the lifestyle aside from a few drunken make-out sessions and heavy petting when loneliness took over. She probably doesn't want those details though.

She bends down and grabs her things from the floor, then quickly stands. "I need to go."

My brows pinch. "What? But the movie is—"

"Let me through." Her words are rushed, choked, and she looks like she's ready to bulldoze past my legs come hell or high water. It's the only reason why I stand and watch as she very carefully and quickly passes me while making sure not a single piece of us touches.

The hell? I didn't mean to hurt her feelings. I was only trying to be honest. "You're going to miss the film," I point out stupidly as she pushes open one of the double sets of doors.

When I see her retreating back disappear for a third fucking time, I drop down into my seat and hear it groan under the sudden weight.

"Fuck," I mutter to myself.

I'm getting real sick of her running.

Should have just skipped class.

Chapter Six

SKYLAR

"GOOD, YOU ANSWERED" IS how Dad greets me a few days after my great escape from film class. "How are you, pumpkin?"

Pumpkin. He hasn't called me that in a long, long time. He only uses it when he wants me to do something. Sadly, it usually works too. I may not be a daddy's girl or have him wrapped around my finger like my sisters do, but I'm still a sucker.

"I'm...okay?" I mentally slap my forehead at how unbelievable that response sounds, which he takes notice of with a chuckle.

"You sound it," he muses. I can picture him leaning back in his office chair at our house, legs tucked under his big oak desk that was custom-made just for him. His mouth is probably tilted into a soft smile that makes the corners of his dark blue eyes wrinkle a little. While my sisters take after our mom more, both in looks and personalities, I have a little bit of both my parents. Dad's height, like my sisters, Mom's blond hair, a combination of both my parents' blue eyes—not too light or too dark—and Dad's social anxiety.

Like me, he also isn't big on talking over the phone. Though, to his credit, he checks in with me whenever he can now that I'm clear across the country.

"If this is about Serenity's event…" I give an awkward smile to a few people who are walking down the library steps as I huff up the steep stairs toward the main entrance. "I've already told Mom and the girls I wouldn't be able to come. It's the weekend before midterms and I need to use the time to study."

I only have three midterm exams and one paper to write. My film class doesn't have any examination, though Professor Vincent says he may have some project due around that same time. Considering I always held a 4.0 GPA without much effort throughout high school, I'm not that worried about locking myself away with my books and notes leading up to the test days.

Dad doesn't need to know that, though, even if he's probably thinking the same thing. Where I may not have the outgoing, shiny personality of my sisters, I've always had the brains. I'd feel giddy whenever my parents praised my school reports, especially since they usually scolded me over other things like shutting myself in my room to read or how often I rolled my eyes over things I thought were stupid. Like Mom getting two new pairs of Louboutin stilettos even though she already has at least thirty she never wears. Or Sienna paying for tennis lessons even though she usually skips them.

"…a lot to her. Don't you think?"

Oh crap. I swing open the heavy glass door to my favorite place on campus and walk through the metal detectors. "I zoned out a little, Dad. Sorry. Can you repeat that?"

His sigh is light but not unsurprised. He's always called me out on daydreaming in the middle of conversations. "I think taking even a day off to support her would mean a lot to Serenity, Skylar. She's worked hard planning this event, and she wants her family there."

She wants to show herself as a family-oriented person because she thinks her boyfriend, Anthony, will look at the full picture and finally seal the deal. He's always wanted a big family—a close one. She's been trying to show him that's what ours is, whether it's true or not. It isn't like any of us are on the outs. I text my sisters often and stalk them on social media since they're always posting. I just don't want to have to fly across the country every time Serenity plans something, especially if it's just so she can secure a rock on her finger.

They've been dating for three years and still aren't engaged, even though I'm almost positive my oldest sister has dropped hints a time or five. It's only a matter of time before she gets frustrated and decides he isn't worth it. It's happened before, though I actually like Tony, so I hope she sticks this one out. I think she'd be depressed without him in her life, but what do I know? My experience with relationships is limited.

The only time my sisters gave me any advice on the matter was when I started seeing a boy in high school. I'd been on one date to the movies with him when they told me I needed to take him out for a test run to see if I liked the model, and since they'd passed me condoms with wicked grins on their faces, I knew they didn't mean an actual car ride.

Considering I graduated with high honors *and* my virginity intact, I obviously didn't follow their instructions. I wasn't ready, Ryan was, and neither of us compromised, so we went our separate ways.

I find myself walking on autopilot to the third floor where my favorite table is located. The third and fourth floors of the library have study rooms and quiet sections for students, separate from the open computer labs and tables near the indoor organic café.

"If the tables were turned, she'd do the same for you," Dad insists. I'm not entirely sure that's true though. Serenity has always been about...Serenity. She can be overprotective when she wants to be, but she's been so focused on her future lately that she seems a little too preoccupied to worry herself with me.

I stare at the little café and debate on getting something. It's pricier than other options around, but it's better than bumping into my roommate and her posse when they do nothing but make me feel bad about myself. I've been spending most of my free time here instead of in my room, where Becca and I have created a clear divide between our spaces.

I don't care if she thinks I'm lame for finding our room or the library to be a safe haven away from the things that could happen when alcohol enters the equation. Especially when *DJ from Boston* made it abundantly clear that I was so bad in bed the first time, he didn't want to ever have sex with me again.

I was already mortified over the situation, but the short conversation with him made it approximately a billion times worse. And him making it clear that he'd been around the block a time or two only made me positive he was the person I had to thank for the parting gift that he left me with. When the clinic called with confirmation results days after I went to see them, they'd asked me for the name of my partner so he could be informed.

I'd given them nothing after a long, awkward stretch of

silence, so they told me to pass along their number to him, because that way, they could treat him too once he called. But how was I supposed to broach that topic? *Hey, remember me? The girl whose virginity you took and then gave chlamydia?*

No thanks.

If he's going around playing the field with a new girl every week, it'll be a campus-wide problem. The clinic told me as much, lectured me on getting the problem treated immediately before it got out of hand. I just was too chicken.

Too...scared.

Because what if it isn't him?

"You're not even paying attention." My father's voice cuts back in, instantly peeling me from my horrid thoughts.

"I'm sorry," I apologize again, dropping my things onto the table. "I've just been busy with school and...stuff. Listen, I'll think about the banquet, but that doesn't mean I'm promising to go. Okay?"

There's a pause where I wonder if he'll ask if I'm all right. I don't know if I should be relieved or not that he doesn't. "That's good enough for now. Hopefully it'll get your mother off my back for a while."

We both know that'll never happen.

"Love you, kiddo," he says.

"Love you too." My voice is no more than a whisper as we disconnect, and I find myself staring off into the distance and listening to the dull voices carry from downstairs.

Easygoing conversations with friends.

Laughter with peers.

All things I find myself lacking in.

My eyes go to the few people who are on this level, and they're staring at me. One of them leans in to whisper to the other. They giggle.

An eerie feeling creeps under my skin and anxiety settles into my bones.

Are they talking about *me*?

~

I don't know how long I have my head buried in my textbook highlighting various passages, but it isn't until someone stops beside my chair that I peel my tired eyes away from the tiny print and up to the person standing next to me.

The first thing I notice is the small stain on the white T-shirt, partially covered by a half-buttoned striped shirt over top of it. When I glance up, I'm met with a set of brown eyes and friendly smile. "Hey."

Stupidly, I glance around as if he's talking to somebody else. My hands grip my textbook, feeling the edges of the thin pages cut into the pads of my fingertips as I make sense of why he's here.

"I'm Caleb," he tells me, smothering a small smile when he sees me give another quick look behind me. "We don't know each other, but I'm friends with DJ. We play on the football team together."

My spine straightens as I sit taller in the chair, connecting the dots. He does look a little familiar. I see them walking around together on campus with a few other guys that I can only assume are part of the team too. "Oh." I flinch at my social awkwardness. "Hi."

He doesn't ask to sit down or make a move to pull out one of the three empty chairs. For that, I'm grateful. "I just wanted to say that DJ isn't so bad. He's a little quirky, but that's just him. Usually, he says something stupid without realizing it." When he sees that I'm too dumbfounded to reply, his smile grows. "I don't know what's going on between you two, but you've got him all twisted up. Haven't seen him quite like it before. Honestly? It's pretty funny. But I saw you over here and thought it'd be nice to put in a good word."

I blink silently, unable to fathom a response. He's here to put in a good word for DJ, which tells me he has no idea what his friend even wants from me.

Or what he already got.

Caleb continues, oblivious to my internal confusion. "He probably inserted his foot in his mouth again. Once, a girl slapped him across the face during freshman year when he was trying to flirt with her. Definitely didn't come off that way. I swear he had a handprint on his cheek the rest of the week."

I glance down at the book I've been reading. "I bet he deserved it."

"He did," Caleb agrees lightly. "But he felt pretty bad about it. All I'm saying is, give the guy a shot."

Give him a shot? The anger I've been shoving away starts rising, heating my blood as I grind my teeth. "I know exactly what kind of person your friend is, and I'm not interested in involving myself with him. You and I obviously know two very different versions of him."

His puzzled expression meets mine. "I usually don't misread this kind of stuff. He's mentioned you a couple of times, and I've seen the way he looks at you when we cross paths. All I'm saying is that whatever happened—"

"'Whatever happened' is none of your business," I cut him off coolly. I take a deep breath, trying to fight off the panic rising in my throat. "Look, Caleb, I don't have a problem with you. You're just trying to help your...friend.

But I don't want anything to do with him. He can be sorry all he wants. It doesn't change anything."

He frowns, scratching the side of his neck. "Okay, well… Sorry that I bothered you."

Sorry.

He's sorry.

Apparently, his friend is sorry.

But where does that leave me?

He watches me for a second, still frowning, before nodding once as if he's reluctantly backing down. "If you change your mind…"

I shake my head. "I won't."

He glances over his shoulder before sighing lightly. "What's your name, anyway?"

Why does he want to know? I debate on whether to answer. Indecision swirls in my head before I finally say, "Skylar."

His smile returns, friendly with something else woven in that I can't discern. "I'll see you around, Skylar."

Doubtful.

Even after he's gone, I can't focus on my homework, so I pack up and head back to my empty dorm room, where I think about the interaction.

DJ feeling bad about what he said doesn't add up. And his friend obviously thinks there's something way different going on besides a few short-lived conversations.

Flopping onto my bed, I groan.

When Tyler texts me about meeting up to hang out, I accept it without hesitation, hoping it'll be a welcome distraction from the feeling building deep in my stomach.

The less I let myself think, the better.

Chapter Seven

DANNY

I JOG UP TO Aiden and smack him in the shoulder before falling into step with his long strides as we head toward the locker room. "What the fuck is Coach's deal?"

He gives me a blank look. "Why would you think I know?"

I refrain from rolling my eyes. "Because he tells you everything."

The brute doesn't argue but also doesn't indulge me with an answer. I have no doubt he knows what crawled up Coach Pearce's ass, but I decide not to push because Aiden seems to be in a mood. About what, I don't know. He's not the type you can pry much from.

We're all in the process of showering, drying off, and changing when Coach storms into the room. "Listen up." His loud voice booms throughout the room. "I don't want any questions. Just listen and do what you're told. There's some shit going around that needs to be taken care of, and I want all of you to get tested to be sure you're in the clear from it."

That's definitely going to raise some questions, whether he wants them to be asked or not. He might as well have told us we were all going to die but couldn't ask when or how.

"What shit?" one of the fresh asks.

Coach deadpans. "What the hell did I just tell you, O'Keefe? No questions."

I snicker at his irritation. "Sorry, Coach, but you have to admit that sounded ominous."

A few people murmur their agreement, and a couple players even look a little worried as we all focus on the aging man.

Coach scrubs a hand down his wrinkled face and sighs. "You want me to give it to you straight? Fine. I know how some of you act. I also know that most of you think with the wrong head. And I've been informed that there's a rise in STD cases going around campus. You all signed forms that agreed to go through testing when the coaching staff sought fit. This is me telling you hussies you're getting tested. I can't have any of you out on the field if you're not in tip-top shape because you got your dicks wet one too many times. Understand me?"

Now there's way more conversation, mumbles and curses going off across the room that can be heard over the running showers.

STDs? Christ. I remember all the lectures in health class. I also remember the uncomfortable as hell sex talk my mother gave me when I turned fourteen. I'd entered high school, which apparently meant in her mind that I was looking to get laid. I think my face was bright red when she passed me a condom and asked if I knew how to put it on.

I didn't, but I wasn't about to ask her to show me, that was for fucking sure.

If what Coach says is true, I can't help but wonder if

some of my teammates didn't get the same awkward talk melded into their brains early on.

We get tested randomly for drugs throughout the season, and we signed our names on a dotted line agreeing to other lab work if something came up. For those on scholarships, it's do or die when it comes to following the rules. Am I worried? No. It's been a while since I buried myself between a woman's thighs, and I always wore protection.

The thought of having kids at a young age is terrifying, especially seeing what it did to my mother. She was only fifteen when she had me. Probably why she felt the need to tell me all about the birds and the bees when she did. Parents are always trying to make sure you don't make their mistakes, and that was one she could rest assured I wouldn't be making for myself.

Coach ignores the groans and complaints coming from the team and tells us the info we need to get the testing done. Based on the atmosphere from the guys, I'd say there are plenty of people who are going to sweat it out until they get their results back.

I can't help but snicker.

"Something funny?" Caleb asks, sidling up to me while towel drying his hair.

I shrug, slamming my locker door once I have my fresh clothes in hand. "I guess the advantage of a dry spell is that I don't have to worry about shit."

He pauses. "You sure about that?"

Snorting, I drop the towel hanging low on my waist. Like most of the players, I'm not bashful. My body is lean and toned with all the right muscles in all the right places. And my dick isn't bad to look at either. What's there to want to hide? "Don't you think I'd know if I had sex?"

He shakes his head as he grabs his clothes from the locker beside mine. "I don't know, man. You were fucking hammered at the party. Don't you remember grinding on Amber? I honestly thought you were going to start having sex in the middle of the living room. It was disturbing."

My face twists in thought. I did indulge in a little too much beer, but they bought my favorite kind, knowing I wouldn't protest the party then. I knew Aiden would have a shit fit when he found out about it, so they bribed me to keep quiet. And I took that bribe and drank to my heart's content because why the fuck not. It's not something I do often, so I let loose.

I don't remember grinding on Amber though. She's been passed around most of Lindon's sports teams, always hooking up with whoever wore a jersey and cleats and was willing. And while I've never been one to slut shame, I have no interest in participating in that sort of thing. Like I told Jesse Owens—an appropriate nickname I gave the brunette in film class considering her love for running—I don't do jersey chasers, and there's an unspoken rule between teammates not to screw a chick they already slept with.

Clearly not everybody follows that rule, because some of them may be needing to take some heavy medication along with their morning protein shakes soon enough.

"I vaguely remember," I tell him. "But I know I didn't sleep with anyone. I was drunk, but not *that* drunk."

I slipped into the basement and locked up when shit started getting crazy. I brought one more beer down with me, turned on *SportsCenter*, and fell asleep on the couch.

Alone.

It wasn't until Aiden woke me up looking pissed as fuck the next morning that I knew the upstairs must have been trashed. Not surprising considering how many people were up there before I made my escape.

Caleb chuckles. "Whatever you say, man. Forgot you were practically a monk these days. Maybe that's part of your problem."

"I'm *selective*," I correct. He's not one to talk, since he has a serious girlfriend he can get some from any time he wants. He may get attention from the same women the rest of us do, but they don't try nearly as hard because it's obvious how much he loves Raine. An annoying amount. They're the disgusting-cute type.

"And I don't have a problem," I add.

"So why does the one chick you can't seem to keep your eyes off of look like she wants to murder you?" he quips.

My mouth twitches. I've noticed the way the brunette catches my eyes when we're out walking around campus and quickly looks away like she refuses to acknowledge me. I can't say I blame her. I sounded like a dick last time we spoke. If she didn't run every time she got near me, I'd apologize.

"Because I'm an idiot," I tell Caleb, fastening the button of my jeans and zipping them. "Anyway, it could be worse. I may not get a lot of action, but at least I'm not Aiden."

He grins before a hand comes up and smacks me upside the head.

No doubt the man in question is standing there, looming like the silent creeper he always is. The team's star tight end definitely doesn't have anything to worry about from these tests.

~

I'm hungry as hell once we're dismissed from practice a week later. The closest place with food that probably isn't

54

swamped is Reavers in the student center, which serves some of the best pizza and subs around. Even though I'm supposed to keep a strict diet, all I can think about is the chicken, bacon, and ranch pizza slices waiting for me.

It only takes me a few minutes to grab a couple from the heated display case, slap them onto a paper plate, pick a water from the cooler, and let the cashier scan my student ID to pay for it all. Sitting down and taking my first bite, I stop midchew when a shadow casts over where I'm trying to see what ESPN is talking about on the flat-screen above the fireplace across the room.

My eyes trail over to the feminine frame standing there, legs covered in black leggings that hug her hips, hands fidgeting with the hem of an oversize black sweatshirt, and long, brown hair cascading over her shoulders.

When I meet her pretty baby blues staring directly at me, one of my eyebrows arches up in curiosity. I can't help but smirk, mouth still full of food that I slowly begin chewing as the runner shifts her weight in obvious nervousness.

The girl who reminds me of the famous runner says, "I need to talk to you."

Christ. Her voice.

Low, raspy, and even with a slight rattle from her nerves, still oddly sexy. Swallowing, I sit back in my seat and stretch my long legs out in front of me. "That so?"

Her eyes dart away, like she's second-guessing herself. I'm surprised when she stands a little straighter, drawing her shoulders back as if she's going into battle.

I've seen her around campus, usually around the snotty group of girls she keeps in her company. I also notice the guys who linger, the way their eyes always find her wherever she goes. It makes me wonder what truth there is to her roommate's jab about the guys she keeps around. But what constantly draws my attention to the brunette is the fact that she's either oblivious to the interest she gets, or she chooses not to pay the guys any attention.

For some reason, I like that she's not invisible to the public eye but not basking in the attention either.

"You ever going to tell me your name?" I ask, cocking my head.

She blinks. "I'm surprised your friend didn't tell you when he came up to me pleading your case," she states after a few moments. Not that I know who she's talking about.

"Which friend is that? I have a few."

Her jaw ticks. "Must be nice."

My eyes study her tense jaw. "I'm surprised that dazzling personality of yours doesn't draw more people in begging for your friendship."

Hurt flashes in her eyes, causing her to look away.

I cuss to myself and swipe at my jaw. "Do you know who Jesse Owens is?" I question, picking up the pizza and taking another bite while she watches skeptically.

Her throat bobs in a heavy swallow. Her right eyebrow twitches. It's lighter. Almost blond, which makes me think she's not a natural brunette, even if she can pull it off. I almost hate that the dark color of her hair brings out the bright color of her blue eyes.

Her hands clasp at her sides and then loosen again. She's losing her feigned strength.

She eventually nods. "He was an Olympic runner."

I hum past the food I'm eating, finishing off my first slice in another two large bites and brushing crumbs off my fingers. "Did you use to run track or something?"

It's hard to refrain from laughing at the weird expression she gives me. "Why would you ask something like that?"

The grin already on my face stretches higher. "You run a lot, so I've been calling you Jesse Owens in my head. Thought you were trained in high school. Five-thousand-meter? Hurdle? That could be it. You seem to be good at avoiding things."

Like me.

I don't add that part.

"You're...you're—" Her nostrils flare in agitation, and it's pretty amusing. "Rude."

"I haven't been called that since I was at least eight," I tell her, shaking my head and snickering as I eye my second piece of pizza. I want to eat it. Badly. But if Ma were here, she'd be glaring me down until I showed some of the manners she raised me with. "You eat something yet?"

That gets another blink from her.

"It's chicken, bacon, and ranch." I pick it up and wave it around, watching a piece of bacon fall off and bounce onto the table. "Freshly made every day. Delicious. I even added a little parmesan on top."

Now I'm just making myself drool. I mean, when was the last time I offered up my food to anybody? I don't even remember. Fairly sure I threatened to stab Caleb with a fork when he tried taking one of my chicken wings during our championship celebration last season.

"You...want to share your pizza?"

Not really. "Yeah." Though I'll probably buy myself another one once she's gone. "Don't you know sharing is caring?"

She chokes on air.

"What?" I ask.

All she does is shake her head, but there's color creeping up her neck and shading her face an unflattering shade of pink.

I wiggle the pizza again, this time watching ranch drizzle off the side. "So pizza?"

Her lips part, then close again. It isn't until her eyes linger on the food I'm offering that I heft out a sigh, slide the paper plate with the food on it to the seat across from me, and gesture toward the empty chair.

I don't think she's going to accept the offer, but she pulls out the chair and slowly sinks into it. Before she can take the food, though, I pull it away.

She gapes.

"Gonna need your name if I'm sharing my food with you," I bargain. "It's only fair. Or else I'll have to get creative with what I call you. And believe me, my imagination is weird."

My lips press together to stifle a smile when her eyes widen, then lower to the pizza I'm holding hostage.

Quietly, she murmurs, "It's Skylar."

Skylar.

I repeat it a few times in my head while I give her a once-over. Those pretty eyes are framed by thick lashes that she watches me through. Fidgety fingers rest on the tabletop as I do my not-so-subtle investigation, the nails painted a blue darker than her eyes. From what I can remember, she has a nice rack, perky ass, and some grab-me hips, but it's not noticeable in the clothes that swallow her right now. Little to no makeup covers her fair skin, but she definitely doesn't need any. I like the bare-faced girl sitting here. Vulnerable yet strong. I can see the fight in her eyes.

Skylar is fitting for her.

Not overly girly or tomboyish.

Somewhere in between.

"Huh" is the only intelligent thing that comes out of my mouth as I shove the pizza toward her again.

She lets her hair fall around her face like a shield as she studies the food.

"It's better than Jesse Owens," I offer, crossing my arms over my chest as she stares at the food without touching it. "My real name is Daniel Bridges Junior. That's why people call me DJ."

There's a moment of pause. "Why?"

"Why not?" I counter, lifting a shoulder. The gray T-shirt stretching from the movement was a gift from my ma before I bulked up. It started out looser than most of the ones I own because she always sizes up like I'm going to keep growing. But ever since I began hitting up the weight room more often, most of my clothes fit snugger on my body. Something Skylar seems to take notice of, even if her eyes never stay on me for long.

My new lunch partner is silent.

"You're not eating."

Her hand goes to the pizza, stalling on the garlic-butter-coated crust. God, why did I give that to her? The question grows tenfold when she blurts, "I'm not supposed to take food from strangers."

The deep laugh escapes me before I can cut it off. Her cheeks darken until the faded pink dusting her skin turns red. "Aw, babe, don't look at me like that. I thought that was cute. Funny, even."

She stiffens, something in her changing drastically. Her voice is suddenly sharp when she says, "Don't call me that."

I think about what I said before lifting my hands in surrender. "Fine. But seriously, why would I ruin a perfectly good piece of pizza? Anyway, it's drinks you shouldn't accept from strangers. Isn't that, like, rule number one for college chicks?"

Suddenly, her body jerks as she stares between me and the pizza. Why does she look so pale?

"What? I'm not trying to be a creep, but it's true. I heard the lectures given to people at orientation. Even heard that they started giving out rape whistles, which is fucked up. Not fucked up that you have them but that you'd need them."

The choppy exhales from her make my eyes narrow. She's freaking out. Why, I have no idea. What I do know is that she's obviously reading too much into my rambling. Any smart person would know better than to do that with someone like me.

"I didn't drug your food," I grumble, feeling offended I even have to tell her that. Jaw ticking, I shake my head. "I didn't even know anyone was going to bother me when I bought it. I'm not keen on giving away my lunch, especially after being run ragged on the field."

My rough voice makes her wince.

Good. I hope she feels bad. I've never considered myself a bad dude. Maybe a little too eager, even a little too unfiltered at times, but I've never wanted to do any harm to anybody. She doesn't know me, which means she has no right to assume I'm someone to look out for.

"*You* approached *me*," I remind her, trying to calm myself down and figure out what the purpose of this interaction is. "What did you want to tell me? You said you had something to say."

Her eyes don't lift from the pizza. I'm not used to girls avoiding eye contact. I should like that she's different, but there's something off about her. She's too jumpy. Too accusatory in her silence.

"It's... I..." Her faltering words only make me impatient. Whatever she came here to say is stuck in her throat as she blows out a deep breath. "This isn't easy for me, okay?"

All I do is blink.

"I think you—"

Just as she's about to answer, my phone goes off on the table. When I see who's calling, I bite back a groan and glance at Skylar. "Need to take this," I mutter, not bothering to move as I lift the phone to my ear. "What's up, Coach?"

"Letting everyone know a few people on the team will be sitting out for a couple weeks" is his monotone response.

"Shit." I don't realize I say that out loud until he grunts in agreement. "This have to do with the tests you made us take? Is that why they're being benched?"

Skylar sits up straighter, obviously eavesdropping. I don't worry about it since there's no way she'd guess what test I'm talking about. We're in a college, so for all she knows, I'm referring to one of my exams.

Coach Pearce sighs heavily, giving me the answer without confirming as much. "Not at liberty to say. I'm just letting you know that we're going to need to adjust. Gonna need your help getting some of the second string ready for the game next week. Think you can handle Bigby?"

William Bigby is one of the newer wide receivers on the team. He's a damn good one too, from what I've seen, so it shouldn't be that difficult. Could be worse. "Got it, Coach. I take it I'm cleared to play?"

Another grunt. "Were you worried?"

"Nah. Always been picture-perfect health. The guys don't call me 'the monk' for nothing these days."

He grumbles something unintelligible.

I shrug it off. "Anyway, same practice time?"

He confirms before disconnecting, making me drop the phone back on the table. When I meet Skylar's gaze, there's something different about it.

She's studying me carefully, not quite as intensely as I was doing to her. Softer, somehow, but still full of caution. There's also a lot fewer nerves cloaking her otherwise doe-eyed expression.

When she stands abruptly, gripping the strap of her bag hanging off her shoulder, I stare at her with a cocked expression. "You going to leave me hanging or what? What did you need to tell me that was so urgent you had to interrupt lunch?"

Dickish? Sure. But untrue? No.

Skylar shakes her head, brushing some of that thick hair behind her ear. "It's nothing. Doesn't matter anymore. Um, thanks for the pizza."

Like always, she leaves me without a single look back as she speed walks out of Reavers. My right eye twitches as I trail her retreating back until she's out of sight.

I shake my head, grab the plate, and eat the rest of the slightly cold food while trying to figure out what the fuck just happened.

At least she didn't bolt on me this time.

Though I could live without the hot and cold treatment from her.

I get distracted from my irritated thoughts by the single buzz from my phone, looking down and snorting over the message on the screen.

Grandma M: Did you know that Brad Pitt is officially single again? That boy needs to settle down with a real woman. Think he'd go for a cougar who could show him a thing or two?

Chapter Eight

SKYLAR

Blond hair.

Big hands.

Hot breath.

It isn't much to go on, but I can't help but repeat those three things in my mind. The man from that night smelled like liquor, not the cheap beer that was being served at the keg. But once that was tapped out, a lot of people started indulging in the more expensive stuff they found hidden away. My roommate had given me rum and coke after rum and coke, and I liked the sweetness of the soda combined with the bitterness from the rum. Or was it *him* who kept passing me the red cups?

The blond?

DJ.

I shake my head, struggling to focus on what my math professor is saying. Something about multivariate data. I glance down at my notes and wince when I realize I've barely taken any. Math has never been my strongest subject, so I need to refocus.

But…

DJ said things I can't help but obsess over. It's been a few days since our encounter at Reavers, and it's all I can think about, because nothing about what I heard him say on the phone adds up.

"…have the answer?"

Complete silence fills the room as I pull myself away from the conflicting thoughts.

I blink a few times and notice that the professor is staring at me. I feel my cheeks burn under the waiting gazes of my classmates.

Sinking into my seat, I shake my head at the teacher. "I wasn't paying attention. What was the question?"

Professor Albertson hums. "Stick back after class if you have a few minutes to talk. Rodney, do you have the answer?"

I squeeze my eyes closed, ignoring the murmurs from people around me, and do my best to stay focused the rest of class.

When Albertson continues her lecture, I inhale slowly and notice a sympathetic look from a black-haired girl across the room. I think her name is Alba. We've exchanged small smiles in greeting, but nothing beyond that. She's quiet like me, always observing and doodling in her notebook.

I should say hi. Ask her what her major is. Make another friend, since Olive has become the only real one I can depend on.

But I don't.

Because part of me wonders if I can even be a good friend since I can barely keep Becca, Dee, and Aliyah's attention without my mind wandering.

When class is dismissed, I wait too long in contemplation, probably looking like a fish out of water while figuring out how to introduce myself after so long of being classmates, when Alba grabs her things and leaves with the others.

My shoulders drop a fraction and I promise myself I'll say something next time.

"I'm going to be honest, Skylar," Albertson begins once it's just us. "I'm surprised at you. Your entrance exam scores were top notch, which is why it was suggested that you be placed at a higher-level course. I wouldn't have signed off on it if I didn't feel you could handle it. If it's too much for—"

"No!" I blurt, horrified over the thought of having to drop the course. My parents would hound me for answers if that happened, and I wouldn't be able to tell them why I've been distracted.

Her light eyes soften. "Is there something going on in your personal life that's taking up your concentration? This isn't the first time you've zoned out on me. You barely scraped by with a C on your last exam, and the homework assignments you've handed in lately are hardly up to par with what I know you can do. I've seen it before with my students and always want to reassure them that I'm here if needed."

Swallowing down the truth, I lift a stiff shoulder and stare down at my Timberlands. They were a Christmas present from Serenity. Usually, she gets me something gaudy that I always pretend I like but eventually give to one of my other sisters. "I don't know what's going on," I lie, hearing the tiny quake in my voice. "I promise I'll pay better attention though."

There's a twinge of guilt knowing that it's not going to be that easy. I can barely focus when I'm alone in my room, much less in a lecture full of other students.

"And put more effort into your assignments. If you need the extra help, I can meet with you during office hours. The student center also has tutors lined up for those struggling in their classes," she adds, her eyes burning into my face until I force myself to look up.

I nod at the graying woman. "I don't need a tutor. Can you tell me what my current grade is so I know what I need to do to raise it?"

When she looks at the computer in the corner and tells me the low number attached to my name, my jaw drops.

No.

No, no, no.

She studies my expression and offers a partial smile. "I know it seems damning, but if you study for the midterm and continue doing well the rest of the semester, you'll pass. And there's nothing wrong with accepting help from people. Me, the tutors, your classmates are all here. There's a study group made up of a few of your peers I'm sure you could join. You have options, Skylar. Be open to them."

There's nothing wrong with accepting help from people.

Why does that hit me deeper than it should?

I can't speak, so I jerk my head up and down before walking out with a tight grip on my backpack strap until my fingers hurt.

I'm walking absentmindedly down the path that leads to the residential side of campus when I hear my name being called from somewhere nearby. I turn in time for some guy with a bright smile to jog over and match my pace. "Hey," the stranger greets.

He's not that much taller than me, with red hair and the freckles to match, and his eyes are a dark shade of brown that don't take their focus off me as I study him. He walks with the kind of swagger that Becca says is indicative of all sports players. Confident because he knows he's good-looking and unafraid to own it.

"Hi," I eventually say, wincing at the weird tone of my voice. It's squeaky, uncomfortable, and his lips waver upward as if he hears it.

"Hi," he says, amused. "It's Patrick. We've seen each other around campus."

We have?

He's oblivious to my cluelessness as he keeps pace with me, one hand in his pocket and the other holding his bag on his shoulder. "I've been trying to get you to talk to me for a while. Your friend said I'd have a shot."

My nose scrunches. "My friend?"

He grins. "Yeah. The tall one. Rachel? I forget. She was at one of our parties over the weekend with a few other people. Noticed you two hung out, so I asked if you were coming."

He must be talking about Becca. "Oh, well...parties aren't really my thing." It sounds lame, but I don't care. I vaguely remember Becca telling me she and Dee were going to some lacrosse thing. I thought she meant a game, but it was getting late, so she must have meant this party. "Do you play lacrosse?"

Patrick smirks. "So you *do* know me."

I try not to make a face at the way his lips tilt up into a flirty smile as he gives me a once-over. I'm not sure why Becca would tell him he has a shot with me, but I'm tempted to find out.

"I don't follow sports" is all I tell him.

He makes a noncommittal noise. "Well, that doesn't matter, I guess. I was wondering if you wanted to hang sometime. Me and my buddies have get-togethers every Friday. Nothing big. You should come."

"Like I said," I tell him slowly, stopping at the crosswalk

as a car passes, "I don't like parties. Thanks for the invite though."

He follows me across the street. "Aw, c'mon. It's small. Barely a party. It'll be fun."

Doesn't he understand when a girl isn't interested? Clearly not. "Listen, Patrick. It was nice meeting you, but I don't have time to hang out. My schedule is busy, and I've been swamped with classwork."

And I don't like parties. Since saying it a third time seems pointless, I keep that to myself.

He looks genuinely disappointed, so I feel a smidge bad. Before I can apologize, a group of guys walks by and captures my attention. A few of them seem to know Patrick, smacking his back and grabbing his hand in a weird guy handshake as they pass.

One of them in the herd is none other than Daniel Bridges Junior, and he doesn't look particularly thrilled when we lock eyes. I'm not sure what I did to cause the furrow of his brow as his eyes go between me and the lacrosse player beside me, but it doesn't make me feel great.

"See you around," I tell Patrick, giving a small wave and avoiding the look DJ gives me as I shoulder past where he's standing. Thankfully, he doesn't bring up our previous interactions or offer so much as a greeting. And it's probably for the best. I don't know where somebody like him would fit into my messed-up life.

When I get back to my room, Becca and Dee are sitting on her bed watching something on her laptop. They both ignore me as I set my things down and pull my hair back into a messy bun.

"Do you know a lacrosse player named Patrick?" I ask my roommate, finally pulling her attention toward me.

Her lips curl up. "Yep."

Dee looks between us before her gaze settles on Becca. "Is that the guy who asked—"

Becca cuts her off. "Yeah, that's him." I don't like the cool tone she uses, but I'm so used to it at this point, I choose to brush it off.

"Why would you tell him I'd be interested in hanging out?"

I'm not prepared for the scoff that comes from her in return. "Oh please. Tyler? DJ? I see you around guys all the time. It's not like I'd be far off guessing you wouldn't be down to hang with him. And who knows what else."

I gape at her. Tyler is the only one I hang out with, and that's barely been happening because he's started acting weird, getting touchy and then cold if I tell him I have to go before things change between us. The few conversations I've had with DJ haven't been anything to write home about either, and besides the short conversation with Caleb in the library, I barely say anything to any other guy who decides to stop me and make a comment about how my jeans fit or my ass looks.

"What is *that* supposed to mean?" I pry, crossing my arms over my chest.

My roommate doesn't answer right away, only fueling the fire as the seconds tick by. When she does look up at me, the hostility in her gaze pins me to my spot. "You know exactly what it means. Stop playing the quiet, innocent girl. Everybody can see right through the act."

I can't help but look to Dee, hoping she'll defend me in some way, because I don't know what act I'm supposed to be putting on.

But Dee only shrugs at me when Becca goes back to

whatever they were doing before I walked in, not giving away her thoughts. I can't say I'm surprised. If sides are chosen in the war waging between us, I know Becca will have the most people on hers.

I try thinking of something to say.

A defense. An argument.

But what would it matter?

I make a choice then.

Kill her with kindness.

~

After my eyes start crossing from all the math equations I force myself to work on, I find myself staring out the tiny window by the foot of my bed facing the track and soccer field.

As I grab my key card and walk out, I hear Becca murmur to Dee, "I'd convert her bed into a couch if she left and finally have some peace around here."

Grinding my teeth, I let the door to our suite close harder than normal behind me. They can trash-talk me however much they like, but I don't want to be around to hear it.

I shoot a text to Olive on my way to the track, examining the blue skies and white clouds rolling through.

> Me: Meet by the sports complex for a walk on the track?

I'm waiting by the large brick building with a huge painting of Lindon U's dragon mascot on the side of it when I hear footsteps approach me from behind.

My spine straightens when the footsteps stop directly behind me, causing my heart to jam itself into my throat.

"Heading to the track seems appropriate, Jesse Owens," the voice teases.

I let out a tiny breath that releases the tension in my back when I turn to see DJ standing there in a pair of athletic shorts and sleeveless muscle top that shows off impressive arms. I quickly look away before he notices me checking him out.

My phone buzzes, and I glance at it.

> Olive: Sorry! Meeting a few people at the library to study. Rain check?

DJ grins when my wary eyes meet his playful ones again. "I'm just messing with you, Skylar. You want some company?"

The question makes me gape before I thumb out a quick reply to Olive.

> Me: Yeah, next time.

He laughs at my silence. "One lap around?"

I stay quiet, wondering what his game is.

He tilts his head, slightly amused by my lack of reaction to him. But what did he expect?

I don't understand how we got here considering our other interactions have been unpredictable.

He jabs his thumb behind him. "I can just fuck off if you want. Say the words and I'm gone. But I just got done with a workout and usually take a lap or two to cool off before heading back to the house to work on homework."

The house.

An involuntary shiver rakes down my back until the hair on my arms stand up.

The more I look at the boy in front of me with an easygoing smile, the more I find it harder and harder to paint him as the villain in my story.

He hasn't necessarily done anything that makes me think he's to blame for what happened to me. He was at the house, his hair is the same color as the hair replaying in my mind, but I can't fit any other puzzle pieces together to prove he's someone I should be cautious over. I've seen him interact with people and he's nice. Friendly. People seem to like him. Wouldn't somebody with bad intentions give people the ick that makes them stay far away?

I replay his phone call in my head for the umpteenth time, picking apart the casualness of his conversation.

Since hearing him say "Coach" when he answered his cell, I've made it my mission to do Google searches on not only Coach Pearce, coach of the Lindon U football team, but the players as well when insomnia strikes. I've studied the players' faces, the level of smugness, and I try to rule out the features that appear fuzzy in the depths of my mind until sleep would find me. But it's never enough to pinpoint any singular face—somebody to place the blame on so it isn't just crushing me. Not DJ, and not anybody else on the football roster.

The only face that I stare at longer than the others is the one currently waiting for my response. I take in the glint in his blue eyes and eased stance of his lean body. He gives off no warning bells, unlike with other men who give me their undivided attention, and I wonder if that's a sign.

Maybe not one to trust him. Not yet.

But to give him a chance.

So I find myself saying, "You can walk with me."

Chapter Nine

DANNY

I DO NORMALLY WALK off my brutal training sessions after I get my ass kicked in the weight room, but I wasn't expecting her to tell me yes.

I figured she'd put on her big girl pants again like she started to at Reavers, stand her ground, and tell me to fuck right off. Hell, I was looking forward to hearing my favorite f-word on those lips.

But I'm not disappointed either.

The way she regards me with caution makes me curious about her. She doesn't act like a lot of girls I know, especially not the jersey chasers I assumed she was part of. That's on me, and it's something I plan on fixing so long as she gives me an opportunity to.

As we walk, I'm tempted to ask where her snobby friends are or about her connection to that dickhead Patrick Malone. He's got a pretty boy smile that make girls think he's a good one until he shows his true colors. I've seen it before. He leaves broken hearts in his wake while carving another notch on his bedpost with somebody new.

I'd warn her away, but if he's not following her around like a lost puppy, she probably doesn't need my say in the matter.

We're a few minutes into the walk when the silence between us starts to make me itch. "I hear we're watching some French flick this week. We have to read the subtitles."

I hate reading subtitles. I have enough trouble paying attention to movies themselves because I'm a naturally antsy person, so adding more work to understand what the hell is going on is too much.

My walking buddy murmurs, "Yeah, that's what's on the syllabus."

Formal. Withdrawn.

My eyes go down her body, covered in another pair of black leggings and a loose shirt with—my eyes narrow. Are those cats with glasses on them? Huh. It's kinda cute on her.

Innocent, in a way.

"You're staring," she points out, quickly looking forward again after our eyes meet for a couple seconds. Her Timberland boots scuff against the red rubber track, holding her focus.

I pop my lips. "You can't decide if you like me or not, can you?"

It's pretty obvious to me, but when her eyes widen as they bolt back to me, I can see she's surprised at my observation. She must be one of those chicks who thinks all jocks are dumber than a box of rocks. And some of them? Yeah. I can name at least three people I'd never want to work with on any group project or trivia team. But that's not the case with me.

Once again, her silent assumption grates at me. "Do you judge everyone you meet, or am I just one of the lucky

74

ones?" I grumble, stuffing my hands into the pockets of my athletic shorts.

"I could say the same about you" is her firm response. "You haven't exactly been Mr. Sunshine toward me, so you're hardly one to make any assumptions. I don't judge anyone."

My brows arch, but I remain looking everywhere but at her, because I don't trust what my face looks like. I guess she's not wrong, but it still seems like a cop-out response. I've never had to pull teeth to get answers from anybody before. "That seems like bullshit to me since you've made a lot of half-assed assumptions about me since we've met. You don't know me either, princess."

There's only a short pause. "You were rude to me the first time we talked, made me feel like crap about...things. Said stuff that embarrassed me. Did you know that?"

My eyes narrow in confusion. "When?"

"At your house!" She stops walking, her clipped voice matching the frustrated expression pinching her. "Then you did it again during class. *You* came up to *me* at the bakery and then made it seem like *I* was chasing *you* when you brought it up during film. Just because some girls may be after you doesn't mean we all are. You embarrassed me by making assumptions that weren't even true. You made me feel like..." Her words fade, cheeks flushing as she lets out a frustrated breath. Her throat bobs. "You made me feel *less than*. I'm so sick of people here making me feel that way when I deserve better."

I feel like shit now. "I'm sorry for hurting your feelings. But I don't see what the big deal is. If this is because I watched you doing the walk of—"

"*Stop calling it that.*" Her voice cracks, her eyes darting away quickly, but not before I see them glaze.

What the hell? "Are you crying?"

"N-no."

Shit. Fuck. "Hey, don't... Look, I'm sorry. Okay? I'm not always the best at wording things. I was just trying to say that we've all been there. It's not a big deal. Shit, that house has seen a lot of jers—er, women who come and go the morning after. It's a rite of passage for college kids these days."

"Well, it's not for me!"

I shake my head at her shriek, not understanding the issue. Some women must not want their business out there like men do. Half the time when a woman leaves one of my teammate's rooms, they're walking downstairs like they won a fucking Heisman and give the dirty details to anybody who will listen as soon as they can.

"Fine." I put my hands up to show her I surrender. "I'm obviously not making this any better. If you want to know my awkward firsts, the first time I did something like that, I didn't know the protocol. Do I stay? Leave before she woke up? Stick it out? Grab breakfast? Pay for a cab home? There's a lot to think about with one-night stands."

The dirty look she gives me has me clamming up. She *really* doesn't want to discuss this. The scathing look practically peels the skin right off my bones.

Deciding I'm not ready to end our time together, I wait until she's beside me before matching her steps as we continue to walk.

"You from around here?" I have a talent for these things, and her sun-kissed skin gives me Cali vibes, but one can never be too sure.

Skylar lets out a small breath before answering. "No." Another awkward pause. "I'm from California."

I give myself a secretive smile.

Called it.

"Boston," I tell her, even though she doesn't ask. There's a pep to my step as those baby blues find their way back to me. "In case the accent didn't give it away."

I'd been tempted to stay in Beacon Hill and attend Suffolk University to stay closer to my family because of our close-knit relationship, but when Ma and I visited the private school one summer, the stuffy atmosphere was an instant turnoff. She would've paid for it if she knew it was where I wanted to go, but she knew the second we stepped onto the campus that I'd never have it in my top five to apply for.

The corners of Skylar's lips start to move, but by the time I blink, they're back in their guarded state. I sigh to myself and shrug it off. You win some, you lose some.

Doesn't mean you stop playing. And there's something about this girl and how she doesn't trip all over me that I want to get to know better. "I have this crazy proposition for you." I ignore the stiffness in her shoulders over my chipper proclamation. "I propose we be friends. I'm not saying besties. We have to work up to that. I'll need to grow my hair out some more so you can braid it, but in the meantime, we can gossip about men, make friendship bracelets, and paint each other's fingernails."

She stumbles to a stop, tripping over who knows what. I reach out to steady her, but she jerks her arm away before I can even make contact. "You're *gay*?"

What the fuck? Not that I have anything against gay people. Live your best life and all that. But seriously. The fuck? And why does she sound *hopeful*? "I'm not gay. Why would you even ask me that?"

"I don't know any other man who would gossip about men with me. Or let me paint their nails."

I blink slowly. "I was being funny." Shaking my head, I palm my face and stifle a partial laugh. "Sorry, I guess my sarcasm didn't come through there. I wasn't joking about the friend thing though. I still think we should be friends. Everybody needs a supportive friend group to get them out of their comfort zone. And, well, you look like you could be one of those people. But fair warning. I'd be a shit gossip, I don't know how to make friendship bracelets, and I doubt I'd be any good at painting your fingernails. We could try, I guess..."

"Why?"

"Because practice makes perfect, and I won't get any better at if I—"

"Not about the fingernail painting," she cuts me off, rolling her eyes. There's something playful about the gesture that makes me smile. "I meant why do you want to be my friend? We don't necessarily get along."

"That's because we don't know each other, but when we become friends—"

"If," she corrects.

"*When* we become friends, we'll both realize we're better off. I'll pull you out of the shell you're hiding in"—she makes a weird noise—"and you'll...well, I don't know what you'll do. Entertain me somehow, that's for sure."

She stares wide-eyed at me, like whatever I said is unfathomable to her. Replaying the words, I snort at what she must be assuming I mean.

"Mind out of the gutter, Skylar. I didn't mean sexually." Though the idea makes my dick twitch, which is probably a sign that this proposal is a bad one. But whatever. A girl can't look at you with her mouth open like that without your mind wondering how your cock would fit between her lips.

It's a fact. "You don't like me that much, and I find that sort of amusing. Girls usually say and do whatever it takes to get my attention. I like that you don't. Except that one time at Reavers. Could have gone without you ditching my ass after I offered you my last slice of pizza. My ego is fragile, and I don't offer my food to just anyone." I offer a shrug and show her a teasing smile. "But considering you ditched without even telling me whatever you were set to, I guess it doesn't matter."

Her face turns red. "What I wanted to say to you didn't matter anymore."

"And why is that?" I ask, genuinely curious. She seemed determined to make me hear her out, then left like her conviction disappeared.

When she doesn't answer, I want to shake her. But I don't. If there's one thing I've learned in life, it's that patience gets you a lot further than impatience does.

"You're flighty, but we'll work on that," I inform her, tipping my chin toward the track and walking again. Whether she follows or not is up to her, but I keep talking. "You need to stand your ground more. Like with your friends. If that's what those chicks were from the bakery. Didn't seem super friendly to me."

They were at the party that night too. I don't know when they left or if they planned on leaving Skylar behind from the moment they showed up, but that's none of my business. And the idea of Skylar *wanting* to spend the night with anyone there makes me feel things I have no right to, so I force myself to brush it off.

For now.

"They're…" Her voice fades and footsteps jog closer until her body is a few inches away from mine. "Becca is my roommate. The redhead. The others are people I met when I first got here. Deanna and Aliyah."

"I don't know them, but they seem two-faced." I think back to what her redheaded roommate said at Bea's and feel my eye twitch. How's that saying go? With friends like that, who needs enemies? "This just proves that you need me."

"I don't *need* anyone."

I shake my head, giving her a solid stare down. "That's total bullshit and you know it. Everybody needs an ally in their life to stay sane. If those are the types of people you hang out with, then you'll need some reinforcements who will be there for you and *mean it*. I'll be your guy."

Guy. Friend. Ally. Whatever.

I'm not exactly a poet. Never been great with words. Hell, I threw up once in public speaking in high school and never lived it down. Granted, I'd eaten way too much at lunch and knew I was probably going to regret it. The fact that it was the first real speech I ever had to make was only part of the reason the food made its debut all over the classroom floor.

"So what do you say?" I prompt, watching her carefully to gauge her reaction. Her bottom lip is sucked in by her top teeth as she listens to my proposal. "If the nail painting or gossiping about men thing are deal breakers, I guess I can agree to those terms. If you're interested, I can help you hook up with the guy from the party again if you're into him. Be your wingman. Help a girl out and all that."

The Cali girl turns pale. "You..."

She blinks.

Swallows.

Blinks again and turns redder than before.

Then her eyes go to the track, her feet shifting slightly.

"No," she whispers. "You don't need to find him. I'm not interested."

"You sure?"

"Yep."

"You okay?" I ask, knowing she's not.

"Yep."

"Friends don't lie to other friends," I point out just as quietly as she answered. "But we'll work on that too. We've got time. I'm determined to show you I'm not as much of an asshole as I've come off to be. Want to head back?"

Letting whatever is on her mind go for now seems to be the best option, because Skylar picks her gaze up and manages a tiny nod. We walk back in silence, even though the quiet is slowly eating at me.

Who the hell did she hook up with at the party that makes her look so...empty?

I tell myself friends like to know those things, but my conscience laughs at the ridiculous lie.

~

Film class hits different from the back row because you can get away with more. It's one of the biggest reasons why I *don't* sit here. When I was eight, I was diagnosed with ADD, and the medicine they gave me mellowed me out too much for comfort. Mom told the docs I was a zombie, a shell of myself, so they pulled me from them and tried other methods. I still struggle to pay attention to things, and sitting front and center usually helps me stay on track.

But that's not where my new brunette bombshell of a friend sits. She's in the last row, six seats in, blue backpack placed strategically in the seat next to her so nobody can claim it, moveable desk trapping her inside the stiff theater seat, and a laptop resting on top of it that she types on to get every word Mr. NYU says.

Leg bouncing as the man up front drones on about the history of foreign film, I lean over the seat positioned between us and whisper, "Do you think he's hot too?"

The look she gives me is comical, and I have to swallow my snort before I draw attention to us. Her response makes it harder. "Are you sure you're not gay, Danny?"

Danny.

When is the last time someone called me that? My friends pull out Danny Boy once in a while to mess with me ever since my ma and grandma called me that after one of our games that they attended. But Danny coming out of Skylar's mouth? I like it. Probably too much.

"Danny, huh?" I muse, tapping the end of my pen against my empty notebook. She stares at me fidgeting, watching my moving leg and pen, then the easy grin stretching my lips upward.

I can't say anyone in my life has ever wondered about my sexuality before now. Ma spent my entire teenage years worried I'd knock someone up, while Grandma Meadow constantly warned me against getting into anything serious since I was moving away. When she told me to "have fun being young" while women still wanted me and my body, I think Ma tried glaring her to death. And good old Dad? Well, his opinion never mattered.

Point is, my family never thought I'd bat for the other team. Doubt they'd care if I did. Ma would probably be relieved. Even though we've gotten past the whole teen dad barrier, she now freaks about the college dad scenario. Once in a while, her care packages include Trojan condoms, which the guys give me shit over if they snoop through my stuff, knowing there's usually food in there they can steal too.

"Not gay," I answer with an amused smile. My head tilts toward the rows of seats that primarily consist of twenty-somethings who are on high alert every time the professor speaks. "How much you want to bet these girls are only here because they heard Pretty Boy was teaching the course?"

Her typing pauses as she contemplates her response before lifting a shoulder. "You don't know that for sure. I'm here because I enjoy deconstructing the process of filmmaking. I'm sure some of them are too."

That's a nonanswer. "So you agree he's hot then?"

Closing her eyes for a moment before letting out a small breath, they open to show exasperation. "Why do you care what I think about our professor? If this is you attempting to gossip about men, I'm not interested in that. Especially not in the middle of a lecture. Or if the subject is the person teaching it. That's"—her lips twitch in distaste—"kind of weird."

She would totally bone him.

"Yeah, you do think so," I decide for her, sitting back in my seat and studying the man, whose pants are tighter than those of most men I know. That's red flag number one. The fact that his eyes linger on some of the girls in the front row a little longer than they do on the guys in the room is the second one. Plus, there's the whole prejudice against jocks thing that makes him a total douche canoe. And he's got chicken legs. No meat. I don't know why that pisses me off, but it does.

I'm sure if Pretty Boy paid Skylar special attention like he does the girls who started showing up with a little more cleavage on display, she'd be batting those thick lashes his way and finding ways to stay after class like the other girls.

Would I stop her? I'd sure fucking try.

"Why does your face look so weird?" she asks, making me wipe away whatever expression is pinching my features.

I sink into my seat and grumble, "No reason. Shh, I'm trying to pay attention."

I hear the scoff and smirk to myself as the professor finishes the first part of the class. We always get ten or fifteen minutes in between the lecture and movie, then after the movie finishes, we have a ten-minute discussion before leaving.

My stomach growls loudly as people pass by for bathroom breaks and a quick walk to stretch their legs. Suddenly, a granola bar is tossed at me, smacking me in the arm and bouncing into my lap.

When I pick up the chocolate-covered granola, I grin. "Shit, I haven't had one of these since I was a kid. They used to be my favorite." I look at my seatmate. "You sharing your food with me, sweet cheeks?"

She cringes. "Not if you call me that. I want my granola bar back."

I hold it tightly to my chest, probably melting the chocolate coating. "No way. I'll figure out a new nickname, give me time. Everyone I hang with has one."

"Everyone?"

Nodding, I rip open the food wrapper and take a big bite. "Yep. By the way, did you want half of this? 'Cause I'm a big dude and it'd take probably a whole box of these to even sate my hunger, but I can share this once."

Her head shakes as those long fingers pull some of her dark hair out of her face and into a partial updo. "You already shared your food with me, remember? And no, you don't have to share that. I had one before I came here."

"You didn't even eat the pizza I offered, so it doesn't count. And no dinner?" I question. The class ends at nine, only an hour before the dining hall closes. And the good food is always picked through by then, so it's basically scraps left over.

She murmurs, "Wasn't hungry."

My eyes narrow as I take another bite of the snack, but she avoids looking at me as she types something into her laptop.

"I haven't noticed you around Huden as much," I comment. I'm not ashamed to admit I've kept my eye out for her. At first, I thought she was busy, but then it became a pattern. The guys, Caleb especially, would mess with me when they realized I was looking for someone whenever we were in there together.

She keeps typing away. "We must miss each other."

Doubtful. My eyes narrow at her. She moves some of her hair to shield her face. I flick a couple of the strands. "What's your natural color?"

One of her lighter brows flicks up. "Why do you think I'm not brunette?"

I eye the various strands that are darker and some that are lighter. Plus, she showed up at the party with black hair. "I've seen you before now, remember? And something tells me the Edgar Allan Poe look isn't your normal either."

She snorts. "Edgar Allan Poe?"

"The poet. Your black hair reminded me of him because of his poem about the—"

"Raven," we say simultaneously.

We both smile, mine wider than hers.

She says, "I'm familiar with it. And you're right. I'm a natural blond." Her eyes go to my hair. "I think it's a little darker

85

than yours. Sometimes in the sunlight, I'd have highlights that made it look almost brown. It used to make my sisters jealous."

"Why'd you dye it?"

She sits still for a while. Too still. "I needed a change," she murmurs. "Something new for my freshman year. I wanted to be different."

There's more to the story, but I don't think she'd tell me if I asked, so I decide not to push the subject. Instead, I ask, "You *are* eating, right?"

I've noticed the slightest change in her face. It's narrower than it was the first time I saw her, like she's lost a little weight. My eyes have raked over her a time or two to see if it's noticeable anywhere else, but I never get to look long because someone always catches me.

She scoffs. "Yes. Quit worrying, *Mom*."

I grin at the quip. "Friends worry about each other, Blondie."

Skylar eyes me at my new nickname but doesn't turn it down like the others. All she says is, "I'm not blond."

I snicker. "It still works. Blondie." I rub my chin and nod. "My friends will probably call you something else when you meet them, but this can be our thing."

"*When* I meet your friends?" Her head shakes rapidly, making one of those loose strands of hair fall into her face. I itch to reach over and move it for her but force myself to keep my hands to myself.

"Yep. We're friends, remember? So you'll meet my other friends. Mostly guys from the team. Not all of them." I can think of a few I'd keep her far, far away from. Wallace comes to mind as the top spot, but there are other horndogs on the team who I wouldn't want her around unless at least ten feet separated them.

"No, I'm—"

"Aw, they're not that bad." And it's true. Aiden, Caleb, and our captain, Justin Brady, are good people. Over half the guys who live at the house are easy to get along with. A little loud. A little too obsessed with *Call of Duty*. But still overall okay humans. "You met Aiden. He was the giant with me when you, er, left the house that one time. He may not seem it, but the guy is a total teddy bear. I swear."

Maybe that's a little bit of a lie, but I feel the need to convince her. Why? I don't know. I've never actively tried getting a girl to meet my friends before. Mostly because there's never been one who seems cool enough that I'd want to hang with. Hook up with? Sure. But the girls I did that with were a little dense. I may not know Skylar that well, but she doesn't seem like any of the women I've stripped bare and become physically acquainted with.

"What's your last name?" I wonder, balling up the empty wrapper and stuffing it into the pocket of my jeans.

My new friend doesn't answer right away. Her eyes are staring at her computer screen, but I don't think she's actually paying attention to whatever is on it. "Allen."

Hmm. "Okay, Skylar Allen. I've just now decided that I want to shoot for best friend status. I know it's soon, but I think we've got what it takes to make it work."

She slowly turns to me, confusion on her face that makes my lips waver upward. "Didn't you tell me the other day it would take time to become besties? Why now? Because you know my natural hair color and we know each other's last names?"

I lean back, kicking my boots up on the empty chair top in front of me. "Nah, because I like you. You're mysterious, cute, and awkward. Three things that intrigue me.

There's an air to you that's refreshing. Do you know what that means?"

To nobody's surprise, she's silent.

"It means," I answer for her, pointing my pen in her direction, "that you can't get rid of me easily. I'm like a pest."

"A really big pest," she mumbles under her breath.

I chuckle. "Oh, baby. The *biggest*. I make all the other pests jealous."

Like I figured, she gets the innuendo and openly glares at me before declaring, "I'm never sharing my food with you again."

We both know she will, so I sit back comfortably and find myself watching her throughout the film instead of the subtitles moving across the screen.

Guess I'll have to get notes from her, which is another excuse to spend time with her.

I smirk to myself.

Chapter Ten

SKYLAR

"Come on. It'll be quieter up here."

Big hands on my shoulder.

On my lower back.

On my hip.

Roaming hands.

Strong ones ghosting over my butt.

A sour breath cascading over my face.

"What do you say?"

I say nothing.

Kissing—I liked kissing him.

The touching started making me feel uncomfortable.

Long fingers wrapping around my arms to hold me still against the—

Bolting upright in bed, I frantically look around the room with sweat dotting my forehead. My heart is racing at record speed as I take in my surroundings like I've done the past few times I've woken up to memories from that night. I look at the purple curtains closed on the window, the small wooden desk covered with textbooks, my laptop, and two picture frames with photos of my family in them. I absorb my favorite romance and fantasy novels lining the shelf and let myself breathe.

Deep breath in. Deep breath out.

Again.

Again.

I grip the black-and-purple comforter in my fists as a light flicks on across the room, temporarily blinding me. My roommate's disgruntled voice sleepily says, "Really, dude? That's the second night in a row you woke me up freaking out."

I woke up the night before in a startled cry at three a.m., sweat coating my body and making my pajamas stick to my skin uncomfortably. I'd gotten up, heard Becca's grumbles as I collected clothes from the wooden armoire the university provided each of us with, and took a shower. I never went back to sleep, which is why she came back to the room after class that afternoon and woke me up from a midday nap to say, "Seriously? Don't you have something better to do with your time?"

The circles under my eyes have gotten darker, and Olive showed me how to cover them properly with makeup, so I don't look like a walking zombie. That is, after she grilled me about why I look so dead on my feet all the time.

I'd said insomnia.

A white lie.

I feel bad for waking Becca for about ten seconds before her pager goes off. The pager that the fire station gave her when she signed on to volunteer there. It's gone off in the middle of the night twice since she got it, along with the scanner she plugged in on top of her desk. Did I complain about that like she complains about my nightmares? Only internally when it'd woken me up from the first night of peaceful sleep I'd had in I don't know how long. Other than that, I keep quiet. I have no right to be irritated when I disturb her sleep too.

Kill her with kindness.

She throws the blanket off her as she reaches for the pager. "I don't know what issues you have, but it's messing up my sleep schedule. If you're homesick, then *go home*."

That's what she thinks this is? It's on the tip of my tongue to correct her, to tell her just how wrong she is, but I swallow those words instead. She wouldn't care. She wouldn't understand.

Rubbing my eyes with the heels of my palms, I shake my head and push away the thought of ghost hands on my body and whispered words against my ear.

It'll be quieter up here.

What do you say?

Those words haunt me, replaying over and over no matter how hard I try to forget them.

I kissed him back.

Let him touch me.

I wanted it.

Some of it.

A thick ball of emotion jams itself in my throat that clearing it can't even budge. "I'm not homesick," I tell Becca, voice hoarse with exhaustion as I pull the covers over my body and lie back down. "It doesn't matter, so why bother trying to make you think otherwise? Turn the light off before you leave, please."

There's a pause where she takes in my cool tone, one she's not used to from me, before she mumbles, "Why did I ever agree to room with you?"

My teeth grind. "I don't know, but I'm asking myself the same thing."

The light turns off and we're bathed in darkness again. I clench the blankets tight in my fingers and face the painted white cement block wall with a frown. I can hear her rustling on her side of the room, sliding on her shoes, and snatching her keys up from where she keeps them hung by the door.

It's only when she leaves that I let out a breath of relief.

My nose scrunches as if I can still smell the strong scent of liquor lingering from the nightmare clinging to my consciousness. Rum and coke. Fingers grazing my bare skin. A weight being pressed against me.

"Stop," I whisper to myself, clenching my eyes closed.

It's just a dream, I chant to myself.

I say it a few more times but never believe it once, even when I succumb to temporary darkness.

~

I stare at the football player who I've since learned is the Dragon's wide receiver. And based on the horrible sketch DJ drew me in his notebook when we should have been studying, his position is on the offense catching and running the ball. Or, in his terms, being "a badass" on the field.

"Are you serious?" I ask.

He nods again, gesturing for me to turn around. "Totally serious. I watched videos on YouTube. I know what I'm doing."

I blink, hesitating only a second before he physically turns my chair. When he starts separating my hair into sections, I can't help but giggle in disbelief. Because who would have thought someone like him would be adamant about this sort of thing? "Why would you look up braiding tutorials?"

"Because," he answers in exasperation, "I need to know this shit now. None of my other friends have long enough hair, so you're the guinea pig on my new skills. I had to practice on shoelaces. Do you know what a pain in the ass that is? To be perfectly honest, though, the friendship bracelets I promised are going to take some time. Those strings are tiny. I could barely keep ahold of the laces I was practicing with."

I sit completely still in my chair while the "badass" footballer puts my hair into a simple braid. He's not bashful about it either. There are people watching from where they're perched on the second level of the library, some taking pictures, some just smiling. I think a girl is glaring at me, but I ignore it. I shouldn't be surprised at the mixed reactions, considering Daniel Bridges is an attractive guy—definitely not one you'd expect to be braiding some random girl's hair in the middle of the day. Especially when he's doing it willingly when I don't remember one time when my sisters mentioned one of their guy friends doing this for them, much less anybody they dated.

The last thing I want to do is complicate things by questioning DJ's motives. He wants to be friends. I can do the friends thing. I think.

"How long were you watching tutorials for?" I ask as he takes the hair tie from me and twists it around the end of the finished product.

"A couple hours."

I want to turn my head and gape at him, but he won't let me. "Why?"

"Because I'm a perfectionist" is all he says, tone casual as he pats my back twice in indication he's done.

I pick up my phone and examine myself in the camera

app, then look at him. "It looks good." I touch it lightly and smile.

He leans back in his seat, stretching out his legs as he watches me proudly. "I know how to dye hair too. My grandma used to make me help dye hers when the white started taking over. Hate the smell of the stuff, but I'm pretty damn good."

I bite down on the inside of my cheek to stop myself from grinning like a fool. The mental picture of the brawny boy sitting in front of me helping his grandmother is too much.

"C'mere." He yanks on my chair until it's as close as it can get to his before he grabs my phone and presses our faces together. "Smile, Blondie."

I obey, albeit confused, as he snaps a few pictures and glances at them after. We look…oddly cute in them. He's beaming, and my smile may not be as big, but it's as genuine.

"What was that for?" I accept my phone when he passes it back to me, examining the images again. The dark circles under my eyes are almost invisible thanks to the primer and foundation I put on this morning. If I hadn't, DJ would have asked me for a third time if I was sleeping.

He pulls himself back over to the table where our things are scattered everywhere. "It's to make memories."

I stare at him in silence, blinking slowly as he opens his notebook and begins scanning the pages of scribbles across them.

He's nonchalant when he asks, "Do you think Mr. NYU is going to quiz us on this week's content? Because all I wrote down is 'douche,' and something tells me that's not going to help me very much."

I can't help but snort as he peers up at me with a slick grin across his face. There's a twinkle in his eye that's dangerous.

"I knew I could make you laugh," he says.
My head tilts. "I *do* laugh, you know."
He's quiet for a moment. "Not enough."
We stare at each other for a long time.
I can't make myself look away.

Chapter Eleven

SKYLAR

OLIVE HOLDS OUT A large iced coffee with whipped cream and caramel drizzle on top, shaking it when I don't take it from her. "Girl, you look like you need this more than I do right now. You okay?"

I want to tell her no, but I feign a smile and accept the much-needed caffeine along with the straw she passes me. "Yeah, I'm good. Not sleeping well, that's all. And thank you."

We fall into step on our way to Intro to Comm class. "Did Becca have to go into the station again? I heard a fire alarm going off in the building next to me. I guess someone set a paper plate on fire in the oven trying to heat up chicken nuggets in the middle of the night."

I blink with the straw halfway to my mouth for the first sip of salvation. "Are you kidding me?" Even though my family had people who cooked for us most times, even *I* knew better than that. What's next? A fork in the microwave?

Olive shakes her head, looking as exasperated as me. "I

wish. Did Becca have to respond to that one? I guess the RA put out the flames with an extinguisher, but the department had to inspect damage for insurance purposes or something."

My mouth waters when I finally get some of the coffee, my taste buds exploding with the sugary flavor. "Heaven sent," I say, nudging Olive with my shoulder. She's become the closest friend I have at Lindon. Our mutual love for *The Voice*, chicken tenders, and fries helped us bond after picking up said fried food from Reavers and binge-watching the newest episodes of the singing competition together. She helps me with my makeup, hangs out just to be lazy, and gossips about anything happening on campus. Our friendship is easy, uncomplicated. "And yeah, she went to it."

"How are you two?"

I choose my words carefully, because Olive may know about the strain between me and my roommate, but she still likes Becca to some degree. I don't want to stoop to my roomie's level and talk out of pettiness or expect Olive not to like her simply because my roommate can't stand me. "We're the same as usual. I don't think it's going to get better at this point. But what can I do?"

Olive holds the door open for me, and I wait until she slips through before we head toward the stairs leading to the basement where our class is held.

"I don't think I'm going to survive this winter if I'm already freezing now."

It's only October, which makes my friend snort next to me. "You're in for a ride. In about three weeks, we'll start seeing single-digit temperatures, and then you'll probably regret ever leaving California."

I make a face at that, thinking about all the reasons I left. For freedom. For independence. To prove to myself that I could handle things on my own. Not that I've done particularly well in that department so far. "We'll see."

We drop our things in our normal seats and sit while a few other students shuffle in. I keep forgetting Olive is from Vermont. She's used to colder weather. When she told me that she, her nieces, and her nephews enjoy going hiking through the woods behind their houses after the first snowfall, I thought she was going to pee herself from how hard she laughed over my horrified expression. Then she may have *actually* peed a little after I admitted I'd never seen snow in real life before. Only in movies.

Olive fiddles with her pen for a few seconds before looking over at me. "Hey, so I was thinking about something."

"What?"

"I know you said you don't do parties."

The coffee I'm drinking suddenly feels heavy in my mouth as I swallow it.

"I normally wouldn't ask you or even consider going," Olive continues, "but there's this guy I like who I'm positive is going to be there. And it's not technically a party. It's outside, which means way more room to mingle. It'd be the perfect opportunity for me to try making a move."

My eyes shift from her to the coffee, which I now realize is a bribe. Eyes narrowing suspiciously, I lower it to my desk. "Did you buy this to soften me up?"

She looks apologetic. "You skipped out on the last bonfire that Aliyah brought up, so I was hoping if I gave you caffeine and *then* asked, there'd be a better chance of you agreeing to come with me. But I'll understand if you say no. I don't want you to be uncomfortable."

Despite the bribery, I can tell she means that. I'm about to speak when she cuts me off to add, "Oh! And Becca and

Dee won't be there because there's something going on at the fire department. It'd just be me and you, most likely. *If* you say yes. You know I won't ditch you."

I do know that she wouldn't ditch me like the others, which is the only reason I'm actually considering this. A bonfire at the end of October, though? "Who's hosting it?"

Olive nibbles her lip. "The hockey team. But the football team will be there," she continues, voice a notch or two lower than before, like she senses my reasoning for asking. "Which draws a pretty big crowd. They sort of run in the same circles since they all play sports. Lacrosse players will probably make an appearance too. I know Patrick Malone made a move on you, but he hasn't since, right? I heard somebody told him to leave you alone, so I'm sure he'll be preoccupied if you're worried about him. He's the captain, so he's going to have to keep his guys in check."

Somebody told Patrick to leave me alone? "Who told him that?"

She shrugs. "I'm not sure. It's just gossip. A friend of a friend of a friend told me that you were, like, off-limits or something."

I gape, unsure of what to say to that. It probably isn't a bad thing that Patrick or other guys think I'm off-limits. At least for a while. It'll give me space. That is, unless Becca intervenes like she's done before. It doesn't matter that I tell her not to. She thinks it's a game.

I decide not to dwell on it. "And you're interested in…?" I take another sip of the coffee, trying to let it calm me even though the idea of being surrounded by that many people makes me want to vomit.

"Alex O'Conner. He's a left wing on Lindon's hockey team." Her mint eyes brighten as she perks up. "He's probably going pro, not that I care about that. It's just facts. He's an amazing player. If you've never been to an actual hockey game, you need to come to one with me. There's nothing quite like seeing big, muscular men beating on each other on the ice."

I blink a few times. I know my seatmate is a big gamer because I've watched her play the violent games in her room before. Her liking hockey for the violence isn't that surprising to me after seeing her yell at the TV screen and curse out the game console she plays on.

She waves it off. "Anyway, I'm positive Alex will have, like, twenty other girls all over him, but I know the game. I can impress him with my stats knowledge. Speak his language, you know? Stand out."

I don't know how guys would react to that. I'm not well versed in anything man-related, especially when sports are involved. If what DJ has to say means anything, this Alex guy would either enjoy her knowledge of his game or assume she's only trying to get laid by employing it during conversation.

Not that I would judge her for it if she was using it to her advantage, as long as it's what she wants. "What exactly do you want from him?"

She shrugs. "I'm not stupid enough to think he'll want to date me, Sky. I mean, maybe. I'm pretty awesome. Why *wouldn't* he want all this? Not only do I know most sports references, but I kick ass at most video games that guys like. And I have great boobs. I'm practically a guy's wet dream."

I smile at her confidence, trying not to laugh as she glances down at said assets and lifts them with her hands to make a point.

"*But* if he does go pro, that means he'll have way more

to focus on than a girlfriend. I just want to go to the bonfire and shoot my shot, then see where it goes." Olive's perfectly tweezed eyebrows wiggle. "Get it? Shoot my shot. Like—"

I giggle. "I get it. Hockey. Clever."

She clasps her fingers together and bats her long, painted lashes at me like that'll somehow influence my decision. "What do you say? Will you come with me? I promise I'll protect you from Patrick and Tyler and whoever else you don't want hitting on you if they try something."

I make a face. "Tyler is just a flirt, Olive."

The noise she makes is a cross between a snort and scoff, making it sound like a pig on crack. "Girl, open your eyes. That boy has got it bad. Didn't you notice the way he glared at Patrick when he came over to you at Huden the other day? He scootched closer to you like he was trying to claim his territory. You're lucky he didn't cock his leg and pee."

My face scrunches in disgust. "That's gross and not the visual I needed. And it's hard to tell with guys like Tyler." I shrug. "Last week, he was all over some girl from Econ 101. I don't take him that seriously."

She gives me a sympathetic pat on the hand. "I don't think he takes himself seriously either. The point is guys pay attention to you. They have for a while. You just don't pay any attention to them."

I'm not completely naive. I've seen the way some guys look at me when I'm around them. They see a freshman who looks like a puppy in need of some guidance and want to help in any way they can. For a price.

Pass. Hard pass. The thought of pursuing any of them makes me physically uncomfortable because eventually they'll want *more*. I don't think I can give them that.

Then there are some guys I pay way more attention to

than I should. Like the wide receiver who's braided my hair twice now and told me all about his favorite TV show—*Friends*—and insisted we start watching it together when he found out I'd never seen a single episode. I notice how his muscles stretch and flex when he does things, and I notice how his blue eyes linger on my lips when I talk, and I notice how often his hand twitches when I'm near, like he wants to touch me but doesn't.

I don't want to like DJ, but I'm starting to. I just haven't quite figured out how much yet or how much he may know about the night at the football house. My stomach tightens whenever I think about the information he could be holding on to if he's heard guys talk.

"I don't need your protection from Tyler," I tell her honestly, sitting back in my seat and gripping my drink. "Or any guy, for that matter. But I appreciate the offer."

I watch the professor walk in, in his usual eccentric, hippie-like clothes. He sets his messenger bag on the table and walks over to the computer to setup for class.

"Hypothetically," I say, "what would happen if your shot made it past the goalie?"

She pauses, then beams at me. "Oh my God, are you making hockey references?"

"Only for you. Anyway, what if he's interested and wants to whisk you away?"

"Then I'll tell him he has to wait."

I shake my head, grateful she'd keep her word and stick by my side even if the reason she showed up gave her a chance. "If he's as popular as you say, turning him down if he's interested probably isn't the best way to go. But as long as you tell me you're leaving, then I'll go be your wingwoman for this thing."

She reaches over and squeezes my arm, clearly shocked by my answer. "You're the best! I'll buy you a coffee every morning from now until Friday!"

I don't point out that Friday is only two days away because she's clearly too excited to think straight. "Let me know when you want to meet up. I need to figure out what to wear so I don't freeze to death."

She's giddy. "Thank you for doing this."

Part of me wonders why she needs me if Aliyah will be there, but I don't question her because it's nice that she wants me to come. It makes me feel like I belong for once.

When you spend a long time wondering where you fit in, you hold on a little tighter to the people who make you feel like the perfect-sized puzzle piece in their jigsaw puzzle.

Chapter Twelve

DANNY

I KNOW I'M IN trouble when I see Skylar walk up to the crowd gathered around the crackling fire and think, *damn, she's cute.*

She's bundled up like it's ten degrees instead of fifty, with a bulky jacket that does little for her figure and a knit beanie covering her loose hair. Her hands are stuffed into the pockets of her coat, and her legs are covered in a pair of jeans that are a little tighter than what I've seen her in around campus.

Because I've looked. A lot.

If I see her walking by herself or with others, I'm giving her a once-over before I realize what I'm doing. Granted, she's not the only woman I check out, just the only one my eyes linger on a fraction longer.

Cute.

Fuck.

A hand smacks into my chest. "Who you got your eyes on tonight? Going to be lots to choose from."

I give Caleb a look before passing him one of the beers I got for us. "Don't have my eyes on anybody," I lie, trying to be subtle about searching for Skylar in the crowd. I lost her though. "Where's Raine? She coming to this?"

His head shakes. "Nah, the girls had some pre-Halloween bash at their place or some shit. I was going to go, but Raine told me their ringleader was in a mood and I don't feel like dealing with her."

I'm tempted to ask, since he complains about the platinum Barbie every time he's there, but I bite back the curiosity.

"Hey, did Aiden mention anything about Ivy?" Caleb asks.

The question pulls me away from my search of the masses of people gathering around the building fire. "Nah. He hasn't said much to me since the party."

Caleb smothers a smile with his hand before raising his bottle to his lips. "You did promise to keep an eye out on people and then got bribed by a six-pack to let things slide. Should have held out for more, you cheap fucker."

Grinning, I shove his shoulder and say, "It was *three* six-packs. And whatever, asshat. Why are you asking about her anyway?"

All he does is shake his head. "It doesn't matter. Anyway, I'll probably leave early and head back to the house. Just want to say hi to a couple people. You want a ride back, or are you planning on getting laid for once?"

I contemplate my answer when I see Skylar pop up again. Her friend is a little shorter and a little curvier than her and looking for someone, based on the way she stands on her tiptoes and scans the crowd. "Uh...can I get back to you on that?"

He nods, eyes trailing to see what's caught mine. "Mmm.

Word of advice? Be careful. You know how small the grape-vine is here, and there's been…talk."

My spine straightens. "What does *that* mean?"

He holds up his hand. "I'm not judging what anyone does. All I'm saying is that the guys have been talking, and she"—Caleb's chin dips toward Skylar—"has been the center of their conversations. Some chick is talking about how your girl gets around. I'm not sure what's true or not, but if there's talk, there's got to be some thread of truth to it. She seems nice, but you never know. Just because you basically pissed all over her in front of Malone so he'd back off doesn't mean everybody else is going to listen. You basically made her a challenge."

I don't like the sound of that one bit.

When I confronted Malone the other day, he'd been a smug fucker like he already won Skylar. I made sure to remind him of reality. He had no claim on the timid brunette, just like I didn't have any.

Do I want to change that? Yeah. The more I hang with her, the more I like her down-to-earth personality. Regardless of the talk apparently going around, there's been no proof of her rumored reputation. It only enhances my need to get down to the bottom of it—of *her*.

My nose twitches. "Got it."

He smacks the back of my shoulders before squeezing one. "I'm leaving in thirty. Find me and let me know what your answer is, or I'm ditching your ass to fend for yourself."

We both know I could get anyone to give me a ride wherever I need. All it takes is flashing my dimple and shoot-ing a wink, and most of the women here would wiggle their keys *and* their panties at me.

Weaving through a few people who slap me on the back

or try making small talk, I make my way to the small opening by one of the kegs where Skylar and her friend are. "Wasn't expecting you here," I tell the cozy-looking brunette. Her cheeks are already red, and I don't know if it's from me or the nipping wind. "Why didn't you say you were coming?"

Her brows go up. "How would I have?"

I open my hand. "Give me your phone."

"What? No."

Her friend laughs. "He wants your number, Sky." She turns to me and smiles. "I think I know you. DJ, right? Wide receiver for the football team? You had the most hundred-plus-yard games since you started playing for the Dragons."

I give her one of my charming smiles, impressed she knows that. "Yep, that's me."

Skylar looks at her friend. "Be careful with this one, or he'll think you're flirting with him. He thinks every girl is a jersey chaser if you stare at him for more than two seconds."

Her dry warning gets a laugh out of both me and her short-haired companion. I deserved that.

"He thinks *you're a* jersey chaser? That's hilarious. You know nothing about sports."

Most of the women who chase after athletes know nothing about the game. They aren't after our stats; they're after our short-lived fame. All colleges have sports stars who are bigger than life, and with them the fanatics who think they can get a taste. Most of that ends once we get the diploma slapped in our palms. Then we're nobody again, forgotten. I'm not sure how I feel about that—relieved or nervous.

I know my marketing degree can get me work, especially if I move back to Boston after college. I just haven't pinpointed what it is I want to do. After realizing that the damage to the ligaments in my shoulder would make it near impossible to pursue anything in the professional sports field, I had to accept that going into anything sports-related may be a little too crushing for me.

It's a reality I find a little heartbreaking because I love the game, but then I think about being around my family again in Massachusetts and figuring out a job there. I'd have red wine dates with Grandma Meadow as she tells me about a game of bridge she won during commercials of reality TV we binge together or brunch dates with Ma as she fills me in on the charity work that she's passionate about. My family grounds me. Reminds me it'll be okay.

"That's not true," Skylar argues, crossing her arms in defense. "I know Daniel Bridges Junior is a wide receiver who had the most hundred-plus-yard games since he started playing for the Dragons. And I also know that Alex O'Conner is the left wing for the school's hockey team and he's probably going pro."

She's a hockey fan?

Her friend shoves her shoulder playfully. "You just repeated exactly what I said. And hands off my man, Allen. I called dibs on Alex." She goes back up on her tiptoes and eyes the various people around us. When she comes up blank, she sighs and turns to me. "Sky hasn't even been to any of the school's sports games. Did you know that? When I asked what sports she's watched before, she told me *none*."

That gets my eyebrows rising at the cheeky girl standing in front of me. "You haven't even seen a game on TV? Your parents never had the Super Bowl on or anything?"

She shakes her head, which explains the lost look she was giving me when I tried explaining what position I play for the team. "I don't come from a sports family. None of them care about any of that. One of my sisters plays tennis, but it's mostly because she thinks the clothes are cute. My dad plays golf sometimes with his business associates, but he's not very good at it. Otherwise, we all think sports are kind of…" Her words fade before she lifts a shoulder, hesitant.

"Kind of what?" I press, holding back the smile tugging on my lips.

She sighs. "We all think they're boring, okay? I don't see what the big deal is. It's just people running after balls and pucks and stuff."

Hand flying to my heart like she shot me, I squeeze my chest. "Wow. Them are fighting words, girl."

All she does is roll her eyes.

Her friend laughs. "I feel like I'm missing something vital here. How do you two know each other?"

Skylar never mentioned me. Interesting. Not sure if I should be offended or what, but I don't let it get to me. "We have class together and find ourselves bumping into one another around campus more and more these days. I'm trying to convince her to be my best friend, but she's stubborn. I guess her hating the sport I play is probably a big factor, since it can't possibly be my charming personality and good looks that makes her hesitant."

A groan comes from the girl I'm teasing while her friend grins, flicking an intrigued gaze between the two of us. "I never said I hated football," Skylar points out. "I said sports seem boring to me. It's nothing personal."

Seems personal, but I let it drop. "Does that mean you'll give me your number so you can tell me when you're coming to these things? I can be your escort. Your wingman. Remember?"

"I practically had to drag her here after bribing her with

caffeine." Her friend sticks her hand out. "Give me your phone. Maybe you can get her out more often since none of us can."

I let myself wonder who the "us" is that her friend refers to, noticing the small wince coming from the girl in question over the statement. But when I accept it's none of my business, I don't think twice before depositing my beat-up phone with a small crack in the screen into her friend's hand.

She types something in before passing it back. "There, now you have her number so you can let *her* be *my* wingman tonight. I need to meet Alex before somebody with bigger boobs steals him away."

Snickering, I glance at the ballsy chick with her sights set on one man in particular. It's hard not to glance at the things she's hoping to reel him in with, but it's not her I'm hoping to snag tonight, so I keep my attention strictly on her face. "You think Skylar is going to help you get introductions with O'Conner even though she doesn't know him?"

They're both quiet.

I slip my phone into my back pocket. "I'll help you. I happen to know him *and* where he's chilling. On one condition."

They both stare at me.

My finger points at Skylar. "Blondie has to leave with me once I introduce you to your knight in shining ice skates."

Skylar is about to protest when her friend pipes up with an enthusiastic, "Deal! I'm Olive, by the way. Yes, I know how stupid the name is. No, I haven't chosen something better to legally change it to. Now, can you introduce me to Alex?"

Our mutual friend gapes at *Olive* like she can't believe

she sold her out. Me, on the other hand, I'm happy as ever. "Follow me, ladies."

A pair of jean-clad legs matches my strides. "Blondie? Still? I thought that was something you were testing out."

I bump her shoulder and watch her make a face and casually inch away from the playful contact. "It's fitting. Blondie was one of my ma's favorite bands. She met Debbie Harry when she was younger. Said she's spunky."

"And you think I'm spunky?"

"You've got fire in you, yeah." I smile down at her as she studies me skeptically. "You just need to let it burn a little more often."

She lets it go. "You can't expect me to leave with you after this. Olive only agreed because she's excited to meet Alex."

"One of my buddies is driving me back to our place. We're going to order some pizza, probably watch a movie or play video games for a bit and just kick back. Nothing big. That seems more your speed than this anyway."

I'm not wrong, and we both know it, which is why she doesn't disagree. "Even if that's true, I don't want to go back to your place."

I want to ask what she has here that's better, but I'm not sure I'd want to hear the answer. So I decide to ask, "What do you have against the house?"

No response.

In fact, she tenses.

"If it's back to the whole—"

Her hand raises to stop me. "Nope. Not going there again."

"You need to stop being so sensitive, babe," I tell her calmly.

That's when the real fire comes out.

111

"And *you* need to stop calling me babe and assuming you know what's going on in my head," she snaps at me, causing us to halt in the middle of the crowd.

Olive inches forward. "Um…everything okay, you guys?" Her eyes are on Skylar only, not paying an ounce of attention to me. At least this friend seems to actually give a shit about her.

"Peachy," Skylar murmurs in an unconvincing tone. "Let's go meet your hockey guy."

I watch as she starts walking off, obviously having no idea where she's going. "It's the other way, Blondie," I call out, trying to lighten the mood instead of letting my confusion take over.

She stops, shoulders drawing back, before turning slowly to me. Her sigh is heavy before she crosses her arms on her chest and waits for me to take lead again.

Grinning as I pass by her, I guide them to where O'Conner is sitting with a group of his followers flocking him as usual. I don't know the dude that well, just that he definitely enjoys the attention. He's tight with our captain and OG quarterback, Justin Brady, so he can't be too much of a dick.

"You sure about this?" I hear Skylar whisper to her friend.

"I'll make sure he considers naming our future daughter after you" is Olive's response.

I snort and stop in front of the hockey player. He stands and slaps my hand before noticing the two women lingering behind me.

"You bring me more fans, Bridges?" he asks cockily, his eyes going to the taller brunette instead of the shorter one. There's recognition in his eyes that makes me think back to Caleb's warning about Skylar's reputation.

I step in front of Skylar to block his view, nostrils flaring with irritation over his roaming eyes. "Got a friend of a friend who wanted to meet you. Big fan. Olive, this is Alexander O'Conner. Not that you need me to tell you that. O'Conner, this is Olive. Don't know her last name. But she's a feisty one and could give you a run for your money."

Thankfully, that's all it takes for his interest to be diverted to the chick practically bouncing where she stands.

I turn to Skylar. "Look, I'm not big on these things. I plan on heading out soon, and I don't want to leave you by yourself. If you don't want to come have pizza at my place, then let me and Caleb drop you off at your dorm, yeah? Unless there's somebody here you want to hang with instead..."

Her eyes go to her friend, who's already in deep conversation with O'Conner about game talk, before they trail back to me. She draws her bottom lip in and nibbles, thoroughly capturing my attention. In the dim light, I see they're painted some sort of pink color. Almost neutral, but enough to make any man want to stare for a little longer than necessary. "Olive looks like she'll probably want to stay..."

"Doesn't mean you have to."

She takes a deep breath. "I don't really feel like being alone tonight," she relents. "But if I want to leave, you'll take me back to my dorm anytime?"

I stand straighter. "Of course."

Her eyes are weary, yet she says, "Okay."

~

While Skylar uses the bathroom, I eye the guys in the living room fighting over who gets to play the next round of their game. "Hands to yourselves tonight," I say, grateful it's only a few of them here. Justin, Caleb, Stephen Marks, another wide receiver, and Aiden are here. Everyone else who lives in the house is scattered. Probably at the bonfire or the Halloween bash at the sorority a block away.

Justin and Caleb both look over at me while Marks grabs the controller from our captain's distracted hands. "This chick your girl or something?"

His question doesn't sit well with me. It makes my skin itch. My hands fidget. "No. She's a friend. Just...don't act like assholes."

"Wallace isn't here," Marks muses, shooting something in the game and whooping when the target goes down. "So your girl will be safe. Though I hear she can hold her own with the guys."

My girl. I should correct him, but I don't. I also choose to ignore his little tidbit in the end, not meeting Caleb's knowing eyes as if to say, *What'd I tell you about her?*

I gesture toward the TV. "Maybe put a movie on or something. You've probably been playing this shit for hours. Didn't your ma ever tell you it'll rot your brain?"

Caleb laughs, standing up and stretching his arms. "Like any of us actually listened to our moms. Probably the reason they're all going gray. I saw yours at the championships last year, Bridges. Poor woman barely had a streak of blond left on that pretty head of hers."

As we walk toward the kitchen, I shove him to the side. "Don't talk about my mother."

He elbows me before walking over to the fridge and grabbing a water. "You want a beer?"

"Nah, man. One was enough."

Skylar appears at the doorway, sheepishly glancing between me and the team's running back, who's taking a swig of his drink.

Caleb smiles at her. "Hey. You're in luck. Most of the idiots we live with are out partying, so it should be pretty quiet tonight."

She gives him a small nod, even though she looks uncomfortable as hell scoping out the place.

I grab the menu to the local pizza shop and drop it onto the counter. "Coach is going to have their asses if he finds out. Last thing we need is them coming to practice hungover."

Caleb cringes. "Yeah, you're not wrong. We have enough players out for…" His eyes go to my guest before stopping. "Well, let's just hope they're smart tonight."

There were a few guys who got delivered the bad news and needed some heavy doses of medication and reality checks after the tests we had to take. I don't envy any of them. Most of them were the newer rookies who obviously didn't get the same wrap-it-before-you-tap-it lecture by parentals and school health officials that I did.

I pull out my phone to dial the pizzeria and shake my head at the text message on the screen from my grandmother.

Grandma M: Your mom tells me you're still single. Maybe you need to expand the age range you're looking for. That JLo girl seems to date men a lot younger than her.

"Christ," I murmur, unable to stop myself from chuckling as I thumb out a reply.

Me: I'll take that into consideration

Caleb asks, "Meadow?"

I nod. "She's trying to play matchmaker. Again." My

sigh comes next before I glance up at Skylar. "You'd like my grandma. She doesn't take my bullshit either."

Pride swells in my chest when I get a small smile from her again. It's tiny. Microscopic, really. But it still counts. The girl is too damn pretty to frown as much as she does.

Cute, I think to myself.

Shaking it off, I jab my finger toward the basement door. "Going to go see if Aiden wants any pizza before I call in. You and the guys good with your normal?"

Caleb nods before going back into the living room where they're hollering over something I have not the slightest clue about.

I look at Skylar. "They're passionate about their video games."

"And what about you?"

I wink. "Nobody can beat my high score."

That gets me a huff of a laugh.

"I'll be right back. Help yourself to whatever you want. There's water, beer, and juice in the fridge. Glasses are in the cupboard closest to the sink unless the lazy dicks didn't do the dishes."

I open the door to the basement that leads to where our tight end sleeps and call out, "Hey, Griff, the guys are ordering—Oh, shit."

Nearly tripping on my feet when I jerk to a stop at the bottom, I take in the scene. The blue-haired girl with a feisty attitude, Ivy, is straddling the giant football player on the couch. And...

Is her hand clutching his throat?

Shit.

Wasn't expecting that.

"We're a little busy," Ivy informs me, looking over her

shoulder with a bored expression plastered on her face despite whatever kinky shit is happening between them.

"I can see that." My eyes trail from her to him, eyebrows quirked up at the interesting position they're in. Guess it's always the quiet ones that'll fool you. I start to back toward the stairs with my hands up. "It's about time, Griff. That's all I'm saying."

Maybe once he gets his dick wet, he'll loosen up a bit.

Door firmly closed behind me, I spot Skylar exactly where I left her. No drink. No snack. Same skeptical, wary expression. "So, Blondie, what kind of pizza do you like? Hope it's not that pineapple shit, but I guess I'd order you a small if it's a deal breaker."

"A deal breaker?"

I hum, pulling my phone back out and ignoring the text reply from my grandma. Love her, but she can wait. "Yeah. I'm not that picky about my friends, but I usually draw the line at their bad food habits."

There's only a minimal pause before she lifts her shoulders. "Lucky for you, I'll put just about anything in my mouth."

My cock grows uncomfortably hard.

Skylar seems unaware of what she just said and especially ignorant of the growing bulge trapped behind the zipper of my denim.

I position myself behind the counter to hide my hard-on and adjust myself before dialing the pizzeria and ordering three large pies for me and the guys and a small Hawaiian for the dark-haired girl studying the kitchen.

Clearing my throat once I stuff my phone back in my pocket, I lean against the edge of the counter. "You look like you're about to freak out on me. Say the word, and I'll take you home."

Her eyes go from me to the other room where the guys are hollering over something stupid again. When those blue eyes slink back in my direction, I can see the indecision in them. "Do they know?"

It takes me a second to realize what she's asking. "Maybe some of them. They're not going to say anything about your time here. Trust me, they would have by now. You're basically one of us at this point."

She cringes. "One of the guys…"

It could be my imagination that tells me she sounds disappointed, but I don't let myself think about that too hard. "I highly doubt any of the guys in there would call you one of them."

She blinks, confusion taking over.

I let myself give her a quick once-over while she watches me. Even without tighter clothes, a face full of heavy makeup, and done-up hair, she's a knockout. Curvy, which means she's got more to hold on to in the right situations. A natural beauty instead of a phony under layers of foundation and lipstick. The windblown hair gives her a sexy just-been-laid kind of look that men are drawn to. Me included.

And I'm the lucky bastard who she's looking at right now, oblivious to the way my dick is standing to attention simply as she is.

Scratching my jaw with one of my fingers, I stifle a sigh and grumble, "Yeah. Definitely not one of the guys."

Which is a problem.

Because if she were, I wouldn't be thinking about the positions I'd bend her in to show her a good time or feel like shit for picturing her in compromising positions when I promised her friendship.

Chapter Thirteen

SKYLAR

DANNY'S LAUGH IS LOUD and obnoxious, but it's also contagious. He's poking fun at himself and the things he used to get in trouble for as a kid, making it hard not to be amused. "It's really no surprise that Ma didn't have more kids," he tells me, grinning as he shakes his head.

No kidding. "You really jumped out of a two-story window for fifty bucks?"

He puffs out his chest. "Sure did. I almost didn't land on the grass either. There was this strip of pavement leading up to the building's side entrance that I was probably a foot or less away from landing on instead."

Caleb grabs the last piece of pizza from the greasy box. "You could have broken both your legs, dumbass."

"Or died," I point out, wide-eyed from the possibility of his stupidity.

His other teammate, Stephen, chips in with, "Definitely would've ended your football career. Then you'd just be some washed-up rich boy from Boston. All sad and lonely and shit."

My eyes snap to Danny. In all the time we've spent together, we've never discussed backgrounds. I know he's an only child. I know he grew up with his mother and grandmother. I know his father is out of the picture. I guess I'd be a hypocrite if I was upset over not knowing about his apparent wealth since I'm in the same boat. Just because his family has money doesn't mean *he* does. It doesn't really change anything.

His cheeks pinken when he notices my curious gaze and lifts a shoulder as if to say *it's not a big deal.*

I get it. There's no real reason why I haven't said, "I come from money too. Want to trade country club horror stories?" With Becca, my hesitancy comes with the attitude I'm sure I'll receive from her. She likes being the smart one who will walk away from Lindon debt-free thanks to her full ride. If she knew my parents paid for everything, it'd be another reason for her to dislike me. But DJ? I doubt that's the case.

He's never brought up the rumors of my reputation that I know are circulating around campus. I'm not one hundred percent certain where they come from, but I have a feeling it's from the six-foot redhead I live with who always feels the need to comment on the men who supposedly surround me. But sometimes I see the look he gives me, like he wonders about where the tales come from. He doesn't ask, so I never elaborate, because what is there to say that would convince him that I don't sleep around?

Would it matter to him? *Should* it?

If it does, then everything changes between us.

The man in question tosses one of the throw pillows from the couch at his friend. "I wouldn't be sad and lonely. Football was never going to be my endgame."

"It wasn't?" I ask before I can stop myself.

It's none of my business, and he confirms as much when he doesn't enlighten me on the subject. "What about you, Blondie? These guys already know all about my embarrassing and dumbass stories. You should share one of your own. Make me feel less like a loser."

"That'll be hard to do," Justin muses.

Someone snickers before everyone's attention is directed to where I'm sitting cross-legged on the end of the couch. "Oh, well…" Would they believe me if I said I didn't have any? I sort of pride myself on not being anything like my sisters, who were always getting into some sort of trouble. "I don't really have any stories to tell."

Even Caleb looks skeptical. "You've never done anything embarrassing?"

Stephen snorts, chugging the rest of his beer before wiping his mouth off with the back of his hand. "We've got ourselves a good girl, fellas. Haven't had one of those around here in a hot minute."

My face burns, and my gaze quickly drops to the floor. What could I tell them? That the most embarrassing thing that's ever happened to me is getting chlamydia? I'd rather not advertise that to a room full of strangers who may or may not include the one who bestowed upon me the experience of treating an STD. I'd like to think I'd recognize the person when I see him—their blond hair, the gut feeling that screams at me to run away. None of them give me that.

Being here already makes my skin crawl. DJ's stories keep my brain occupied so I'm not stealing glances toward the stairs every five seconds. It's bad enough my brain wanders to that night when I'm on my own. Being at the scene of the crime brings on feelings too heavy for me to sort through because too many questions are left unanswered.

I shake my head, toying with a loose strand of hair that fell from the messy bun I tossed it up in to eat. Maybe I should dye it again. Something lighter. Maybe something fun.

Another change. I need a change.

I clear my throat. "Guess I'm boring."

It's DJ who says, "Boring isn't a bad thing, Blondie. And something tells me you're far from it even if you didn't jump out of a two-story window."

"Or try rescuing a cat that mauled you," Caleb chirps, shooting a smirk at the boy whose hand is a mere inch away from mine.

I subtly move my hands to my lap, fiddling with my fingers so he doesn't try touching me. He's never tried before beyond hair braiding or grabbing my books and carrying them.

Olive shoving my shoulder or giving me a bear hug? Not a big deal. Dee? Aliyah? Even Becca? Although not as welcome, I wouldn't mind it...that much. I might even welcome something as mundane as a hug from one of the girls who look at me like an outcast. Because then I'd be one of them. A friend. Part of something that would make me feel like Lindon wasn't such a bad choice after all.

Even though the charming smile and easy-on-the-eyes facial features directed at me right now say I'm safe with DJ—that I'm part of something with him even if I have my hesitations—I find myself cautious all the same. Because he's done nothing to make me feel uncomfortable, yet I know the lingering gaze is one I've gotten from men who have far fewer good intentions.

All I can think about are hands on my hips. On my back. On my butt. And I can't remember a face or a name. I can't remember when I stopped enjoying being kissed. Or *if* I did. I don't remember the word *yes* or the word *no*, and it kills me. Every single day, a tiny piece of me withers away from the lack of knowledge I have from that night.

And every time a piece of me cracks, I force myself to think of better memories that replace the bad ones. Like Olive's hilarious rants during her video games or how easily she drops things to hang out with me. I think about how simple it is to be her friend—to be lazy without feeling bad about it. To go makeup-free without her judgment. To eat something bad instead of something healthy without her eyes judging me.

And I think about DJ. My mind wanders to the photo we took together in the library. I have it saved on my phone—even considered posting it online to show people I have more than one person here for me. But the second I upload it to any of my social media, my sisters would be demanding details from me that I'm not willing to share.

And I don't want to share DJ.

Not yet.

DJ groans at his friend's quip, pulling my attention back to him. "That was *one time*. And that motherfucker gave me an infection from scratching me up so bad. I was just trying to help it. Damn nurse I went to see thought I was a cutter and called my ma because she was worried for my mental health."

All I can do is stare.

It's Stephen who remarks, "We all worry about your mental health. You pay too much attention to the wrong kind of puss—"

"*Watch it*," the cat-loving man growls, smacking his teammate upside the head.

Stephen looks at him, then me, rubbing where our mutual friend hit him. "Damn. Sorry. I figured she of all people wouldn't care if I said—"

Another warning look from not only DJ but Caleb too has Stephen shutting up.

I offer him a limp shrug, confused over their reactions but choosing to let it go. "It wouldn't be the first time I've heard guys say that. Don't worry about it on my account."

Caleb looks between me and his buddies before standing up. "Well, I'm whooped. Going to head upstairs. Skylar, it was nice chilling with you. Hopefully, you can mellow this dipshit out. None of us can seem to manage it."

Something tells me that's an impossible task since DJ is always bouncing around with the kind of energy I can only muster after at least three cups of coffee. "I'll do my best," I reply grimly.

Caleb chuckles and slaps hands with the guys before walking around the couch and jogging upstairs.

Stephen stretches out and drapes an ankle across his bent knee and throws an arm over the back of the couch. "You were at the party we held, right? Came with a couple of other chicks."

"Marks," DJ warns under his breath.

His teammate smirks. "I'm making conversation with your girl, not moving in on her. Calm your brovaries. Plus, I just want to know what her friend's deal is."

I blink at his inquiry, having a hard time ignoring the fact that DJ didn't correct his teammate when he called me his girl. "My friend?"

"Tall. Hit-me-red hair."

Becca. "Oh." That's the best I can do.

I don't want to tell him anything, which would make me

petty. But would that make me any better than her if I held back simply because things aren't great with us? I don't make any of our friends pick sides like she seems to. I don't make derogatory comments about her weight, exercise routine, or clothing choices. And I'm not about to lie to a guy who's interested in her just because I can.

Nibbling my lip, I release it and say, "I don't know if she's seeing anyone if that's what you're asking. I think she has her eye on somebody from the fire station in town though."

His brows go up. "Is she their receptionist or something? Why would she know anyone there?"

"Dude, that's sexist," Justin pipes in. He's been so quiet I almost forget he's sitting in the same room. His braced leg has been propped up on the ottoman in front of the armchair he's sitting in. His attention has mostly been on the textbook on his lap.

"She volunteers there," I correct Stephen, agreeing with their captain. I may not like my roommate that much, but that doesn't mean I want to set women back fifty years by letting his comment slide. "Women can be firefighters too, in case you didn't know."

He holds his hands up. "Shit. Fine. So she's not seeing anyone? I see her around parties a lot. Seems like she's the type to know what she wants. My kind of girl."

As much as I wish I could be excited for my roomie, I'm not. In fact, I secretly hope he forgets all about this conversation and seeks out someone else instead of her. "Yep. That's Becca. Fun, fun, fun."

"Becca..." He cocks his head as he repeats her name, making me share a look with DJ before shrugging.

"Um, anyway, she seems into the sports stuff, so maybe you have a shot." The information isn't a lot, but it seems to perk him up. "Can't be sure though. I've seen her reject guys pretty openly for weird things, so don't get your hopes up."

Stephen laughs like I'm joking. "Babe, don't worry about that. I can handle her."

I murmur, "Don't call me that," at the same time as the guy beside me snaps the same exact thing, leaving Stephen gaping at the both of us.

He stands. "Christ. Just bone already." His eyes go to me before they roll at whatever he sees. "Nice meeting you. Thanks for the info on your friend."

"Becca," I remind him, ignoring his boning comment while fighting a furious blush.

He nods once before disappearing upstairs too.

Danny is quiet for a moment. "Sorry about him. A lot of these guys aren't used to having girls over to hang out. Except for Raine."

"Raine?"

"Caleb's girlfriend."

Ah.

"Anyway, you want to watch another movie, or are you ready to head out? Caleb told me I could borrow his truck to take you back whenever you were ready."

I look at the time on my phone and frown. It's getting late. If we start a movie, I won't get back to the dorms until at least one, and I don't feel like fielding all the questions that I'll get from Becca or my suitemates. I don't know the other girls I live with well. It's mostly Becca who hangs out with them in our common room because my anxiety makes it too hard to have basic conversations with them. I've heard my roommate make comments about me to them before, so who knows what they must think of me?

It's a few seconds longer of me debating my options when I decide, "I think I should head back."

Saying goodbye to Justin, I follow Danny out to the truck in the driveway. "You should probably convince Stephen not to try anything with Becca."

His brows go up as he unlocks the doors for us. "Why?"

"She's…" I pause with my hand on the door handle. "Look, I don't think she's a very good person. You've said you thought so too, and you've barely talked to her." *I hope.* God knows what he's heard if they've had more than one conversation. "Her attitude is mostly just to me. She doesn't like that I'm not like her. Or maybe that she can't control me, I'm not sure. We're too different and she doesn't like that. And I guess I could—well, I *know* I could try harder. It's difficult for me to be social like her though. It gives me anxiety to put myself out there. But it wouldn't be fair if Stephen had some preconceived notion about her that isn't true."

He's quieter than I expect as he contemplates how to respond. Studying me with his lips pressed together, he nods once. "You know, something didn't sit well with me about her the first day I met her at Bea's."

"What did she do?" I feel the need to ask, even if part of me doesn't want to know.

He shakes his head after a long stretch of time. "Get in. It's not important. All that matters is that it's good you're nothing like her. She's the type of person the world only needs one of. Trust me. And as far as Marks goes, he's a big boy. He'll do whatever he wants, no matter her reputation or what one of us tries advising him against doing."

It's too quiet in the cab once we're inside as I sneak a peek at him. I envy the way he seems to get along with everybody and not care what people think. I've always cared too much about that sort of stuff and been bogged down by the weight of people's opinions.

"What are you thinking about?" he asks.

Too much.

I lift a shoulder. "I've always had social anxiety. It used to take me at least twenty minutes to prepare myself for a phone call. My sisters would tease me for asking our mother to make doctor's appointments for me, but they're not like me. Going out, being able to talk to whoever, isn't easy for me. My chest gets tight, and I start feeling like I'm going to hyperventilate." It's embarrassing to admit, but I find myself going on because he's listening to me without one ounce of judgment on his face like I'd get from Becca or one of the other girls if I tried opening up to them. "I was hoping I could reinvent myself here where nobody knew me. I could be anybody I wanted. A girl with any color hair, who wore whatever she wanted and did whatever she felt like. I could be quiet or loud or introverted or extroverted because I didn't think people would care. College was supposed to be different. *I* was supposed to be different."

But maybe I'm too different now.

Shaped by all the wrong choices.

I feel his eyes on me, but I can't make myself meet them.

"College can be if you stop letting people try tearing you down," he says.

Easier said than done.

"Hey, look at me," he murmurs, fingers gently touching my chin and turning my head toward him. His eye twitches when he sees me flinch, but that doesn't stop him from saying what he wants to. "I know a few of the guys go through the same thing as you with their anxiety. Some people can just play it off easier than others. Channel it in things like sports. And I know ignoring what your roommate says is probably difficult, but once you stop showing her that it upsets you, she'll stop having that power over you. She only says shit because she knows you'll react. It feeds her. People like that aren't worth it. Eventually, they'll get what's coming to them."

His fingers remain on my chin, his thumb caressing the underside of my jaw in a light brush that causes goose bumps to pebble on my skin.

I let his words sink in. *Really* sink in. I do let Becca walk all over me. I thought killing her with kindness would be enough, but all it's doing is killing me instead.

Being somebody that I'm not has only made me more confused. Even when I'm wearing something frumpy and warm with a face naked of makeup, I have people who enjoy being around me.

That's enough for me.

"Skylar?" he asks quietly, glancing briefly at my lips and watching me do the same to his.

I'm not sure who moves first. Me or him. I don't even know why I let it happen. I just need it to. One second we're staring at each other talking about my roommate, and the next his lips are on mine.

The kiss is light. No tongue. No teeth. Just lips pressing against lips. Soft. Nondemanding. It's almost one of comfort rather than desire. Almost like he...

I pull back quickly, startling him into falling forward. My body moves closer toward my door as I play with the seat belt and stare at my lap. "Sorry, I shouldn't have..." I shake my head and buckle in, unable to look at him.

"I thought we were thinking the same thing. But if I crossed a—"

"It's fine. I don't..." I lick my lips, staring out the passenger window and trying not to think about the kiss.

He feels sorry for me, that's all.

But you still let him kiss you.

My chest feels heavy again, panic threatening to absorb into the drumming organ trapped in its cage. But then I repeat those words and remind myself of something important.

I *let* him kiss me.

It's enough to inhale for three and let the tightness finally ease with the weighted exhale of my breath. "When Becca convinced me to go to the party you guys were having, I thought it'd be a good chance to become friends with her. To prove to her that I'm not as boring as she thinks I am. But that party..." My head moves back and forth, remembering the little things about that night that I wish I could change.

I choose not to voice them. "That party just proved to me that she wasn't interested in being my friend. The girls I came with left me, and the sad thing is I don't even remember when."

When I flick my gaze upward to his face, I see confusion. "What do you mean you don't remember?"

"Can we go, please?"

His hands grip the steering wheel. "No. I want to know what you mean."

"DJ—"

"It's Danny to you."

I file that away for another time. "I got too drunk." My cheeks warm under the scrutiny of his attention. "I drank way too much and don't remember much about that night. I don't remember who I danced with, who I talked to, or who I..."

My eyelids squeeze closed. He can figure the rest out himself since he's so keen on bringing up sex.

His eyes soften when I open mine. "You don't remember who you hooked up with?"

I shake my head, avoiding the look he's pinning me with.

"Shit, Sky. I'm sorry. That's…"

He's at a loss for words for a few seconds, and that makes two of us.

Until he says, "Look, it happens. I mean, I've had my fair share of drunken flings. There's nothing to be embarrassed about."

"That isn't my thing," I inform him.

"How do you know?"

"Because I do." I'm getting snippy, defensive, but the way he prods me isn't helping the downward spiral I've been in for weeks because of that night. "Not all of us are as happy as you admitting we sleep around."

His eyes narrow. "What's that supposed to mean?"

"Like you don't know." I cross my arms and stare out the window, fully ignoring the way he adjusts in his seat to glare at me.

"I *don't* know. Enlighten me, Skylar." The challenge in his voice isn't one I want to take, so he keeps going when he realizes I won't answer him. "If you're not the judgmental type, then care to explain why you're basically calling me a man whore? I'm not the one who's apparently got at least two men around me at all times."

Something inside me cracks, splinters.

"Wow," I breathe. "I guess that explains why you kissed me. Did you want to be part of my personal harem, *DJ*? Did you think it'd be that easy?" My voice cracks as I fight back the tears that prickle my eyes. "Just because you feed me pizza and offer to drive me home doesn't mean I'm going to take my pants off for you and spread my legs. I know what people say. That doesn't mean it's true. Whoever started it"—*Becca*, I silently accuse again—"doesn't know me at all. You obviously don't either."

And that probably hurts the worst.

When, in the short time we've known each other, have I ever given him the impression that I pay any attention to the guys who are apparently always flocking around me?

"Aw, fuck," he cusses, swiping a hand down his face. "That isn't what I meant. And that's definitely *not* why I kiss—"

"Don't." I hold up my palm to stop him, and he obeys. "Do not apologize if you don't mean it. Don't make up excuses either. That makes it worse."

"But I do—"

"No," I cut him off again. I peel my eyes away from the glass to level with him. "You're only saying you're sorry because you think it'll make up for being an asshole. But you don't know me. You want to be my friend, but friends don't treat each other like this. They don't make the other feel bad because they get hit on. They don't make their friends feel *cheap* and *easy* when that's the furthest thing from the truth. If you want to sleep around, then fine. I don't care. It's your business. Just like what I do or don't do is none of yours."

His jaw ticks, but he stays silent.

I swallow past the lump clinging to my vocal cords and try calming my tone. "I don't know why you think that I'm dragging along half the campus's male population, but I'm not. If they're interested, it's one-sided. But did you ask that? No. You chose to believe the worst in me to make yourself feel better for whatever you've done in the past." His eyes dull and his lips start weighing at the corners, but I don't let the guilt he's showing stop me. "You have no clue what happened that night, do you? You don't know anything about that party."

He rears back. "Me? Why would I?"

I can't form the words. The question.

Blond hair.

Big hands.

The truth is, I've long accepted it wasn't him that night. I wouldn't have agreed to meet up with him if I believed he's the one who took my virginity.

His eyes widen, slack-jawed in awe as he stares at me. "You thought it could have been me that you slept with this whole time, didn't you? That's why you were acting weird around me at first."

Again, I'm quiet.

One of his palms scrapes down the side of his face as he leans back in his seat. "Guess that explains it."

He doesn't even know the half of it, and I'm not sure I could ever tell him. Not about the nightmares I've been waking up from that aren't really nightmares at all.

No, they're little memories piecing themselves together. And I'm afraid of the day when they come together fully because then...

I'll remember everything.

And I'll either hate myself for putting myself in that position or hate somebody else for it. But hate gets you nowhere.

My throat thickens with emotion. "I remember enough to think that it could have been. I didn't completely rule you out as much as I probably should have at first. Like I said, I'd been drinking a lot, so it's fuzzy."

There's a deep breath coming from the driver's seat that makes me look at him with pinched brows. "Skylar..."

I blink.

"It wasn't me. I wish... Shit, it doesn't matter what I wish. But it wasn't me, I swear. I would have said something by now if it were. It had to have been someone else on the team if you were upstairs all night..." After a second, pink creeps up his neck and settles all the way to the tips of his ears. "Look, I don't know how to ask you this because it's none of my damn business, but, uh..." His wince makes me flinch too. "Shit. Okay, well, it's just that Coach made us all get tested for...er, things that are going around campus. And some of the guys tested positive for those...things." He grips the back of his neck. "Fuck, I'm bad at this. I don't know how to ask you, but I think you should know. Just in case it's something you need to take care of..."

He's stumbling through one of the most awkward conversations of my whole life. Next to the one I had with the doctor.

Biting the inside of my cheek so hard I can taste blood, I whisper, "You guys wanted to know what the most embarrassing thing I've ever done was. Well, now you know your answer. I lost my virginity to some random guy at my first college party, and I can't even remember it."

He goes stock still.

"And now one of the few people who seemed like he genuinely wanted to be friends thinks I sleep around with every guy who smiles my way."

Pain crosses his features, but I don't look for long.

"Don't worry, DJ," I add, voice nearly inaudible as I stare out the window again, bringing my thumbnail up to my lips. "I already know about what you're warning me of. I found out for myself the hard way."

He cusses again.

Smacks the steering wheel.

Mumbles under his breath.

Then, "I don't think you sleep around. I was talking out of my ass. I was…am—" He stops himself abruptly. "It doesn't matter what I am. I don't think that."

We drive.

Stuck at a red light, he asks, "You were really a virgin?"

I don't answer him verbally.

Only nod once.

When he drops me off at the curb by my dorm building, we say nothing else. The short ride to campus was thick with tension and an unspoken truth lingering in the air.

I had a one-night stand.

Lost my virginity.

Caught an STD.

And have no recollection of any of it.

When I close the passenger door, I almost turn back around and ask him if he still wants to be my friend. That's a lot to put on someone who barely knows you, especially considering he thinks of me as just another one of the women who normally chase after him.

A catch and release.

Easily disposable.

But before I can even open my mouth, before I can so much as gather the courage to ask him about where we stand or tell him that his friendship would still mean a lot to me, he drives away.

Quickly.

Not looking back once.

Guess that's my answer.

Chapter Fourteen

DANNY

SKYLAR DOESN'T SHOW UP to film class on Wednesday, and I know I messed up. Bad.

Who the fuck kisses a girl they like and then basically calls her a slut?

Me. Because I'm a fucking idiot.

Granted, I didn't mean for it to come out the way it did. Then again, half of my conversations with the opposite sex usually end up the same way. Badly.

Me: U okay?

It's only the second text I've ever sent her since Friday night, the first one just being my name and a short apology so she could save my number.

I get nothing back.

Not five minutes later.

Not ten.

Not when class starts.

I've barely seen her around campus when we usually cross paths. Not in the dining hall when she and a few other girls usually show up. Not walking along her normal short-cut in between the science building and Smithson Hall. She's practically vanished since I dropped her off at her dorm.

When I passed Olive yesterday, she glared at me. I knew then for sure she was okay enough to tell her friend about what a dick I am.

I screwed up.

If I were a better man, I would have stayed and asked Skylar if she was okay after what she'd admitted before driving away. Considering she never actually said the words, it's hard to confirm my suspicions about what she went through, not that it's a valid excuse for rushing off on her.

What little she did tell me was enough to set me off because it's obvious something royally fucked up happened at the party. Whether she's acknowledging it or not, nobody should have gotten near her when she was drinking. Whoever it was knew damn well what he was doing.

I've been *pissed* for days.

Not at her. Christ, how could I be? She's a freshman trying to make friends and settle into college life. I was in her shoes once, doing stupid shit to fit in. But I never went through *that* and couldn't imagine putting any girl I meet at a party through it if she was too drunk to consent. There are always other, sober options.

After going back to the house, I barged into Caleb's room and interrupted him and Raine doing something that made them flushed and breathless. If I didn't look ready to blow, my teammate probably would have kicked me out without a second thought. But I needed to talk to someone, and Aiden and I haven't been on great terms lately.

A simple "I did something stupid" had both Caleb and his girlfriend hearing me out and offering advice when they could. I'd talked out of my ass with Skylar. Kissed her because I wanted to—because I thought *she* wanted me to. Said shit I didn't mean because I was jealous of her being with other guys. I had no right to feel that way, but I did.

Do.

Watching guys hang around Skylar is never my idea of fun. Not when I know their minds are on one thing only. Me? I want to know what makes her tick. Why she keeps her head down. Why she sticks around the group of girls who obviously don't give a fraction of a shit about her as she does them. Why she colors her hair so much.

She's made me curious.

So yeah. One conversation with Caleb and Raine made me realize I lashed out to blame Skylar because I didn't want to acknowledge either of our truths.

That I'm a selfish bastard who wants her all to myself, even when I probably shouldn't.

And that Skylar was sexually assaulted at the party I was partly responsible for.

Which means that there's going to be a lot of layers to peel back until she's actually comfortable around me.

Raine's psychobabble made sense, even if I didn't want to hear it. Skylar needs time. Patience. A friend. *Friend.* I'd promised her I could be that before, and I stand by it, even if I know—deep down—I want more.

When they did push me out the door to finish whatever the hell I walked in on, I only sulked in my room down the hall, staring at my phone and debating on what to say to the girl to whom I owed an apology.

Not texting her sooner than I did probably wasn't the best

thing considering how we left things. But I had no clue what to say, even after twenty minutes of staring at my blank screen.

The simple message I did send didn't really touch on how awful I feel, but I figured I'd have something planned out to say to her when I saw her tonight. I wanted to get my head on straight after our last conversation went wrong so quick.

Yet here I am.

Leg bouncing more than usual.

Focus deterred from the lecturer.

My fists clench on my lap as I attempt to listen to the professor drone on. The truth is, though, I don't want to be here. Not right now. I'll make Coach give me an excuse and lie through my ass about it later.

All I can think about is her.

I need to see Skylar.

That's how I find myself slipping out of class despite the pause and probable glare I get from Mr. NYU at the front of the room.

The air is nippier now that it's November, more comfortable in my opinion. I can wear a T-shirt and jeans without sweating my ass off like usual, even though everyone else starts reverting to their winter wardrobe. My mind goes to the bundled-up frozen brunette who I hung out with Friday night at the bonfire.

When I arrive at Morris Dormitory a few minutes later, I don't know what I'm going to say when I walk over to where one of the RAs is sitting behind the counter near the entrance. Thankfully, I don't have to say much.

"You're DJ Bridges," the nerdy-looking guy says, pushing his glasses up his nose. "Me and my suitemates watch the football games all the time."

I shoot him an appreciative smile and lean on the edge of the counter. "Thanks, man. Means a lot. Hey, I was wondering if you could help me out with something."

He perks up. "Sure, anything."

"I need to find somebody who lives here."

A smirk curves up half his lips. "A girl, huh? I'm technically not supposed to tell people where students live. But for you? Sure. What's her name?"

"Skylar Allen." I drum my fingers against the edge of the counter as he grabs a binder and flips through a couple pages.

"Yeah, yeah. She's actually right here on the first floor. Walk through that hallway, and she's in suite two. Only door on that side."

I glance in the direction he's gesturing to before pushing off the counter. "Thanks, dude. Hey, shoot me an email or something with your details, and I'll give you and your suitemates tickets to the next home game."

His eyes grow huge behind those thick glasses. "Fuck yeah. I'll definitely do that. The guys would freak."

I wave him off and head over to the door with a big number two in the center of it. Knocking a couple times, I stand back and stuff my hands into the pockets of my jeans, waiting for someone to answer.

When I hear the lock click, it's a short, curly-haired girl standing there with a nose ring and surprised smile. She looks vaguely familiar. Can't put my finger on it though.

"Hey. Is Sky here?"

"You want to see Skylar?"

My lips flatten over her gaping expression. "Yep. She here? She missed class, so I wanted to make sure she was okay."

That stirs her into action. "Yeah, sorry. Come in. I'll get her for you."

Following her inside, I stop far enough in to close the door and study the common room. There are two other girls lounging on the cheap couches, both staring at me with interest. The leggy, tan blond farthest away works at the diner across from Bea's, always has a smile on her face, and used to be in an on-again, off-again relationship with our last quarterback before he graduated. The other chick is undoubtedly Skylar's roommate: red hair that looks similar to what I imagine Lucifer's skin color is, narrowed eyes, and something weighing down her lips.

My presence is the only thing I can guess.

When the girl who answered the door knocks on the one closest to the exit and says, "Sky, you have a visitor," I notice the eye roll that comes from Skylar's roommate.

I'm tempted to ask her what her problem is, but I don't have time before the door cracks open and a disheveled, tired, familiar face peeks out.

When Skylar sees me, her eyes widen.

"Hey," I greet.

A pause. "Hi."

The girl who answered the door winks at her and gives an approving, "Good going, girl," before turning to me with a soft smile and then walking to sit next to Skylar's roommate on the couch.

Tipping my chin toward her room, I ask, "Mind if we talk for a minute?"

Skylar's hand grips the door before she lowers her shoulders, opens it wider, and steps aside so I can enter.

She keeps it open as I study the small space she shares with the piece of work currently sitting outside the room. Somehow, I know quickly which side is hers before I even walk over and look at the pictures on her desk.

It's the colors. Bright like her. The books all lined up strategically. She told me before she loves to read.

When I pick up the picture frame, my eyebrows dart upward at the clones surrounding a blond version of Skylar in the image. "Christ, genetics did your family a solid."

A quiet snort causes me to turn and watch her sit on the edge of her unmade bed. Has she been sleeping all day? "Yeah, we get that a lot."

I set the frame back down where I found it. "They're all pretty, don't get me wrong, but I think you take the cake, Blondie. I never liked flashy women much, and based on that picture alone, it seems like they're the opposite of your laid-back personality." Seriously, one of them is in brand-name designer sportswear holding a tennis racket, and another one is covered in gold jewelry that looks more expensive than my Jeep back home.

She doesn't offer any insight as to if I'm right, so I switch gears.

"You didn't come to class."

Her eyes drop from mine to stare at nothing in particular on the floor. "I wasn't feeling very well."

Something tells me that's not entirely true, but I don't know whether to call her out on it. "He's going to deduct from your grade if you keep skipping. You already ran out once."

When a shoulder lifts, I frown.

"Tell me what's wrong," I prod, crossing my arms over my chest. "That's what friends do, isn't it? They talk about what's bugging them."

Her nostrils twitch. "Last time we spoke, you didn't seem to like what I had to say."

My arms drop to my sides. "I can't imagine a lot of people in my position would like hearing that."

Her lips curve even further down.

I walk over and nudge her leg with mine before saying, "We should probably talk about that. What you said."

Her eyes dart between me and the door.

Sighing, I walk over and close it so people—namely her roommate—won't eavesdrop on whatever Skylar is hesitant about. When the door clicks shut, I hear giggles from outside it and an enthused, "Shit's about to go down in there."

I roll my eyes at their cracked assumptions. When I turn back to the only other person in the room, her hands are twisted in her lap and her shoulders are hunched.

Not sure how to broach the topic, I decide to try lightening the mood. "The first time I ever got drunk here, I woke up spooning one of my teammates on the living room floor of the football house. Had no fucking idea how I got there. All I knew was that I had morning wood and a massive hangover and there was a dude pressed against places I definitely didn't want him touching."

A choking sound comes from her throat as she eyes me. Pink creeps into her cheeks as she shakes her head. "Why are you telling me this?"

I shrug. "Because I want you to know that we all do dumb things when we're finally given some freedom. I know I poke fun, but I'm being real. We're not defined by the decisions we make when we let loose. And you have to know by now that the choices made that night at the party weren't all on you."

"I don't want to talk about that."

Blowing out a breath, I nod once. "Look, we're all bound to make some mistakes, but we learn from them and move on. But there are going to be some things harder to move on from, and I want to be there for you if you need help with it. Okay?"

She blinks, contemplative. "Your situation and mine are different. You got drunk and woke up cuddling someone. I…" The color in her cheeks deepens, spreading all across her face before she lets her hair fall around her like a force field for protection. "I woke up alone and found out a couple weeks later that the guy I slept with gave me an—" The words cram in her throat. "You know. An…" She murmurs the words in a shallow whisper, but I hear the letters anyway.

STD.

I knew it already, but hearing her say it makes me rage even more than I was all week. It's been stewing, boiling in my blood. Not as much as her downplaying it does. Is she really going to keep harboring the blame here?

Our situations *aren't* similar. The outcomes of each were about as fucking different as you could get. "Are you okay now?" I ask quietly, despite wanting to figure out who the fuck the guy is so I can have a one-on-one with him about what the fuck consent is. Her tomato-red face picks up to meet mine skeptically. "You got…seen? Maybe even talked to one of the school counselors? That's a lot for one person to handle on their own."

The groan coming from her is drawn out as she flops backward. Her hands cup her face, the words she murmurs through her palms muffled. "Most friends gossip about their celeb crushes and favorite movies before they get to this stuff."

I can't help but crack a grin even though a weight is still resting on my chest. "Selena Gomez can get it anytime she wants, and I don't have a favorite movie. I guess if I *had* to choose, it'd probably be *Ocean's Eight*, because Sandra Bullock is up there in celeb crushes too. Maybe *The Proposal* if she and Ryan Reynolds can be a package deal. I wouldn't mind waking up next to him in the morning." All I get is silence, so I pull out her computer chair and sit in it backward, straddling the back of it to face her. "And I'm shooting for best friend status, so it's no wonder we're getting to the heavy-hitter topics. Like the time my grandma walked in on me jerking it."

She sputters out a laugh. "Oh my God! Why would you tell me that?"

I snort. "I knew it'd make you laugh."

She sits up on her elbows. "So it's not true?" Her tone stings with disappointment.

"Oh, it's true," I confirm. Grandma Meadow didn't say a word as she turned around and closed the door behind her. The next day, I found a bottle of lube and box of tissues on my bed. "I couldn't look at her for a solid week after it happened."

Skylar nods slowly. "I bet."

"I could keep going, you know. There was one time when one of my friends walked in while I was—"

"No! Stop!" She makes a choked cackling noise, then giggles before dropping back down onto her back. "I can't believe you told me that. But I needed the laugh, so thank you."

"Anytime, Blondie." Hearing her laugh is more than worth it. "You *are* good, right? Because I could borrow Caleb's truck and take you somewhere if you need me to. I know I was an asshole on Friday, but I really didn't mean it. I'll do whatever it takes to prove that to you."

Her body stiffens on the bed before loosening as she turns onto her side and looks at me from where her head is propped up against the pillow. "You mean that, don't you?"

I frown. "Of course I do."

The humming noise she makes as she watches me carefully is the only thing that fills the room between us. That and whatever her suitemates are watching outside.

Eventually, she sighs. "I'm okay. Olive took me to get seen already and I...haven't thought too much about counseling. I'm dealing."

I don't believe her, but I don't feel like calling her out when it seems like we're slowly patching things up.

"But I appreciate the offer. Really. I don't know many people who'd do that."

My brows pinch. "Then you need better people in your life, Sky."

She doesn't argue with me.

I lean back and perch my elbows on the edge of her desk behind me. "Who's your celebrity crush?"

A small smile curls up her lips. "Selena Gomez can totally get it."

The unexpected answer makes me laugh until her smile stretches higher. "We're going to get along just fine," I determine.

But I already knew that from day one, which is probably why I wished she *was* a jersey chaser. Easier to ignore that way.

Her hands rest under her cheek. "I didn't think you wanted to be my friend when you drove away," she admits quietly, eyes looking a little cloudy from the thought. "But if you're here, I guess that's not the case."

Pressing my lips together, I shake my head as I watch her face go back to its natural color.

It's then and there I'm determined to prove to her just how much I want to be in her life, friend or not. Preferably as more, but I'll take as much as she'll give me.

I make a cross over my chest. "I promise I'll be better. I let my emotions get the better of me, and you didn't deserve it. But name the price, and I'll pay it. Want me to do your nails? I can figure it out."

She nibbles her lip, fighting the smile that I know wants to widen. "No, Danny, I don't want you to paint my nails. You'll just mess them up and I'll have to fix them."

Danny. "Fair. Movie then?"

"You want to watch a movie?"

My shoulder lifts. "It's either that or gossip about guys. I doubt you want to talk about other stuff with me. Your pick."

She doesn't hesitate. "I've got Netflix on my laptop." Sitting up, she pats the empty spot on her bed in silent invitation.

I happily plop down beside her, using the wall her bed is up against to rest my back on. "I don't like people calling me Danny normally," I admit, settling in. "But I like it coming from you."

She pauses logging into her laptop to glance at me. "Okay...Danny."

All I do is smile.

Chapter Fifteen

SKYLAR

OLIVE TEXTS ME WHICH study room she's in as I weave through the maze of book stacks in the library until I spot the right door.

Spotting the Styrofoam cup in my hands, Olive wiggles her perfectly sculpted brows before yanking out packages of candy from her backpack and proudly holding them up. "I brought contraband too."

The library doesn't mind food and drinks inside so long as they're not next to the expensive computers they offer students to use in the labs. I don't take the fun away from her though, so I note the different sugar options she brought and wonder if she robbed the campus store before coming here. "Did you get one of every option?"

"I'm indecisive." She throws me a Reese's cup. "You might as well claim that. I saw the half-empty jar of peanut butter on your nightstand the other day. Do you just eat it plain?"

"Doesn't everybody?" I remark. The first time Becca saw me pull out the jar of my favorite creamy peanut butter, she eyed me distastefully but didn't say a word as I grabbed a plastic spoon and dove in.

Olive blanches. "Uh, no."

I shrug, unfazed by her disgust and ready to start working on some practice problems for math class so I don't bomb my next exam.

Her sea-green eyes roll. Today they have winged black liner around them and shiny pale pink dusted across the lids. She taught me the same liner method and I almost have it down, wearing it today in a less impressive manner than her.

"So," I pry, peeling open the candy wrapper and carefully removing the chocolate cup. "Are you ever going to tell me about what went down with you and Alex?"

Olive feigns an innocent look as she leans her chin on the palm of her hand. "Are *you* going to tell me what happened between you and DJ Bridges?"

My stomach flutters hearing his name, both with nerves and something else I'm afraid to read into, so my eyes train solely on the processed sugar in front of me.

I woke up to a text this morning from the boy in question. Two words.

Danny: Morning, Blondie

Two words and an instant smile formed on my face. I'm glad Becca had already left for her early study session, because I didn't feel like her digging into my business and asking what had me so happy. Especially not when she'd walked into our room halfway through the movie Danny and I were watching on my bed and gave us a look of disgust even though nothing was happening.

Our arms were touching, that was it. I wasn't fondling

149

his goods or shoving my tongue down his throat. But the way Becca looked at us would make anyone think otherwise.

"There's nothing to say," I say, breaking the peanut butter cup in half and studying the contents inside. "We're friends."

A weird look pinches Olive's eyes. "You haven't said a word about him since the weekend you hung out, and I haven't seen you two make googly eyes at each other at Huden nearly as much from across the room," she remarks.

My face blasts with heat. "We don't make googly eyes at each other!" Do we see each other in the dining hall from time to time? Yes. And do I find myself catching his eye more than I like from where we sit with our respective groups of friends? Also yes.

But *googly eyes*?

I meet Olive's knowing eyes for a millisecond before casting my gaze downward at the table, which has little phallic carvings in the wood top.

One smile from Danny has my stomach filling with little butterflies that I don't trust one single bit. It wouldn't be the first crush I've had, but it'd be the first one where the person *might* reciprocate, the first once since the night of the party. I'm not sure how I feel about that. How I could fully trust it.

When I told him I didn't know what I wanted to do with my communications major, he didn't say anything condescending or make suggestions like Tyler or others have. He simply shrugged and said, "You'll figure it out."

Melted chocolate coats my fingertips as I pull myself out of thoughts about the school's wide receiver. I lick off the sugar and stifle a sigh, causing Olive to study me.

She says, "Those pictures he took of you two don't seem very friendly to me."

"We take selfies like that all the time," I remind her.

"But neither of us were smiling with our eyes," she counters, grinning. "If I saw that posted online, I'd assume he's your boyfriend."

My stomach dips.

She taps my hand with the end of her pen. "I heard a few people talking about what a total flirt he is. Just be careful with him. If you're friends, then that's great. But if you decide to be more…"

It hurts to swallow as a swarm of emotion rises up my throat. "I already know what he's like, but duly noted. Can we talk about something else, please?" I don't acknowledge the hoarseness in my voice that isn't there when I think about Tyler hanging around other girls and shooting them winks and panty-dropping smirks.

It doesn't make me feel great to acknowledge that most of the guys who pay me attention also pay plenty of other girls the same amount, but it isn't like I laid claim to any of them. I'm not interested in Tyler or any of the others who shoot me looks, so I don't even care what they do. But Danny? I don't know what to think about his ability to make me laugh when I want to bawl or how he braids my hair without a care of what people think of him as they watch. Every time I find my mind wandering to Danny, it gets trapped there for too long.

On how his shoulders shake when he laughs. How his eyes brighten when he's up to something. He can't sit still for too long without fidgeting, hates taking notes in class but still gets good grades, and puts one hundred and ten percent into everything he does.

Like always, my friend delivers with a much-needed subject change that successfully draws me away from my brain before I slip into a void. "I slept with Alex."

I blink slowly. "Can you repeat that?"

She nods sheepishly, her cheeks turning red as she fiddles with the pen in her hand. "We hooked up after the bonfire. He and my brother are kind of mortal enemies. Like, my brother Sebastian can't stand Alex."

I'm lost. "So...? *Huh?*"

"I'm pretty sure Alex figured out who I was and slept with me to get back at my brother," she concludes, her shoulders lifting like it's not a big deal. "I mean, I met Alex last year when I visited Sebastian here to get a feel for the campus. They both play hockey. They were teammates battling it out for top spot to get noticed by pro scouts. Alex obviously didn't recognize me because he had a band of followers around him at all times. My brother and him didn't get along at all when Seb still went here, and he drilled it into my head to stay away when I announced I was enrolling. He and Alex would get into these prank wars and try to outdo the other the entire time my brother was at Lindon. It was borderline hazing."

I slowly begin processing everything she lays out for me, but I'm only buried even deeper in a pit of confusion. "Let me try getting this right. Your brother's enemy is your idol and crush?"

"Which I ignored," she confirms matter-of-factly.

I lean forward so my crossed arms hold me up on the edge of the polished table. "So you slept with him despite Sebastian's warnings that he wasn't a good dude."

"Just because Seb doesn't think he's a good person doesn't mean he isn't one," she defends quickly. "And come on, Sky. You saw Alex. How could I not want to get involved with him? Isn't hooking up with a bad boy part of my life journey as a woman?"

Snickering, I say, "Whatever helps you sleep at night."

Grabbing a snack-sized Snickers, she chucks it at my head, which I somehow manage to dodge. I snort when I hear it smack against the wall behind me.

"Do you think he really slept with you because of the silly war between him and your brother? If Sebastian graduated, what would put you in the middle of it?"

She drops the candy bar she's playing with and scrubs her palms down her face. "I think it was this unspoken thing that I'd take over the prank war since Sebastian is gone. But I've never been any good at that sort of thing, so I went to the bonfire not only hoping to meet him and prove I'm better than the puck bunnies he hangs with but also to call a truce. It took a turn."

"A turn?" I repeat.

"I slept with him instead."

I can't help but smile no matter how hard I try fighting it. "That definitely seems like a good way to seal the deal on a peace treaty."

This time, she throws a York Peppermint Pattie at me. I laugh when it smacks me in the cheek and lands on my notebooks stacked in front of me. "Stop laughing! The worst part of this whole thing is that he wouldn't give me my panties back," she says.

I choke on my chocolate. "I'm sorry, he wouldn't give you back your *what*?"

She drops her head back and groans. "I bet he's going to priority ship them to my brother to brag about it."

That's cringeworthy. "You think he'd really do that?"

Olive considers it. "You're right. He wouldn't spend the money. I bet he took pictures and plans on posting them all over the internet with a caption that says, 'Property of Olive

153

Henderson' and then tags Sebastian." Her hands smack into her face before she face plants into the table and stays there.

"Or," I offer, trying to be the glass-half-full type of person since her theory is creepy, "maybe he just wanted to keep something to remind him of you and has no plans whatsoever."

When she does look at me, it's with a doubtful expression at best. After a few moments, a big exhale leaves her as she straightens and murmurs, "At least the sex was amazing. I would've hated my brother murdering me not knowing what it felt like to have a man like that show me his true talents at least once."

My nose scrunches. Then I snort, causing her to grin.

"Sorry, is that awkward? I know some people don't like talking about sex. Especially if they've never..." The smile she gives me is sheepish when I realize what she assumes.

Staring at my chocolate-coated fingertips, I mumble, "I'm not a virgin."

Nausea rises up my throat.

Something smacks the table. "I knew it! Was it DJ? Was he good? Was it *horrible* and that's why you don't want to talk about it? I can totally—"

"Stop! Oh my God, breathe." Is it possible for me to blush any harder? I shouldn't have bothered with makeup at all today. "And lower your voice."

Olive looks far too giddy. "Was it him?"

I wish, I instantly think, reeling back.

Oh my God.

I don't know where that came from, but I realize it's true. I wish it'd been Danny who'd taken my virginity.

My friend's brow furrows. "Why do you look like that? What's wrong? I'm sorry for prying, but I wasn't sure. I mean, from what I hear, DJ knows what he's doing, but you never really see him with anyone, so it's fair to be curious. He's totally got eyes for you. That selfie of you two that you showed me proves it."

My voice goes up two octaves. "No, he doesn't. We're friends. *Friends.*"

Maybe if I keep saying it, it'll be more believable.

She leans forward, clearly invested. "But do you *want* to be friends? Or more?"

Quickly, I shake my head. Despite where my thoughts wander, I can't go there. I have no idea what to do in a relationship or who I'll become if I let someone in. "I'm not ready for more, even if I wanted that. Which I'm *not saying I do*, so get that creepy Joker grin off your face. He's been really nice to me. And as for the other thing…"

She laughs. "Sex. But okay. Please continue telling me about the 'other thing.'"

I deadpan. "Sometimes I wonder why I like you."

She flips her short bob. "Because I'm awesome, especially compared to your other choices."

Well…she's not wrong. The curvy, boobalicious girl in front of me is full of confidence that I wish I had even a fraction of. "I lost it a while ago," I go with, avoiding any kind of detail. "The person doesn't matter."

Blond hair.

Big hands.

I swallow down the last of my chocolate before wiping my hands off on a tissue from my bag. "Anyway, you ready to study?"

The abrupt end to the conversation has Olive looking disappointed. "Yeah, sure. Are you still going to see your family this weekend? I know you wanted to try cramming as much study time as possible before you leave."

I can't help but make a face when I nod.

It took one bad weekend where I thought Danny was going to ghost me after he drove me home to finally agree to fly to Cali for Serenity's event. I think everyone was shocked when I texted them saying I got a plane ticket for Saturday morning. But what was I supposed to do? Staying in my room as I hide from Danny and what I assumed he thought of me didn't sound like a fun option for weekend festivities.

I open my notebook. "I won't have a lot of time to study when I'm home, so we should probably start."

Thankfully, she lets go of what we were talking about in a teasing tone. "Does this mean you don't want to know how Alex managed to get my panties off in the first place?"

I roll my eyes and fight an amused smile from forming. "Like you said, I've seen what he looks like. I doubt it took much."

She hums dreamily. "So true."

~

I'm halfway to the Latte Lounge when a group of guys I recognize from the bonfire start laughing as they eye a couple girls waving at them in passing. One of the guys takes notice of the extra swivel in the dark-haired girl's hips as she walks by, but one of his friends yanks the back of his shirt to stop him from following her like he obviously wants to.

I force myself to smile as I get nearer, remembering all the times when Mom told me my resting face was a scowl that I needed to fix before I scared everyone away.

I find myself forcing a tight-lipped smile as the men pass by me. My head tips in an awkward greeting at a couple of them who give me a fleeting look. Just as I turn to face forward, a body breaks from their group and steps directly in my path.

Jerking back on my heels, I glance up at the tallish boy with broad shoulders encased in a Lindon U black T-shirt who's giving me a smile I've seen far too often around here.

Cocky.

"Hey."

I don't allow myself to look at him as I return a nervous, "Hi." My eyes go around him for a split second before I clear my throat. "I'm late to something, so…"

"You've been hanging with Bridges, right?" he asks despite my obvious discomfort. Either he's oblivious or doesn't care.

I move to the side so he's not blocking me, but he shifts his feet to mimic the movement.

My breath shutters as fear prickles the back of my neck.

From behind me, someone says, "C'mon, Wallace. We've got to get to class."

The guy—Wallace—waves the person talking off while eyeing me with something glimmering in his eye. "So go without me, Rigger. I'm trying to have a polite conversation with a pretty girl. I know where the building is."

Taking a small step back, the tight smile on my face inches higher. *Don't let him see you're afraid of him.*

Brown eyes.

Not dark or light.

Plain.

And they shine with the same kind of certainty that his smile gives off. He's not a bad-looking guy, but I want nothing to do with him.

So I say, "Yes, I know Danny."

Those eyes light up. "*Danny*, huh?"

I bite the inside of my cheek and nod.

He cocks his head, letting his hair, a lighter brown that's a few shades darker than my natural blond, fall into his eyes. "I've seen you around. Wanted to say hi a few times, but you're always with other people."

"Oh, well…" I shrug awkwardly, not knowing what to tell him. I take another step back and grip my backpack strap.

"I've heard some buddies of yours say you like to have a good time. If that's true, maybe we could—"

"*There you are,*" someone new says, dropping an arm around my shoulders.

It takes everything in me not to lock up, but I manage to loosen my stance when I take in the familiar cologne belonging to the witty football player I've been texting on and off with.

"Thanks for finding my girl, Wallace," Danny tells the guy in front of us in a clipped tone. "I've been looking for her everywhere."

Those two words echo in my head, but I press my lips together and don't say anything.

My girl.

My girl.

My girl.

Wallace takes a few seconds of staring at Danny before he backs up and smirks. It's a different kind of smile than the one he gave me. This one is challenging. Amused.

When his gaze shifts between the two of us, he chuckles. "My bad, *Danny.*"

From the corner of my eye, I see Danny's mouth twitch downward before going back to neutral. "No big. You should probably head out before you're late. Coach wouldn't want you getting marked down for tardiness again. It'd suck if you didn't get to start in the next game."

Whatever threat lies between the lines is loud and clear to Wallace. His smirk disappears and is replaced with a scowl. "Whatever," he grumbles, almost pushing into my shoulder as he walks toward the few guys still waiting for him.

I notice their attention turns to me and Danny, who still has his arm around me, until they shake off whatever thoughts they have and start walking away.

A few seconds later when I decide it's safe to, I move out from Danny's hold and offer him a weak smile. "Thanks for that. He's…" I'm not sure what Wallace is, but my stomach twists trying to figure out the right word.

"He's a dick," he finishes for me. His blue eyes aren't as bright as normal as he looks at me, and the way his brows furrow until there's a crease between them makes me frown. "You good? He didn't do anything, did he?"

Blowing out a breath, I shake my head and glance in the direction his teammate wandered off to. "I just get a weird vibe from him."

He chuckles. "Most people do. He's a player. Be careful."

"People say that about you too," I comment, daring to look at him. "Should I be careful around you?"

His lips twitch as mischief dances in his eyes. "I'd really rather you weren't, Blondie. It'd be way less fun."

My nose scrunches at the word *fun*.

"Where are you headed? I'll walk you there."

I point toward the Latte Lounge. "I was going to get something to drink and do some studying before my next class. I need to up my math average before my parents have a conniption when they see my current grade."

His eyes go toward where I'm pointing before an

overdramatic noise rises from his throat. "We can't go *there*. That's an epic betrayal to Bea's I couldn't live with."

I gape at him. "Um…"

"Come on," he urges, tipping his chin. "If you're down with walking, I'll take you to the bakery. My treat. It's a good place to study, and the food and drinks are better anyway."

"What's wrong with Latte Lounge? It's right here."

"*That*," he practically spits, glowering at the popular college hangout, "is a dishonor to Bea's. She's worked hard to build her business and all for this joke of a place to open and steal her customers. They overcharge for everything on their menu, and their pastries are brought in from some random supplier. They're not even homemade or bought from Bea's! We can't support that, Skylar."

I find his dedication to the local bakery oddly adorable. Then he sweetens the deal with one statement that would have me following him toward Main Street.

"Your roommate doesn't hang out at Bea's," he says, grinning like he knows it's the winning blow.

And it is.

"Lead the way," I tell him, feigning reluctance.

When he offers me his arm, I stare at it for a solid ten seconds before he says, "Grant me the chance to properly escort a pretty girl to my favorite place. Just this once."

My eyes flicker up to his hopeful face.

His eyes are soft, his smile softer.

I tell myself the reason why I wrap my arm around his is because it'll protect me from the nipping wind that blows around us.

But I'd be lying.

Chapter Sixteen

DANNY

I SET DOWN THE white cloud mocha in front of Skylar, along with a plate of Bea's famous pumpkin pound cake that's only for sale this time of year. When she glances at the frosted treat, she flicks her gaze up as I sit down with my Mind Sweeper—coffee with a double shot of espresso.

Grandma Meadow says she doesn't know how my heart is so strong with all the caffeine I consume on a daily basis, but she doesn't complain whenever I make sure she gets her dose of it anytime I'm back in Boston. I've been told enough times in the past by the batty woman not to come home unless I have something from Dunkin" for her, so it's become a habit to stop at one of the many stores Boston has before going to the house.

I take a sip of my drink. "Best pound cake you'll ever taste," I promise her, pushing the plate and one of the forks in her direction.

She eyes it with uncertainty.

Grabbing my bag and pulling out my anthropology

notebook, I smack it down in the empty spot to my right. "Don't think I've forgotten what you said. You'll put anything in your mouth, so give that a try."

Her posture stiffens. "I was hoping you'd forgotten I said that." The telltale sign of a blush makes its way to her face.

Trying my best to hide my smile, I shake my head as I glance at the notes and study guide that Ivy helped me with. "Trust me, Blondie. When you tell a guy that, there's no way he's forgetting. Chances are he—" I stop myself quickly, clearing my throat. "Never mind. Go on. Try a piece of the cake."

She picks up the fork and cuts a small piece off. "What were you going to say?"

I click my tongue in contemplation. She's flighty about topics like the ones constantly on my mind, and the one I've been thinking about nonstop since her little remark? I'm not sure she can handle it.

But I give her the chance to try. "You can't tell a guy you'd put anything in your mouth without him thinking about his favorite appendage going there."

Her blush doesn't deepen, but she does glance down at the cake still on her fork. Quietly, she says, "Oh."

I tell her I've thought about my cock in her mouth, and all I get is "oh." It'll do for now. My fantasy and right hand have brought the image to life more times than I can count already. "Anyway," I redirect. "The pumpkin pound cake is my favorite fall special here. But in the summertime, Bea has these really awesome sponge candy chocolates that I have no clue how she makes. They're the fucking bomb though."

My rambling only makes her gape harder at me. "Did you really just go from talking about imaginary blow jobs to sponge candies in, like, three seconds?"

Hearing her say the words makes my dick react on the spot. I shift in my seat and stifle a groan as it salutes her in my jeans. "Yeah, so?"

She watches as I reach down and adjust myself under the table before blinking slowly. "Are you...um...?" Her eyes dart toward what the tabletop is hiding.

I scrub my face before nonchalantly reaching for my notebook and flipping it to a random page of half-assed scribbles. "I'm a dude. I get hard easily."

"Obviously," she mumbles.

"Just eat your damn cake," I murmur.

To my surprise, she laughs lightly.

Through my lashes, I watch her take a bite of the pound cake. I can tell she likes it by the way her face lights up. It makes me smile when she does a little shimmy in her chair. I'll never understand why girls do that when they eat, but it's fucking—

Don't say cute, my inner voice says.

"Good, right?" I ask instead, shooting her a victorious grin. "I know the best food in a fifty-mile radius. In the mood for pizza? Bridgeport has the best pies in the tricounty area. Treats? Definitely Bea's. The diner has the greatest fish fry on Fridays and the best chicken parmesan I've ever eaten, but don't tell my ma that. She'd beat me with a newspaper if she heard me say someone else's chicken parm was better than hers."

She goes for a second helping of the cake and asks, "How would I tell your mom? It's not like I'd ever meet her."

I shrug loosely. "She comes to my games sometimes, which I was hoping to convince you to do. Actually, we're playing a big one this weekend that I planned on bribing you to attend." When her shoulders drop a fraction at my invitation, I instantly backtrack to make it sound more convincing. "My ma won't be at this one, but she'll probably be at the next one. And this is a home game. We're playing a team that we should beat no problem. It'll probably be a little cold, but I know you've got the gear for it. Bring your friend Olive. I bet she'd like it. I know how much she likes sports."

"Danny..." Her lips twitch. I already know she's going to turn me down before she confirms it. "I'm going home this weekend. Or else I would."

I frown. "Why are you going home?"

"Family event." Skylar doesn't sound enthused about it. Her sigh is light as she pushes the plate of food toward me and fidgets with her drink. "I really would have gone if I were around. Olive would make sure I knew what was happening. It's the least I could do with everything you've done for me."

My head cocks in curiosity. "What is it that I've done for you that makes you think you owe me?"

She nibbles on her lip. "You've been my friend."

Oh, Skylar. "You don't owe me anything for that. If anything, it's the other way around."

Now she looks confused.

"I know you've had your reservations about me, and I've given you some good reasons for that. You've been through more shit than I probably know. Yet you gave me a chance. You still are. Every time you say yes to hanging with me, you're giving me a shot that I probably would have gotten on my knees to beg you for otherwise."

The thought of me on my knees gives me a lot more images in my head to use tonight when I'm alone, but I push them away for now.

"So no, Sky. You don't owe me shit." I hear her small intake of breath as we watch each other from across the table. I decide to let her process that for now and change the subject. "Are you close with your family?"

She accepts the turn of conversation smoothly. "I get along with my sister Serena. She and her twin, Sienna, are twenty-four, so there's a decent gap between us. But not as much as the almost ten years between me and my oldest sister, Serenity. They're all very..." She searches for the word as she stares at her coffee. "Excessive. It's not really their fault though. Our parents are the same way. We grew up in Beverly Hills."

No shit. "And you came *here*?"

"You came from Boston," she points out. "The Hills scene was never for me. And like I said, my family all enjoys living off the riches and reputations they've built for themselves. I've always felt like an outsider. I had a few friends that my sisters called the misfits, but I never really fit in fully. I was rich but didn't dress or act it. My sisters were outgoing and extroverted while I was shy and introverted. I figured coming here would give me a chance to mold myself into someone without money or my sisters' shadows."

I wouldn't have pegged her as a rich kid, but people probably say the same about me. When I first arrived, it'd been clear I came from wealth. I wore expensive clothing with brand names stitched on each piece. Over the years, it's become less obvious. I blend in now. "Have you molded yourself into who you want to be here?"

There's a moment of hesitation where she stalls to take a sip from the cup she's grasping on to. I don't know if she realizes it or not, but she's playing with one of the dyed strands of her hair, twirling it around her finger thoughtfully. "No.

I didn't realize how homesick I'd be, so I sort of shadowed Becca and tried being like her. But it was obvious from the start I couldn't live up to her social prowess. She loves going to parties and dancing and drinking, and there's nothing wrong with that. Unlike her, I'd never judge somebody just because they live differently than I do. It just seems like being myself hasn't exactly made me a lot of friends."

"As far as I'm concerned, that's a good thing. The more people in your circle, the more drama that's in it. It's about quality, not quantity. And Olive seems like a cool chick to me."

That gets me one of those rare smiles from her. "She is. She was one of the first people who gave me a chance here. No judgment. No assumptions. She just lets me be my awkward self."

Curiosity sinks in. "And who are the other people who gave you a chance?"

Her expression turns shy. "You." Her fork pokes at the cake. "Just you."

Just me.

I reach out and flick her hand playfully to grab her attention. "Are you finally acknowledging our best friend status?"

She challenges me with a single look. "I don't know. Do best friends give each other boners?"

The boner in question that *had* deflated turns into a semi in its confinement. Flashing her a devious smile, I lean in and say, "You have no idea, Blondie."

Her lips waver as she tries to hide a smile, but she fails. It grows on her face like my dick grows in my pants.

She really has no clue at all.

"So," I prod, "tell me about that new book you started. You basically blew me off last night because you said it was getting good."

Her eyes widen. "You want to hear about the book I'm reading?"

I sip my drink. "If that's what makes you happy, then yes."

She stares.

I stare back.

Slowly, she shakes her head. "Okay. Well, it's a brother's best friend romance..."

I listen to every word, hanging on to the way her expression lightens as she tells me all about the story.

Chapter Seventeen

DANNY

OUR TIGHT END'S BLUE-HAIRED obsession sinks into the chair next to me, sniffling through the first ten minutes of biological anthropology. Her cheeks are flushed and her eyes are red as she furiously scribbles down notes as Professor Relethford talks.

"You sure you don't need to go home?" I ask her, frowning when her lips twitch into an irritated frown. Aiden wouldn't like knowing Ivy's here when she looks so run-down from the cold she'd been fighting for days.

She side-eyes me before gripping her pen tighter and stares back at the balding professor at the front of the room. "DJ, I don't wake up and strive to be a hard-core bitch every day of my life, but you're about to see that side of me if you ask me that one more time."

My lips threaten to shift into a smile. The more I get to know the fiery personality of the person sitting beside me, the more I like her. And I can see why our star tight end does too.

One of my teammates snickers at her frosty reply from the other side of me, but I don't know who. Whoever it is stops as soon as she leans forward and shoots him a small scowl.

I nudge her arm half-heartedly. "I'm looking out for you, and not just for the tight end either."

Ivy flips gears. "Did you take any decent notes while I was away?"

She should know better than to ask me that sort of thing. I'm lucky if I even absorb half of what this guy says. "No, but—"

"You can borrow mine." I recognize Wallace's sleazy voice and press my lips together to fight from glowering. He's had his sights set on Ivy since Aiden showed interest. Just like the douchebag is doing now with Skylar too.

My teeth grind at the thought of him hanging around her. The shit Wallace has been saying in the locker room about her isn't worth repeating to her face, but I'd been two seconds from throat punching him every time he grabbed himself and talked about what he wanted to do to her tight—

Jaw clenching, I force myself to stop thinking about it. Caleb had to steer me out while Aiden talked to the dickhead before I lost it. With my luck, Coach would have blamed me for the altercation and let Wallace off the hook.

When I see Ivy giving the douche an appreciative smile at his offer, I want to snap at her to quit it. I vowed to dislike the guy as soon as he took over Justin Brady's position and started acting like he owned the place. But when he makes moves on women he has no claim to? It makes me rage.

"Watch out for that one. He thinks because he's the new quarterback he can charm his way into anyone's pants."

Ivy stiffens at my useless warning. "You don't need to

worry about that. I'm not interested." There's a heavy pause. "In anyone," she adds, which makes me snort.

Her saying she isn't into Aiden is like me saying I'm not even a little into Skylar. I'd be fucking dumb not to be. She's gorgeous even when she tries not to be, funny even in her awkward moments, and mysterious as hell. All things that make me want to unwrap her like the total package she is.

I'd be lying to myself if I said I wasn't bummed she wouldn't be around to see our game this weekend. When I'm playing, I'm in my zone—as confident as I'll ever be while flying across the field, helping my team walk away with another win, or dancing on the sidelines to get a little extra noise from the crowd.

The turf is a high I'll miss when I graduate. Miss like a piece of me is gone for good.

I think about what comes after Lindon for the rest of class until I'm hauling it to the dining hall for a quick bite. I'd told Skylar that I changed my degree because I didn't want to be around sports until I was retirement age, but that's not completely true. Truth is, it'd wreck me if I had to watch from the outside.

My stomach growls with the scent of food surrounding me as I scan my ID and head toward the prepackaged sandwiches from a fast grab-and-go before meeting the guys.

Walking back toward the front door after swiping the last two chicken sandwiches wrapped in aluminum foil, I see Skylar sitting at a corner table with two other girls, one of whom I recognize as Aliyah.

Skylar looks uncomfortable as she scans a few nearby tables, all full of people who occasionally glance in her direction and talk among themselves.

As soon as she sees me approaching, she sits taller, ignoring the barely touched food on her plate and the girls clearly gawking as I stop at their spot. "Hey," I greet, giving each of them a smile. Thankfully, Becca isn't around. Last time I passed Skylar's roommate, she'd looked at me like I was a challenge she wanted to take on, if for no other reason than to say she got me before Skylar did.

It'll never happen though.

I've already been claimed, even if the person who has me doesn't know it yet.

Skylar offers me a weak, "Hi." Her eyes look a little glassy, and the way she pushes her vegetables around with her fork has my smile dropping.

"You feeling okay? Did you catch what's going around?"

The choked noise escaping her has me fighting back a cringe.

Bad choice of words.

"The cold going around," I murmur. "Did you catch the cold going around? My teammate's girl just got over it. Took a few days, but he got her back on her feet."

Her friend with glasses asks, "Is that your way of asking if she needs your help getting her back on her feet?" She and the darker-haired girl next to her share a light laugh as Skylar rolls her eyes at them.

I simply smile, rocking back on my heels as my eyes return to the one person I'm here to talk to. "I'd do whatever Sky needed. All she has to do is ask."

It's true, and I can tell it takes her by surprise. "I'm fine, but thanks. Just a little tired lately trying to prep for exams. Are you grabbing lunch?" Her chin dips toward the wrapped food in my hands.

I nod. "Need to head to practice soon. We've got a big

game coming up, so Coach is riding our asses hard to make sure we dominate at tomorrow's game."

Her lips twitch downward, and I want to do anything in order to get them to stop.

I continue, "Hey, I was thinking about something earlier. Do you need a ride to the airport tomorrow? Depending on when your flight is, I can probably squeeze it in before preparing for the game."

Coach wants us to meet at our usual spot to go over game tapes of the team we're up against. It feels like we've studied everything we can about them, but he seems to think we need all the help we can get.

"You don't need to do that. I have to be up and at the airport really early, and—"

"What time?" I press anyway.

"Danny—"

Aliyah hiccups and stares between us. She nudges Skylar and whispers, "Girl, say yes."

"Yeah, Skylar. Say yes."

She makes a face at my sheer determination and then sighs. "I need to be there at four thirty in the morning so I have time to go through security and everything. My flight leaves at five."

The girls both make unintelligible noises at the early as hell wakeup call.

Me? I shrug, unfazed. "Okay. I'll pick you up at your dorm a little before four."

Skylar gapes. "Really?"

I snicker. "I'm usually up around five to get my run in anyway. It's not that much earlier."

The comical expression I get from each of the girls staring at me makes me chuckle. I'm going to assume none of them are morning people, which will make driving Skylar that much more entertaining.

"I have to get going, but I'll text you later. Sound good?"

Those blue eyes fill with something close to uncertainty for some reason, but she nods before I wave to her and her friends. I'm out the door and walking to the sports complex when I pull out my phone with a last-minute idea.

> Me: Come over and watch a movie with me. It's Caleb's turn to cook and he's not half bad. We can hang for a bit before you leave for the weekend

A few people pass me as they enter the building I'm standing just outside of. One of them is a teammate who smacks my shoulder and gestures toward the door, but I wave him off.

Bubbles appear at the bottom of the screen as I take a big bite of my sandwich and wait for her reply.

> Blondie: I'm not sure...
> Me: I'll let you choose the movie

The guys will probably join us and complain about it, but they can suck it up for a night.

> Me: Caleb is making his famous fish tacos

I overheard Skylar tell Olive how much she missed fish tacos back in Cali, so it was worth a shot. I'd say about anything to get a few extra hours with her.

> Blondie: Fish tacos, huh?

I grin, knowing I got her.

Me: I'll pick you up. Name the time

Walking into the building with a grin on my face, I fist-bump Caleb and drop onto the bench in the locker room.

"Dude, it's gross you're eating in here," he remarks, staring at my half-eaten lunch.

I shrug a shoulder. "I need a favor."

His brows go up as he changes.

"I need you to make fish tacos tonight."

~

Caleb smacks my back as he exits the kitchen, his keys in hand as he walks over to his girlfriend by the door. Raine gives me a wave and peeks at the brunette currently sitting on the couch scrolling through Netflix before a secretive smile tilts her lips. I eye her to stay quiet, she giggles, and the two lovebirds head out to her place for the night.

I don't know where Aiden and Ivy are, but when I brought up the movie night, I was glad when Aiden said they wouldn't be around for it. Justin is at the library studying his ass off because he's stressed about some exam he has bright and early on Monday, and the rest of the guys aren't my problem.

Walking into the living room with a bowl of popcorn, I drop into the spot beside Skylar, leaving enough room to set the snack between us. If she knows it's just us, she doesn't say anything, and I'm afraid to offer the information in case she chooses to bolt.

"Find anything?" My eyes go to the screen as she reads

the description of some awful-sounding mystery movie featuring a comedian as one of the lead roles.

"Not yet. Are you against a family movie?"

My phone buzzes in my pocket, distracting me from the outlandish question. I pull my cell out and grin at the screen. "No. Choose whatever you want. I'm good with anything."

> Grandma M: Your mother told me you weren't coming home right away for Thanksgiving. After everything I've done for you boy...
>
> Me: We have a game against Wilson Reed that weekend

My grandma has an unhealthy appetite for competitions, and the problem with mine against the Wilson Reed Raiders is that I'm not sure Grandma Meadow would root for Lindon.

The Raiders are from Massachusetts, and the older woman who could whoop my ass on any given day, she says it's woven into her existence to be loyal to any Mass sports team, no questions asked. It doesn't matter that her only grandson plays for a New York team.

Ma thought her mother was going to have a heart attack when I surprised her with tickets to the Red Sox game that would end in their fourth World Series title back in 2018. I'd managed to get tickets for the three of us, and the world exploded around us when the game ended. You could hear the whole fucking city celebrating for days afterward.

> Grandma M: No wonder she told me we couldn't go

I snicker. Ma knows Grandma would be wearing my

number but waving a Raiders' foam finger in the air. It wouldn't go over well.

"What's so funny?" Skylar asks, eyeing my phone for a moment as she crosses her legs under herself to get comfortable.

I wave my phone. "The traitor I'm talking to is a Raiders fan—that's our enemy over at Wilson Reed. If she came to our game in a couple weeks, she'd cheer for them."

Her eyes go back to the TV screen. "She?"

Not wanting to read into her mumbled inquiry, I fight off the crooked grin that wavers on my face. "Yeah. Grandma Meadow. I mentioned her before. You two would get along. Wouldn't be surprised if she had you waving a Raiders flag."

Clarity eases her tight shoulders until she settles into the couch cushion, and I know it's jealousy subsiding. "Oh." There's a pause as she scans a kids' movie I watched when I was little. "You two seem close."

I nod, smiling over the thought of the eccentric sixty-four-year-old. "My grandma is badass. Even my friends love her because you never know what to expect. The woman is obsessed with reality TV and those annoying gossip table shows that spew rumors about celebrities all the time. Once, I saw her watching one of those tattoo shows, and I think she was considering getting some ink."

The smile on her face is light as she watches me talk. "I didn't know my grandparents, so you're lucky. They died when I was too little to remember them. But my sisters said they were all snobby, so maybe it's not a bad thing. My mom's parents came from nothing and didn't like that my father started making a fortune from some investments he made early on. I guess they thought their wealth changed them." She lifts her shoulders. "All I know is who my family is with money. Maybe they *were* different. Money tends to change people."

"Only if we let it," I counter. "I couldn't even tell you where my family's money comes from. All I know is that it'll be mine someday. It paid for what my football scholarship didn't, and it'll pay for grad school when I'm done with my bachelor's degree. I'm grateful for it, but I don't think it'll ever change me." Lindon is a hell of a lot cheaper than any of the other schools I applied for, but it was always the better choice. We never cared if there was a higher price on an education as long as it had what I wanted. So here I am. "People think money will buy us happiness, but the material things it gets us are only temporary. If your grand-parents were that pissed at your parents for having money, the problem was them. Sounds like it isn't so bad you didn't know them."

All Skylar does is hum, clearly contemplating my response.

After she chooses a movie, we fall into a comfortable silence as it begins playing. I grab a few handfuls of popcorn, prop my feet on the coffee table, knowing Aiden won't be around to smack them off and scold me, and Skylar stares solely at the screen with her hands in her lap.

She's too still.

I subtly study the distance between us. It's not much, but it's there. Space. Comfort. My eyes trail to where her bent knee is an inch or so away from my thigh, and I debate on moving over and making an excuse for it.

Sensing my lingering gaze, she turns her head. "What are you looking at?" Her eyes go down to our legs, examin-ing her leggings as if there might be something on them.

I rub my denim-clad thigh. "It's nothing. Don't worry about it."

My strained voice makes her squirm until her knee knocks into my thigh. "No, it's not nothing. What's going on? You're acting...weird."

"I'm always weird" is the smart thing I decide to reply with.

Her eyes lighten playfully. "True, but you're usually weird in a fun way."

I debate my options. I could play it off as something trivial, or I could brush it off completely and just watch the movie. But the way Skylar's eyes are roaming over me makes me choose the best option: the truth.

"You don't seem that comfortable right now, and I'm not sure if it's me or what. It..." My nose twitches as I palm the back of my neck. "I don't know. It bothers me. Maybe 'bothers' isn't the right word. I just don't like seeing you uncomfortable."

She fumbles with her fingers as she stares at the distance she put back between our legs. With a sigh, she slumps her shoulders. "It's going to sound stupid, but I have these dreams that wake me up. Nightmares, I guess. Except I'm pretty sure they're actually memories from the party here. It's weird being back when I don't remember much about it. It's not you."

My body tenses. "Tidbits like what exactly? Do you remember who—"

"No, and that's why I get uncomfortable around certain people. You. Guys in general. You may think because guys seem to stare at me or whatever that I'm doing something on purpose to attract their attention, but I'm not. I'd rather be left alone. It's pathetic, right? Olive crushes me in strangely intense hugs all the time and I'm fine. But if some guy did that, I'd get all squirmy."

"That's not pathetic," I tell her quietly.

She doesn't seem to believe me. "All I remember is hands on me while I'm dancing and...when I'm not dancing. Hands on my skin. It's like I can *feel* them even after all this time. I can't get it out of my brain. I vaguely remember someone telling me to come upstairs. I don't know how many times I was told not to go with a guy who I didn't know, especially not when I was drunk. But I did anyway. I remember kissing him. I remember...liking it. A lot. I thought he was blond and I'm pretty sure he'd been drinking too because he smelled—" Her nose scrunches. "He smelled like something stronger than the beer you guys had. Like the rum I'd been drinking with soda." She stops talking for a few seconds and nibbles on her thumbnail. When her eyes meet mine, they're sheepish. "Honestly? I think I know why I kept suspecting it was you, why I was so determined to believe it."

"Why?"

There's a brief pause.

"I wanted it to be different," she whispers. "I wanted to believe that I went upstairs with somebody cute who I wanted to be with. I don't know. I just...knowing you now, I would have preferred I'd made the choice. I would have chosen you."

Her admission does something screwy to my heart. It makes it pound. Hard. Fast. Heavy.

I stare at her as she says, "As much as I don't want to, I think about that night a lot. Because I have no clue who I let lead me upstairs or who I let touch my body. And you're so nice, everybody seems to like you, which makes me think you'd...you would have taken care of me. Made it good. But I don't know. And that sucks. It's...yeah. It just sucks." Her eyes go to her lap. She picks at her leggings and shakes her head. "When I woke up in the room, I was tired, so tired, and I was confused. My head hurt, my…other things hurt. I was bleeding a little."

My teeth grind.

"I knew what I'd done," she whispers, voice thick with emotion that I wish I could help ease somehow. "I knew what had happened from the stories my sisters would tell me about their experiences with exes. I've read books, seen movies. The harder I tried putting the pieces together, the more confused I'd get. Believing somebody like you had taken my virginity made it not seem so bad."

Her cheeks heat, and her eyes stay on anything but me no matter how bad I want her to look.

"The thing is, I never thought sex was a big deal. I always made light of it like you did. But that night changed my opinion. Because I should have remembered having it, but I don't. I should have figured out by now if I told him to keep going or to stop, but I haven't. Just because I liked kissing him didn't mean I liked…other things. And part of me doesn't want to remember at this point."

"Why not?" I find myself wondering.

Her eyes finally travel to my face. "If you had the chance to forget the choices you made instead of looking them in the eye, wouldn't you?"

Lips pressing together, I study her. "What if your choices weren't entirely yours? Wouldn't you want to know? There'd been alcohol, and that makes people do stuff they wouldn't normally. You're putting too much pressure on yourself, Skylar."

She swallows. "I didn't say no, so how could the choice not have been mine? I just told you that I liked—"

"I liked the women I kissed too," I say bluntly, seeing her wince. "But that doesn't mean we had to do more. I've never once hooked up with a drunk woman because I always wanted them to be sober when they made that choice."

When her eyes return to the screen, I nod to myself, knowing she doesn't want me to keep going. The longer the silence lasts, the antsier I get about what the hell happened at our party.

Aiden was right.

It should have never fucking happened.

As the movie goes on, the bowl of popcorn empties, and Skylar becomes restless. Her body squirms and her focus shifts until she moves a fraction.

One little fraction until her knee is touching my leg again.

Except this time, she doesn't move it.

The move may be tiny, but the leap is big.

And I'm diving headfirst after her.

Chapter Eighteen

DANNY

INCOHERENT MUMBLES COME FROM the girl whose hair is the only thing between her face and the cool passenger window as we drive. I'm not surprised she's dead to the world considering she fell asleep right before the movie ended last night. Not wanting to move her, I let her sleep until my legs were numb from the way they were tangled with hers. She looked peaceful, carefree when she slept. Only when she shifted enough to lie down on the other cushion did I get up, cover her with one of the blankets that Caleb's ma gave him for the house, and set an alarm on my phone to get us up early enough to head back to her dorm and grab her bag before driving to the airport.

When she walked out of her dorm this morning, her face was clean of the makeup she slept in, and her hair was brushed and resting over her shoulders. She changed into a pair of baggy sweatpants that looked like they could fit two of her inside, and she was wearing that puffy coat again.

Did she still look ten times better than most girls I know?

Yes. Sexy in a laid-back sort of way. To me, there's nothing hotter than a girl who's completely comfortable around you in anything.

I roll my shoulder, which aches ten times worse than usual because of the armchair I slept in all night, as I steer. I didn't want Skylar waking up in an unfamiliar place and freaking out. Not when she already experienced that once in our house. If stretching out at a weird angle to make sure she saw me across the room when she woke would make her feel secure, I'd do it again in a heartbeat.

Even though Coach will probably give me a lecture when I wince through warm-ups.

"You doing okay over there, Blondie?" I muse chipperly, causing a groan to escape her. I refrain from snickering as I glance into the side mirror that faces her. I'm pretty sure she's drooling, but I know better than to tease.

We drive over a bump, making her head knock into the window. Her hand comes up and swipes at her mouth, cracking my lips into a bigger grin that I try keeping to myself. When she peels herself away from the glass and turns her head toward me, I make sure I'm solely focused on the road so she can't see the waver of my lips.

"Do you know who else was this peppy early in the morning?" she asks me gingerly.

I shake my head. "No. Who?"

She reaches for the travel mug of coffee I poured for her before we headed to grab her bag and draws it to her naked lips. "Hitler," Skylar answers.

I choke on a surprised laugh at her little offhand joke as she takes a long sip of the caffeine.

Then she adds a murmured, "Probably."

Scrubbing my jaw with my palm, I swallow my laugh

and clear my throat. "For someone who looks ready to face plant into the dashboard at any second, you've got one hell of a mouth on you."

There's a mild pause before she makes a face at herself. "You're not Jewish, are you? I should've really chosen somebody else, but I was trying to think of someone evil. And if it were between Hitler and Satan, I feel like Hitler would be the worst out of the two."

I blink, giving her a quizzical glance. "You think *Hitler* is more evil than Lucifer? Lucy is the devil himself."

She clasps onto the mug like a lifeline as she shrugs. "Mm-hmm. Lucifer was an angel, just a fallen one. Who was Hitler before? A baby. And I've heard it on good authority that babies can be evil. I'm pretty sure my mom struggled deciding to have more kids after my sister Serenity was born because of it. I mean, Ser is the oldest, so obviously Mom got over it. But still."

There's no stopping the snort that comes from me. "Wow. That's…" I have no real words for how twisted this conversation got. "For all intents and purposes, I'll agree with you. Mostly because I don't know where to begin with this conversation or your whack train of thought. I'm concerned."

"Why?"

"You're comparing the devil to babies."

"No, I'm comparing him to Hitler."

"Who was once a baby."

Another hum comes from her.

I snicker. "You're something else when you're half-asleep. I already found you interesting as hell, but this? I'm glad I offered to take you, even if it's the ass crack of dawn."

Her head thumps against the glass like she can't hold it up any longer. "Like I said. Evil."

"Because I like being around you?"

"That *is* questionable," she mumbles, probably more to herself than me. "But I'm mostly judging your affinity for mornings."

I roll my eyes. "Don't go fishing for compliments, Skylar. We both know I like you just fine. I wouldn't subject myself to getting lectured on the dos and don'ts of driving my buddy's truck for just anyone."

Since Caleb has to open his dad's hardware store bright and early to get things going before his pops can come in, I had to ask Aiden to borrow his truck. After twenty minutes of being berated about not fucking up his property—or fucking *in* it—he passed me the keys with his usual charming glower.

Skylar finds the energy to turn her body toward me, eyelids still heavy as she rubs one with her closed fist. "Why do you like me anyway? It's so…random."

"How is it random? You're a cool chick. I like cool people. Chicks especially." My brows wiggle, not that she can see it well in the darkness.

"At first I thought it was pity. You made it pretty clear from the start that you didn't want to sleep with me, so what else was there? Especially after I gave you a perfectly good reason not to ever sleep with me—"

I grip the steering wheel tightly. "Hold up, Blondie. I'm going to stop you right there before you go spewing more bullshit. In fact, I've wanted to talk about this for a while, but you always find ways to shut me down. Now's as good a time as any."

She stares at her coffee mug in silence, knowing she has no other option as a captive audience.

"I already apologized for what I said when we met," I

185

begin, eyeing her for a moment before my eyes return to the road. "And I meant it. I *am* sorry for how much of an asshole I came off as when we first started talking. I have a thing against going after girls who like men for their sports stats. Jocks get bad reps for being only good for one thing, and that shit pisses me off. I made a dumbass assumption and rolled with it because I'm used to women treating me like I'm only worth a quick fuck. I shouldn't have lumped you in with them without getting to know you. And yeah, I said some shit about hooking up that was obviously misplaced, so I get why you'd be wary of me."

"Danny—"

"No. When the driver is talking, the passenger shuts their cakehole."

"Did you just misquote *Supernatural*?"

"Unimportant," I reply dryly. "Just listen. We don't have that much longer until we're at the airport, so if nothing else, I want you to hear me out before you head off for the weekend." When she makes no move to cut me off, I nod and take a deep breath. "I don't always take things seriously. I know, I know. Shocking. So when I saw you trying to sneak out of the house, I wasn't really thinking. Sex has always been sex to me, so I joke about it. And then when I saw you again, I kept pushing you on it because I thought everyone had the same mindset. I was wrong. I remember you at the party. Even remember dancing with you."

Her body tightens.

Scratching the back of my neck, I grunt to myself. "Don't know if you remember that. Honestly, I barely do. We were both drinking quite a bit that night. You'd gone back with your friends, and I didn't see you again until the next morning when you were leaving. Thing is, I don't dance and joke around with just anybody. I don't go up to random people at bakeries and try hitting them up for their number. That's what I was trying to do, by the way. Failed miserably too. Guys still pester me about it."

The girl riding shotgun winces at her epic rejection all those weeks ago.

"But I'm glad you didn't give it to me," I admit casually, lifting my shoulder. "It made you stand out. Could've done without you running out on me. Have to admit, that habit was a little grating after a while. But I get why you did it. When you told me about the party, about what happened, it made sense. This is where I need you to listen—to *really* hear me." I fist the wheel until my fingers bite with pain. "There isn't one time when I've seen you and haven't wanted to get you alone, strip you down, and get to know your body on a personal, intimate level. It's not that I've never *not* wanted to sleep with you, Skylar. I just have my own set of rules to follow through on when it comes to you. But make no mistake. You're the kind of girl any guy would be fucking lucky to have in any way you'd let them. And what I'm about to say is going to be awkward and you're probably going to tell me to shut up, but this needs to be said."

I can hear her suck in a breath and hold it, so I choose not to relent until the words are out in the open. We pass by the airport sign with the short number of miles to get there printed in bold white lettering.

"I'm not sure what excuse you've concocted in your head about the party, but what happened at it isn't your fault. What that asshole, whoever the fuck he is, did should have never happened because you were drinking too much. Everything about that night is on him." My fingers hurt from their grip as I force myself to take a deep breath and release it. "You were drunk. Nobody should have taken advantage of a college girl having a good time, even if you'd…said you wanted it in the moment. Even if you enjoyed doing things with him. Anyone in that room could've seen how wasted you were. I'm not saying that to embarrass you, I'm simply stating facts. Don't think for a second that I think any less of you because of everything that happened that night. If you gave me the chance, I'd happily replace that night with new memories in any way you'd want me to. Name the time and day and I'm there. Understand me?"

I slow down as we near the exit that'll take us into the drop-off section where I'll watch the passenger who's stiff as a board next to me disappear behind closed doors.

There's a long stretch of time where she doesn't say a word, doesn't move. I'm not sure she's even breathing properly.

I reach out and gently touch the hand still holding tightly onto the coffee. "Think about it, okay? Maybe getting some sunshine and fresh air away from Lindon will help. I'll even leave you alone, although I'm sure you'll miss me."

The last bit is accompanied by a small smirk that she glances at warily.

I pull up to the curb in front of the drop-off section where only a few other cars are unloading at. "So what do you say? Want me to fuck off or no?"

Her tongue swipes across her lips before her eyes dart toward the window. A guard wearing a yellow reflective vest is walking down the sidewalk, ushering people to move along. It'll only be a matter of time before she's telling us to hurry up too.

When Skylar glances back at me, her bottom lip is between her teeth. Releasing it, she lets loose a sigh. "I don't want you to fuck off, Danny. Not at all. We're friends."

It's something. A start.

"As for everything else you said…" Her eyes dull and I can see her retracting into herself, something I don't want her doing.

"Just think about it. That's all I'm asking. No pressure. No expectations."

The woman in the vest taps the passenger window and makes a gesture to hurry our goodbyes along.

"Danny…" Skylar's voice is small as she puts the coffee mug back into the holder.

I shake my head, stopping her. "Don't say anything right now. Get that cute ass of yours on the plane, Blondie."

She blinks.

I smile wider.

She swallows.

Leaning forward, I lean my forehead against hers and move some of her thick hair away from her face. The silky strands fuel a lot of late-night fantasies that may or may not involve a fistful of hair exactly this color in my hand while I'm—

Clearing my throat, I let out a breath and brush her nose gently with mine until I hear the smallest intake of breath. "For the record"—my voice is huskier than I intend—"I wish that night were different, that we hadn't been drinking, that we'd danced and made the *choice* to go upstairs together. If we'd made that decision, I wish it would have been me. I would have made it so fucking good for you, there would've been no way you'd forget."

I feel her breath against me, sharp and hot, as I lean in. My intention was to peck her cheek in a chaste goodbye, but she moves her head until it's our lips brushing instead.

We both freeze.

One second.

Two.

Three.

One of my hands flattens against the side of her head, interweaving into her hair, cupping her skull, and absorbing her warmth.

I move back a fraction to gauge her reaction before closing the space between us again, deepening the kiss. Her lips part hesitantly, inviting me in, but I don't dare cross that line. Not yet.

We stay like that, lips caressing one another's as we breathe each other in.

Sharing oxygen.

Sharing a moment.

She pulls away after a few moments, her eyes looking rattled but not scared.

I can work with that.

"You don't want to miss your flight," I rasp, pulling my hand away from her head and putting distance between us even though I'd rather she stays right here.

She blinks, biting down on her bottom lip before nodding once. We watch each other as she pulls her bag out of the back seat and drapes it over her arm. I can read the confusion on her face even from the feet that separate us as she heads toward the building.

She looks back once.

I wave.

She clenches her bag tighter in her hand and disappears past the sliding doors.

Chapter Nineteen

SKYLAR

I'VE BEEN IN CALIFORNIA for an hour and a half, and I've already got a migraine. I could blame the altitude from the flight, the significant weather change, or the conversation I walked away from at the airport, but it's really the people surrounding me who are causing the not-so-subtle knocking in my skull.

And that kiss.

Our second kiss. The stress of figuring out what it means consumed me the second I stepped into the airport. I almost missed final call for boarding because I was sitting and staring at the grubby floor while touching my lips, which still buzzed from the contact.

You're a mess, that pesky inner voice chides as I close my eyes.

"We already had Starbucks three times this week," Serena complains from the passenger seat. Her bare feet are perched on the dashboard of Sienna's Lexus, her toes painted a sparkly pink that fits her bright personality.

When my two sisters pulled up at the airport in the bright-red convertible, I wasn't shocked that Serenity wasn't with them. She sent at least twenty texts to the group chat freaking out about various problems with her event tonight: the caterers messed up the menu, there wouldn't be enough drinks, they were one table short. It went on and on and on until I stopped reading them and put my phone on silent.

Rubbing my temples, I glance down at my phone. I turned off Airplane Mode as soon as we landed, but there were only messages from my family asking if I'd arrived yet beyond the panicked texts Serenity sent. And when an hour went by and *still* nothing from the boy who played guard dog for me all night, then kissed me goodbye, I couldn't help but feel a hollowness take over my chest.

When he leaned in, I moved on instinct. The pull was there, tugging me toward him, to the comfort of his closeness and firm, genuine words. I have fun hanging out with Danny no matter what we're doing—more than I thought I would considering our rocky beginning. It doesn't matter if we're studying in silence and kicking each other underneath the library table or teasing each other while watching movies, he never makes the moment dull.

He has no expectations, and I like that.

Need it.

So the blank screen in my hand taunts me as my temples throb harder, making the pressure behind my eyes intolerable. He'd said a lot before I walked into the airport, and every word soaked into my skin and clung onto my bones ever since. I barely listened to the flight attendant's protocol spiel because all I could think about was what he said about the party.

It wasn't your fault.

I set my head against the headrest carefully and close my eyes again, letting those words absorb into my tight chest. *It wasn't your fault. It wasn't your fault. It wasn't your fault.*

Clenching my eyelids, I let loose a strangled breath. "Can you guys please stop? I've got a horrible headache and your arguing isn't helping."

It's Serena who says, "I have Motrin in my bag. Want a couple tablets?"

Out of the whole family, Serena has always been the most nurturing to me. Anytime I was sick, it was her checking up on me when Mom was too busy. If I was sad, she'd do something dumb to try making me laugh. Once, she even suffered through an entire marathon of all the *Star Wars* movies because she knows how much I love the franchise.

"Yes, please." I hold out my hand as she passes me two tablets and the bottle of water she's been drinking from. "Thanks, Rena."

It's Sienna who turns on the blinker and slows the car down. "You know what also helps with headaches?" She turns into the busy Starbucks parking lot. "Coffee. I'll even pay."

Serena scoffs. "We all know *Dad* is paying since you lost your job at Nordstrom."

My eyes go to Sienna as she pulls up behind the long line of cars in the drive-through. "When did you lose your job? Last I heard, you were up for some sort of promotion."

"Yeah, and when she didn't get it, she threw a fit and the manager had to let her go," Serena cackles, taking her water back and dodging the hand that Sienna aims toward her.

"They all knew I deserved that position!"

"You weren't working there for as long as the woman who got it," Serena points out. "I don't think you can blame them for giving it to someone who has more experience. Plus, the fit you threw was in front of the customers. You looked like a psycho."

"You were there?" I question.

Serena bobs her head excitedly. "Sky, I thought Sienna was going to tackle her new boss. The one who got the promotion. What's her name, Si? Gladys. Yeah, Gladys. The poor woman looked like she was about to pee herself in the middle of the store."

I gape at Sienna. "Were you really going to fight her?"

"No! *Rena* likes to overexaggerate." The line of cars starts moving, so she inches forward and releases a sigh. "I have a degree in business, and *Gladys* doesn't. It doesn't make any sense why she'd get it simply because she was there longer. It was only by a year. Eleven months, to be exact! I think it's because she's older than me and looks more professional. But Gladys doesn't know the kind of marketing and business tactics that I do. Our store's demographics need to be targeted specifically to gain the most profit. I had a presentation and everything for the assholes who canned me."

I'll admit, I feel bad for her. She's had that job for years—she even worked through college to build up to the manager position and whatever was above that after time in the hot seat. "I'm sure you can get something better. Like you said, you have a business degree. You can apply that sort of knowledge at way better places. Who needs Nordstrom?"

Serena sighs as she studies the menu we're driving up to. "I'm going to miss your discount though."

"It's about integrity, Skylar," Sienna informs me bitterly, ignoring our other sister's remark. "I spent a long time at that store, and they booted me like I was just another employee."

"I mean, you were—"

"Rena," both Sienna and I say at the same time. My tone is more scolding than Sienna's bitter one, but Serena holds her hands up all the same in surrender.

"Fine, let's drop it," she grumbles. She looks back at me and smiles. "I really want to ask you for all the tea that you won't want to spill when Mom and Dad are around, but if you're not feeling well..."

It's Sienna who laughs. "Like that's ever stopped you before." Her eyes move toward the rearview where they lock with mine. Unlike Serena, hers aren't painted with nearly as much makeup. Between the twins, Sienna's style is a little more like mine—less flashy but still stylish. Professional and chic. "What's the gossip, Sky Sister? Any cute boys? Girls? Professors?"

Fighting the frown that always comes when my sisters hound me over these things, I shake my head. There's a lot I plan on keeping to myself during this trip—maybe forever— and the few months I've been in college take up most of that territory. "Nothing you'd be interested in hearing."

They both frown at that. "You've got nothing? What about that roommate you don't like? And don't pretend you do. We can all read between the lines whenever we ask."

My brows pinch. I haven't divulged much about Becca to my family, but I suppose it shouldn't surprise me that they've caught on to my struggle with her. They've always been good at detecting stuff like that. "There's not much to say. She and I are opposites, so it's hard to get along."

The girls share a look before Serena shakes her head and glances back at me. "That's no excuse. We're all opposites but we get along."

Sienna murmurs, "Most of the time."

Serena shrugs, relenting. "Fifty-fifty, but we're siblings.

We're supposed to get on each other's nerves. What makes you and her so different? It's been a few months. There has to be some common ground between the two of you by now."

I think back to the few TV shows we both enjoy, but that's about it. Even when I bring those up, she sounds pained to have the conversation. It doesn't seem to matter what I do because Becca finds a problem with it.

If I wear the same clothes too often, she rolls her eyes. If I tell her I don't want to go to the gym with her and the girls, she'll make a comment about me gaining "more" weight before the year ends. If I mention not wanting to go out, she'll call me a social recluse and hound me about being a college reject.

We eat differently, listen to different music, and have different tastes in guys. Trying to be her friend has become pointless. As pointless as killing her with kindness. She doesn't respond any differently when I try proving I'm not going to stoop to her level, so what's the point?

It's exhausting.

Because real friends don't need to try so hard to gain acceptance. It isn't about impressing them. It's about letting them see who you are to begin with.

Sinking into my seat, I cross my legs under me and stare out the window to avoid my sister's curious gaze. "I've tried, Rena. Honest. I went out with all the girls, agreed to do things she and the others like to do. But for me? They never meet me halfway. Don't get me started on the comments they make."

"The comments?" both girls repeat.

I wince. "Just silly stuff." Judgmental is more like it, but Serena is starting to get that look on her face that probably matches what Sienna looked like when she found out her coworker got the promotion she was working so hard for. "It doesn't matter. We're never going to be friends."

"Maybe that's why you haven't been feeling well," Sienna says from in front of me. "I know Mom mentioned you were getting a lot more headaches recently, and you look kind of pale. It's probably stress wearing you down. Being in that kind of environment isn't healthy."

Serena studies our sister. "Have you been reading from my psych textbook again?"

"As if," Sienna muses, shooting her an exasperated look. "It was bad enough having to take that intro course with you when you begged me to so you had someone to talk to. It was boring. If I'm going to free read something, it'll be one of Sky's smutty novels that she left behind."

My cheeks heat. "They're not *that* smutty. And hands off my books. You bend the pages and stain them."

"Like that shirt I let you borrow?" she asks, glaring at me from the rearview mirror.

I groan at the memory. "I was thirteen! When are you going to let that go?"

"Never."

Her dramatics make me want to roll my eyes. I rest my head back again as Sienna rolls up to order. I zone out since she already knows what we all get, closing my eyes and enjoying the AC blasting through the vents. It's nice to have the sun beaming down on my face and the air to contrast it. Sienna's right. I haven't been feeling well. Between lack of sleep from the night terrors and stress from trying to bring up my grades, I've been drained. Add in Becca's mood swings, and it's a recipe for disaster.

Danny is right. Fresh air might be exactly what I need. Time away from Becca will be a huge bonus.

The thought of him makes my lips twitch into a frown.

He packed a lot into the short ride to the airport, and I still haven't quite unloaded it all. It's all there, swirling in my thoughts among math equations and literary analysis.

I've always been book smart. But when it comes to guys, I'm clueless.

Sienna pulls up to the next window and pays, distributing the drinks as they process her card. Serena passes me a little baggy that smells like my favorite pastry, making my stomach rumble with approval. When I unroll the top to peek inside, I smile at the contents. "Thanks."

It's Sienna who says, "Eat. Your sugar may be low, and the last thing any of us needs is Serenity losing her mind because you passed out and couldn't make it to her banquet."

Serena smacks Sienna.

Sienna glares at Serena.

And I find myself...smiling.

I'm not sure why, but their kindness makes me feel bad I haven't divulged more about my time away. So I blurt, "I made a friend." The person who comes to mind is tan, tall, and toned from athletics. But I find myself chickening out when two pairs of the same color eyes stare at me expectedly. "Her name is Olive."

The image of Danny vanishes, along with that twinge of *something* in my chest that comes along with the idea of him.

Serena's lips twitch, but I can't tell if she's disappointed or amused. "That's a very Hollywood name."

I lift my shoulder. "She knows it. Once, she said she was just glad her parents didn't name her Apple or Fifi."

Sienna huffs a laugh and thanks the man behind the window as she rolls hers up. "Well, at least you're not lonely and lame at Lindon."

"Sienna!"

She sounds unapologetic. "Skylar is way too introverted for her own good. It isn't like we weren't worried about her making friends when she went there. We can't pop in like we normally did before and drag her out to places."

They did do that. A *lot*. Out to the mall and restaurants and nail salons. I never liked the activities, especially when they disrupted me when I was reading something, but I enjoyed the time with them.

"Don't worry," I say, putting a straw in my iced coffee. "Olive does that too."

Serena beams. "I like her already."

The way she seems genuinely happy for me makes the smile on my face curve even higher as I sip my drink.

Once we're pulling out of the parking lot and back onto the busy road, I relax against the seat and stare at my carry-on bag next to me.

Quietly, I say, "I missed you."

They both stay quiet for a second.

"We missed you too," Serena replies, warmth in her tone as she reaches back and squeezes my knee.

Sienna snickers. "Just remember you said that when Serenity is driving you crazy tonight. She hasn't slept in days, trying to make sure this event is perfect."

We all know that's never a good sign. Serenity on no sleep is like me without coffee. It's dangerous, especially when I'm the target of her breakdowns most of the time.

Serena pats my knee sympathetically, reading my mind. "Welcome home, sis."

Chapter Twenty

DANNY

AFTER INHALING A SLICE of pizza and two energy drinks, I haul my shit up to my room and unpack the notebooks I plan on going over before exams next week. Coach chewed us out hard today after nearly losing the game. I didn't blame him. We played like shit—barely like a team. And the ice bath and hot shower did nothing for my screaming muscles that resulted from the intense hours on the field.

Not even five minutes into staring at my notes and jotting some shit down onto the study guide the professor passed out, there's a knock at my door. Turning my neck makes pain shoot down my spine, but I try brushing it off when Caleb appears.

Unconvincingly, it seems.

"You don't have to pretend you're not in pain with me," he says knowingly, tipping his chin toward my stiff body. His shoulder rests against the doorjamb as his gaze roams to the mess of books on my unmade bed. "A few of us planned on hitting up the library tomorrow to study. You in?"

"Sure, man. Who's all going?"

"Raine, Matt, Justin, Wallace—don't make that face. Aiden's got enough shit on his shoulders with Ivy. I don't know what's going on there, but the last thing he needs is to deal with the little prick too. I told him I'd look after him."

I shake my head and carefully lean back against the headboard. The pain radiates through my body, forcing me to breathe through it. "You mean babysit. He's old enough to make his own damn choices. None of us should have to look after him."

Caleb doesn't look like he disagrees, but like always, he plays the mediator. "For some reason, Aiden sees something in him. Even Justin said he's a good player."

Justin Brady is officially out the rest of the season thanks to his ACL injury—his second major one—which means Ricky Wallace was put in his place as quarterback. I wish he wasn't any good, because then we could easily write him off. But even Coach sees something in him, and if it's anything like he was with Aiden, he'll blow smoke up his ass and train him for the big leagues as another NFL hopeful.

Lifting my good shoulder and ignoring the tightness in it, I murmur, "Still don't see why he has to join us."

"He's got to study too," Caleb points out, walking in and dropping into the desk chair by the door. "Did you schedule an appointment with the physical therapist?"

His eyes are trained on the shoulder I'm trying not to move. "It's not that bad, *Ma*. I just tweaked it a little."

"DJ, come on."

I pick up one of my notebooks. "Coach already handed me my ass about getting seen. But you and I both know there's not much that can be done at this point. The tendonitis has set in and made things complicated. You don't need to add to it by nagging."

"Coach knows what he's talking about. If you get some therapy on it—"

I sigh, scrubbing my face tiredly. "Bro, I'm fine. You know we all took a beating out there. I'm just sore from that. I saw you dragging yourself off the field. Hell, even Griff was looking extra ragged."

Caleb blows out a long breath, giving me a solemn nod. "Coach definitely hasn't been easy on us. But I know you've been hurting more than usual lately. The Motrin in the cabinet is almost gone and you and I are the only ones who use this bathroom. The others may not see you pushing past it, but I do. Is it getting worse?"

Pressing my lips together, I stare at my nearly illegible ink across the page.

The biggest reason I'd never make it to the NFL like Aiden or Wallace isn't just because there are others better than me to choose from. It's because my body wouldn't be able to handle the extensive training, much less the hits I'd take if I was drafted by some miracle.

I wouldn't make it through a season.

I know it.

Coach knows it.

Caleb knows it.

Doesn't make it fucking suck any less.

So I keep acting like it doesn't bother me because there's nothing else I can do about it. Some people are built for the stress professional sports puts on their bodies. I'm not. I come from a family of ill health. I had a great-grandpa who had an extensive case of inflammatory arthritis and a great-grandmother who had osteoporosis. The beatings I take on the field will only make it ten times worse for me down the road if I keep doing this to myself.

Coach Pearce once called me a quitter when I told him I wouldn't push myself to go further than college football.

I told him I was a realist.

Thankfully, Aiden transferred to Lindon shortly after that and took Coach's impatience with me and channeled it toward him instead. To Coach, I was a lost cause, but I was okay with that because I don't measure my worth based on how many touchdowns I assist or yards I run.

"The pain is about the same," I finally admit with a heavy sigh, shoving my notebook off my lap, knowing studying is pointless tonight. "But the mobility is getting worse. I don't know, man. I was hoping to end my last season with a bang. Kick ass and celebrate with my buddies while doing it. I know Coach gets pissed with me when I fuck up a play, but he doesn't want to understand that I'm starting to physically struggle out there." Swiping a hand through my mussed hair, I shake my head and let it fall however it wants to. "He thinks we're all here to make a name for ourselves, so that's what he wants to focus on. I've yet to hear him give Justin a hard time for working toward med school instead of the league like they planned since he got starting position sophomore year."

Stretching back until the chair creaks, Caleb rubs his jaw. "I don't know about that, dude. I've heard some of the shit Coach says to Justin on the sidelines. Justin just doesn't give a shit because he knows what he wants. I think he's kind of glad he got hurt because Coach wrote him off and found other people to bitch at."

My nose twitches. "Coach makes it hard to like him sometimes."

Caleb grunts from his seat.

From somewhere in my mess, my cell dings. Considering it's about the time Grandma Meadow would be doing her nightly gossip reads online using the tablet I bought her for her birthday, I expect to see something about a Kardashian on my screen.

So when I see BLONDIE(x2) on it instead, I perk up, nearly forgetting the bite of pain traveling across my shoulder blades.

> Blondie: I was thinking about something you said...
> Blondie: You told me you'd help me replace the
>   memories from the party with new ones. I think
>   I'd like that.

I'm staring at the phone with a huge smile on my face as I reread the messages when the other person in the room snorts. "Man, that's weird to see. First Aiden, now you. That who I think it is?"

"Skylar," I confirm, not bothering to look over at him as my eyes scan each word she wrote me carefully.

Before I can reply to her, she sends another message.

> Blondie: Oh. And hi

Snickering, I shake my head. "She's awkward as hell sometimes, but it's kind of endearing." I drop my phone for a second to glance at him. "But I'd hardly compare our situation to Aiden and his girl downstairs. Not from what I've personally witnessed."

Caleb grins. "Not yet anyway."

I wave it off. "She's got her reservations and I can't blame her."

Rubbing my jaw, I replay what happened in the cab of the truck before she left.

"Mind if I ask you something?"

My teammate shrugs. "Shoot."

"How did you and Raine get together? Everyone knows you've been dating for years, but it couldn't have been easy. Why her? Why still work at it after all this time?"

He looks contemplative for a second, but the soft smile on his face is the same one he always has when his woman is involved. "Raine is a good person. I was always into her, but she never really looked at me that way until we were probably about fifteen. We were awkward growing up around each other as it was, and when we were teens, we got dared to make out during a stupid party game. Seven minutes in heaven. Ever played?"

All I do is grin.

He snorts. "Anyway, once we got into the closet, we just sat there. It was probably about five minutes before I told her we could lie to everyone and say we did it." His smile spreads at whatever memory he's having. "So that's what we did. I wanted to kiss her, man, but she didn't want anything to do with me in that moment. And afterward, I was glad, because she deserved more than a kiss in the shadows with twenty people outside waiting."

"So what? You chased after her until she was so annoyed she finally agreed to give you a shot?"

"Nah. She was saving up to buy a car and looking for work during the summer. My dad talked to her mom, and she ended up getting a job at the hardware store. We spent almost every day together over summer break. Kind of forced us to talk, or else it would have been awkward as hell. It all sort of...clicked into place then."

"That simple?"

"Nothing about a relationship is simple, dude. Just because you don't see us arguing or getting on each other's nerves doesn't mean we don't. We just work it out privately."

I wiggle my brows. "I bet you do."

He takes one of the pens from my desk and chucks it at me. It misses and lands on the other side of my bed. "Shut it, ass. What I'm trying to say is that sometimes there doesn't have to be some huge love story involved. I didn't chase her, but I didn't give up. We got to know each other and decided we liked each other. That grew to love. By the time school came around, I'd convinced her to go on a date with me. That turned into two, three, you get it. And here we are. Shit isn't always easy, but if you find a good one, it's worth a little stress."

There's a moment of silence between us as I think about what he said, giving me time to pick up my phone and thumb out a response to the person still waiting to hear back from me.

Me: Hi

Caleb breaks the silence. "Is there a reason you think she wouldn't want a relationship with you? Did you open your mouth and say something stupid again?"

My glare makes him grin wider. "The fact that you'd assume that's why she wouldn't be interested offends me."

He doesn't look like he cares. "No, it doesn't. So what's the deal? You're friends, right? I know you have class with her. You got up early to drive her to the airport. I see you texting with her all the time, and you never text with chicks unless you're trying to get a hookup. I don't even know the last time you got laid."

"She needed a ride" is how I choose to reply. "And for the record, we *are* friends. It's just a little complicated right now."

"Why?"

My nose twitches, so I swipe it. "I kissed her. Twice. And now she's in California."

His brows dart up. "You didn't talk about it before she left?"

I wince. "She would have been late for her flight." I wave my phone. "And this is the first time we've talked since she left. I wanted to give her time with her family instead of bugging her about shit that is better said in person."

He almost frowns but stops himself. Out of all the guys I hang around, he's the relationship guru. He and Raine are a package deal that can offer some wise words when needed, but I've never needed any until recently thanks to my conflicted feelings surrounding Skylar.

"She's skittish," I tell him. "And I don't want to make it worse by laying it on thick. The kiss wasn't even that big of a deal."

Lie.

My thoughts wander to the party, trying to scrape together any clues as to who she was with that night. I'd been preoccupied doing my own thing, trying to get people to stop breaking and stealing shit that Aiden would find out about if we weren't careful. Not to mention the jersey chasers who would come up and pull my attention away one dance at a time. I didn't pay a lot of attention to Skylar that night, but I wish I had.

When I glance down at my phone, I see her next message.

Blondie: I want a redo

A redo.

"Christ," I murmur.

Caleb shifts. "What is it?"

"Nothing," I mumble, rubbing my neck and quietly groaning to myself. "I need to figure some shit out, I guess. I don't want to make the wrong move with her. I'd rather have her as a friend than nothing at all."

"I get that," he says. "You sure that's it?"

"Yeah. Don't worry about it. I've obviously been watching one too many sappy movies is all. Getting all up in my feels. I need to finish up some homework before crashing. When are you all heading to the library?"

"Probably noon. I think Raine requested a couple study rooms for a few hours." He looks between me and the phone in my hand. "Is everything okay?"

More than. "I'll go with you tomorrow. May need to cut out early." I click my tongue. "I also may need to borrow someone's truck to pick up Sky when she flies back."

He studies me for a split second before nodding. Whatever he sees, he chooses not to push. "Fine with me. I don't have to be anywhere tomorrow night, so you can borrow mine." He stands and starts walking out. From over his shoulder, he says, "Take something for your shoulder if you didn't already. It might help."

It won't, but I say, "Will do."

Once he leaves, I stare at the messages Skylar sent me to make sure I read them right.

Blondie: What do you say?

What do I say?

I meant what I said in the truck. I wish I'd been the

one to take her virginity—to share that experience with her. Make her feel good, feel beautiful and valued and so many other things.

But sending her a picture of the hard-on in my pants would probably be too much if she knew how much I liked this idea of hers, so I settle on something a little more subtle.

Me: Anything you want, Blondie. I'm your guy

And I mean it.

Anything, no matter how small or how large, I'd give to her. She wants someone to hold her hand around campus? I'm down for that. She wants someone to snuggle up to during movie night? I'm more than happy to be her human-sized pillow.

Everything else…shit. It's dangerous territory to even think about those things. Especially because I'm too fucking sore to jerk it right now.

Then again, a cold shower may be exactly what I need.

Chapter Twenty-One

SKYLAR

THERE'S A KNOCK ON my bedroom door as I tug at the hem of my new cream-colored dress. It cracks open, and Serena's head pops inside before I can answer.

"Oh my God! Look at you, hottie!" She slips inside and closes the door behind her as she studies the tight material encasing my body with a wide smile on her face.

"It's short," I complain, trying and failing to get the material to stay midthigh. All it does is slide back up to a place that makes me nervous to do anything other than stand.

Serena shakes her head and walks over to me, hands on my exposed shoulders as she examines me with a proud look on her face. Her loose curls are in a braided updo that looks like a crown around her head. "Don't tell Mom this," she whispers, "but I'm totally jealous of your body. Your thighs are life."

My face scrunches at her admission as I glance in the mirror at the thickness she's referring to. I used to be more self-conscious about my legs, but I've embraced them. None of my sisters can catch food with them when it falls quite like I can. As far as I'm concerned, I've won. "Why don't you want Mom to know that?"

She steps aside and looks into the reflection as she brushes something off the simple yet elegant dress. "Because I promised I'd go to that new juice bar with her, and I really don't want to. It's something to do with fasting, which sounds awful."

The last thing she and Mom need to worry about is fasting. Not only do they eat something green, leafy, and lean with protein at every meal, but they also work out almost every single day. Me on the other hand? Green is my least favorite color, especially in the form of food, and the only particularly lean thing about me is my fingers. Working out? Well, running from my problems is probably as close as I've gotten at this point.

"You can tell her no," I point out as she plays with my hair. I haven't even touched it yet beyond washing it earlier in the shower. It's air-dried into a frizzy mess.

She shrugs. "I know, but it's Mom."

Not sure what to say, I stare at my reflection in silence. I'm surprised Serenity approved this dress. There's nothing necessarily fancy about it. It's sleeveless and tight and has a plunging neckline that shows off my boobs.

I look...hot. I'd be surprised if Dad *doesn't* give me a disapproving once-over.

"What shoes are you thinking?" she asks, guiding me over to sit in front of the makeup table. I never used it much over the years. It's white like the rest of the room is with a mirror attached that has bright stickers and lights lining the sides of it. Nightlights that Serena bought me because I was afraid of the dark and stickers Sienna bought me because I was obsessed with collecting them.

Now they look silly, but I keep them up for the nostalgia.

"Serenity laid out a pair of black heels." I point toward the strappy things resting beside the bed and make a face at the height of them. "I think she's trying to kill me."

Serena snorts as she puts a brush through my dark locks and begins working her magic. She's always been great with styling hair and doing makeup—though nothing like Olive, which makes me miss being in Lindon a little bit. "She wouldn't try killing you until after the photos were taken."

Smiling at the truth, I return my gaze forward to watch her work. "Has Tony hinted at any kind of proposal? I know there's been a lot of speculation surrounding this, but Ser doesn't seem to know what's going to happen."

The easy expression on Serena's face diminishes for a second before her smile returns, a little lower than before. "No. Serenity thinks this event will cement things for them, but that's it."

I shake my head, but she holds me in place in a silent chide. "Why can't she just make the move? It's the twenty-first century. Women can ask men to marry them. It isn't like Tony isn't head over heels for her." Any man who has the patience to deal with our oldest sister's craziness is the real deal.

"Don't all women like to feel special?" Serena asks, braiding two small sections of hair on either side of my face and pinning them back so they stay out of my eyes. "Serenity has always liked the spectacle of things. She isn't going to settle for anything less when it comes to a proposal."

I watch my sister comb my hair with her fingers until the frizzy waves fall over my shoulders. She goes to my bathroom connected across the room and comes back with a curling iron. I make a face that she chooses to ignore while plugging it in, then goes to stand behind me.

"What about you, Sky?"

My brows go up. "What about me?"

She smiles into the reflection of the two of us, resting her chin on top of my head. "You've always marched to the beat of your own drum. Would *you* go after the guy or let the guy come to you?"

For some reason, my mind wanders to Danny, and my traitorous lips turn upward into a goofy smile.

She gasps dramatically, fingers gripping my shoulders until they pinch. "Oh my God! There *is* a guy coming after you!"

The shriek of her voice makes me hiss out a low, "Keep your voice down!"

Despite that, she claps and does the same dance she always does when she's excited. "I can't believe you've been keeping this to yourself. What's his name? What does he look like? Is he pining for you? Or—"

I groan loudly, smacking her hands away from my shoulders. "It's not like that, Rena. His name is Danny—" More high-pitched noises come from her that make me glare in warning until she zips her lips. "His name is Danny and he's on the football team. We've been hanging out a little."

"Hanging out as in hanging out? Or hanging out as in"—her hands twist together in a weird gesture that I think is supposed to symbolize something sexual—"*hanging out?*"

I turn in my chair to eye her. "Never do that again. It looked like you were stroking out. And we're *just* hanging out. He took me to the airport. We have a class together. Sometimes, we study and watch movies. It isn't a big thing."

Lie.

Lie, lie, lie.

The text I sent him becomes front and center in my mind, making me internally groan. I can't believe I even told him that I wanted a redo of that night. That I wanted *him* to replace those memories. I never thought I had it in me.

So maybe Serena is right. I guess I am the type to march to my own beat.

My sister gets a doe-eyed look about her. "I have a feeling you're thinking about him right now, and it doesn't look like it's in a friendly way. A football player, huh? I never would have thought you'd go after a jock. That's so...Allen of you. Very Sienna. She'll be so proud—"

"You can't tell her!" My eyes narrow in warning that she looks none too pleased about. "I mean it, Serena. You can't say a word to anybody. You know our family will blow it out of proportion. Remember Ryan?"

Her shoulders lift. "He was different. He was your first boyfriend."

"And Danny is..." My lips curve downward as I let loose a sigh. He isn't my boyfriend, but I care about him. "Danny is a great person, and I just want it to be as uncomplicated as it can be. If Sienna or Serenity find out, they'll tell Mom and Dad, and the group chat will be nonstop questions pestering me about him. That's hardly fun or uncomplicated."

She checks to see if the curling iron is hot enough and murmurs, "I don't see what the big deal is. You have no problems ignoring our messages most of the time anyway."

Guilt creeps into my chest and scrapes a nail down my heart. I *do* tend to ignore the messages until I have no choice but to answer them. "You have to admit, most of the messages in that chat aren't even geared toward me. I can't have my phone out twenty-four seven replying to Serenity's crises or Si's work meltdowns. If I put it on silent for *one* class, I find at least twenty texts waiting after I'm done. It's…a lot."

She picks up the iron and walks over to me, picking up a section of hair. "Did it have to be New York?"

My brows furrow at her question, but I think about it while studying her sad eyes. After a few extended seconds, I offer a small smile. "Yeah, I think so. I just needed some distance."

"From us?"

This time, I don't answer.

"We're not that bad, Sky."

It only makes me feel worse. "I know you're not. But…I don't know what you want me to say, Rena. Isn't it normal to want to explore? Leave home? Serenity went to Yale, clear across the country, so why is it so different that I did? College is a perfect chance to figure things out." I gesture toward the outfit I'm wearing. "I was never totally happy doing stuff you guys wanted to do. I never liked dressing up and attending these events and getting my photo taken a million times. What's wrong with trying to figure out who I am?"

She considers it while moving on to a new section of hair. The curls aren't tight but loose and bouncy as they slip past my shoulders. "I get it. I do. Honestly, I'm not a fan of these things either. In fact, I think only Serenity and Mom are. Everyone else just does it to make them happy because it means something to them."

I find myself silently agreeing, even if I'll never fully understand.

"But I get it, Sky. You want to be your own person. We're all happy for you. Even though Mom and Dad have been worried since you got back."

"What? Why?"

"You've lost weight…"

My nose scrunches. "Hasn't Mom always hinted that I should?"

Her frown deepens. "I know she can be a little…brutal sometimes, but she never means anything bad by it. I think she's a little envious of your curves too. You rock everything you wear and not many can say the same. It's no wonder you've got a football player after you."

I blush.

"Anyway," she continues, "they just worry that something is up. You've never considered joining us at the gym or club or actively tried losing weight. You've been sick. Even now, your eyes are dull, and your poor nose is red even with your makeup on. Are you sure everything is okay?"

I used to think I was the invisible one, but it's obvious I'm wrong. "It's been harder than I thought to fit in at Lindon," I admit quietly. "That's all."

I don't tell her that I avoid Huden when I know the rush of people are there. Or that people staring has made me too self-conscious to make appearances places when I don't need to. My natural tan from being in the California sun has faded considerably from all the time I spend in the comfort of my own little space.

"Have you considered moving out of your room and away from your roommate? It sounds like she's a big part of the problem. Stress causes people to get sick easily, and if you're always surrounded by it…"

I haven't considered that. "I'm pretty sure Becca is the one who's spreading rumors about me. It's… You're not wrong. Moving out would be easier. But I'm not sure there are even other rooms available."

"You should check, because if she's responsible for something that crappy, you shouldn't be around her. I can help." Her hand squeezes my arm. "We all want what's best for you, Sky Sister. And if it takes flying to New York to put a bitch in her place, you know we'll do it. All of us would."

The offer makes me ease into my chair, knowing she means it. My sisters would book the first flight out to deal with Becca if I said the word. It's endearing.

"For the record," she remarks, "you look super sexy even with your little Rudolph nose. And you look amazing with the dark hair. I don't know why people wouldn't want you as a friend, but they're clearly idiots."

I smile softly at her and think about what Danny said about quality over quantity. "I'm starting to see that it might not be a bad thing having one or two really good friends."

"You're right. It's important to have people who will have your back no matter what. It sounds like Olive and Danny are those people for you." Her wistful look turns into something mischievous. "It's too bad your football player isn't here to see you all dolled up. Your ass would probably make him drool."

My football player.

I fight a goofy smile as I listen to my heart thud, thud, thud in my chest. "He had a game this weekend."

She pauses. "Would you have invited him if he didn't?"

My instant thought is *no*. But for some reason, I don't answer it right away. If I'd asked, would he have come? He definitely would have found a way to make this banquet fun. And anywhere there's food, Danny is at his happiest.

Plus, he told me anything I wanted, he'd do. *I'm your guy*, his text said. And while I'm afraid of having any big expectations about what that means, that annoying, fluttery feeling in my stomach tells me that it's something to look forward to rather than be afraid of.

"I don't know. Maybe."

All she does is hum in response as she finishes up my hair and helps me with my makeup. It takes five minutes of arguing before I relent and let her do a bold color on my lips.

Bright red. A statement piece.

By the time I'm finished, I look...

Nothing like myself.

I look sexy and elegant and much older than my almost nineteen years. Standing and flattening my palms down the front of my dress, I examine the final product while Serena stands off to the side looking like a proud mother.

Grabbing my phone, I pass it to her. "Can you take my picture?"

Her eyes flash knowingly. "Sending this to a certain athlete?"

I nibble my lip before nodding.

She tells me how to pose, takes a few different shots, and then passes me back my phone with a proud look in her eye. "You realize even if you don't tell me anything about this guy, I'm going to look him up on your school's website and then stalk him on every social media platform known to man, right?"

I slide on my heels, wobble a little as I strap them, grab the hideous clutch that matches, and say, "Fine. Just don't blurt your findings to the others."

She pouts. "You're no fun."

I roll my eyes and tell her I'll meet her downstairs. After looking at all the pictures she took, I select one and send it to Danny.

It's after I walk downstairs and get fussed over by Mom and Dad that I get a reply.

Danny: Damn, Blondie
Danny: You look beautiful

I find myself smiling at the screen until Serena gives me a Cheshire cat smirk, wiggling her eyebrows until I nudge her with my shoulder.

I don't get a chance to reply before another text bounces back.

Danny: I'm partial to those baggy clothes you wear tho...

Serena must have read the message from over my shoulder because I swear she swoons.

And she's not the only one.

What the hell are you doing to me, Danny?

Chapter Twenty-Two

DANNY

WALLACE IS GOING ON about some party that one of the fraternities on the row hosted last night. The fucking idiot doesn't know when to stop bragging about shit he shouldn't be talking about.

The hockey team is notorious for their ragers and even more infamous for the drugs supplied at them. Most of the people who go are snorting something, smoking something, or a combination of the two out in the open where anyone can record it. Since most of the guys on the hockey team are part of the frat, it wouldn't surprise me if more than one of them partook in the party favors while they were there.

Caleb shoots me a look from across the table where we're studying at the library and shakes his head to stop me from saying anything.

It's bullshit.

I pull my phone out.

Me: Someone needs to drug test this moron to
    knock him down a peg
Caleb: Don't get any ideas
Me: Stop coddling him

Caleb rolls his eyes and goes back to his homework. Raine murmurs something under her breath as Wallace relays some action he got with one of the girls at the party. That's what gets Caleb to sigh and look over at the douche talking.

"You do realize other people can hear you, right?" he asks, gesturing toward the other students on the level within hearing distance. "If you were smart, you'd be careful what you say and where you say it. And show some fucking respect to the chick you're talking about."

Wallace has the nerve to roll his eyes and throw a piece of paper at him. "Like the girls who get involved with us don't tell everyone they know as soon as we pull out." A few of the guys snicker. Wallace shoots them a smirk before turning back to Caleb. "Quit giving me that look. None of you are any different. Butt out of my fucking business if you don't want to hear about it. It's not my fault you only get to have the same puss—"

In a deadly tone, Caleb says, "*Do not* finish that sentence."

It's rare he loses his shit, but whenever he does, it always has to do with the quiet girl beside him.

At least Wallace is smart enough to lift his hands up in mock surrender. I don't miss the wiseass remark muttered under his breath, but Caleb must have, because he's back to staring at Raine with that longing look on his face. I won't be surprised if there's a ring on her finger by graduation.

Flipping through another page of anthropology notes

that I conned Ivy into giving me, I grow bored and grab my phone again.

Me: What's the latest gossip?

My eyes trail to my buddies surrounding the table as they jot down shit on paper and read through textbooks. Justin is a table over, a table to himself because he's got a massive workload this semester. His leg is propped up on one of the chairs, his crutches resting against the sides, as he thumbs through a book bigger than three of mine combined.

The dude is smart—smarter than any of us on the team. Last I knew, he had a 4.0 GPA, and he was beating himself up over applications into a decent med school. I know the biggest reason he got hurt is because he was too distracted from the stress of postgrad.

My phone goes off, drawing my attention from our main QB and to the screen.

Grandma M: Your mother has been on my case about you calling her. Says you haven't spoken in almost two weeks. She thinks you're avoiding her for some reason

I roll my eyes. I told Ma the last time we talked that I probably wouldn't call home for a while. Classes started packing on assignments, Coach was drilling us hard, practice was grueling, and then there was Skylar. I've been busy as hell trying to balance everything.

Me: I'll call tonight
Grandma M: You better, boy.

Boy. It doesn't matter that I've got a foot and a half on the short woman, I know she could take me down easily. She'd smile as she did it too.

Grandma M: You better bring back some of those cookies with you for Thanksgiving since I won't be up to that bakery you love so much to get them myself

I snicker quietly and promise her I will before looking up at Caleb's curious eyes. All I tell him is, "Grandma M says hi."

He smiles easily. "She giving you shit about the next game still?"

"Acts like I've banned her from coming," I grumble, earning a chuckle from him and an amused grin from his girlfriend.

Caleb sits back. "Remember last time she was at a game with Aiden's grandma? They started that brawl with those younger dudes. I still think they would've won if his parents didn't break it up first."

Shaking my head, I smile wider. "I told Griff next time they're at the same game, we need to split them up. Less chance of security having to get involved."

I check the time on my phone and feel my leg start to bounce when I see how late it's gotten. I've been antsy knowing I'll be driving back to the airport and seeing the girl whose picture I saved to my phone the second it came through.

Because Skylar looked fucking heartbreaking. She always does, but it's never as obvious. If she showed up to our party like that, goddamn glowing, there would've been a line of men waiting to ask for her name and offer her drinks and then some. And the thought pisses me off.

Glancing at the picture in question, I bite back a groan and exit out of the photos app before pulling up our messages.

Me: If u HAD to choose between killing baby Ted
    Bundy and baby Jeffrey Dahmer who would u
    pick?

I'm reading the same three sentences in my notes, trying to drill them into my head—rather pointlessly—when I get a response.

Blondie: What kind of question is that?
Blondie: Nvm I forgot who I'm talking to for a second
Blondie: Bundy has more kills than Dahmer so I'd
    have to kill baby Bundy

Her answer makes me chuckle, knowing she more than likely didn't have to Google that information. She made me watch a fucked-up documentary on infamous serial killers not that long ago, so now I know way more than I ever thought I would about the subject.

Me: When are you supposed to land?
Blondie: 5:15
Me: Want dinner?
Blondie: Should I be concerned that you're ask-
    ing about dinner in the same conversation you
    mentioned Jeffrey Dahmer?
Me: I eat people in a very different way, Blondie. I
    can demonstrate if you want

As soon as the message sends, I freeze up and rub my forehead. "Aw shit."

Caleb stops highlighting something. "Is Grandma M okay?"

"Uh…" I stare at the message as it's marked DELIVERED and then changed to READ with no bubbles appearing below. "Yeah. She just lost some sort of poker game."

"Your grandma plays poker?" Marks muses.

Caleb frowns. "Since when?"

I just shrug, going with the lie. She does play cards, but bridge is more her thing. Guess it wouldn't surprise me if she kicked ass at poker too. Once, she came home with a thousand bucks from a game she wouldn't disclose, and Ma scolded her for it.

Finally, my phone buzzes.

Blondie: Not sure what to say to that

I sink into my seat.

Me: I'm messing with u. Sorry

Bubbles appear.
Disappear.
Appear.
I cuss.

Me: Flirting is second nature to me. If it makes u uncomfortable tell me to fuck off

Those bubbles disappear again.
For a minute.
Two.
Three.

Blondie: You don't want to flirt with me then?

That's not the answer I'm expecting.

Me: Do u WANT me to?

The tension in my shoulders must be visible because Raine asks, "Is your grandma okay, DJ?"

Almost forgetting the lie, I reply, "Yeah, she's good. Lost some money is all. No big."

They don't push me on it as I stare at my screen, focused only on one woman.

Blondie: Would it be weird if I said I didn't mind if
     you did?

My lips start to curl upward, but I force them to stay neutral, knowing there are people probably watching.

Me: I don't always know where I stand with u so I try
     keeping it low-key

Me and low-key usually aren't in the same sentence, but I never want Skylar to feel uncomfortable around me.

Blondie: If it makes you feel better, I don't always
     know either
Blondie: But I meant what I said about wanting a redo

How could I forget? It's been on the forefront of my mind every time I close my eyes. The shit I woke up to in my head this morning led to a very long cold shower and some suspicious looks from more than just Caleb when I finally emerged from the bathroom.

Me: We'll have to discuss that over dinner. The diner
    or Bea's?

One is more casual than the other, so I hope she picks the diner. What I want with her isn't a casual thing.

Blondie: Birdseye

I grin.

Me: It's a date

I don't let myself wonder if I shouldn't have called it that before flicking off my phone's screen and setting it down.

"What are you smiling at?" Marks asks, trying to look at my phone.

I place it facedown on the table and shove his chair back with my foot, nearly making him topple over.

"Christ, Bridges! We have enough crippled players on the team."

Justin glares.

I snort.

And Caleb stares at me, clearly wondering what it is I'm trying to hide.

All I do is shoot him a wink.

~

Skylar's barely looked me in the eye since I grabbed her bag at the airport and set it in the truck. We stared at each other in silence for a few seconds before she snapped out of whatever thought she was having and climbed in once I opened the door for her.

Now, she's staring out the window as we drive down Main Street looking for a spot to park. Sundays are always busy on the main drag, especially with the start of exams. People are getting their caffeine fixes as they cram in some last-minute studying.

"You ready for exams?" I ask, heading for a spot at the end of the street that a car just pulled out from.

It's only then her eyes peel away from the window. "Mostly. I'm a little nervous about my math one."

"Why?" When we've studied before, she looked like she knew what she was doing. Her nose would do this cute little scrunching thing in concentration as she copied down formulas from her textbook and figured them out on a scrap piece of paper.

"I tend to zone out in class these days. I always paid attention in high school, got good grades, never had an issue. My mind's been preoccupied here. The professor told me I have a good chance at passing the course if I get a good grade on this exam. If not…" She makes a face. "I've never failed a class before. Ever."

I note the disappointment in her tone as I put the truck into park and wave at a couple familiar faces that pass by.

Turning off the ignition, I turn to her. "I don't know if you're interested, but I can help. I've had to take a handful of math courses with my degree. I'm not bad with numbers. Maybe after we're done, we could grab your things and head somewhere to study."

Her fingers fumble with the seat belt. "I think the library is going to be packed."

"True. We could do it at my place, but the guys are all there. It'd be loud."

She nibbles her lip and looks over at her bag resting on the seat behind us. "We could go to my suite. It'll be quieter than a lot of the alternatives." As soon as the suggestion is out there, she tries taking it back. "I mean, we could probably go to the student center or—"

"Blondie," I laugh. "Relax. If you're cool with it, I'll stop by my place and grab my books, then we can head to yours. But let's grab food first, because I'm starving."

On cue, my stomach rumbles loud enough for her to crack a smile. She nods once and follows me into the diner, our arms brushing as we're guided to an open booth in the back where there's fewer people. Skylar gives me a shy smile as we slide into the benches opposite each other and thank the waitress, who gets our drink orders and leaves us with menus.

I already know what I'm getting, so I don't bother touching the one placed in front of me. I fiddle with the saltshaker and ask, "Did you have a good time with your family?"

Her eyes move from the list of food to me, her lip between her teeth. The same lips that I may or may not have woken up from a dream about the night before. They'd been painted the same bright red as they were in the picture she sent and doing very dirty things to me.

Releasing her lip, she lifts a shoulder. "It was okay. My oldest sister, Serenity, the one hosting the event, stopped being melodramatic after all the family photos were taken and her boyfriend—well, fiancé now, actually—whisked her away to pop the question. He did it in this beautiful lit-up garden at the venue. It was full of flowers and lights and really cheesy classical music. She loved every second of it though. I think my other sister Serena got it on video as soon as she realized what was happening."

"Wow. That's quite the weekend."

"For her," she agrees quietly. "It was good to see them. I needed it more than I thought I did. Anthony—he's Serenity's fiancé—is really cool. We were all waiting for him to ask her to marry him because she's been trying to get him to do it since forever. Maybe she'll stop being so nutty now that she's got a huge rock on her finger."

I snicker. "You don't sound that impressed with the ring. I thought all girls liked that kind of stuff."

She makes a face. "Not me. I've never been into jewelry that much, in case you haven't noticed. The diamond that Tony got Serenity is pretty, but it's huge and flashy and *expensive*. I prefer smaller, less obvious things. Simple." Her shoulders lift as if embarrassed. "That's just me though. I guess I'm weird."

"Nah. You know what you want, and that's going to make some guy"—my jaw ticks—"one lucky motherfucker."

She snorts. "Especially if he's broke."

I chuckle. "Especially then."

We fall into silence for a few seconds as she studies the menu some more.

"I had a nightmare," she says. "Like the ones I've mentioned before. I guess I...I screamed. It woke up a couple of my sisters."

I gape. "You screamed?"

She winces, still not meeting my eyes. "I don't think I've done that before. I don't even fully remember what the nightmare was. But Serena and Sienna were freaked out. They thought I was being murdered."

She's never told me about her nightmares in depth before, only that she has them and they make it hard to sleep. "Did you tell them what you remembered? Did you tell them about...?"

230

Skylar presses her lips together and shakes her head.

My eyebrow twitches. "You should tell them. Or somebody. It doesn't have to be me. I know you don't like talking about it. But it might help."

"There's nothing to say." Her tone is clipped as she grips the menu tighter.

"Sky—"

"Danny, stop." Her eyes flick up to mine, the color pleading. "There's nothing anybody can do."

"You don't know that for sure."

She's silent.

"I'm trying to look out for you. I'm sorry if that upsets you."

Her lips curl down. "I know." She sighs heavily, dropping the menu. "I know you are. I'm sorry. I just don't think anybody can say anything that would help. But I'll think about it."

The timid smile she gives me makes me drop it.

"Tell me about your sisters."

Her blue eyes widen a fraction as the waitress comes back with our drinks and collects our food order. I don't think Skylar pays much attention to whatever she asks for before passing the menu over to the woman's extended hand.

As soon as it's just us, Skylar tells me all about her family. How her sister Serena is in grad school to become a psychologist. Skylar gets irritated with her whenever she psychoanalyzes everyone. She tells me about the modeling her other sister, Sienna, does and how their mother is obsessed with getting her new campaigns now that she's unemployed. Their oldest sister is some hotshot lawyer with a bad case of OCD that makes her a perfectionist. I can tell who Skylar is closest with and who she's not and just how much those distinct lines affect her, even if she won't outright admit it.

When she tells me about how her father earned a fortune by being a smart businessman and investing in the stock market, I can't help but become ten times more interested. From the smile on her face as she explains the marketing campaigns he's helped build from the ground up, I can tell she's proud of him.

"Maybe you could have a conversation with him sometime," she says lightly. "He could shed some light on possible career paths. Give you advice. He loves talking business. Sometimes I think he's sad more of us didn't go into business or marketing at school so he would have somebody to talk to about these things."

Her face makes me grin. "I take it you don't enjoy talking about those things."

Her head shakes, a sheepish smile gracing her face. "Not really. Especially not during dinner. There were some nights that was all he wanted to talk about until one of the girls cut in and started telling us about some guy they were crushing on or local gossip about neighbors they wanted to discuss."

My chuckle is quiet. "I can't picture you participating in either of those conversations, Blondie."

"I'd rather hear about the male escort that Mrs. McKenna, our ninety-year-old neighbor, hired over stock portfolios and projections on the latest sneaker trends."

Her deadpan expression makes my grin widen. "Touché. And what, exactly, did Mrs. McKenna do with said male escort?"

She leans in like she's about to share a secret, so I do too. "Word on the street is that they were in the middle of doing very naughty things when she had a stroke. Sienna saw the ambulance rushing her away while cops spoke to the escort. Because he didn't want to get arrested for prostitution, he lied and said he was her nephew."

"How do you know he *isn't* her nephew?"

She giggles. "Because Mark Pemberley across the street also uses his services for the same reason Mrs. McKenna does." Her wink about stops my heart, and I want her to do it again.

"Damn, Blondie," I say, letting out an impressive laugh. "Sounds like you left behind a lot of entertainment."

Leaning back, she rests her crossed arms on the edge of the table. "California is the land of entertainment, after all. Our street might as well have its own reality TV show."

"I'd tune in."

In exchange for the history lesson that she gave me on her family, I tell her all about the Bridges family.

I tell her about being raised by my mother and grandmother and all the awkward conversations I had with them, especially throughout puberty. I brag about the homeless shelter Ma runs and the charity she heads to fund the local food bank south of Boston. My smile grows when I mention the trouble Grandma Meadow gets into since her retirement as a schoolteacher, trouble usually pertaining to sporting events and gambling.

Money becomes common ground between us when I mention the old money passed down between the generations.

Our families both have it.

We grew up around it.

With Skylar, none of that shit matters. I could probably show up in a holey shirt, scuffed shoes, and dirty jeans and she wouldn't give a shit. And considering where we are, she's not that interested in people with Ivy Leagues associated with their names.

I know if Ma were here right now, she'd take one good

look between Skylar and me and deem us kindred spirits. I think part of me acknowledged as much even when she was running from me—when she pissed me off from avoiding rather than confronting me.

We talk as our food arrives, going back and forth on books, movies, and music. I'm not a huge reader, but I can hold my own with some of the classics thanks to the lit classes I took earlier in my Lindon years. She doesn't know many action movies, so I promise to catch her up on the films worth watching during our movie nights, which she casually agreed to with a secretive smile on her face that I haven't quite decoded. And when we both talk about what a queen Taylor Swift is, I think her eyes nearly pop out of her head when she challenges me to finish the lyrics of random songs by the artist and I get them right.

Every. Single. Time.

Both of our plates are almost empty when I finally nudge her foot. "What exactly did you mean about wanting a redo?"

Her eyes stay glued to the plate as she pokes around one of her fries with her fork.

"I want to help, Sky," I tell her softly. "I just need to know what it is you want help with. If it's about being comfortable enough drinking and dancing at parties, I'll happily take you to some and be your own personal guard dog. Help you work your way up until you don't feel so uneasy. You have my word. You'll be safe. But it's up to you, completely in your hands, so you need to tell me what your expectations are."

Her lips part for a moment before she lowers her fork until it *clanks* against the ceramic plate. "It's not so much…" She pauses, shaking her head and looking up at me. Vulnerability is plastered across her face. "That's part of it, I guess. I want to have fun and try experiencing college life. Just not how some people do."

"You don't want casual hookups."

Her cheeks start turning pink. "No."

"Okay, so you want to try giving parties another go. Easy," I say, leaning back with my glass of sweet tea wrapped in my fingers. "What else?"

She looks pained. "Are you really going to make me say it?"

"This is in your control," I remind her, making sure she knows exactly what that means. "I told you before that I'd do anything you wanted. Tell me when. Tell me what. I'm there. Trust me, my imagination is vast on the open possibilities here, but I won't share those thoughts because I don't want to scare you."

We stare at each other for a long moment before she drops her hands into her lap. She's uncomfortable, but in this moment, I don't care. I want her to say it—to tell me what it is she wants from me.

I *need* her to.

"I want…" Her voice is strained, unsure, as she stares at my relaxed position across from her. I'm surprised when her shoulders pull back and she leans forward, hesitantly brushing my hand with hers. I let her move my palm until hers is sliding into it, closing her fingers around mine.

I try to calm my heart.

Try to ignore the twitch in my pants.

Skylar studies our intertwined hands like they're some sort of anomaly. "I want to feel normal again. I want to hold hands and dance and touch and…" The red in her cheeks encases her whole face. "I want to do other stuff too. I don't want to think about that night. I want to think about new ones. Fun ones. Calmer ones. Maybe then my brain will stop taking me back to that night. Maybe the nightmares will stop."

Her voice is heavy and low, and it drives me fucking crazy. I squeeze her hand until her eyes cast upward to meet mine. "Do I make you comfortable?"

She nods without hesitation.

My fingertip trails up her wrist, tracing the vein that goes up her forearm. "Does this make you uncomfortable?"

There's a brief pause before she releases a choppy breath and shakes her head.

Instead of pushing, I let my fingers rest there on her bare skin. Her palm flattens against my forearm as we sit and stare in silence. Only the murmurs around us fill in our surroundings as we soak in each other's company.

A few moments later, the waitress comes back and breaks the moment. "Aren't you two the cutest," she gushes, smiling at the blush on Skylar's face and the easy smile on mine. To my surprise, Skylar's hand doesn't move from where it's resting even when the waitress collects our plates and sets our check down.

With my free hand, I grab the slip before she can and pull out my wallet. "There's a little get together to celebrate end of midterms next weekend. A buddy of mine hosts it every year. It's never wild or anything, so it'd be a good starter for you."

I slap a couple of bills down over the check and slide my wallet back into my pocket.

My hand slips back into hers, a movement she watches carefully, quietly. "If this is what you want," I say, "I'm down. We'll take it a day at a time. Be friends. Be...whatever you need. I won't push or expect anything that you're not willing to give. But, Skylar?"

She stares, silent and waiting.

"There's a lot of things I'd love to give you," I admit. "Things that would make you feel so fucking good. The second that moment comes, you won't remember anything other than my mouth on your pussy and my hands on your body. It'd be the best thing you ever felt. I promise."

I see her throat bob as she swallows, and I wait patiently for her to wrap her head around what I'm offering.

"A party," she repeats quietly.

"A small one."

We catch each other's eyes.

In a breathy tone, she says, "Okay."

I don't know what exactly she's saying okay to, but the heated look in her eyes tells me it's more than going out together.

Chapter Twenty-Three

SKYLAR

EXAMS ARE BRUTAL. WAY more than they should be for someone with my GPA. When Mom asks how they went during our phone call, I lie and say they were fine.

"I had no doubt," Mom chirps, something clicking in the background that I realize must be coming from the chef my parents use. "Blake, please make sure that's gluten free. I don't need to look puffy for the photos. Oh, Sky! Did I tell you that your father surprised me with anniversary photos with Martin Redford?"

The famous photographer's name has even *me* impressed. Go Dad.

"I'm so excited, but now I need to make sure I'm in top shape. Margo down the road worked with him and her photos looked immaculate. I know if mine don't measure up, I'll never live it down."

I roll my eyes. "You'll look fine, Mom."

She huffs. "We'll see. I swear Botox is looking better and better every day. Anyway, have you looked into a different room yet? Serena mentioned you'd considered moving out. If you need us to make a call—"

"God, no," I say quickly, walking toward the door to my next class. It won't be until another week at least before we see our exam grades, but I can't help but feel anxious stopping in front of the door to mathematics. "The housing department said there's space when I emailed them about it, but that's as far as I've gotten. I tried talking to Becca about the situation, but she won't even make time for me."

I was tempted not to say a word while I searched for a new room but realized it wouldn't go over well if I just up and left once I found something. Olive knows, and so does Aliyah, since I slipped the information to her during the class we share. I think Dee might even suspect too, but none of them has said a word to my current roommate. I've noticed a small rift, something off in their dynamic that has to do with Aliyah. She's been jumpy lately, quieter than normal. I don't ask why whenever we see each other, whether it's for food or class, because I have a feeling she wouldn't tell me.

And I get it. More than she knows.

Ever since Danny suggested I talk to somebody about my nightmares, I've become hyperaware of the flyers on the student center activity board that include therapy sessions near the campus clinic. It's free for all Lindon U students. I tell myself that's the reason I snap a photo of the information and save it on my phone, even though I've yet to look further into it.

Because…could they help? If I'm not willing to talk to Olive or Danny, what could a certified stranger do?

"Darling, Becca's going to find out if you and your things magically disappear," Mom points out, almost sarcastically.

I grumble, "I know." Sighing, I lean against the wall outside class. "I have to go, but I'll keep you updated. They may make me wait until next semester, but I'll let you know what happens."

After we say goodbye, I head in and smile at Alba—the black-haired girl who's moved her seat closer to mine ever since I made my official introduction. Once I sit down, she says, "I didn't mean to eavesdrop, but you're looking for a new room, right?"

I rub my lips together before nodding. "I am. Things with my current roommate aren't working out, so my family thinks it'd be a good idea to find something else."

She frowns. "That sucks. I know a few people who were in the same situation at one point. But it's actually kind of perfect for me. I'm one of the room advisers for Ellis Hall, the building on the hill. I know it's pretty steep, but they keep it really well maintained in the winters and it's pretty empty right now. They usually put freshmen in there, but they spread the incoming class out this year because enrollment was down. They're looking to fill some of the rooms, and the first floor has a ton of singles available."

My brows lift. "Seriously?"

Alba nods enthusiastically. "Yep! And I'm the only girl on the first floor, but my room is actually on the other side, so you'd have your own bathroom and everything. How cool would that be? No roommates. Your own personal bathroom. Oh—except for weekends. Girls would probably stumble in there and use it. But the janitors are really good about cleaning."

That is pretty cool, I silently admit.

She claps. "If you're interested, you should meet me over there. I can show you around, maybe get you to see one of the rooms in case you'd want to make the move. They're offering discounts to students who move there right now."

I'm not worried about the money, knowing my parents

already offered to pay whatever necessary if it means getting out of the environment I'm in. The nightmare I paired with the dark circles under my eyes was enough to encourage me to leave Becca behind. "Are you free after this class?"

"Yeah. You?"

I nod.

Her hands squeeze together, trying to contain the excitement blooming across her face. It makes me smile. "It would be really cool to have someone I know living there. The other floors are a mixture of people, but none who I know that well or have classes with. We sometimes do fun mixers to help people get to know one another, but it's not mandatory to go to."

"Alba…" I sigh in contentment. Hope starts spreading in my chest. "I'm glad I said hi to you."

She laughs. "Me too, girl. Me too."

~

Sitting in front of the bathroom mirror rubbing my lips together until my pink gloss is evenly applied, I give myself a once-over, fuss over my hair until it's mussed, and walk back into my room.

I bite back a groan when Becca sets her lanyard with her keys and ID down on the desk and tosses her bag on her bed. "Where are *you* going?"

Her dry question as I slide my ID into my back pocket and pick up my phone from where it's charging on the mini fridge has me holding back the deep frown that wants to curl my lips. I ignore the tone though. "I'm going out."

I don't miss the scoff.

"To a party," I emphasize, not that I owe her any explanation. Our suitemates are all already scattered around the town—most of them at Fishtail, the local bar. One of them is stuck at her shift at the diner until closing—Sammi. Out of the group of girls, she's always been the friendliest, yet I find her the most intimidating anyway.

"Which one?" she asks.

I slide on the brown suede boots that Olive let me borrow that go midway up my shins on my skinny jean–clad legs and flatten out the black sweater that I'll probably melt in later. It's a basic but cute outfit. My makeup is simple enough, nothing too showy. My plans are to blend into the crowd, even though Olive pointed out that most of the girls would be wearing far less than me.

"Danny said Alpha Sigma Phi was hosting it or something," I tell her, examining myself in the little mirror I keep in the corner. I should probably do something more with my hair, but I decide to toss a beanie over it that I stole from Serena and call it good.

"Alpha Sigma Phi only has exclusive parties" is my roommate's reply. When I glance at her, she's gaping at me as if she can't believe it.

I shrug and look at my phone to message Olive back.

Me: You sure you can't come?

Becca makes a noise as she digs through her closet. "When are you leaving?"

I blink, watching her pull out a few shirts and examine them. "I told Danny I'd meet him outside at nine." The clock on my phone screen tells me I have a couple minutes. "How did your last exam go?"

She gives me a dumbfounded look at my attempt at small talk. "It was fine. I need a few minutes to get ready."

I blink again. "Uh… You want to come with me?"

Yanking one of her favorite party shirts that shows a lot of cleavage from the hanger, she tosses it on her bed and finds something to go with it. "Dee is out, and I have no clue what's wrong with Ali. She's been acting weird. So yeah. The Alpha parties are hard to get into."

My phone goes off in my hand.

Olive: Sorry, can't :(Sebastian is home and mom is making us bond before he leaves again. Home until Sunday night

I frown, slipping my phone into my pocket after telling Olive to have fun and then cross my arms over my chest. "I don't think I'm allowed to invite people, Becca. Like you said, it's exclusive."

The look my roommate gives me could burn flesh from bone if possible. "Are you serious right now?"

Is *she*? "I am." My teeth grind. "Why should I invite you when you've been nothing but rude to me?"

She glares. "I've only ever been honest with you. It's not my fault you don't like hearing the truth."

The truth. "I have no idea what kind of truths you think you're informing me of, but they're skewed. Sorry, but you're not coming. You'll have to figure out something else to do tonight. The last thing I want is to be ditched again because you get tired of me."

The shock on her face is almost comical.

Almost.

I'm irritated that she thinks she could invite herself along after all the nasty things she's said to me since I got here.

"*You* ditched *us* at the parties we took you to," Becca

practically hisses. She clutches her clothes. "Do you know how long we looked for you at the football house? You went on and on about not being left behind and then you just randomly disappeared with some guy you didn't even know. So don't get pissed at *me* for your bad decisions."

What is she talking about? "That's not what happened!" *Is it?* "We were drinking and then—"

And then what?

There's a mental block, a total eclipse of memories. I was drinking with the girls, dancing badly to some rap song I'd never heard before, and then…I don't know. I was kissing somebody. Being groped. Not really thinking. Then I woke up in bed the next morning alone.

"That's exactly what happened." She whips a piece of clothing onto the bed. "And then we go to *another* party together, and you ditch us *again* within twenty minutes. With a different guy. Tyler was bragging about you two going at it that night to anybody who would listen. You act like you're so fucking innocent, but I know the real you. The second a guy gives you any attention, you'll ditch anyone for them. Real classy, *Skylar.* Who are you opening your legs for tonight? Daniel Bridges? Or one of his teammates?"

My throat tightens as I swallow past the harsh words being thrown at me. Why the hell would Tyler lie about us getting together? I assumed Becca was the sole person spreading things about me, but I guess Tyler could be a culprit too. It's no wonder he hasn't bothered me as much lately. He must have realized those rumors were all he'd get out of the weird friendship we had.

"I don't know what you're even talking about." I can't look at her, so I decide to evade her eyes and collect my thoughts. Taking a deep breath, I decide to choose my battle wisely. "You know what, Becca? You can think all you want about me, but you don't know the real me at all. You believe in some screwed-up version that makes you look good. I'm sorry you're pissed off that I'm not inviting you. I'm sorry that you think I ditched you guys at the parties we went to. There's nothing I can do about that."

"You could own up to it."

"I'm not owning up to something I didn't do," I inform her gingerly. I should tell her about moving out, tell her how I found a single room that Alba showed me earlier in the coed dormitory across the street. But I don't.

I don't tell her that I called my mom and asked if I could get the room or that my parents already paid for it in full within an hour of me seeing it. I don't tell her that, buried at the bottom of my book bag, is the key to my escape.

I say nothing about the paperwork I signed or how I can move by the end of the weekend once I sign off on papers with the current RA here in Morris Hall and hand in the keys weighing heavy in my hand.

Becca wouldn't care if I left anyway.

She wants me gone.

When Danny texts me that he's outside, I double-check to make sure I have what I need before calling out a murmured, "Bye," to my roommate and leaving her to steam on her own.

When I push open the front door and see the tall football player waiting exactly where he says, his eyes go straight to the smile on my face. "Not that I'm not flattered you're so happy to see me, but what's with the smile?"

I stop beside him, zipping up the jacket I grabbed on my way out and stuff my hands into the pockets to protect them from the nipping wind. "Nothing. I'm just...glad we're going out tonight."

He beams, draping an arm over my shoulder and tugging me into his side. "I knew you wanted me, Blondie."

I playfully push him before settling into his side as we walk side by side.

His eyes flash with something that I can't distinguish before he starts walking us toward his friend's truck. Opening the door like he always does, he waits until I climb up before gripping the roof and watching me buckle.

My brows pinch when I see him staring, wondering what's on his mind. "What?"

"I was just thinking that you should smile more," he says, almost to himself more than to me. "That's all. It's nice."

It takes me a couple seconds to grapple with that as the smile wavers. "I'm working on it" is all I say.

He drums the roof of the truck, nods, and closes the door.

When he hops into the other side, we share another look. His eyes go to my lips, and I wonder if he wants to see another smile or if there's another reason.

I swallow.

Force my lips to stretch upward again.

He blows out a breath and starts driving.

Chapter Twenty-Four

SKYLAR

THE PARTY ISN'T AS big as I'm expecting. Unlike the one Danny's friends had, there's not as many people crammed inside or music thumping at an ear-piercing volume.

As we walk through the front door and weave through the small crowd in the foyer, Danny's hand keeps mine in a firm grip as people call out his name in greeting. I don't know any of them, not that I'm surprised. What does make my brows arch is that he barely acknowledges them and gets us to the living room where there's more room to mingle instead.

I notice Alex O'Conner in the corner, surrounded by his usual gaggle of girls, and am suddenly thankful Olive couldn't make it. She hasn't said much about her hookup with the hockey player currently sucking face with some purple-haired girl, but I know there's something she's holding back about their situation.

"Olive couldn't make it, right?" he asks, tracing my eyes over to Alex. He doesn't look shocked, just indifferent. If anything, maybe he feels a secondhand sense of responsibility for Olive simply because she's my friend.

I turn my back so I don't have to watch the very public display and nod. "Why do people do that? Olive is a catch. I don't understand why he'd want to be with other girls." I make a face, then remember what Danny has said about his past. "No offense. I know you used to...uh..."

His lips waver. "I haven't done that in a long time, Blondie. Especially not now."

My brows pinch. "Now?"

"My attention is focused on one person only. I don't need anybody else." One of his shoulder lifts casually, as if he isn't implying something big.

Choosing not to read into it, I decide to focus back on my friend. "Olive drove home to spend time with her family. Have you heard of Sebastian Henderson?"

Recognition lights up his face. "Bash? Sure. The whole campus knows him. Why?"

I give him a wary look. "He's Olive's older brother."

His eyes widen. "No shit?"

I nod.

His look becomes contemplative. "I wasn't expecting that. Not with her fangirling over Alex, since he and Bash had some sort of rivalry."

"Does everyone know about their war?"

His shoulder lifts. "Pretty much. I guess we all assumed it was over when Bash graduated and got drafted. But, I mean, the competition is always going to be there between them." His thumb hooks in Alex's direction. "Once O'Conner is released into the world, it'll be ten times more brutal."

"What do you mean?"

Danny pulls me toward the refreshments as a group of

guys come barreling in. He shoots them warning looks that they mostly ignore as he offers me an unopened beer. I accept the slightly chilled can with a small smile. He grabs one for himself. "O'Conner and Henderson duked it out all the time on the ice. They worked well together to get Lindon plenty of wins, but off it? It was always stiff competition to get scouts' attention."

My eyes wander over to Olive's obsession. Thankfully, he isn't making out with anyone now. A couple guys who look as massive as him joined his little group and they're all talking about something. "You think the New England teams are holding out for him?"

Danny presses his lips together for a second before sighing. "Probably, yeah. It's what I would do if I were in their shoes."

I soak in that tidbit of information before following him off to the side so people can get drinks from the table. "It's not as packed as I thought it'd be."

Danny leans against the wall, keeping me close to his side as he examines the room. "The frat can't get another complaint, or they'll be shut down. They've had to keep it low-key."

Ah.

He nudges me. "Did you want something else?" His chin gestures toward the unopened can in my hand that I'm fidgeting with. "There's probably water around here I can grab you. You don't have to drink that."

"Stop being such a buzzkill," Becca tells me, pushing a plastic cup in my hand. "Drink another one of those and loosen up."

"Sky?"

My eyes stay locked on the beer.

"Blondie?" Fingers carefully graze my chin before lifting it up to meet his eyes. "You good? Do you want to go?"

Swallowing, I shake my head. "No, I—" I cut myself off and think about that little piece of information I didn't remember before. "I'm good. Sorry. Zoned out. Um, I'll just keep this for now."

He smiles. "Want to dance?"

There's a group of girls on the opposite side of the room huddled together and moving to the beat of the music. I have absolutely no rhythm whatsoever.

So on second thought…

I crack open the beer and take a long sip while Danny's curious eyes watch me. It's only after I force myself to roll my shoulders back that I take his hand and smile up at him. "Yes. I'd love to dance."

His eyes look a little wary as I take another sip, but he lets me pull us away from the wall until we're facing each other much closer than before.

My free hand grips his shoulder as his hesitates by his side. I say, "You can touch me."

He studies my face before one of those large hands palms my hips. It's he who guides my body to match the music playing, and I don't mind it at all. Bits and pieces from the football party come back to me, and it involves a lot of gyrating, grinding, and fumbling on my part.

But this? This is nice.

"What are you thinking about?" he asks, leaning closer since it's gotten louder with the arrival of more people.

I bite my lip. "The first party I went to."

His eyebrows go up.

I don't indulge him on more information, and he doesn't ask. But I can tell he wants to. "I told Becca that she couldn't come tonight."

My admission makes him blink.

"It felt good." My smile is sly, even though her hurtful accusations make it fumble.

"No wonder you looked so happy when you left. I take it she didn't like that very much."

I shake my head, gripping his shoulder a little tighter when someone accidently bumps into me. Stepping into Danny until our chests are flush, I look over my shoulder when a girl already partially drunk apologizes and stumbles away with a friend. "No, she seemed pretty pissed. But I don't care. Is that bad?"

"She doesn't seem to care about hurting your feelings," he points out matter-of-factly.

I frown.

"Sorry if that was blunt," he apologizes quickly, misinterpreting my reaction.

My sigh is probably too quiet for him to hear over the voices and music. "No, you're right. I wouldn't be surprised if she's trash-talking me right now to whoever will listen."

Anger takes over his eyes. "Is she the one who's been spreading shit about you and guys?"

My nose twitches. "She's at least one of the people. There could be others, but she makes the most sense."

"That's fucked up, Sky."

"I know it is. A lot of stuff she's said to me is. And she and I seem to remember the football party differently." I nibble the inside of my cheek, thinking about my conversation with her. "Becca told me she and the girls were trying to find me before they left, but I'd already disappeared with..." My nose scrunches. Does my roommate know who it is I walked away with? "Whoever I was with that night. But I don't remember that at all. One second I was with them, the next I wasn't."

Danny is quiet, quieter than I expect. "Do you remember anything else from that night? What room you were in?"

"I could probably show you sometime. It was empty when I woke up, obviously, so there's not much to go on. But no. I don't recall much else other than what I've already told you."

He hums.

"What is it?"

"Nothing." His hard tone doesn't convince me though.

"Tell me," I prod, resting my chin on his shoulder and staring at him until he admits whatever he's thinking.

"I don't want to ruin the night," he grumbles, tipping his head back and letting out a heavy breath. "I'm thinking about the bad things that happen at parties, and the last thing I want to accept is that something bad happened at one I was partly responsible for."

His response makes my brows furrow. "I don't think you can take responsibility for what other people do, Danny. That's putting too much pressure on yourself. It's not fair."

The first song moves flawlessly into the next, and we keep going, not picking up the pace like others or slowing down like a few couples who've joined in.

Danny eventually looks back down at me, brushing hair out my face and running the pad of his thumb across my cheek until a lone shiver travels down my spine. "I know it's not completely my fault, but I was there—"

"So were a lot of others," I remind him. "We didn't know each other. I wasn't your responsibility. As much as I wish I could blame Becca and the girls, I wasn't theirs either. I chose to drink. I chose to dance with random people. And I...I chose to go upstairs. Trust me, I know what you're feeling. But the blame isn't on you. It never was."

"It's not on you either."

"We all have to own up to our choices," I murmur.

This time, he says nothing for a long time. His chin rests on the top of my head after he guides my cheek to his chest.

Sometime later, he mumbles, "I wish you were treated better by those girls. You don't deserve the shit Becca says to you."

"They're just words."

His answer is felt deep in my bones, soaking into each one slowly. "Words can hurt too. Sometimes more than physical blows."

"You're right," I whisper.

"I'm not close with all my teammates. Caleb and Aiden are the two I'd probably call my friends. Justin too. The rest? We get along fine. But none of us are openly dicks to each other without justifiable reasons. Not like your roommate is with you. It pisses me off."

Danny always seems to get along so well with everybody, so I'm surprised he's not very close with the guys I've seen him hang out with around campus and at their house.

"My sister told me I should find somewhere else to live next semester," I admit. I haven't gotten around to telling him about Alba or Ellis Hall yet.

"Serena?"

I nod, smiling that he knew which sister I'm referring to. "Yeah. I've been distracted for a lot of reasons this semester, but constantly being around Becca when she's in a mood doesn't help."

He sets his drink down on an end table and puts both hands on my hips. "She's not wrong. I could help you try finding something off campus if you want."

"I appreciate it, but I think I want to stay on campus.

Even though I don't go out and do much, it's kind of nice to be part of the lifestyle. Plus, it's closer to the dining hall and academic buildings."

He relents. "If you change your mind, let me know. If nothing comes up, I have a few options in mind."

One of my brows quirks. "Already?"

His grin is sheepish as his fingertips twitch on my hips. "Aiden is leaving after this semester. He's got some intense training before the combine in February. His girl Ivy, you know the blue-haired chick from Bea's, will probably stay downstairs, but we've got room if there's nothing else available. It's just something to consider. I don't want you to be miserable with your roommate, but I know the house isn't your favorite place right now either."

"Isn't Aiden a senior? I thought his last semester is this spring."

I feel his long exhale. "Yeah, we've all told him to finish it out, but he's dead set on dropping. The school will probably give him an extended leave of absence and let him re-enroll to finish his degree if he wants to later on. College has never been his thing though. He never really wanted a degree, even though he's smart as hell. He's only ever been here for football. And once he reunited with his best friend from childhood, he was all about her to. Man is suddenly obsessed."

It seems silly to me to quit so close to getting to the finish line, but I guess that just shows he's passionate. "You said football wasn't your endgame, so what do you want to do after Lindon?"

There's a pause between us. "Grad school, probably. Started looking at different programs here and at a few other places. I haven't quite got it figured out yet."

"No football at all?"

His body stiffens, making me pull back to study his tense expression. "No. Not all of us are cut out for it like Aiden."

The change of his voice makes me realize we're stepping in dangerous territory, so I change the subject. "Remember that girl from my math class I told you about before? Alba? She's an RA for Ellis Hall and found me a room."

His brows dart up his forehead. "Shit, Sky. When did that happen?"

"It only happened this week. I've tried bringing it up to Becca, but she hasn't wanted to hear me out."

"So don't tell her. That's on her."

"She'll be pissed."

"She's already pissed."

He has a point. Still... "I don't want her to come after me worse than she already has. She's made my anxiety here worse because she runs her mouth to everyone who will listen. People I don't know who will obviously believe anything. I know you've heard the stuff people are saying. A lot of people have."

A dark look shadows his face.

"Yeah," he mumbles. "I've heard. I've also threatened to knock a few assholes' teeth out if they keep feeding into it."

"You did that?"

"Don't act so shocked. I like you, Skylar. I don't like to see you upset. I know shit people say isn't true, and it pisses me off that more people don't say so. I mean, shit. Sleeping around isn't that uncommon on campuses. Your roommate shouldn't have made you an isolated target like you did something wrong, especially because she's spreading lies. So yeah. I've thrown around some threats. Nearly punched a fucker who was talking smack to his buddies. And I'll keep doing it until they stop."

I swallow past my words. What can I say to that? Olive has hinted that Danny was doing this, but I wasn't sure if I should believe her. I never asked him to defend me—never expected it. So knowing he is makes me feel…

A lot. I feel a lot.

Nervous over the tension between us, I bring my drink to my lips and take another healthy swig. It tastes bitter as it slides down my throat, and I make a face as I take a third sip while my dance partner watches closely.

I'm halfway done with it when he reaches up and plucks it from my fingers. "You might want to slow down."

Heat creeps under my skin. "I…"

"Am I making you nervous?"

"It's not *you*."

"Do you want to head out?"

My eyes go to the people around us. They're all having a good time, laughing, talking, drinking, and dancing. Then there's me. Despite the person holding on to me and obliging my silly quest for comfort, I'm not having that much fun.

Because I suck at dancing.

And obviously suck worse at conversing.

"I was kind of hoping the alcohol would help," I mumble dejectedly.

"Look at me," he says softly, eyes burning holes into my face as I slide my gaze toward him shyly. "Alcohol should never be used as a coping mechanism. Okay? If you're uncomfortable, tell me. If you don't want to stay, tell me. I don't want you to drink to get through it."

"I'm sorry," I whisper, fighting the heat prickling my face.

He flicks my nose playfully. "Don't apologize. If you're not having fun, we can head out and do something else. You wanted to go to a party"—he gestures around us—"and you did. Mission accomplished."

"You wouldn't think I'm lame if we left even though we just got here?"

Instantly he shakes his head. "I don't think that's lame at all. There's more to college than parties. It gets old after a while anyway."

I think about it. Study the room. Look back at the person waiting patiently for my answer.

"Want to watch a movie?" I ask him.

"Only if it's the next movie in that magical pants series you got me into. I need to know what happens to Lena and her Greek god of a boy toy."

I laugh, shoving his shoulder playfully.

When he takes my hand, I happily weave our fingers together and let his steer us out.

Nobody stops us as we exit, but plenty of people stare.

For once, it doesn't make my skin crawl.

~

The entire suite is pitch-black when we arrive, and I'm able to breathe a sigh of relief knowing it'll just be us for a while. No assuming stares or expectant giggles will greet me when they see Danny trailing behind. No glares from Becca or lectures on roommate rules when it comes to guys being here.

Danny stretches across my bed, propping my pillows up behind him as I grab my laptop and log on. He grabs the paperback next to my bed and reads the back. "Is this a *sexy book*, Skylar?" His teasing tone has my cheeks coloring as I watch him flip to the first page.

I quickly grab it from him and set it on my shelf, tucked safely between others. "They're *romances*."

"What's that one about? The guy on the cover had nothing but dog tags on, so color me intrigued." He looks genuinely curious as he bends an arm behind his head to use as a headrest.

I say, "You wouldn't like it."

"Says who? Maybe I want to read it."

"Be serious, Danny."

He grabs one of the smaller throw pillows and tosses it at me. "I am! Choose a book from your shelf and I'll read it. I want to know what you like, Blondie. Let me into that head of yours."

All I can do is stare for a few seconds. "I don't think you're being real right now."

He snorts. "I *am*. What book? Pick one."

I blink slowly. "Um, okay." I turn and stare at my small collection of romances and choose one of my favorites. "Here. But I'm telling you, it's a romance. You probably won't like it."

"Am I not allowed to like a good romance because I'm a dude?" he questions, making me realize how unreasonable I'm being.

I shake my head. "You're right. Read away." Waving my hand at the book clutched in his hands, I shift my focus back to the computer on my desk and start the movie.

He doesn't give me a chance to wonder where to sit when he scoots over and pats the section of mattress beside him. Safely tucking the book on the other side of his body, he lifts an arm to welcome me next to him.

Only slightly hesitant, I kick off my shoes like he did and crawl up to the bed after hitting Play. As soon as I lie down, he wraps his arm around my shoulder and tugs me into his side.

He lets out a contented sigh.

No words.

Just a sigh.

We watch the movie in silence, cuddled up beside one another as the lives of the four women play out on the screen. Unlike the first movie, he doesn't ask questions. He takes it in, thoroughly invested in what's going to happen to each of them.

I told him last time these movies were based on a book series, which he said he would consider looking into.

What's hotter than a guy who reads?

Nothing.

And the way he watches whatever movie I want—no matter what kind—gives him major brownie points. There's never any complaint over the cheesy plot or dialogue. He doesn't even look at his phone during them.

And now he wants to *read* my favorite romances? Sometimes I wonder if this man is even real or if he's some twisted figment of my imagination that my loneliness has conjured up.

Well over halfway in, I can feel Danny's breath on my forehead and his eyes scanning my face. "I can tell you're thinking something. What's on your mind?"

Through my lashes, I glance up at him.

Our lips are so close I can practically taste his. "You're missing the movie" is my answer.

"Mm. I can watch it anytime." His voice is quiet, barely a notch above a whisper. "I want to know what you're think-ing right now."

Right now?

God, I'm not sure it'd be smart to tell him exactly what I'm thinking. Especially since he made me drink an entire bottle of water once we got back to make sure I was sobered up and thinking straight. I can't blame alcohol for the thoughts of his body pressed against mine or the way his lips could potentially graze my own if we shifted just right.

"Sky."

I swallow, my throat bobbing as my heartbeat echoes in my eardrums. "I was thinking that I want to kiss you," I admit.

His breath hitches and I feel it against my face. "Yeah?"

My head nods once. "But if you want to watch the movie..."

"Shut up, Skylar." That's all he says before his head dips down and captures my lips. It's tender, unrushed, and sweet. I silently demand my heart calm down in my chest before it propels right out of its cage, but it doesn't listen. It pounds heavily, thumping until I worry he can feel it as I press my body closer to his. One of his hands reaches over and cups the side of my face as he parts my lips with his and teases my tongue.

It's slow.

Painfully slow.

Cautious.

Beautiful.

His hand is warm on my cheek as his thumb brushes my jaw and coaxes me to open deeper, angle my head, and kiss back.

And I do.

God, do I ever.

I inch closer, resting one of my palms flat against his own racing heartbeat. The groan tearing up his throat as I taste his tongue and move my hand from his chest to his shoulder has me squeezing my legs together.

I shift until the seam of my jeans is rubbing against where I need it to, pressing my lips harder against Danny's until he moves his hand to the nape of my neck and squeezes, tracing his tongue along the back of my teeth, then my lips, and nipping at my bottom one.

"Fuck, Sky," he rasps after pulling back, resting his forehead against mine. Our breaths tangle in the small space between us as he nuzzles our noses.

I can't help but squirm until his leg is pressed between mine, applying the perfect amount of pressure against the needy bundle of nerves begging for attention. A strangled moan escapes my lips as he captures them again, sucking my bottom lip into his mouth, then the top, and moving his leg to give me friction.

"That's it," he coaxes against my lips. "Just like that," he whispers, trailing his lips to my ear. "I love the noises you make."

Biting my lip and tilting my head back as his leg works its magic against me, he uses the access to graze my sensitive skin with his teeth, nipping at my pulse and biting down until I arch into him further.

He draws back, flicking his tongue against the same spot his teeth bit into, and peppers kisses up and down the column of my throat. "When does your roommate get back?"

The question sparks something dangerous deep inside me, shooting desire straight to my core and fear straight to my heart. "I don't know. But I'm not ready to—"

"No sex," he promises, pushing up to look down at me. "I just want to make you feel good. Do you trust me?"

The question captures my breath, storing it in my throat as I stare at him with unblinking eyes.

Do I trust him?

He brushes his thumb along my cheek until it rests against my lip. "We don't have to do anything. We can go back to watching the movie. Cuddle. There's no pressure here."

I know he means that too.

But there's a burning ache between my legs that may cause me to combust unless it's taken care of.

So I breathe out, "I trust you."

His eyes flash as he bends down and kisses me again, this time deeper, harder, like he needs me to feel how badly he wants this too.

Lips trailing down my neck, he pays attention to every piece of exposed skin—against my collarbone, the opening of my V-neck leading to the exposed tops of my breasts cradled in a new lace pushup bra. His hands move down my sides, tracing my curves like he's mapping them for future memory. When his fingers land on the waistband of my jeans, he stops and looks up at me.

"Is this okay?" The question comes out hoarse as I feebly nod, unable to vocalize past the nerves and anticipation as he pops the button and lowers the zipper.

I bite my lip hard when he grips the denim and starts tugging them down. Arching my hips so he can slide them past my butt and down my thighs, I watch as his eyes take in the black panties exposed as he whips the denim somewhere behind him.

Whatever they hit falls, but neither of us look to see if it caused any damage.

"These," he says, "are sexy as hell. And as much as I'm dying to see if your bra matches, I want you to fall apart on my tongue before any of your roommates get back."

His words do something to me that only fictional men in the past have ever made me do. They make me wet. I tighten my thighs as his fingertips dance along my smooth legs until they stop at the edge of my panties.

"May I?" he asks. "I want to taste you. Make you come."

My lips tremble. "I–I've never..."

The blue in his eyes darkens, full of heat and lust. He presses a kiss against my bent knee and curls one of his hands around the upper part of my calf. "It'll feel great, I promise."

He waits until I nod before he disposes of the panties the same way he did my jeans.

Flawlessly.

With experience.

I'm self-conscious when he slowly peels my legs open, baring me to him. He stares at the trimmed curls and wet, pink skin like he's dying a little inside.

"Beautiful," he whispers, his palms moving up my legs until they grip my thighs and part me wider.

I lock up when he descends, self-conscious of the fact that I have no idea what I'm doing or what to expect. Nerves weigh down my stomach as he positions his shoulders between my open legs to keep them in place. I start to close them, but he glances up at me with a look of admiration that halts my movements.

My hands go to the blanket under me, gripping fistfuls of the material as he lowers his mouth to my slit and presses an open kiss against me. I bite my lip so hard I can taste blood as he parts me with his fingers and flattens his wet, warm tongue against my clit.

My back arches at the unexpected feeling bursting through my body, earning another sexy noise from the man who licks me from the bundle of nerves down to my entrance. The tip of his tongue teases me before he moves back up and sucks me into his mouth.

"*Oh God.*" I can feel it building already. My stomach tightens as my body heats up and tingles shoot down my spine when he grabs one of my legs and positions it over his shoulder.

He keeps a solid hold of my hip as he licks, sucks, and teases. My butt lifts from the bed with need that he happily fulfills, the hand on my hip moving to knead my bare ass, squeezing one of my cheeks in his hand as his other hand moves to work alongside his tongue.

While he flicks my clit, his finger circles my entrance before moving inside slowly.

In.

Out.

Suck.

Lick.

In.

Out.

Curl.

Suck.

It's too much.

"D-Danny—" I can't even get the words out before I'm moving my hips forward into his mouth, feeling him take me over the edge. I come fast and hard until white dots my eyes and electric shocks shoot throughout my body.

It's nothing like I've ever experienced before in my life.

Danny kisses me one last time before pushing himself up, licking his lips, which are coated with my arousal, and shooting me a devastating smile.

He crawls up my body, positioning himself to the side so he's not completely hovering over me, and stares at my lips.

I make the move, experimentally pressing mine against his, tasting myself and making him groan into my mouth.

The kiss is chaste, brief, but it means so much more than words can.

I begin lowering my hand down his flat stomach to return the favor, but he shakes his head. "This isn't about me." His breath is uneven as he settles beside my half-naked body. Grabbing one of my throw blankets, he covers me up. "Plus, the noises you made alone took care of my little problem."

My brows pinch.

Then I realize what he means.

I made him come in his pants.

I find myself laughing. It's unexpected and loud, and he grins at me before joining in.

"Laugh it up all you want," he muses, moving over me and grabbing my panties and jeans from the floor and passing them over.

My legs are jelly and body weak and sated, but I'd rather not be naked when Becca gets back.

He gives me a chance to redress before joining me back in bed. "Anytime you want me to do that, text me."

"What if you're at practice?"

"Coach will have to deal."

"At a game?"

"I'll happily let the other team win."

I roll my eyes at his playfulness, listening to the drum of my heartbeat and replaying everything that just happened in my head. Words can't describe what I'm feeling, so I settle under the arm he lifts again and curls around me, trying to enjoy the moment without letting the past ruin it.

Becca comes back half an hour later to see us in the same position.

There's no doubt she knows what happened based on the look on her face.

And I don't care.

Chapter Twenty-Five

SKYLAR

A HEADACHE FORMS IN the back of my skull as I finish proofreading my paper on Jane Austen's *Emma*. After the last paper earned me a C, I had to get my act together and make this one perfect. I learned the hard way that the professor doesn't hand out easy As in her class.

"Wait a minute," Danny says. He's sitting in the cushioned seat across from me with his booted feet crossed on top of the corner of the table. "This dude has a *pet tortoise?*"

He's holding the book I lent him, flipping to the next page with intrigue.

I glance at him, studying his relaxed posture as he reads. Pen cap in my mouth, I think about the night in my room. I expected our dynamic to change, but it hasn't. Not outwardly.

We steal little glances when we hang out, sit closer, with some part of us always touching—our hands, feet, arms, or legs. I don't feel weird from the contact but warm. At peace. He's not pushy or forward, and he respects my boundaries.

He's still a flirt, but now there's a different connotation attached. Whenever he makes eyes at me, brushes my hair away from my face, or says something sexual to be funny, my mind takes me back to the image of his head between my legs and his tongue on the most intimate part of my body.

And when I start blushing over it?

He grins because he knows exactly what's replaying in my head.

Releasing the pen, I say, "Yep. It's a pretty cool pet to have in college."

Danny looks up from the page he's reading. "The guys and I have always wanted a pet, but our lease states no dogs or cats are allowed in the building." He's contemplative for a moment. "Doesn't say anything about turtles."

"Tortoises," I correct.

"Would you help me name it?"

I blink. "Where would you even get one? There isn't a pet store around here last I checked. Plus, you're graduating soon."

A factor I haven't let myself think about for too long. What's going to happen when he's gone? Who will I have then? Olive will be around, but she's been busy traveling back and forth to see her family or hanging out with Alex, who apparently is her friend with many, many benefits, and I don't want to monopolize her time simply because I can't seem to make any other friends. Alba and I talk on and off, but it's mostly in class and to meet up to study in the RA's office when she's on duty for the night.

"He could be Sheldon. Get it? *Shell*-don." He cracks up at himself before going back to the book. "Is it weird I have a man crush on this dude? He's so laid-back, *I* want to be with him."

Snorting, I shake my head. "Get in line. He's got an entire fandom after him and his cookies."

His brows pinch, obviously not far enough in to get the reference yet. "Don't worry, Blondie. You'll always be number one to me."

I nibble on my lip to hide the smile.

"Caleb said he'd help with your move," he says after a few minutes. He closes the book and sets it on the table. "We can use his truck to load up your stuff instead of making multiple trips. That hill will be a pain in the ass otherwise."

"He doesn't have to—"

"He knows, but he wants to help. Raine will probably be there too. She's got a cousin who lives in Ellis, so it's perfect. Maybe she can introduce the two of you."

"Are you trying to help me make friends?"

"Nah, then I'd have to share you. But Raine is. Apparently her cousin hides out in her room watching anime or some shit all the time. She's worried about her."

I've learned that forcing those things doesn't usually end well. "You guys don't have to spend your bye week helping me lug stuff around. I don't have that much anyway."

A smile blossoms across his face. "Look at you using proper sports terms." He drops his feet and leans forward, plucking my nose. "I'm going to make a football fan out of you yet. Wait and see."

My eyes roll.

"Anyway, he said he's got nothing else going on. Neither do I, and I'd be hanging with you anyway, so might as well make the most of it. Does Becca know you're leaving tomorrow?"

My shoulders tense. She's avoided me as much as possible since our spat about the Alpha party, which has made our time in the room together awkward. Our suitemates know it too, because they constantly watch us like one of us is going to snap. I'm sure they placed bets on Becca winning that fight.

I would too.

Blowing out a sigh, I shake my head and tap my chewed-up pen cap on my paper. "I tried texting her saying we needed to talk, but she blew it off. I don't really know what else to do. Olive told me to forget about it. That she'd get over it eventually."

"Which she will," he agrees.

"She's vindictive."

He hums. "Something tells me she'll find a reason to complain about this one way or another, Blondie. With people like Becca, you can't win. They're going to find reasons not to like you even if it's unjustified."

I know he's right, but it doesn't make me feel any better about it. "I know I can't make everybody like me, but it's hard when I can't figure out what I did wrong."

His eyes sadden. "You didn't do anything. Not everybody needs an excuse to dislike people. Want some advice that Grandma Meadow told me a while ago?"

Silently, I nod.

"She told me that there would come a time when I needed to stop making myself so available to people," he says, brows going up knowingly when I sink into my seat. "The more we try helping people, understanding them, the more we lose ourselves along the way. You don't always have to be nice to everybody, Sky. Being nice usually only gets you used."

The frown is instant, weighing down my lips like lead is attached to either corner. "That's a sad way to look at it."

"It's not untrue though."

I think about it, something clicking inside my head as I stare at him. "Danny, do you feel like *I'm* using you? Please be honest because I don't want to—"

"Skylar," he cuts me off, seriousness washing over his usually playful features. "I'm going to tell you this once, so listen real good. There's a big difference between agreeing to help somebody when they ask because you care about them and having somebody assume you'll help because they think you owe them something. You never have to worry about me feeling used when it comes to anything we do together. I'll bury my face between those pretty thighs of yours any day of the week. I'll bury plenty of other things there too if that's what you want."

He says that as a couple guys walk by the table, earning amused snickers from them. "Oh my God," I grumble.

He chuckles. "I recall you saying those exact words when I was doing that thing with my—"

"Stop!" I squeak, tossing my pen cap at him. He dodges it artfully, grinning like a fiend.

He raises his hands, waiting until the bystanders pass us by. "Okay, okay. But do you understand? I don't feel like you're using me. Not in a bad way. If you knew the things I was thinking about right now..."

"I'm not sure I want to."

"You do," he counters, still grinning. "I have a feeling you'd be very interested in them."

The blush starts to subside, despite the images in my head that I can't seem to brush off as easily. Clearing my throat, I change the subject to something safer for public. "What time is Caleb free to help me move?"

"Sure, *now* you're accepting his help."

I shrug. "You're both offering, so I'd be stupid to turn it down. Plus, I don't have nearly as many muscles as you all do. It'll be way easier for you to carry my fridge and bigger items versus Olive and I struggling with them."

"True." He flexes his arm and wiggles his eyebrows. "And for the record, I totally have bigger muscles than him."

He doesn't, and we both know it. Just because Caleb is taken doesn't mean I haven't noticed how ripped he is. It's not in an overdone way either, but that guy's biceps are as big as my head, and I've seen the way Raine drools over them when he's wearing a T-shirt.

I almost do too.

Danny claps his hands once loudly, causing somebody from across the room to *shush* him. "So how are we attacking the Becca situation?"

My brows pinch. "What do you mean?"

"Is she going to be there when we pack?"

"Probably not. She usually has study group in the mornings, and she said something about meeting up with a guy from the station in the afternoon. We'll probably get most of the stuff out of there before she's back."

The nagging sense of guilt smacks into me, making me stare down at my forgotten assignment. Am I being petty because of everything she's put me through? Stooping to her level? The last thing I want is to give her ammunition.

"Hey," Danny says softly. "From one recovering people pleaser to another, don't do that to yourself. I know what you're thinking. There's nothing wrong with putting yourself first. She's stressing you out, making you upset, and that's not doing any good for either of you." Moving his chair closer to me and picking up the book again, he glances up at me with a lopsided smile stretched across his face. "Now, get back to work and stop distracting me, woman. I want to know all about my next man crush."

I shake my head but settle back into my seat in contentment. Especially when he uses the armrest on *my* chair to hold my hand.

He goes back to reading.

I go back to editing.

But my mind is completely wrapped up in him.

~

Stephen Marks hauls the mini fridge out of my room effortlessly as Caleb talks to one of my suitemates in the corner. I didn't know they knew each other, but the moment he showed up, she started beaming. Even Danny looked a little perplexed when they hugged and started talking.

Danny is currently grabbing the last of my boxes and stacking them on top of one another to pick up when I eye him.

"I can take one of those, you know," I tell him, reaching for the smaller one on top.

He smacks my hand away. "I've got it."

I notice the small flinch in his face when he lifts the cardboard boxes containing odds and ends—trinkets, snacks, textbooks, and shoes.

"Are you sure that I can't—"

"I said I got it," he replies coolly, making me gape at him. He closes his eyes for a second before shaking his head. "Sorry. My shoulder is just hurting a little today, so I'm in a mood."

Walking over to him, I grab the box on top and give him a don't-argue-with-me look. "I know you want to show off all those muscles"—I glance at his bare arms, which must be cold since he's been loading up Caleb's truck parked at the curb outside—"but I can carry things too. What would happen if you got hurt and couldn't play?"

"That wouldn't happen, Skylar. I'm carrying"—he looks for the label in black Sharpie that Olive and Raine helped me with, so we knew what was in each box when we got over to Ellis Hall—"shoes and textbooks. Why did you put these things in the same box? That's so random."

I laugh lightly. "I didn't realize I was in the presence of an expert packer. But for your information, Olive packed those. We couldn't fit all my textbooks in my backpack, so we just sort of tossed them in there. It isn't like my shoes would get ruined."

He shakes his head. "I'd hardly call myself an expert. Lived in the same house my whole life up until coming here. But Grandma M loves watching those get-organized shows, so the proper methods to these sorts of things are officially drilled into my head."

Before I can reply, I hear, "What the hell is going on?"

Both Danny and I turn to Becca as she stops at the doorway, keys in hand and backpack hanging from her shoulder.

My half of the room is bare—the bed stripped of its bedding, the desk rid of its scattered contents, and the area between where the bedframe was pressed against the wall and the armoire now empty of the mini fridge Sienna bought me before I left. I might feel a *tiny* bit bad about taking that with me since she used it quite a bit, but not enough to let her keep it.

"I'm moving to a different building," I answer, glancing at Danny. He nods once in encouragement before gesturing toward the door and leaving, letting me have my moment with Becca. She looks shell-shocked. "Look, I tried talking to you about it, but you'd never let me say anything. When I was asking you to meet up, it was so I could tell you I was doing this."

"Are you kidding me?" Becca snaps, throwing her things on the bed. Her arms cross over her chest as she glares at my old pieces of furniture. "Unlike you, I actually have friends and a life. I couldn't come meet up with you every time you asked because I was hanging out with them. I had better things to do."

"*That!* That is exactly why I need to leave. If you just agreed to meet with me *once*, I wouldn't have kept bothering you. But you're always so dead set on making me feel like shit about myself that it's impossible to tell you anything. You always say what you'd do with my side of the room if I were gone, so now's your chance. Convert my bed into a couch for all I care. It's not my problem anymore."

"You're such a—"

A throat clears from behind her, cutting off whatever insult she was about to call me. Bitch. Asshole. Slut. Whore. I've heard it all from her, so I'll use my imagination to fill in the blanks this time around.

Except this time, I'm not going to give a shit.

Danny and Caleb are both waiting for me at the door with Sammi in the background. She's frowning, and I'm embarrassed she had to witness the rift between me and Becca. I know she likes my roommate—that they get along well and always have something to talk about. But none of the girls have ever showed me any judgment despite what Becca might have told them. My grudge has never been with them.

"Ready?" Danny asks.

Caleb is looking between Becca and me, lips twitching into a frown but staying silent.

I give a feeble nod before turning to the angry girl in front of me. "For the record, I'm sorry. I wanted to tell you in person so you didn't find out this way. I did try though."

That's all I say before walking around her and joining the athletes, who look like pseudo bodyguards. It's Danny who drapes his arm around me, not taking the box from my white-knuckle grip like I'm sure he wants to. He guides us out, Caleb says goodbye to my suitemate Sammi, and I feel eyes glaring into my backside until we're out of sight.

"You okay?" Danny asks as soon as we're outside. I huddle into him, fighting the shiver from the cold weather that smacks into me.

"I was expecting that, so I'm not shocked. Like you said, I can't make everybody love me. Trying is pointless. It didn't work out. We'll both move on."

He squeezes me in a side hug and presses his lips against the top of my head. Caleb notices and smirks at us, making me dip my eyes down toward the sidewalk.

It only takes twenty minutes to get Caleb's truck unloaded and put my stuff into my new room. It's surreal to stare at the small space and realize it's all mine.

I'm finally getting a fresh start.

A new place to live.

No roommates or suitemates around.

And a boy I like who will spend time with me without anyone around to judge.

Caleb kicks the baseboard heater as if that'll help. "You may want to get maintenance to do something about this," he tells me, kneeling and putting his hand next to it. "It's barely giving off any heat."

The wall by my bed is white, glossy cement blocks, similar to my old room, and reflecting the cool air as I set some things onto the naked bed. "I'll ask Alba about it. She's supposed to come by later after she's out of her meeting with her adviser."

While the guys ask where I want certain furniture set up and begin moving the bulky pieces, Raine and Olive help me start unpacking my clothes and hanging them up in one of the closets. Olive wiggles her brows as she waves around a pair of my silk panties, causing me to shoot her a glare, while Raine sneaks a peek at Caleb with a strange look on her face.

I don't ask if she's okay and she doesn't offer any information as she turns back to the clothes and helps fold, hang, and situate everything. It isn't like we're very close.

Within an hour, my fridge is plugged in with food that I definitely didn't purchase since most of it is things Danny loves eating, my bed is made, my clothes are all put away, and my textbooks are scattered on my desk.

There's a knock at the door that has Olive and I turning.

Aliyah stands at the door, her arms crossed over her chest as she looks at my new room. I told her where I'd be staying a few days ago. Maybe part of me hoped she'd slip that information to Becca. Clearly, she kept it to herself.

"Hey," I greet, noticing the wary look as she glances at the guys and then back at Olive and me.

"Hi." Her tone is emotionless, not completely unlike herself but not necessarily normal either. She fidgets with the thick sweatshirt she's wearing before shifting to focus solely on me. "Can I talk to you?"

Everybody seems to understand she means only me, so they find reasons to scatter. Caleb goes to find Raine, Danny squeezes my arm and tells me he'll be waiting down the hall, and Olive says she's going to get ready to meet Alex. Her eyes light up, but I don't comment on that before telling her to have fun.

I sit on the edge of my bed as Aliyah closes the door behind them. "If this is about Becca—"

"It's not," she tells me, studying the shelves next to her. They've got some cleaning supplies, two small wastebaskets, and some of my extra shoes lining the bottom. "Although you could have told her sooner. She sent a text to the group chat going off on you."

My lips curl. I was never in a group chat with any of them, which is telling enough.

She blows out a breath and stares at my books, all stacked sadly on my desk. "You need one of those desk shelves that attach to the top like you had before. You could ask if there's one available. The school probably has some in storage."

"Ali, are you really here to give me furniture advice?"

Her hands still at her sides, shifting from one foot to the other, she asks, "Do you remember the night at the football house?"

My eyes widen a fraction. "Why are you even asking about that now?"

Her eyes drop to the checkered floor. "I need to know, Skylar. You said that we ditched you, and Becca says you ditched us. All *I* know is that you didn't come back with us that night."

"Does it even matter now? It was a while ago—"

"It matters to *me*," she snaps. The glare she casts me isn't the same angry one I'm accustomed to seeing on Becca's face.

It's…full of uncertainty. Fear.

"Aliyah," I say quietly, watching her stand to full height on guard. Her posture is stiff, her eyes glazed, her face flushed. "Tell me what's going on."

Her nostrils flare as she looks away.

I gape when she says, "I think I know what happened that night."

Chapter Twenty-Six

DANNY

THE TEAM HAS A week to relax before the Wilson Reed game next weekend, which means the guys will be letting loose. With Thanksgiving coming up, some of the team feels the need to party hard before going home to their families.

The last bye week we had is still gnawing on me. Aiden had to help me drag Marks out of one of Lindon's sorority houses where he was blitzed out of his mind. One of the guys almost broke his leg accepting a stupid dare that involved jumping from a roof to the pool below. If Coach had found out the shit the guys did that week, they wouldn't be as eager for any repeats this time around.

With Aiden occupied with Ivy these days, I don't have anyone to help me straighten the guys out. If I had to do a search and rescue, I'd need to either peel our tight end away from his girl or our running back away from his.

And I hate that I can't ignore the pit of jealousy that pokes at my gut whenever I see couples pair off. Getting into something serious had never been my endgame when I officially signed on to be a Dragon. I thought I'd come here, play football, have some casual flings, and get my degree. But two years into playing the game—the one on *and* off the field—I got tired. Physically and mentally. My shoulder started acting up, and I knew playing football would never work long-term.

A hand whacks into my chest, making me grumble and rub the tight pectorals. "You even paying attention, fucker?"

I loosen my grip on the Xbox controller and try ignoring the pain settled into the shoulder. "Knock it off. That hurt."

"You can take it," Justin says. His smirk fades when he sees me wince as I roll my shoulders and twist my back to get my spine to crack. "Shit, you good?"

I wave it off, staring at the screen where my character is dying a brutal death. "Just sore from our last practice. No big."

"You know, Caleb said—"

"*Caleb* is a gossip," I cut him off, knowing what our running back has been blabbering to people. He's *worried* about me. He thinks I'm downplaying the pain.

Am I? Sure. But it's nothing I haven't dealt with before. A few pain relievers later, and the pain is dull at best. Tolerable. When they stop working, I text Skylar. Which usually leads to cuddles, a heavy make-out session, and a little groping. Best distraction ever.

That makes Justin snort. "That's fucking hilarious coming from you, but I'll drop it. You got plans this week?"

I stand from the couch, ignoring the video game we're in the middle of playing. My guy already got taken out, so no sense in me sticking around to get my ass whipped a second time. "Yeah, actually. You finally going to kick back, or are you burying your head in the books again?"

He grumbles something under his breath before pausing the game and setting the controller down on the coffee table. "I got early admission into two of the med schools I applied for, but they're not the ones I want to go to."

My brows shoot up. "Shit, man, that's awesome. Which colleges?"

"Albany Med and Upstate Medical University," he says.

"Isn't Upstate where you were considering?" He'd talked about it a few times in the past as if it was a serious option.

He lifts a shoulder. "Things change."

I get that. I've been looking into grad schools myself now that I've had to come to terms with the fact that football isn't my endgame. "Which ones are you still waiting to hear from?"

His eyes go to the TV screen. "Columbia, Cornell, and New York Medical."

My nose twitches. "Some Ivy Leagues in the mix, huh?"

His eyes snap to me. "Got a problem with it?" When I lift my hands in surrender, he blows out a frustrated breath and drops his head back. "I've been a bit testy waiting to hear back."

"It's all good. I didn't know you wanted to go big league, that's all. Never heard you talk about it before."

"Because I knew I couldn't afford it."

"And that's…changed." It's not a question based on the way he scrubs his jaw.

"I found out that my gramps put money aside for me for med school when he found out I wanted to follow in his footsteps. It's enough to cover most of the expenses."

"That's awesome, dude."

"It isn't if I don't get in."

"You will." How the fuck could he not? Despite his

insane sport schedule, Justin kept up with his grades and stayed top of his class. If that doesn't prove his worthiness, nothing can. "Try not to stress about it. When are you starting physical therapy? That'll definitely distract you."

He makes a face at his knee. "Next week. Supposed to start before the holidays. Coach brought in the big guns this time. Not Sanderson."

"He's sending you to Monroe?"

"Yep."

"He's good."

Only a grunt greets me, so I decide to leave it be. Letting him stew for a while, I grab my jacket and wallet and poke my head back in the living room where Justin is still sulking.

"I'm heading out for a while. Need anything before I get back?"

He chuckles. "*If* you come back."

If I had something to throw at him, I would. "Shut it, cap."

He drapes an arm over the back of the couch and shrugs. "All I'm saying is that you might as well make it official with her. We all know you want to."

I scratch my neck.

That doesn't mean Skylar wants the same thing from me. She's a freshman who's dealt with more than anyone should have. I wouldn't blame her if she wanted to keep me at a distance without putting labels on us.

Doesn't mean I like it.

~

Skylar's room is fucking freezing, so I'm not surprised when she answers with a blanket wrapped around her. "What the fuck, Blondie? Maintenance never came?"

She told me she filed a report with Alba who handed it over to custodial. "Ernie did look at it, but he said he'd need to order a couple of things that the school doesn't have on hand. It was backordered or something."

"Christ." I guide her over to the bed where she was clearly hanging out before I arrived. Her sheets are wrinkled, pillows are propped up, and comforter bunched toward the end. "Climb up. Let's get you tucked in."

She snorts. "You're such a dork."

I ignore her, covering her body and then plopping myself in the tight space next to her. "I have a few chapters left of the book, by the way. Had to force myself to put it down to go to class earlier. I think they're about to get it on."

She blushes. "I still can't believe you wanted to read it."

I shoot her a wink.

"The second one is about his best friend and little sister. I have all the books that are out in the series if you want to read them."

"No shit? His little sister…" I settle against the pillows. "Don't suppose you'd be willing to read that to me, would you?"

"Nope."

Chuckling, I turn to study her. She looks like a wrapped-up burrito. "As fucking adorable as you look right now, Ernie needs to get his shit together and fix your heater."

"Ernie is nice. Don't be mad at him."

"Blondie, only *you* could defend the guy who's freezing you to death," I muse, tweaking her red nose. Settling onto my side, I use my palm to prop my head up and watch as her eyes rake over my face.

She cuddles into the blankets, inching over slightly so we're pressed together. "It's not that hard. Ernie is the sweetest. He said he's glad Lindon gave him a chance to work because nobody else would with his disability. He got into an accident when he was twenty-four, so he's a little slower than others but hard-working. I don't think he *needs* to work, but he likes to. I respect him."

I reach over and move her hair behind her ear, tracing her cheekbones and then her jaw. "I love that you know his story. You've only been here two days."

"He's a talker and I'm a good listener." She points her chin toward the door. "He even made me a doorstop using some scrap wood he found in case I wanted to keep my door open and chat with people. Alba said the people who lived here other years used to do that all the time, but since the building is pretty empty, there's not as much of that happening these days."

I'm not sure I like the idea of her doing that since her room is so close to the side exit where most of the students come in. "That might not be safe. I imagine there's a lot of drunk people who stumble in and out of here during the weekends."

Her lips tilt upward. "Last night when I was moving some stuff to the garbage room, a couple walked in. The girl was so drunk, she stumbled into my room and sat down in my chair, telling me how much she loved all the purple things I owned."

I snicker. "Sounds about right."

"Her boyfriend kept apologizing but I think we both found it funny." Her smile lightens until something flashes in her eyes. I don't need to ask her what when she says, "Can I ask you something about that Wallace guy?"

Why the hell does she want to know anything about him? "What exactly do you want to know?"

285

There's an edge to my tone that I try keeping to myself, but it's obvious she hears it.

"Don't get all weird on me," she mumbles, wiggling until one of her arms is free from her blanket. She rests it under her cheek after turning on her side so we're facing each other. "I'm only asking because Ali told me he made her really uncomfortable during some party she was at. And she and I may not be very close, but that doesn't mean I don't care. She's been really off. Even Becca has said she hasn't been acting like herself. There's something more to the story that she hasn't told me, but I get a bad feeling."

My face screws. "Why would she come to you about him?"

There's a brief pause when I think the absolute worst before she murmurs, "Because he was at the party at your house. He's part of *your* team, and people know that you and I...hang out."

I blink. "Okaaay..."

"There's talk," she tells me. "About Wallace. Aliyah said there were girls at the party who mentioned seeing him slip things into girls' drinks. It's only party gossip, so I don't know how true it is, but it seems like something worth bringing up."

My body stiffens at the information. If Wallace was seen doing that to other girls, what are the chances there's a connection between him and the night Skylar was assaulted? "What exactly is your question, Skylar? Going to need you to spell this one out for me."

The way her teeth sink into her bottom lip as she looks away for a second has me reaching over and gripping her hip, squeezing once until she focuses back on me. "You haven't heard about this, have you? You've said that he's bad news before, but I assumed you meant he played girls and slept around. Not, well, *that*."

"Do you honestly believe I'd let that sort of thing slide if I knew?" I ask her, flabbergasted she even has to ask. "Or that the other guys would? You know Caleb by now. You've talked to Justin. Marks may be an idiot, but he'd never let Wallace get away with hurting women. None of us would let that sort of thing happen on our watch." The fact that she even has to question me tightens the muscles in my chest. Rubbing the tension away with my closed fist, I shake my head. "Look, I don't know what truth lies in that. Wallace is usually all talk and no show, but if he *is* doing that, then it needs to be reported to campus police."

"There's no evidence."

We lock eyes again, hers weary. "It may not matter if there is or not," I reason quietly. "But if there's a report with his name attached to it, then there's something to work with just in case an incident comes up. A paper trail will protect *any* girl he could potentially take advantage of."

She thinks about it before nodding, but I don't think she's willing to put two and two together like I am. Her forehead rests against the crook of my neck, a sigh releasing from her. "I guess."

I move my hand from her hip to her back, rubbing circles on it until she eases into me. "It's nice that you want to help Aliyah even though you're not close. You're a good person, Sky."

This time, she's quiet.

Quiet isn't always good when it leaves you to your thoughts. And mine right now aren't pretty. Because Wallace talks a lot of talk around here and always has something to say about the girls he's with. But how many of them actually *wanted* to be with him? And if one of those girls was the one curled up next to me…

My nostrils flare.

Skylar and I stay like that for a while, listening to the shuffle of feet pass by her door and the opening and closing of the side exit as people come and go. Her nose brushes against the column of my throat, causing me to pull myself out of my head and back into the moment. I bite back a groan when I feel her shift until warm lips brush against the same slice of skin.

"What are you doing?" I ask, voice shaky as her lips move downward.

"Warming up," she says against my skin.

I tip my head back and feel her teeth graze the edge of my throat before skimming toward my collarbone. "Shouldn't it be the other way around?"

I feel her smile against me as her fingertips dance along the front of my stomach. "Trust me, I'm nice and toasty right now."

I fucking bet.

Her fingers stop just above the waistband of the joggers I slipped on before coming here. I look down and see her eyes staring at the obvious bulge growing between us. "Sorry, I can't really help it. You're touching me and all I can think about is—"

"I can stop if you want," she tells me nervously, glancing up through her lashes. "But I don't want to. I want to return the favor from last time. To…touch you. Maybe not, um, the other thing. Yet. But you could teach me how to get you off with my hand."

"You're going to kill me," I wheeze, dropping my head onto her pillow.

"Is that a yes?"

I swipe her face with my thumb, tweaking her bottom lip. "Do you really want to? Because I didn't come here for any of that. I just wanted to hang out. Cuddle. Didn't realize how much of a cuddler I was until you. But that's all."

She watches me for a second before nodding slowly. "I know. But I want to. I'm just not sure how exactly. Show me how you like it."

I close my eyes for a second to try calming the beast down. One little touch could set me off, that's how hard I am right now. My reply comes out husky as I say, "Okay."

She helps me lower the hem of my sweats, paying extra attention to the way the long pipe between my legs is trying to greet her as it tents my boxers.

"We don't have to," I remind her, hands stilling on the elastic of my underwear. She doesn't say anything as she carefully lowers those too until my erection is freed.

Her small intake of breath has me pinching my eyes closed. I can't handle the way she's looking at me right now. It's too damn much.

I jerk instantly when I feel her hand wrap around my shaft and squeeze lightly. "*God dammit.*"

She quickly lets go. "Did I hurt—"

"Do it again," I beg, guiding her hand back to my aching dick. "Like this. Squeeze here and pump up. Just like— *fuuuuck.* Yeah, baby, just like that." Her hand feels like heaven as it pumps me from base to tip. I keep my hand on hers, guiding the movement, helping her find the grip, tightening it for the perfect pressure, twisting it at the perfect place, and moving it at a torturous pace.

My hips move to fill our palms, my dick twitching as she jerks me faster. I'm so goddamn close I'm embarrassed when

I start leaking precum. And when her thumb brushes my tip to trail it down and lubricate me, it's what does me in.

"Coming," I warn, hips frantically thrusting into her palm as she clenches me tighter and keeps stroking.

The gargled noise coming from my throat as I empty onto our fists has her staring at the mess, then up at me like she's mesmerized by it.

With my clean hand, I swipe down my face and shake my head. My legs feel numb as I stare up at the ceiling. "That was better than I fantasized about," I tell her, glancing down at her. I peck her lips and grab a tissue from the corner of the desk, wiping us both off. Blowing out a breath, I pull my boxers and joggers back on, dispose of the dirty tissue, and crawl back onto the bed. "Can I touch you?"

She looks hesitant. "That was supposed to be payback for you since you—"

"Sky." I press my lips to hers to stop her from talking. "There is no 'payback' when it comes to intimacy. We get each other off because we want to, not because we're obligated. And I really, *really* want to fuck you with my fingers until I feel you clenching them so hard I come in my pants again. Feel me?"

Her breath shutters.

"So can I?" I ask again, not making a single move until I get her permission.

One of her arms wraps around my neck, pulling me down to kiss her. Against my lips, she breathes, "Yes."

I grin victoriously.

Justin is right.

I don't come home that night.

Because I make Skylar come three more times long after the sun goes down—once with my fingers, once with my tongue, and once with all our clothes on and her grinding against my leg like two teenagers who can't get enough.

We fall asleep wrapped up in each other in her small bed in sated oblivion in the early hours of the morning.

But when she starts thrashing in the middle of the night, my eye takes the brunt of the impact. I grab hold of her arm to stop her from hitting me again, which only makes her go crazier.

"Skylar!" I say, shaking her shoulder.

She cries out, eyelids closed and twitching as she fights my hold.

"Sky, it's a nightmare," I coax, even though I know the truth.

Whatever is happening isn't a nightmare at all. It's real for her.

My voice cracks. "Wake up, baby."

I loosen my hold once her body starts calming down, and only then do I press my lips against her cheek and watch as her eyelids flutter open tiredly.

"Danny?" she breaths, tears streaming down her face.

"Blondie…" I press my lips together and brush the pads of my thumbs along her cheekbones to dry the dampness on them. "You need to talk to somebody. *Please.*"

She's silent.

"*Please.*"

Chapter Twenty-Seven

SKYLAR

OLIVE IS BOUNCING WITH excitement as we follow a group of people down the stands of the Wilson Reed stadium. I double-check the tickets Danny left with someone up front before studying the numbers on the ends of the rows we're nearing.

"I think this is us," I tell my friend as she takes in the surroundings. A mixture of red for the Dragons and gold for the Raiders takes over the packed stadium, and the noise is already insane. I can only imagine what it'll be like when the game actually starts.

I wasn't sure what to expect, but it definitely wasn't *this*.

Olive grabs my arm as I steer us toward the two seats our tickets are for. "I still can't believe he got you to come," she says.

Her words are innocent enough, but my mind still twists them into something much dirtier. The whole reason I'm in Massachusetts at Wilson Reed University is because I agreed in my postorgasmic state to not only cheer him on during this game but to spend Thanksgiving break with him and his family since mine were scattered around the country for the holidays.

I'm not even sure how we managed to have a full conversation with all the exploration we'd done on each other the two nights in a row we spent together in my room, followed by a whole day of reading, doing homework, and watching movies at his place.

Since my parents are going on a cruise to the Bahamas for Thanksgiving, Serenity is spending the holiday with her fiancé, and Serena and Sienna are doing a trip with their friends to Las Vegas, I planned on staying in Lindon. They invited me to tag along, but I knew I wouldn't have any fun. And after a twenty-minute lecture on how Lindon would be closed down and I'd have nothing to do or nowhere to go, Danny convinced me to come to Boston after the big game with him.

I blame the things he did to me with his hands and mouth, along with his smooth talk, which involved pretty words whispered about my curves and boobs.

Plus, I owed him for the shiner I gave him during our first sleepover. He hasn't brought it up because I always shut it down, but I can tell he wants to talk about it.

"Talk to somebody," he pleaded.

I called the campus therapist but hung up when somebody answered because I'm not ready. Will I ever be?

Olive is holding a huge plastic cup of Coca-Cola and a bottle of water for me, grinning as she takes in her surroundings. I know she smuggled snacks in her bag since she never carries one this big normally.

I settle into my seat and zip my jacket up higher to protect myself from the cold air. "It was hard to tell him no,"

I admit begrudgingly. Besides the orgasms, all he has to do is give me those puppy-dog eyes and I'm weak. "Thanks for driving us, by the way."

Olive wasn't going to say no to going to a football game, especially a free one. Not even when I told her it was an away one. She knows Danny plans on stealing me away to go to his childhood home for the rest of break and has made it blatantly obvious how excited she is for me...and my vagina.

One day during lunch at Reavers, she came right out and said, "Girl, it's about time he gave you the glow. It doesn't matter if you won't tell me the details. It's obvious that he's doing you right based on that look in your eyes."

I was too afraid to ask what look that was because I knew she wouldn't have held back. If seeing the hungry gaze she gives Alex whenever they cross paths is any indication, I'm sure my expression isn't that different when I pass Danny.

I sent him a text when we got here, knowing the team's bus arrived hours before. Hunkering down as people get to their seats and talk among themselves, I pull out my phone and examine the reply I got.

Danny: Don't fall for me too hard when you see how amazing I am out there

I almost snort again, which was the same reaction I had when I saw it come through originally.

When I saw Aliyah, Dee, and Becca at the dining hall yesterday, I was pretty shocked when my former roommate asked what I had planned for the holiday. I even wondered if she was extending an olive branch of sorts by making idle conversation. A branch I would have accepted happily considering I hadn't heard a word from her since moving out.

I barely see Dee anymore, and Aliyah talks to me in class and walks with me when we leave, but she usually disappears to meet up with the others soon after. It's become obvious that sides were chosen, and Olive and Danny are the only two on mine.

I could let it upset me, but then my time is being spent on people who aren't worthy of it. Because the biggest thing I've learned in my over three months at Lindon is that friendship is about the people who walk into your life when everybody else walks out. And the two who I do have are all I need.

An elbow nudges my rib cage, making me turn to Olive. "Alex texted me this morning. He said that the Canadiens have been scouting him."

I stare blankly at her.

"It's Montreal's NHL team," she explains nonchalantly. "Anyway, he's going to check out their arena and speak to some of their reps and then head back to the States for the rest of break. We've talked about meeting up."

"Now I know the real reason you agreed to drive this way," I tease, nudging her back. "I see how it is. You want to link up with him."

She scoffs. "Bitch, please. If I didn't agree to come, you'd be so lost sitting here. Plus, you know how much I love football. Not as much as hockey, but it's a strong second."

She and Alex have been keeping things "casual" between them from what she's said. How casual, I don't know. Unlike Becca, who used to spew details about the men in her life without any prodding, Olive is tight-lipped about her situation with her brother's nemesis. Besides the first time they hooked up, she hasn't been as loose on where they stand. But if they're planning on meeting up over break, it has to mean something.

"What does Sebastian say about that?" I ask, even if her brother's opinion doesn't matter. Still, I know she's close with him—to her whole family. She already admitted she didn't want to cause a rift by getting involved with people they don't approve of.

She shrugs. "He doesn't know. Unless something happens, I don't see why he needs to. He's got too much on his plate with the Rangers to deal with anything else. And Alex hasn't boasted about this and neither have his loyal cronies, so I doubt he'll find out anytime soon."

I'm surprised nobody has said a word, which only cements my suspicions about this being way more than casual. "You're being careful though, right?"

Olive gives me an exasperated sigh. "If you're asking if he's wearing a condom, then the answer is yes."

Heat blasts my face as two older guys a row ahead of us turn and grin, clearly amused by this conversation.

"Oh my God!" I hiss, smacking my friend as she cracks up over my embarrassment. "I was referring to your feelings. The last thing I want is for you to get hurt because he decides to do something stupid to get back at your brother."

Thankfully, the guys in front of us have lost interest. They're pointing at something on the field and mumbling about it.

Olive sighs, wiggling to get comfortable in her seat and passing me my water. "Don't worry about me. I know the risks. Like I've told you, he and I aren't—"

"Anything serious," I finish for her, barely able to contain my frown. When I asked if they were exclusive, I hadn't brought up the party where I'd seen him making out with another girl. Especially when Olive told me, with a sour look on her face, that she doubted they were that serious because of his reputation.

"Anyway, focus on you. You've got Lindon's wide receiver panting after you. I swear, the second you said you were spending Thanksgiving with his family, I nearly peed myself. You two would make adorable babies, by the way. I used that photo app I showed you once to merge your—"

"Why would you do that?" I cover my eyes and try holding back the bubbled laugh that builds in my throat. "He's...we're..."

"See!" She points at me. "You don't even know what you are. So I guess you'll have to keep telling me the same 'just friends' bullshit until you actually believe it yourself."

My nose scrunches. "He *is* my friend."

Who makes me laugh and gives me orgasms.

The best kind of friend.

"Of course you are. And he makes a great friend. A very tentative one based on the way you're biting your lip right now. But if you *wanted* to become more than that to him, I highly doubt he'd say no. Guys don't ask girls to meet their family for the sake of friendship. He's spending an entire break with you when he could be out doing God knows what with other chicks."

"Olive—"

She holds up her finger and then leans forward to tap the stranger in front of her on his shoulder. He turns, smirking. "Hi. Can you tell us if you'd bring a girl home to meet your family if you weren't interested in having more than a platonic relationship with her?"

He instantly shakes his head. "My family is a lot. Wouldn't want to subject any woman to that unless I knew she could handle it."

That hardly proves anything. I say, "Ignore my friend. She's off her meds."

The guy and his buddy laugh, turning back to face the field, where people are starting to move around on the sidelines.

I glare at Olive. "He invited me because he knew I didn't have anywhere else to be."

"You know that's crap. If you'd told me about your family's plans, which you didn't until you'd already agreed to go home with him by the way, I would have extended an invite to my place. My mom adores you. When we FaceTime, she asks if you're around because she wants to know how you are and what Jane Austen book you're discussing in class." Her eyes roll. "But that's beside the point. You could have come to my house. You could have gone with your sisters to Sin City. Yet you chose to go home with DJ. Tell yourself whatever you want, but even you know there's something way more going on between the two of you than whatever you do at night together."

Because I don't know what to say, how to get her to think differently—or myself for that matter—I press my lips together and stare out on the field.

I know one thing for sure. I like Danny.

But thinking about how I see something working with him scares me, because if we change the dynamic between us, I could lose a friend if it doesn't work out. Nothing is promised or guaranteed. Least of all us. I'm not sure I can handle losing him if one of us decides that it's not worth the fight.

Chapter Twenty-Eight

DANNY

"With a six-point lead on their home turf, the Raiders might finally break Lindon's winning streak," the commentator says, getting an enthusiastic response from the audience dressed in white and gold.

I huff under my breath and jog back over to the bench where the guys are hydrating. "If they think they've got this in the bag already, they haven't seen shit yet."

Caleb fist-bumps me. "Hell yeah." We both turn to Aiden, who's eyeing the stands where his girl, her brother, and his parents are. "I think if we get the element of surprise, we can gain on them. What do you think, Griff?"

He snaps his attention back to us, bringing his water bottle to his mouth. "Yeah, pretty sure that'll be Coach's next play."

"We've got this," I tell him, knowing how much this victory means. He's been on edge leading up to this game, and the second he stepped onto this campus, his tension grew. None of us really know the extent of the bullshit he endured during his Wilson Reed days, just the bare basics.

If there's one thing all the Dragons can agree on, it's that we're determined to win this for the guy the Raiders stupidly gave up.

Coach Pearce calls us to huddle and goes over the game play. He looks at each of us, at Aiden extra hard, before breaking. When we jog back out onto the field, I search the crowd for the brunette who I grinned at while doing my little sideline show at halftime. I saw her shake her head while her friend—and a handful of other women—filmed my slick moves.

The girl about to spend a handful of days with my family has her eyes plastered in my direction right now. I wish she could see the grin spread across my face, but my helmet blocks it. I notice Caleb looking in my direction and tipping his own protected head toward the men getting into formation.

We get into positions.

My eyes train on my targets.

Studying.

Cautious.

When the ball flies and my team bolts into action, I block out the noise around me and focus solely on getting Lindon to its next win.

For Aiden.

For the Dragons.

I don't know how it goes wrong.

One second we're flying a yard at a time to the end zone, everybody doing what Coach told us to by the playbook, and then Wallace is breaking free and running his own maneuvers to steal the ball as it passes between the Raiders.

I curse to myself when I see him swerve through the opposing team, catch the ball as it flies in the air, and try making the touchdown himself.

He's getting close, but I can tell instantly that the two guys coming after him will tackle his ass to the ground in a matter of seconds unless someone stops them. I break from formation and try fixing the mess that the dumbass made for himself, ready to take down the biggest guy who's nipping at his heels.

That's when it happens.

I'm jumping to take down the brute chasing after Wallace when my body makes impact with another much larger one. I'm slammed into the ground and sliding yard by yard across the turf.

There's a collective gasp from the crowd, mixed with the cheers from the Raiders fans over the brutal takedown as my body bounces a few feet. Pain radiates down my entire right side as I finally stop moving.

And I know, I fucking *know*, something is wrong.

I heard the pop.

Felt the burning pain through my body like someone took a lighter to gasoline.

Excruciating.

That's the only way to describe it.

A whistle blows when I fail to get up, and someone starts yelling. The crowd starts going wild—over what, I don't know. All I can think about is the fire shooting from my shoulder as I pinch my eyes closed.

Don't fucking cry.

Don't you dare fucking cry.

A few faces appear above me when I finally open my eyes. Caleb and Marks, and one other dude in the other team's gear. He's the one who cusses and extends a hand, unaware of the turmoil coursing through my body. "Fuck, man. I didn't mean to hit you that hard."

Red Bowen.

Goddamn Red *Fucking* Bowen.

Another Massachusetts native. He and I went to high school together for a hot minute before he got himself kicked out.

"DJ?" Caleb asks, worry in his tone when I fail to sit up. "You good?"

I clench my teeth, trying to calm my breathing. "Shoulder" is all I manage to rasp.

Somebody mumbles something about my helmet when I finally force myself to sit up, but I don't know what they say. My head hurts, my arm hurts worse, and I'm *angry*. And at this point, I can't even tell at what.

A ref and one of the members of the medical team jog over to where I'm sitting dazed and pissed. The three guys watching give them access to me to check me over.

People are watching.

My team.

Theirs.

Our fans.

Our enemies.

"Get me the fuck out of here," I tell whoever will listen when I can't stand the scrutiny from the mixed reactions around us. This time, when Red offers me his hand, I use my good one to help get tugged up to my feet.

Every part of my body screams in protest, but I force myself to get past it.

The people here rooting for the Dragons who are decked out in red all start clapping and cheering in support as I'm escorted off the field and toward the locker room.

Raiders fans are clapping for other reasons that I don't let myself think about, or else steam will start coming from my ears.

Coach catches up. "What's wrong, son?"

"It's my shoulder," I grumble, my arm limp at my side. I don't want to move it—don't know how the fuck I'm going to get out of the protective gear that obviously didn't do shit for me today.

Frustration bubbles to the surface, and all I want to do is yell and hit something. A locker. A wall. Red for coming at me so hard. Wallace for his existence. Coach because he'll walk back out and refocus as if he doesn't give a shit one of his own is being looked over.

I run a hand through my hair as I'm guided to sit down on the bench inside the locker room we were assigned.

It takes twenty minutes of fighting, sweating, and cussing before my top half is bare and exposed to the professionals examining my injuries. I have to bite down on my knuckle when Claire, the medical professional who's worked on me a few times before, starts examining my arm.

To distract myself, I look at the massive crack in the back of my helmet from where my head must have slammed against the ground when I landed. No wonder I've got a headache.

"You're lucky," Claire says, seeing what's captured my attention. "I'll need to get X-rays done, but I'm positive your shoulder is dislocated at the least. And I know you already have problems with tendonitis in this shoulder, so I imagine this will make that flare even after its set and healed. Are you dizzy? Blurry vision?"

I've got a headache drumming in my skull that increases with each passing minute, so I tell her as much.

"How many fingers am I holding up?" she asks, holding up two. Why do they always hold up two?

"I'm not blind, Claire."

"I'm trying to make sure you haven't sustained any other injuries. You know how this works, Bridges. Entertain me."

I sigh. "Two."

She nods and goes back to examining my shoulder, careful of how she moves it. I clench my teeth and grind my jaw with every small touch no matter how gentle she tries being. "You definitely need imaging done. I'm not sure if I should set it here in case it's something worse that I could damage more. I'm going to request a full body scan at the nearest hospital so they can check out everything to be on the safe side. In the meantime, I'll need you to wear a sling to immobilize it." She digs through her shit and produces the uncomfortable monstrosity that I've had to wear before.

"I'm not going anywhere until the game is finished," I tell her. "So set the damn thing."

"DJ—"

"Claire," I challenge.

She sighs, shaking her head but doing as I ask. I have to bite back the rapid curses as she works my shoulder back into place, then helps me put on a clean T-shirt before getting my arm into the pain-in-the-ass contraption.

"You know how it works. Once we get the results from the image tests, we'll go from there. Take two of these"—she dumps a couple tablets into her palm and passes them to me—"every six to eight hours as needed."

Long after she's gone to make some calls, I remain in the locker room sulking. My head drops forward, hanging dejectedly between my shoulders until the bite of pain from the muscle movement is too much.

I hear the telltale signs of my phone going off in the locker across from me, so I dig it out and see a string of texts from various people.

Ma: Please tell me you're okay.
Ma: CALL ME RIGHT NOW!
Grandma M: If you need us to come get you, say
　　the word. I'll kick those Raiders' butts myself
Raine: What's the prognosis? That was a hard hit

Yeah, no shit. I can still feel it.

Justin: You doing okay, man?

He didn't end up coming to this game, so he must be watching at home. After his physical therapy session, he said he would be too uncomfortable stuffed in the bus with us. Coach wasn't happy about it, but then again, when is he?

Blondie: Are you okay???
Blondie: Can I come see you?

There are other messages, but I ignore them all after seeing hers. Scratching my jaw and letting out a heavy breath, I listen to the distant rumblings of the crowd and wonder what's going on. Who's scoring? Who's in the lead?

At last count, the Raiders were.

After my fall, they probably will be until the final countdown.

Me: I'll live, Blondie
Blondie: Are you hurt bad?

My eyes go to the arm.

Me: I've had worse

It's not entirely true, but I know it's what she needs to hear right now. Usually I deal with concussions, which I won't be shocked to hear I have yet another of after this game, but that's it. A day of rest, a game or two on the bench, and I'm back to new.

This time? I don't think I'll be so lucky.

Me: I can give ur name to one of the workers and
     tell them to send u this way
Me: If u want...

Ten minutes later, the sound of my voice being called from the doorway has me turning. There's a security guard who gives me a pointed look like he's warning us from doing anything he'll have to hear from outside the door.

"Hey," Skylar greets, walking in hesitantly.

"It's just us," I assure her.

Her body eases as she stops beside me.

I don't think before wrapping my good arm around her waist and tugging her into my lap. She's careful not to brush my bad arm as she settles in, body a little stiff until I loosen my grip to let her know she can move anytime she wants.

I just...need to be near her.

Her fruity scent that smells like peaches and vanilla.

Her warmth that thaws some of my bitterness.

I lean my head against her shoulder and heft out a sigh. "We're going to lose," I tell her, feeling it in my gut.

"You don't know that."

But I do. With me out and Wallace making his own plays, the team is disjointed. We're not working as a unit like we're supposed to. If I'd kept at the play Coach told us to do,

I wouldn't be sitting here. I'd be with my team, geared up, fighting until the end.

I simply shake my head.

Her hand comes down and takes mine, weaving our fingers together. She rests them on her leg, brushing the back of my hand with her thumb. I close my eyes and absorb the moment.

There's a beat where it's silent between us. Then, "I'm glad you came, Skylar."

She doesn't hesitate. "Me too."

I turn my head and brush my lips against her shoulder, covered in layers to keep her warm.

Even then, she still shivers.

In a shaky breath, she repeats, "Me too."

~

Hours later, the doctor in the emergency room points to the lit-up image hanging on the wall, tapping on a few different spots. "See this? There appears to be tearing in the ligaments. Knowing your history, it could have been there long before this point, especially with your sport, but it was definitely worsened by today's injury."

Ma squeezes my hand like the doc is telling me I have six months to live. As soon as she saw the fading shiner I have on top of the sling holding my arm, she about lost her mind.

She insisted on going with me to the hospital despite me suggesting Skylar come with me instead. But when she pointed out Skylar's never driven around here before, she made it her mission to be the one to play chauffeur.

The salt-and-pepper-haired doctor gives me a solemn, almost apologetic look. "The ligaments previously torn were damaged again. Some worse than others. Not going to lie, son. Surgery would be a good option for you. It'd be the best one you have."

I start to shake my head in protest. "I don't think—"

"Will it fix the problem?" Ma asks before I can reject the idea outright. She shoots me a look to stay quiet before turning back to the expert.

"It'll help with stability," he explains. "If treated early enough, there's less of a chance that he'll have permanent damage. But playing football will always increase the probability of reinjury even after the procedure."

Ma makes a disgruntled noise. When she found out I went back out to watch the last quarter despite being told to come here instead, she wasn't happy with me. She was even less thrilled to find out I stormed the field after that jackass took Aiden down.

I rub my neck. "I've been having some problems with my shoulder over the past couple of months. Bites of pain. Nothing too bad. Was that a sign that I'd damaged it before this game?"

I ignore the glare from the woman I get my looks from as the doc nods. "Most likely. You mentioned that you'd done physical therapy, which can help strengthen the injured area, but if it's damaged even in the slightest way without a full chance to heal, that injury can worsen. Contact sports commonly cause these problems. Eventually, you're risking the full mobility of your arm."

"Daniel!" my mother chides. "How many times have we talked about this? You need to be more careful—"

"It's not about being careful," I remind her, gesturing toward the specialist sitting across from us. "Like he said, football players get beat up all the time. Until I stop—"

"*When* you stop," she corrects firmly.

"—I won't be in the clear for good."

We have a stare off before the doctor clears his throat. "Listen, Daniel."

"It's DJ," I grumble, mood souring by the second. I wish Skylar were here.

"DJ," he says. "It's inevitably your choice. But you're not going to be able to play for a while. You need to let your shoulder recover. If you choose surgery, that recovery time will double, but it'll be a better option to ensure the use of your arm long-term. If you've been having trouble with the pain and mobility before, it'll only get worse if you keep avoiding the core reason for it. And if you have the procedure and choose to go back, the chances of you needing another one are highly likely."

I know he's right. I know that Ma's worry is valid. Hell, I know I'd be stupid to say no to surgery. I'd already decided that football wasn't going to be my endgame. But saying goodbye to it now, sooner than I anticipated, sucks.

"I wanted to finish the season," I tell them both, swiping a hand down my face. "That was all I fucking wanted. To end senior year with a bang doing something I loved."

If I choose the surgery now, I'll be done with football for good. If I choose not to get it and let my shoulder heal on its own, I *may* be able to play one or two more games by the time the season ends.

Ma's face softens as she squeezes my arm once. "Sweetie, I get it. This isn't ideal for anyone, but you need to put yourself first. How many times have you told that to me and your grandmother? To your own teammates? Once they hear about this, they'll tell you the same thing we are."

I don't answer her.

After two hours, I'm finally discharged.

I don't agree to the surgery.

But I don't tell the doctor no either.

I accept his card, tell him I'll be in touch when I've decided, and follow Ma out of the emergency room.

When we're in her car, she turns it on, lowers the volume to her favorite classic rock station, and says, "We won't talk about it right now."

My chin dips once in acknowledgment.

"Instead," she hedges, voice lighter and prodding, "we can talk about that beautiful girl who looked worried sick about you and is waiting for you in the guest room."

I shake my head. "Don't go daydreaming about anything, Ma. I already told you where Sky and I stand. Leave it be."

She hums. "All I'm saying is that I've been waiting for the day you brought a girl home to introduce to me."

I snort, turning to her skeptically. "Since when? You've always been worried I'd knock up some poor, helpless girl and come home with news of my impending fatherhood."

Her lips stretch into a coy smile. "I only said that to scare you away from doing it. But if it ever happened, you know I'd love you and that baby no matter what. Just because your father and I made some rough decisions way too young doesn't mean you will. You're responsible. And Skylar? I can see the sadness in her eyes. I don't know why it's there and I won't ask. What I do know is that you're good for her, no matter what you two are to each other. She seems good for you too. Give it time, Danny Boy."

The rest of the car ride is quiet.

She hums along to the songs playing.

I stare out the window and think about football. About grad school.

And inevitably, about Skylar Allen.

Chapter Twenty-Nine

SKYLAR

I LOOK BETWEEN THE crowded market and my own personal tour guide. "Are you sure your arm is going to be okay? It seems packed in there."

Danny was told to keep his arm immobilized for a few days to give it time to heal, and I can tell it still hurts when he takes the sling off to do a few small stretches suggested by the specialist. "You obviously talked to my mother," he grumbles.

Caroline *did* talk to me this morning when she found out our plans for the day. When someone knocked on the door to the guest room, I expected to see Danny standing there. When his mother greeted me with a soft smile, one very similar to her son's, I invited her in, and she expressed her concerns.

His mom is exactly as I'd expect her to be knowing what kind of man Danny is. She's warmer than my own mother, a lot more welcoming, and someone who obviously loves her family very, very much.

"Your mom loves you," I say, watching his face soften from the tense irritation. My voice slightly quieter than before, I add, "And I care about you too. I don't want people to smack into you. Especially if you haven't made up your mind about the surgery."

He steps closer to me to let a large group of people pass on the busy walkway. I gaze down at his boots when he replies, "What do *you* think I should do about that?"

I peek up at him. "It's not my decision to make. You have to figure out what's best for you and your body."

He stares down at me, reaching out with his good hand and cupping my cheek. When he leans down, I think he's going to kiss me, and I hold my breath with the anticipation. But all he does is rest his forehead on mine and nuzzle our noses together. "Four years, Skylar," he murmurs, his breath tickling my lips.

"Four years what?"

That hand cupping my face tightens before loosening and dropping back to his side. With a heavy sigh, he steps away to put space between us. "That's how long I've been waiting for something like this. Didn't even know it until now."

I gape at him in confusion, my chest filling with endless flutters that rise from the bottom of my tummy.

He shakes his head, scraping his hand through his hair before reaching down and taking one of my hands. The way our fingers weave together instantly feels natural. "C'mon, Blondie. You'll love all the food options in Quincy."

We hold hands the rest of the day.

In the market.

Finding a seat on the steps outside.

Exploring the various stores.

The only time we let go of each other is when he pays

for the trinkets I find at gift stores, things I'm sure he couldn't care less about since he's lived in the city his whole life, or when he pays for our tickets into the aquarium so I can see the penguins.

By the time we get a cab back to Beacon Hill, I've got a bag of souvenirs on my lap, a full stomach, and a stuffed penguin perched between me and the boy who's watching me with a huge smile on his face.

That's how long I've been waiting for something like this.

When I meet his eye, nothing is said between us. He pecks my cheek, breathes me in, and squeezes my hand once, twice, a third time.

Skin buzzing with a mixture of nervousness and excitement, I can't help but wonder, *what is it you've been waiting for?*

~

Sinking into the soft mattress, I prop my phone against my stuffed penguin and watch as Serena helps Sienna do her hair in a French braid through FaceTime. "Have you been to the harbor?" she asks.

"We passed by it, but he wants to take me on a boat tour before we leave."

The girls share a look before turning to the phone they have on their hotel bathroom counter and grin.

It's Sienna who says, "Do we need to have the safe sex talk with you, little sister? I know we gave you the condensed version when you were with that douchebag—"

"Si!" Serena chides.

Sienna shrugs nonchalantly. "He *was* a douche. We all thought so. We just didn't say anything because it wasn't up to us to decide who she dates."

I'm gaping, honestly shocked that they didn't say anything when I was with Ryan. It was a short-lived relationship, but still. "You all said you liked him!"

"We lied," Sienna says.

Serena adds, "Duh." She sighs, pausing on the work she's doing on Sienna's hair. "It's not like we thought he was *awful* for you."

That's not exactly a rave review.

"Yeah," Sienna agrees. "As far as first boyfriends go, he wasn't bad. Remember Dylan? Between his on-again, off-again relationship with Mia Bishop, he was Serenity's first boyfriend. That boy screamed trouble from the start, especially bouncing between two different women before finally settling down with one of them."

I'd completely forgotten about Dylan Casanova. The famous singer is married to pop princess Mia Bishop last I knew. When he and Serenity went out, I vaguely remember him coming over and messing up my hair and trying to suck up to Dad because it was obvious that Dad didn't like him. I don't think he and Serenity dated very long because of his weird dating history, so I suppose I see their point.

"Oh, what about Mackenzie?" Serena quips excitedly. "He was a total dick. Remember what he did to Dad's liquor cabinet that one time when we had that huge party?"

Sienna groans. "I thought we were going to forget about the misfortune of my first." She looks at the phone and says, "Trust me, Skylar. Ryan was a saint compared to Mack. He was practically an alcoholic by the time he was twenty. I thought I wanted a bad boy, but he was next level."

Why don't I remember him? "I don't even know who that is."

She looks contemplative. "In hindsight, he mostly snuck

in through the back when everyone was sleeping so we could—"

"She doesn't need to hear the details," Serena cuts her off, swatting her arm. "It's bad enough *I* had to hear the things you two did. Our poor, easily influenced sister doesn't need to learn all the ways you were corrupted by Mr. AA."

"As if you're one to talk!" Sienna points out, eyes narrowed. "Who do *you* want to talk about first? Clinton or Watson?"

Serena gasps. "That's not fair! I didn't even know I was technically dating Watson when I agreed to go out with Clinton. He just assumed we were an official thing."

I snicker, remembering how that went down when the three of them wound up at some event Mom and Dad dragged us to. "Didn't Watson punch Clinton in the face after he found you two at that gala together?"

Sienna bursts out laughing. "Yes! I thought Mom was going to combust from the embarrassment. It wound up on one of those tabloid websites the next morning with pictures and everything. What was the headline? 'Son of multimillionaire defends honor of well-known investment banker's daughter.' What a load of shit, am I right?"

I have to squeeze my lips together to stop from joining her. Serena isn't even half as amused as we are by it. She glares at the both of us before going back to the hair in front of her. "I can't believe you two think it's so funny. Let's move on, hmm? The point is, Ryan wasn't so bad, but he wasn't great. Especially not for you. But this Daniel guy—"

"Danny," I correct her.

"I read people call him DJ," Sienna cuts in knowingly.

My brows pinch. "You 'read' that, huh?"

Serena holds her hands up. "I only told her about him after you texted me to turn down our offer to join us here."

"The last place I want to be is in the land of debauchery with a group of women who love clubbing and drinking. I hate that stuff."

Sienna snorts unattractively. "I've seen photos of your host, Sky Sister. It's obvious you want your debauchery to happen in Boston instead."

I'm glad they're not paying enough attention to see the color washing over my cheekbones. "Shut up."

"She's not denying it."

"Is he better than Ryan?" Sienna prods.

"He has to be," Serena remarks. "Ryan was young and probably not that experienced. I bet he didn't even know what a clit was."

My sisters nod in agreement, Sienna humming. "I bet you're right. Does your football friend know how to score?"

"That was lame," I muse, trying to avoid having to answer. I'm not that lucky.

"Maybe so, but I still expect an answer. Between Ryan and DJ, who's made you come more? Because I've been with jocks before and—"

"You were with *one* soccer player," Serena cuts her off. "That hardly counts."

"Are you forgetting that time I took our professional tennis player-turned-coach into the bathroom of the country club and—"

"You *didn't!*" Serena's outburst means she obviously doesn't remember that little detail. If memory serves, their tennis coach was in his fifties back then...

Huh.

"I wouldn't know about Ryan. We never got that far," I tell them, dispersing whatever is going on in their hotel room. They both turn to me and gape.

"Come again?" Sienna replies.

Serena nods slowly. "Yeah, I thought you two had—"

"Just because you guys threw condoms at me and told me to take him out for a test run doesn't mean I did," I deadpan. The condoms they gave me expired before I moved to Lindon, so I had to throw them out.

"*Are you a virgin?*" they ask at the same time in that weird, shrill voice they use when they're mind-blown about something.

I face plant into the bed when they start tossing question after question at me in rapid succession. It's too much, so I groan into the comforter and regret even telling them the truth. I could have lied and said I had sex with Ryan, and they probably would've dropped it, especially since he's old news.

"Skylar! Say something!" Serena demands.

"I can't believe we've been corrupting our virginal sister all these years," Sienna adds, flabbergasted.

It's almost funny.

Almost.

I blow out a long, dramatic breath and force myself to look back into the camera where they're waiting for my reply. "I don't like talking about this stuff. I'm not like the rest of you."

"Duh," Sienna says at the same time as Serena mumbles, "Obviously."

I roll my eyes. "I didn't sleep with Ryan, and I'm not... I haven't gone all the way with Danny yet. But I want to." The admission isn't surprising to either of them based on their expectant expressions, and it shouldn't be to me either, but it still does something funny to my heart as I replay those words. "I'm nervous."

The usual softness in Serena's face returns. "Of course you are. Having sex is always a little nerve-racking, first time or not."

Tell them.

I part my lips...

And close them.

They don't seem to notice I'm dealing with an internal battle. Not when Sienna pipes up with, "Just be open with each other about what you want, because people you can't communicate with during intimacy will make it awkward."

Serena bobs her head. "It's true. And even though we joke around about sex, it's a huge deal, Skylar. If you're not ready, then don't rush into it. It seems like this guy is decent if he's waiting. I'm sure he wouldn't mind."

"We're not even dating," I tell them, voice hoarse with embarrassment and something far darker bubbling in my blood.

"So? Friends with benefits is great too."

Serena sighs at our sister's response. "It doesn't have to be with somebody you're in love with, but it definitely makes it more special. Every girl wants their first time to mean something to them. They may say they don't, but it's an experience we only get once. It has to count."

My throat thickens.

It's an experience we only get once.

Tears threaten to glaze my eyes, so I blink them away and sit up. My chest burns with awareness. Clearing my throat, I grab my phone and take a slow breath in. "You're right. It's been great talking to you, but I should probably go. I think Danny said something about a card game with his grandma. Have fun at that new club you're checking out, and tell the others I said hi!"

Before they can see the deteriorating wall I've built around my memories, I hang up.

Make it count.

Make it count.

Make it count.

That's the thought circling my head when there's a knock at my door.

The "Blondie?" from the other side makes my heart race rapidly in its cage.

And that's when I know what I want.

Chapter Thirty

DANNY

"BLONDIE?" I KNOCK ON the door to the guest room, strategically placed in a completely different hallway from my own. It took everything in me not to sneak inside after Ma and Grandma went to bed last night like I'm sure they figured I'd do regardless of the placement.

Skylar said she had plans to talk with her family, so I left her be for the past hour and a half, even though I wanted to take her out and hang with her for a while to see the night-life. Footsteps creak the floorboards before the doorknob turns and the door cracks open.

She looks a little pale. "Hey."

"You okay?" I ask, stepping inside when she moves over in silent invitation. Flopping down on the queen-size bed and grabbing the stuffed animal I bought her at the aquarium, I hold it to my chest and watch her slink over to stand beside the foot of the mattress.

I smile and pat a section beside me, watching as she sinks onto the corner, drawing one of her knees up.

Her eyes go to the penguin I'm cuddling against my chest. "My sisters are going to some new club on the strip in Vegas because they saw online that one of their favorite singers is going to be there."

"Anyone I heard of?"

"Cassidy something or other. She's new to the scene. From what Sienna said, she's known for dating some famous boy bander and starring in a sex scandal when a video of theirs leaked."

I chuckle at the way her nose scrunches.

"I can't imagine what that must be like. Anyway, they'll probably club hop if they don't find her, so I'm sure I'll get plenty of drunk texts and video calls throughout the night."

I reach over and tug on her hand until she inches closer to me. Lifting my arm for her to curl up beside me, I peck the side of her forehead and heft out a sigh. "I drunk texted Caleb once. Though, full disclosure, I'd meant to text my friend Candace at the time. It was an honest mistake."

Her nose twitches as she looks away. "I suppose Candace is a special friend like me?"

It's hard not to let my lips curve into a cocky grin. I can taste her jealousy. "Nah. Maybe if Candi Cane wasn't a lesbian, I would've tried my shot at her when we were kids, but I'm pretty sure she still wouldn't have given me a chance. Word on the street is I'm a little too much to handle sometimes." A small laugh vibrates her, so I pull her closer and rest my chin on her head. "I booked us tickets to do a tour that I think you'll like. I've done it before with my old high school history class, and if it's anything like it used to be, it'll be interesting."

"What kind of tour?"

"It's called the Beacon Hill Crime Tour." The way she

perks up has me grinning wider. "It's a foot tour that focuses on the Boston Strangler and his victims. Since you're obsessed with that sort of shit, I figured you'd want to do it before we headed back. We can hit up the harbor beforehand and meet with the group right before it starts. You down? It's not too much walking, but we'll be on our feet a lot…"

She drapes an arm across my stomach and squeezes, her chin resting on my pec as she glances up at me. "I'd love that, Danny. I didn't even know that was a thing when I googled things to do."

"You googled tourist attractions?"

The pink dotting her cheeks has become my favorite color over the past few months. "I wanted to know more about where you grew up. It seems like such a cool place to live. I'm still surprised you ever left to come to Lindon."

"You left California, Blondie," I remind her matter-of-factly. "A lot of people would kill to go to Beverly Hills and see the stars."

She makes a face but nods once. "I'm glad you wound up at Lindon."

Tucking a stray piece of hair behind her ear, I murmur, "I'm glad we both did."

We stare at each other for a few moments, my eyes trailing down to her lips, which part as soon as I lock my gaze on them. My lungs squeeze as she reaches up and touches my lips, tracing them with one of her fingertips.

Her voice is raspy when she speaks. "Can I ask you something?"

Anything. Fucking *anything.*

"Of course you can."

Moving so her cheek is flat against my chest, probably hearing the drum of my heartbeat reacting to her closeness, she releases a breath. "I want to know what you meant when you said you'd been waiting four years for this. Because I don't want to make any assumptions about where we stand or what we are to each other. The last thing I want is to be seen as some clingy jersey chaser who—"

"Stop." I shift us so she's forced to look up at me, two of my fingers gently pinching her chin in place so we're locked. The fact that she's worried about people seeing her as that physically pains me. "I'm sorry for putting that into your head when we met. You want to know what I meant when I said I was waiting for something like this? I meant something *real*, Skylar."

Her eyes widen, fully as in tune with this conversation as I am.

I cup her face, stroking her smooth, flushed skin. "I meant *you*. Somebody who didn't care about who I was or what I played. Someone who could make me laugh even when I was pissed and make me focus on the shit that mattered when I wanted to avoid it. You never expect anything because you're good, so fucking good. You're sweet, but you're never going to just take my crap. You keep me on my toes. I just..." Shaking my head, I press a kiss to her forehead and keep my lips there for a fraction longer than necessary. Against her, I admit, "I've been waiting to find someone worthy of being in a relationship with."

"You want that with *me*?"

"Blondie, if I haven't made that obvious enough by now, I need to try even harder. Yes. I want to put the effort in with you. Take you on a proper date, show you what a true gentleman I am—"

Her snort makes me pull back.

"Excuse you," I tease. "I am one hell of a gentleman when I want to be. I just find my other skills tend to overshadow it."

She nods. "Whatever you say."

"Don't think I don't know you love it when I get flirty and dirty with you." I nip her lip and suck it into my mouth until she shivers against me. I feel her legs squirm until I manage to insert my thigh between them, a position we've gotten quite accustomed to over the past couple of weeks.

I press against the spot between her thighs and listen to her moan into my mouth. The kiss turns into a slow exploration of each other's mouths, teeth against teeth, tongue against tongue. I can taste the lemonade Grandma M insists on making from scratch as I deepen the kiss, weaving my fingers through her hair and holding the back of her head.

She grinds herself against my leg, building a steady rhythm that quickens her breathing with each stroke. I move with her, sucking her tongue, biting her lip, and angling our faces to get just enough air without breaking contact. My hands move down to cup her butt, kneading it, pulling her farther up my leg until she's draped across my body.

"Your arm—" she tries protesting.

"It's fine." I line up our hips, moving her to straddle me until she's pressed against the bulge in my jeans. I'm so hard it hurts, but I don't dare pull myself out. I guide her to start moving again, helping her find the friction as she moves her core over the denim until her head tips back.

"Just like that, baby," I praise, gripping her ass, her hips, squeezing and watching her ride me over our clothes. I can only imagine what it'll look like when we're naked, her taking my cock, clenching me with her tight—

Her breath hitches as she grinds down, her hips getting jerky with each frantic movement. When her fingers go to the button of my jeans, I have to catch her hands.

"Danny, I want to—"

"Come just like this," I tell her. The flush of her cheeks and swell of the lips I thoroughly kissed tell me she's close. I arch upward until she can feel exactly what she's doing to me.

It's like I'm sixteen again, dry humping my first girlfriend until I come in my goddamn pants. I wouldn't even be embarrassed about it this time because it's so hot watching her fall apart on top of me.

When she does, her breath catches as her hips press into me until I have to bite the inside of my cheek to stop from making any noises that my family could potentially hear downstairs.

Her chest crashes down on mine, her face buried in the crook of my neck as she catches her breath. My palms squeeze her ass one more time before moving up her spine. I kiss the crown of her head before she pushes up to look down at me.

"You didn't come," she notes, circling her hips over where she's still seated.

A pained groan rises up my throat. "It's fine. I just need a minute to—"

"I want to make you come, Danny."

Sexiest damn words I ever heard.

"I want...I want to do more." Her admission comes with a crimson face.

I have a feeling the "more" she wants would require a lot less clothes and a foil package that's currently in the night-stand in my own room across the house.

Blowing out a breath, I drop my head back until it's resting against the mattress. "I want nothing more than to do that, Sky, but my family is downstairs." The disappointment on her face swells my chest. "I came up here to see if you wanted to go to the pier with me. After the sun sets, you can see the city light up. It's something you need to see at least once while we're here."

She nibbles her lips. "That does sound nice…"

I can tell there's still one thing on her mind, and I'd be lying if I didn't say it was on the forefront of mine too. "Later," I promise her, voice low. "I want to make sure it's everything and then some for you."

Which probably shouldn't happen at my childhood home where anyone can hear us.

Will that stop me? The way the girl on top of me is looking at me, I'd say no.

I pat her butt. "C'mon, Blondie." I shift her off me and sit up, adjusting myself and wincing. "I may need a cold shower before we go. Give me ten minutes?"

The small smile on her face tells me she's happy with herself. She should be.

This is all for her.

Chapter Thirty-One

SKYLAR

DANNY IS RIGHT, THE pier is beautiful at night. At the waterfront restaurant he took me to, you can see the lit-up cityscape.

After an hour full of conversation and clam chowder, Danny knocks his foot against mine underneath the table. "Just so we're clear, I'm not taking you out tonight just so this counts as that date I promised."

Something deflates in my chest. "Oh."

He doesn't want this to be a date. The dim lighting and beautiful view set the scene perfectly. I may not be dressed to the nines, but neither is he. It seemed like the kind of perfect first date you see in the movies.

"Sky," he says with a laugh, tapping my hand and covering it with his. "All I mean is that I don't want you thinking I asked you out for any nefarious reason. This doesn't mean we have to do anything later. There's no pressure. Just you, me, and good New England food. That's all."

Relief loosens my shoulders. "What if I want something nefarious to happen after we get back?"

His eyes heat. "I should probably tell you that we should wait, at least until we're back to campus."

Hope blossoms in my chest. "But you're not going to do that," I guess, voice a little raspy over the possibilities.

Danny rubs the back of his neck. "When you look at me like you are right now, it makes it pretty fucking hard to want to be a gentleman."

The way he shifts in his seat makes me wonder if something other than his decision is hard right now too.

We walk out after he waves down our waiter and pays the bill. His hand slips into mine the second our coats are on, guiding us outside to stop by the edge of the bay.

I breathe in the cool, fresh air and stare at the ripples of water as I listen to the sounds of the city. Car horns blast, people yell, and it's oddly...calming. Familiar. Like California and the bustling suburbs that I'm accustomed to. Lindon is nice because it's quiet, but sometimes I miss the racket to dull out the thoughts in my head.

"What was your first girlfriend like?" I ask, thinking back to the conversation with my sisters.

He rocks back on his heels before blowing out a raspberry with his lips and leaning on the top of the railing separating us and the water. "That was not what I was expecting you to ask at all." His laugh is short, light. "Her name was Juliette, but everyone called her Jules. She was nice. It didn't last very long. It was mostly a summer romance."

"Why?"

He stares out at the water. "My high school football coach was helping me do some extra practice in my free time to bulk up and train for the new season. During the summers, I went to training camps for at least half of the break. Jules wanted to spend more time with me, and I didn't have any of it to give. She got tired of waiting, I guess."

"That sucks."

"Eh. We were young." His eased tone matches his calm demeanor. "I wasn't exactly heartbroken by it, which is telling."

I nod along.

"What about you?"

His question has me thinking back to my time with Ryan. How many months had we seen each other? Two? Three? Barely. He asked me out just after Valentine's Day, which I think was strategic on his part. He didn't want to invest in the flowers and chocolate that the school always sold to raise money for the events that the student counsel hosted. It didn't bother me because I was shocked he was even interested. No guy had seemed that into me before him. Serena says I was just aloof to the boys who looked at me.

"Ryan was my only boyfriend," I admit sheepishly. Danny's eyes scope out my face. I lean my hip against the rail and sigh. "He was popular, and everyone liked him, so I was excited when he asked me out to a local hangout. But I never felt all that giddy like I think I should have when we were together. He was really touchy-feely and always wanted to do more than I was willing to—"

He makes a face, eyes narrowing.

"—but he never did anything to pressure me. It was the biggest reason we broke up. I wasn't ready to give it up to him, and we were about to graduate and go off to college. It made sense to end things there."

The gruff noise he makes has me cracking a smile appreciatively. "Guy sounds like a dick."

"Apparently my family thought so too," I muse, still surprised they kept that opinion to themselves. "But can you blame him? He was a teenage boy. You can't tell me you didn't always have sex on the brain with Juliette."

The single shoulder he lifts without any confirmation is plenty telling enough.

He turns, using the rail to rest his good elbow on. "I think we need to talk about that."

"Your sex drive as a teenager?"

He snickers. "No, smart-ass." He wraps an arm around me and tugs me into his side. "We need to talk about sex though."

"Oh. That."

The smile he fights still makes an appearance, though short-lived. "Yeah. That. I want to make sure you're ready and not feeling pressured to do anything with me. Like I said, I didn't bring you with me for that. All I expected was to spend time with you and make sure you weren't alone. Nobody should be during the holidays."

His words send little sparks throughout my body. "I know that's not why I'm here, but I want that experience with you. It's not like we haven't done other things already."

"Don't remind me," he mumbles, tipping his head back. "I don't want to embarrass myself in public."

"How would you do that?"

The laugh he gives me is both amused and pained. "Babe, I'm a walking erection when I'm around you."

My eyes widen, but I can't help but grin as I sneak a peek in the general direction he's referring to.

"You're proud of yourself, aren't you?" he asks, pecking my lips and smiling down at me like he doesn't mind that I am at all.

Because I definitely am.

"I'm ready," I promise him.

To leave here with him.

To go back to his childhood home.

To forget the bits and pieces from the beginning of the semester.

~

When we get back to his house, there's anticipation building deep in my bones. He opens the door for me, helps me out of my jacket, and all I can think about is what else he'll help me take off when it's just us.

I think about how he'll slowly strip me of my jeans and sweater and take his time peeling the cute pair of panties I have on down my legs.

We've never been fully naked together in all the times we found ourselves in bed and experimenting on each other's bodies. Sometimes, a shirt will come off, maybe two, and buttons on jeans will come undone and zippers will be pulled down. I've never been fully comfortable stripping bare, even though it's not Danny's fault.

The ache between my legs is intense as we walk hand in hand down the hall until we get to the large open den and kitchen area. His hand moves from mine to the small of my back, guiding me in first to see a reality show playing on the television with his grandmother sitting on the couch with a glass of red wine.

"I thought Doc told you to stop drinking that," Danny tells the woman whose white hair is tucked back behind her ears. He walks over and pecks her cheek in greeting.

Grandma Meadow looks up at him, her eyes narrowed

through a thick pair of glasses and looking ready to fight. "I thought *your* doctor told you to stop playing football and get surgery. Guess we're both shitty listeners, aren't we, boy?"

All Danny does is snicker.

When his grandma turns to me, I try hiding the fact that I've been thinking about all the dirty things I want to do with her grandson. "I heard he took you to the pier. Did you go to Maggie's for dinner? Or did the cheapskate take you to one of the booths before showing you the harbor?"

Danny rolls his eyes, answering before I can with an amused, "Give me *some* credit, Grandma. She needed a proper New England meal. Can you believe she's never had a crab cake before?"

That gets the older woman's attention, her eyes going back to me. "Did you at least like them?"

I can't lie to her. "The seasoning was..." It still makes me want to rinse my mouth out. Turns out Old Bay and I don't get along. "A little much for my liking. But the clam chowder was delicious, and Danny shared his seafood medley with me."

Danny grabs a hold of my hand. "You should know that Grandma M puts Old Bay on anything she can get away with. The woman would snort it if she could."

"Don't give her any ideas," Caroline chides, walking into the room with a glass of wine matching her mother's. "I don't need to rush anyone else to the hospital this week."

I crack a smile when the oldest person in the room huffs in exasperation. "Leave me be to watch my Kardashians. I think Khloe is about to lose it. 'Bout time too."

Danny wasn't kidding when he said she was obsessed. I wonder what she'd say if I told her one of my sisters knew the famous celebs. Before I can offer that information, Danny squeezes my hand and tips his head toward the stairs.

He says good night to his family. I offer them a shy wave when both women look between us and the contact we're making before similar smiles appear on their faces.

Thankfully, we're walking away before they can see me blush. Do they know what we're up to? Do they care? Even though I want nothing more than to spend the night with Danny, part of me feels weird knowing it's in their house.

Make it count.

When we make it to the top landing, Danny stops us. "I thought we could watch that panel discussion you told me about. It was posted today, right?"

My heart does a backflip in my chest. "I didn't know you were even listening when I told you about that." He'd been texting with Caleb about something that made him look distracted while I blabbered on about the question-and-answer panel my favorite author was doing.

"I listen to everything you say, Blondie."

That can be dangerous. "I tend to babble a lot though. That's got to be tedious."

His lips stretch. "It's amusing more than anything. So do you want to? I'm dying to know if she says anything about the next books in the series I've been reading."

The eagerness in his tone matches the excitement in his eyes. He already read the first three books and seemed genuinely upset when I said that was all there was so far. He distracted himself by searching my other books and reading the backs of them, then using my laptop to search pet stores that had turtles within a fifty-mile radius of campus.

When we settle into the guest room, laptop propped between us on the bed and the video in question playing, my body eases. Our hands are folded together, feet touching, breathing in sync.

Ryan never talked about books with me. Most people I know aren't interested in talking literature unless they're English majors. In fact, it's probably a good thing that Aliyah hasn't asked to borrow any more of the novels I brought back with me from Cali, because Danny's been going through them like he's waiting for his next fix.

And that's...*God*. It does something naughty to my lady bits that it probably shouldn't.

"What did Caleb want earlier?" I ask during a YouTube commercial in hopes of sounding casual, even though I'm feeling anything but.

There's a brief pause before he scratches the side of his neck. "He's just going through something and needed to vent."

I frown. "I hope everything's okay."

His lips twitch, heavy contemplation weighing down his features. "Me too."

I decide not to press. "Olive texted me saying Alex might be signing with the Canadiens. Something about an offer he'd be stupid to refuse."

That changes his expression from conflicted to impressed. "That'd be great for him. I'd go to his state games."

I snuggle up to him, wrapping an arm around his and using his good shoulder as a pillow for my cheek. "You're a fan, huh?"

"I wouldn't be able to fight Olive for the coveted number one spot, but I'm somewhere in the top hundred."

I smile up at him. "It'd be impossible to beat her, considering they're together."

One of his brows quirks. "Is that so?"

My lips rub together. "Sort of. I mean, they're together in the biblical sense."

"Definitely can't beat her there," he muses, nuzzling his nose into my hair. "You've got that look again. What are you thinking about?"

What *am* I thinking? I'm thinking about Olive's situation with Alex. How they're basically doing the same thing we are. Alex and Danny are going away, graduating, and moving on to different things. Where does that leave us?

"Just thinking about Olive," I murmur.

He hums, not calling me out on the little white lie. I'm grateful. I'm not sure I want to have "the talk" with him and derail all the things we've been teasing each other with all day.

His next question is random. "When's your birthday?"

"January twenty-eight. Why?" I don't have to ask him when his is, because I *may* have looked it up after we kept bumping into each other at the start of the semester.

His nose tickles the side of my face, then my cheekbone and jaw, before peppering light kisses along my skin until his lips wind up at my ear. "Just wondering. I want to do something special for it. Have anything in mind?"

I peel away to meet his eyes. He wants to spend my birthday with me? Granted, it's not that far away, but still. "I haven't thought much about it. Usually, I go somewhere with my family. A favorite restaurant. That's about it."

"We'll be back for the spring semester by then if you want to go somewhere. I can bring my Jeep back, so I stop having to borrow my friends' vehicles. We can go to Bridgeport or somewhere else. Anywhere. You name it."

I melt into him. "You're too good to me, Daniel Bridges Junior."

"That's sure as hell not true."

It is, and I'm ready to prove as much.

Grabbing my laptop, I hit Pause and close it before moving it away. Understanding flares in Danny's eyes as I move, swinging one of my legs over his lap until I'm straddling him. His hands go to my hips instinctively, his fingertips massaging my flesh as we lock eyes.

"Hi," I say, almost shyly.

"Hi. Whatcha up to?"

He knows exactly what I'm up to. Moving a piece of hair behind my ear, I lean forward and brush my lips against his. It's a soft kiss, basically a peck. His mouth follows mine, going for another, adding more pressure, and curling a hand around the nape of my neck and tasting my tongue.

I can feel him growing underneath me and smile against his mouth. My hands go to his hair, fingering his blond wavy strands and tugging him to my mouth. I roll my hips against him, remembering how amazing it felt earlier. I'm greeted with the same noise too, making me repeat the motion and riding out the yummy friction.

Danny's hands go to the edge of my shirt, hesitating at the hem. "I locked the door," he murmurs, eyeing me as he slowly lifts the material up.

I give him a single nod, lifting my arms as he lifts the soft cotton over my body and tosses it onto the floor. He takes in the simple bra I'm wearing, fingering the underwire pushing up my breasts before running the pads of his thumbs over the pebbled buds poking out from the material under his heated gaze.

Unexpectedly, he leans forward and takes one into his mouth, sucking until I'm arching my back to press farther into him. I bite my lip, knowing I need to be quiet, but it's hard. *So* hard when he uses his tongue and teeth over one nipple, then the other as his hand slides between us and starts rubbing me over the seam of my jeans.

My breath shudders as he pays extra special attention to my clit, rubbing me in circles before slowly starting to undo the button and zipper of my denim. I help him as he nips the top of my breast and tugs the cup of my bra down with his teeth until I'm exposed. And when he takes me into his mouth with nothing covering me at the same time as he slides his hand into my panties, I'm almost at my breaking point.

He sucks my nipple, his tongue and teeth doing delicious things to my sensitive breast as one of his fingers trails down my seam until it teases my wet opening.

I'm embarrassed at how ready I am for him and can tell how much it turns him on when he slips a finger inside me and does that wonderful hooking motion to hit *the spot*. Using his free hand, he undoes my bra and throws it somewhere across the room, so I'm completely bare from the waist up.

His mouth moves to one breast while his free hand tweaks and plays with the other, and a second finger joins the first one inside me as the heel of his palm presses against my clit. I should be mortified by the wet noises coming from each thrust of his fingers inside me, but I'm not. I should also probably be embarrassed by the way I start riding him and quietly begging him to bite me harder. Who knew I even liked that sort of thing?

It's when he obeys, biting down on my breast and fingering me faster that I detonate around him. I have to clench my teeth as the orgasm washes over me, his fingers still moving as I contract around them.

When it subsides, I collapse into him, squeezing an arm around his neck until we're both desperately peeling off other layers of clothes in between brutal, hot kisses.

His shirt.

My jeans.

His pants.

My panties.

His boxer briefs.

When we're both completely bare, we take a long stretch of time to study each and every little piece of exposed skin between us. My heart is pounding as I look at his twitching organ, long, pink, and girthy, and picture exactly where it's about to be.

"We can stop," he tells me, misinterpreting what I'm thinking.

I reach between us and wrap a hand around the base of him, pumping once like he's taught me to do and watching him grow in my palm. He kisses me as I repeat the movement, stroking him from base to tip and back down again. He's leaking, desperate when he reaches for something he must have grabbed earlier.

A condom.

I watch as he moves my hand away and rolls it on, fascinated by the skilled movement. My breath catches as he rolls me onto my back and hovers above me, his knee gently knocking my legs open until he's settled between them.

My hand cups his face, meeting him halfway for another kiss before pulling away and whispering, "I don't want to stop."

His eyelids flutter closed as he kisses me, lining himself up to my entrance and pushing in slowly. The pinch of pain is there, making me hiss out a breath that has him pausing.

But I shake my head and return his kiss, bending my legs and settling them on either side of his hips to urge him to continue.

Inch by inch, he sinks into me, kissing my lips, my cheeks, my jaw, before nipping the crook of my throat. One small thrust later, he's fully seated inside me, and I *feel* it. Him. All of him. I feel his body on me and his hands on me and his breath over me.

My chest tightens, but I try to ignore it.

His fingers wrap around the meaty part of my thigh and hitch my leg around his back before pulling out and pushing back in. It's slow, calculated, and both painful and not at the same time. It's nothing like I've ever felt as he kneads my thigh and whispers pretty words against my lips and sets a slow rhythm with every single thrust of his hips.

My throat thickens, but I try to ignore it.

My lips part when his hand slides between our sweaty bodies and starts playing with the nerves that are still recovering from my first orgasm. I make a strangled noise that he swallows with his lips, his tongue twisting with mine and tasting every single part of my mouth as he picks up the pace.

His hips slap into mine, my other leg moving to join the left one around his back, crossing at the ankles as he slams into me. His grunts become heavier, faster, his kisses stinging but sexy as he tries quieting his noises.

The fingers working my clit press down, tweak, and pinch, building that familiar feeling that travels down my spine and tightens my tummy as his movements become jerky.

It feels good, but my mind starts producing murky, fragmented images that make it hard to focus until he opens his mouth and says, "Need to feel you come on my cock, baby. I need to know what it feels like when your tight pussy vice grips me as you come apart."

His words are all it takes before my back is arching off the bed and a second orgasm completely takes over my body. I clench him so tight I can't see straight. I feel his hands gripping my ass, holding it up as he pounds into me before burying himself deep and releasing a garbled cry into the pillow beside my head as he empties himself into the condom.

I can feel the subtle shake of my body as I absorb the way his hands move along my butt, squeezing once as if to remind himself of who's underneath him.

I take in the way he twitches inside me and the bite of pain from what we've done.

His lips coast over my jaw until they find my lips, the kiss sweet and lingering as he slowly pulls out, anchoring the condom carefully to make sure it doesn't leak before he disposes of it.

My hands shake as images and sounds and emotions I didn't remember until just now smack into me like a freight train.

It'll be quieter in here.

We can just talk.

You're so fucking beautiful.

You like that, don't you?

Hands on my hips.

Hands pulling down my leggings.

Hands tugging off my panties.

Heavy body.

Heavy mind.

Do you want this?

Trapped thoughts.

"Skylar?"

Nothing.

"Skylar, baby?"

You'll love this, I promise.

Hands cup my cheeks before a new face comes into focus above me. It's only then, with Danny hovering above me looking panicked, that I realize I'm crying.

"Did I hurt you? I shou—"

To my horror, I start sobbing.

"Christ, I'm sorry." He pulls me into his arms, our chests crushed together. "Shh, baby. I'm so sorry. Tell me what I did. If I was too rough—"

"I-It's not *you*." My voice is unrecognizably broken, heart shattering piece by tiny piece in my chest. I cling to him like he's my lifeline to forget everything else trying to grab hold of my brain. "It wasn't you. I wish it was you. I wish it *had* been you," I say into his neck, sniffing back the tears that keep leaking from my eyes.

His palm strokes my spine in comfort as he drops his head to peck my shoulder. "Oh, Sky. You have no idea how much I wish the same thing. No fucking idea. Let it out, baby. It's okay. You're okay."

I'm okay, I force myself to repeat.

Okay.

Okay.

Okay.

I hiccup.

Am I?

Chapter Thirty-Two

DANNY

THANKSGIVING BREAK FLIES BY, and the ride back to Lindon U, this time in my precious Jeep Wrangler, is spent listening to a playlist and watching the mixture of suburb, city, and rural sceneries pass by.

I don't push the girl riding in the passenger seat to share what's on her mind. She stares out the window, her thumbnail in her mouth nearly the whole three plus hours we're on the road, while I think about the surgery I finally agreed to after talking to my family more about it. We both have a lot going on in our heads, and pushing her to tell me what's going on in hers probably wouldn't get me very far.

She helped Ma with the late holiday lunch, making idle conversation about where she grew up, what her family is like, and how close she is with her sister Serena. There's no indication of what happened between us after we had sex. I stayed the night with her, door locked, with her in my arms from nightfall to sunrise. She twitched from who knows what, looking empty when she awoke from whatever memory stirred her from sleep. Because I know asking her is pointless, I pretended to sleep so I didn't set myself up for disappointment.

My hands grip the steering wheel as I see the Lindon sign in the distance. "Did you let your family know we were on our way back?" I ask when I can't handle the silence anymore.

Fingers turning the volume dial down, I glance at her drawing her feet up to the edge of the seat so her knees press against her chest. Her head rests against the window. "Yeah, they know. I spoke to my mom this morning when I was packing. Serenity was with her at some new clothing boutique they found."

I loosen my hold on the wheel and settle into the seat. "Sounds nice. Did they have a good holiday? You said your parents went on a cruise, right?"

She hums. "I guess my dad got food poisoning, so their trip wasn't great. They ended up cutting it short once they got to the Bahamas."

"Is he doing better?"

"Yeah."

"Skylar—"

"I'm sorry," she blurts, turning to me and looking nervous.

I'm stunned speechless for a couple seconds.

"I ruined things back at your house. We shouldn't have done that there. Your family must have known because they gave me weird looks—"

"Sky." I stop her, reaching over and taking her hand. I drag it between us and hold it tight. "You've been through so much that I wish I could help you get past. I hope I can do that. One day at a time. Just stay with me."

Her eyes water, making me wish I was in a safe place to pull off to the side of the road and comfort her.

Instead, I squeeze her hand to let her know I'm here and not letting go. "What do you need from me? I'll do anything. Just please don't cry. That damn near ended me, knowing I couldn't do shit to make it better."

Her head shakes as she stares at our hands. "You've already done so much. I've taken up so much of your time and you never complain. You watch the stupid movies I like and read my cheesy romances and indulge in my peanut butter addiction—"

That one makes me chuckle because she really does have an obsession. I made sure Ma picked up a jar of her favorite kind to have at the house.

"Whenever you're not busting your butt at practice or cramming for classes, you're with me. And you French braid really well, which makes me sort of jealous. I'm surprised you aren't sick of me yet. Especially because I haven't been very…open to doing more until recently."

Is that what she thinks I want her around for? "Blondie, I never wanted our dynamic to be about sex. I like our friendship. I like that we can just chill and watch movies or read or study. When I'm exhausted from playing, the last thing I want to do is try getting it up. That's the truth. I like the pace we've set, and if you want to pull back on that, I'm cool with that too. Whatever you want, babe."

She's quiet, making me nervous.

"I've got to be honest," I say, rubbing the back of my neck. "I don't think it's a good idea to do it again. Not right away. After your reaction…"

She physically cringes.

"And I don't want you to apologize for that. But I do

want you to try doing something about it. If you're not comfortable telling me what happened, then you need to open up to somebody you feel comfortable with."

"I *do* feel comfortable with you—"

"Not completely," I disagree, almost grimly. My lips press together. "Skylar, there are some things distractions can't fix. I'll happily make more memories with you, but the old ones you have—the ones you're running from—will still be there."

She's silent.

"I want you to be happy. Happy here at Lindon. Happy with me."

"I am," she whispers.

Why do I doubt that? "Happiness can be temporary sometimes," I murmur.

Her body freezes. "What does that mean?"

What *does* it mean? I take a few minutes to think about it, not wanting to botch this like I have other conversations with Skylar. "It means that I want this to be real with us. I want *you* to be real with me. No dodging subjects or changing the conversation when it gets hard. I never want to force you to tell me anything, but that doesn't mean I don't want to know."

"You said no pressure—"

"I know." I sigh heavily. "I know I did."

"You lied then."

"Blondie—"

"Don't 'Blondie' me, Danny. Do you think any of this is easy for me? Why can't I just move on? Why do you want me to talk about it? To remember?"

"Because it'll help," I say quickly, glancing at her cool expression. She's angry. I get it. "I'm not trying to pick a fight. I'm trying to understand. To help—"

"You can't."

345

My jaw ticks as I twist my palms around the steering wheel in a tight grip. "That's because you don't want any help. But guess what, Skylar? You need it."

Once again, silence greets me.

When I look back over at her, she's staring out the window and ignoring me.

I shake my head. "Don't shut me out. That's what I'm asking of you."

There's a brief pause. "Maybe you're right," she mumbles.

My brows go up.

"Maybe we shouldn't do this anymore."

Fuck.

~

After dropping off Skylar, her words still tangling in my stomach, I head back to the house and walk into a room full of tension. Caleb's leg bounces from his seat in the living room, and Justin's face is twisted with the same nerves I saw on it when he was waiting for his MCAT results. Aiden, on the other hand, is fuming.

"Who pissed off Griff?" I ask, looking between the various guys lounging around.

They all turn to me as I lock the front door behind me and drop my bag onto the hall floor.

All Caleb's text said was:

Shit going down with W.

W. Wallace. It's not like I'm surprised to hear that, but I think I might have underestimated what exactly he did to make our tight end look so murderous.

It's Marks, sulking in the corner like someone took away his favorite video game console, who speaks up. "Coach called an emergency team meeting this morning."

My eyes widen. "What the fuck? I never got a text."

"You were driving," Caleb points out in a somber tone that builds the uneasy anticipation. The fact that Raine and Ivy aren't here for this conversation tells me that something serious is up.

"What the hell did he want?" I pull out my phone, wondering if I missed any voicemails from Coach Pearce. Just because I'm injured doesn't make me any less part of the team.

Aiden swipes at his jaw before one of his massive hands goes to grip the back of his neck. "Coach was contacted by the campus police about Wallace. Allegations have been made against him that he's being investigated for. We're all going to be questioned."

My brows shoot up. *Jesus Christ.* "Care to elaborate on that?"

Caleb shifts in his spot, crossing his arms over his chest and blowing out a heavy breath. "It isn't good, that's for damn sure."

Most things involving the campus police aren't, even if most students laugh off the uniformed officers who ride around handing out parking tickets. But after my chat with Skylar about Wallace, this isn't something any of us should be brushing off.

Aiden drops down in the armchair, shaking his head. "He's being investigated for drugging girls' drinks at parties. We're supposed to talk to the head of the campus police to tell them if we've ever witnessed anything. I guess a few people have filed reports. There's one girl who's claiming he did more than drug her."

My teeth clench so tightly there's probably permanent damage.

"I don't get what the fuck he was thinking," Aiden continues. "He's always talking shit about those parties. Anybody can link him to those allegations even if they aren't true."

"Who says they're not?" Caleb asks.

I nod grimly. "Hate to break it to you, Griff, but the kid is nothing but trouble. You know he thinks he's invincible."

"Why the fuck would he do that?" is Aiden's question. "He has a lot going for him. It doesn't make any sense."

"Power trip," Caleb grumbles.

Marks flinches. "He can, so he does. We've all heard him talking about the shit he does at those parties. The dude is lucky all we had to do this year is get tested for STDs. If he were drug tested…"

We're all silent for a long stretch of time. I think about Skylar's question—about her friend Aliyah.

"Where's Wallace now?" I ask nobody in particular.

I'm not surprised when Aiden is the one who responds. "He and Coach are talking to the campus police. They need to get his side of things to make a full report to the local station. Then they'll talk to each of us."

I'm tempted to text Skylar about this, but I know she needs time to cool off. Our conversation definitely didn't go the way I wanted, but that doesn't mean I'm going to give up. I hope she has the same mindset.

"Coach will let us know what's up," Marks says, standing up. "If this becomes something huge, that's another player out." He turns to me. "You *are* out, right? Coach said it wasn't likely they'd let you play."

It's Caleb who turns to me. "Yeah, what did you decide?

Last we talked, you said you weren't sure if you were going to go through with the shoulder surgery."

They all look at the shoulder in question, which I haven't had in my sling for a few days now. I roll it on instinct, feeling the tightness settled into the muscles, and cringe. "I'm out for the season. I'll know when my surgery is scheduled this week."

"I'm sorry, bro," Caleb says.

"It is what it is." I glance at Aiden. "I know you want to have faith in Wallace, but I wouldn't waste your time. Just because somebody is good at what they do doesn't mean they're a good person. If you keep holding on, he's going to drag your ass down with him."

He doesn't say anything.

Doesn't argue.

But doesn't agree either.

With Aiden, I'll take it.

The guys disperse shortly after that with Caleb hanging behind. He claps my back. "You good, man?"

I know he means my shoulder. "I will be. Sorry to let the team down."

He rolls his eyes. "The team doesn't care as much as you think. And Coach will get the fuck over it, even if he talks smack. You've pushed yourself harder than most of us out there. You didn't let us down."

"The Raiders won."

"They probably would have won even if you didn't get hurt." He doesn't sound happy about it but shrugs it off reluctantly. "But that doesn't mean shit to us. We still have a shot. Semifinal games are a possibility yet."

True, but now with Wallace's situation, that's up in the air.

"Hey." He nudges my arm. "Focus on you. Your

shoulder. Your girl." The smirk he shows me is knowing. "How'd that go anyway? I take it Grandma Meadow didn't scare her away?"

I snort. "They bonded over *The Bachelor* and their love for caffeinated drinks. I had to run to Dunkin" at least ten times while they watched TV together and gossiped about women I don't even know."

Caleb finds it way more entertaining than I do. Then again, seeing two of my favorite people together was always nice. Even if Grandma M would shoo me away because she didn't want to hear me complain every ten minutes during their shows.

Before I left, Ma pulled me into a hug and whispered, "I like her." Her approval of Skylar only makes my feelings that much more cemented. Ever since I was a little kid, I'd been telling my mom that she was my number one girl, but I think she knows that spot is about to be filled with somebody else, and she's okay with it.

Caleb smacks my chest as he passes by me to head upstairs. "You should text Skylar to hang out. Don't worry about any of this shit with Wallace. Like you told Aiden, he isn't our problem. The second we claim him to be, he's going to take us down."

We used to swear that we were a team through everything—thick and thin. But some things aren't worth fighting for.

Some *people*.

"Skylar and I need some time away from each other. Things got a little tense on the drive home." Caleb looks worried, but I wave it off. "I'm good, man. We'll be fine." *I hope.*

"If you're sure…"

I smack his back. "Yep. You and Raine are solid?" Last time we talked, there was some sort of rift between them.

"We'll be fine," he says, the expression on his face looking just as unsure as mine.

I smile. "If anybody can get through it, it's you two." Hell, if they don't make it work, then I'm doomed.

I grab my bag and bring it upstairs, throwing it onto my bed while pulling out my cell to let my family know I got here safely. But Caleb is wrong.

If I want to prove to Skylar that I've got her back, I'll figure out how to deal with Wallace before he ruins shit for all of us.

Chapter Thirty-Three

SKYLAR

I PULL OPEN THE door to Huden with a false sense of confidence that I can do this without freaking out that a million people are staring. It's already packed with students who look about as eager for classes to start again as I am.

My eyes scan the room, hoping to find a familiar face, when I lock onto Dee and Becca in the far end of the dining room. I know nothing good could come from talking to Becca, but I approach them anyway. Why? Because I'd like to think time and space could heal anything.

I forgo grabbing my food, take a deep breath, and walk over to the table they're sharing with a group of people I don't know. The tightness in my chest caused from my anxiety travels down to my gut, telling me this is a bad idea. Do I stop? No.

The smile I offer all of them is shy as I turn to my ex-roommate. "Hey." I spot a tattoo across her forearm that she must have gotten over break. "That looks awesome."

Becca glances down at the fire helmet with a number on

the front that I vaguely remember is the same one as her fire department back home. "Thanks," she responds. Her tone isn't completely dry but far from friendly.

I shift on my feet, waving at Dee awkwardly. She returns it despite the look Becca shoots at her. "How was break?" I ask them, hoping casual conversation will deter some of the tension built between us since my move.

It's Becca who says, "What's wrong with your voice?"

I clear my throat, wincing a little. Ernie fixed the heat in my room the best he could, but it's still cold in there. I woke up this morning with a sore throat and know I'm coming down with something. "I have a cold."

Her lips tilt up as she refocuses on her food, giving Dee a chance to speak up. "I hung out with my family for most of break. You went to Boston, right?"

I nod, surprised she remembered. "Yeah, I spent time with my friend's family after seeing the Dragons game against Wilson Reed."

Friend is a weird thing to call Danny. We're so much more than that. Or we were. Guilt swarms my stomach like bees rather than butterflies every time I think about the car ride home. Danny has always been patient with me, but anytime he gives me leeway, I still feel suffocated when I think of the possibility of what comes next.

My former roommate snorts, bringing me back to the reality in front of me.

Dee gives Becca a look before going back to her food, making me feel weird just standing there. There's no way I'm going to invite myself to sit with them, so I guess I'll have to pay for a container to take food back to my room. Neither of these girls are going to make an effort, and I don't have it in me to do it either. Maybe the failed attempt at making some sort of peace is what I needed to let it completely go.

After all, there are better people here I can focus on. Olive. Danny...

Things between Danny and I haven't been great since coming back. He texts me to see how I am, but I don't always respond. Do I lie and say I'm fine? Or tell him I'm miserable since our talk in his Jeep? Having sex with him changed everything. It makes us real. Everything that comes with a relationship comes with that—expectations, trust, honesty.

He deserves all that from me.

But the words stay jammed in my throat.

I'm ashamed of crying after sex. I'm embarrassed for how I snapped at him when he was just being honest about what he wanted from me. He asked me not to shut him out, and that's exactly what I did.

He doesn't want to sleep with me again until I get help.

And I don't know if I'll ever be ready to ask for it even though I know it's the best option. What's the harm of reaching out to someone?

You'll know the truth.

And the truth is...hard to swallow sometimes.

But with the sudden isolation from him, I feel something dark boiling. Something that I know will destroy me if it bubbles over.

Shaking off the dangerous thoughts, I walk away from the girls with my shoulders tight and hear Becca say, "I bet she's got an STD from all that dick in her mouth."

I freeze, shoulders pulling back in alert as the people at the tables surrounding us all start laughing at her loud quip. My face instantly heats.

Fighting off the burning tears that prickle my eyes, I clench my teeth and walk out of the dining hall.

The feeling in my gut worsens.

My hands start to shake.

My limbs turn weak.

Only when I'm back in my room with my door locked do I let the tears fall until hot streams of anger and embarrassment flood my cheeks.

Talk to somebody you're comfortable with.

I dial a number and lower myself to the floor, not caring that I'm sitting in the salt, dirt, and slush mixture that I tracked in on my boots.

"Rena?" I sniffle.

"Who do I need to kill, Skylar?"

~

Two hours on the phone with Serena, who immediately makes Sienna join the call after I tell her what happened at the dining hall, and I finally manage to calm down. Which is probably good, because I have to convince them *not* to fly to New York to put Becca in her place like they both want to.

If Serena wasn't nearing finals like I am, she probably would have ignored my request and booked the first flight out with Sienna right behind her. "She's *done*, Skylar," Sienna had all but growled into the phone. "When I get my hands on that snake…"

Hearing their voices, their threats, somehow makes me feel better, even though Becca's words still echo in my head. I know I don't deserve them. I know they mean nothing—there's no truth to back them up. And I also know the contented feeling with that acceptance won't last, especially when I have to show my face in classes tomorrow, but it's a start. Words have the capability of hurting or healing people, and some people like Becca only want to use them as weapons rather than cures.

It isn't until almost midnight when I'm finally able to lie in bed without feeling like I'm going to throw up or cry from the events at Huden. I'm cuddled in my favorite pajamas with my stuffed penguin in my arms when I pick up my phone and stare at the screen. I've started and deleted at least five different texts to Danny that usually start with me apologizing for being so hot and cold, but I never hit Send no matter how badly I want to hear from him.

When sleep evades me and my thoughts become too much, I thumb out a message to somebody else.

Me: I think Danny and I are over

I roll onto my back to stare at the ceiling. It's only a few minutes later when my phone buzzes.

Olive: I'm coming over. Give me an hour

Forty minutes later, Olive is at my door with a sleeping bag under her arm, her neon backpack slung over her shoulder, and a McDonald's bag hanging from her fingers.

"Sleepover?" she suggests, waving the greasy food in front of me. "I brought the goods."

I step aside and let her in. "Did you drive all the way to Bridgeport to get that?"

"It's what friends do."

I feel like crying again.

Friends.

Normally, I'd hold back because I hate people seeing me like that: weak. But with Olive, I know she won't judge me for everything building inside me that's desperate to finally come out.

"I heard about what happened in Huden," she says once we've positioned ourselves on my bed with our midnight snacks.

I swipe the back of my hand against my cheek and sniff back the tears that want to keep coming. "I don't know what to do, Olive. I've never done anything for her to hate me so much. The school already thinks I'm a slut, but her comment just made it worse. I thought I was over caring, but..."

"There's no truth in it," she says, making my shoulders drop in guilt. I know it's true, but I still haven't told her about the party. About what happened. About...anything. Friends are supposed to *trust* other friends. "So she's talking out of her ass for attention. People like Becca like the sound of their own voice and making people listen to her. I know ignoring her is hard, but this will blow over. Something bigger is going to happen that will make this seem like nothing."

My blurry eyes meet hers as I feel the truth creep up my throat and over my tongue. I lick my chapped lips and stare at the untouched food in front of me. "I'm not a slut. You're right about that. But..."

Olive's eyes widen when I dare sneak a peek at her.

I swallow, wincing past the pain of my raw throat. I look away from her somber gaze and blow out a breath.

If I don't talk, I'll explode.

I feel it coming.

And I know I won't survive.

So I tell her everything.

From the second I decided to go to the party with Becca to the stumbled walk home to every little thing since.

And suddenly…I felt like I could breathe again.

Chapter Thirty-Four

SKYLAR

WITH FINALS GROWING CLOSER, I spend more time locked away in my room or inside the library with Olive as my bodyguard. Ever since our sleepover, our friendship grew once the truth was out. I couldn't hide behind a mask and pretend I was okay. I told her about the football party. About the morning after. About the real reason I needed her to take me to the clinic.

Truth is an ugly thing, a monster in the dark. It's always lingering, waiting for the perfect moment to strike. But once it's spoken, the power it has suddenly becomes nobody's power except your own. A huge weight has been lifted off my shoulders just like Danny knew it would be.

Olive and I are walking toward the exit of the library after a few hours of exam prep when a few guys come stumbling in, brushing off snowflakes from their jackets. One of them bumps into me, giving me a quick once-over before smirking.

"I know you," he says, eyes going down my body again.

Olive steps closer to me. "Doubtful."

He glances at her in an unamused way that makes me twitchy. "Aren't you O'Conner's latest toy?"

My nostrils flare, but before I can comment, Olive bats her lashes at the jerk and asks, "Jealous that I took your spot?"

The guy's friend laughs, smacking him in the back to nudge him along. "C'mon, Bryant. Leave them be."

"I'm just making friendly conversation," Bryant says, eyeing us. "It's not my fault they're being bitches about it."

"Hey," somebody says from behind us.

I look over my shoulder to see Caleb, Raine, and Ivy standing there.

Caleb gives the two guys a warning look before saying, "That's uncalled for."

It's Bryant who rolls his eyes, which are directed at me for a brief moment before moving away. "Whatever, man. I was just trying to talk to them. I don't need the fucking football team after me for it. Pussy ain't worth that shit. Especially not hers."

Olive's hand finds mine and squeezes as I fight off the blush that wants to take over my entire body under the dickhead's scrutiny.

Ivy, who always gives me a small smile if I find myself at the bakery, steps forward, standing on my other side and leveling with the douchebag in front of us. "I highly suggest you shut the fuck up before I rip your dick off and shove it down your throat until you choke on it."

I hear, "Christ," murmured from Caleb and a small, choked laugh from Raine.

Both the guys throw their hands up and shoulder past us, not saying a word as they go. Probably smart on their part since Ivy looks serious about her threat.

When they're gone, Caleb walks over with Raine trailing right beside him. "You okay?"

It's hard to meet his eyes. I don't know what Danny has told him about our sort-of breakup, so I simply nod.

Raine brushes my arm and gives me a small smile before looping her arm around Ivy's. They start walking toward the doors, but Caleb sticks behind.

He asks, "Mind if we talk for a second?"

Olive looks between us, waiting for me to give a hesitant nod before she gives us privacy.

His hands go to his jacket pockets. "I heard about what happened at the dining hall. People can be real dicks."

That's what he wanted to say?

"And," he adds, making nerves shoot through my body. What exactly am I expecting? Him to officially break up with me for Danny so their wide receiver doesn't have to? "The team has your back. You mean something to DJ, so we'll make sure people don't bug you."

I blink slowly. "I'm not so sure about that anymore."

"You do. DJ is one of the best guys I know. He doesn't always take things seriously, but you...you're the one thing he does."

I can't conjure up anything to say to that.

He scratches his stubbled cheek. "Also, I just wanted to give you a heads-up about something. One of our teammates is in some trouble, and there's a chance he could talk to you and your friends. Lash out or something, I don't know. The dude can be unpredictable. I'm sure Danny mentioned something already, but I figured it'd be good to bring it up while I saw you."

My brows pinch. "What are you talking about? Danny and I have barely spoken. He..." I scrunch my nose. "I thought you wanted to talk to me to end things for him."

"*What?*"

"We got into a fight, and I told him that we probably shouldn't see each other. I just assumed...I don't know. I know his shoulder has added a lot of extra stress to his life, so I haven't wanted to butt in where I didn't belong and make it worse. I'm not sure what to say to him to make it better."

Caleb looks dumbfounded. "He told me you guys talk almost every day."

"We do," I admit sheepishly. "But it's like what you'd text your parents when you want to check in to see how they are. It's my fault, not his. I'm in a weird place, and he wants to fix that for me. But..." Why am I telling him any of this? "It's fine, Caleb. I'm a big girl and can handle it. Obviously there are worse things that could happen. I just wish he would do it himself if he wants to break up."

He slowly shakes his head. "I think you've got it all wrong. He—"

I hold up my hand. "I've had a really bad week. A bad semester, honestly. And maybe this is for the best anyway. He's graduating. I'll be here for a while. Probably." I cringe, knowing I want to stick out Lindon until graduation but not knowing if I'm mentally capable after the shit show this year has been. "I have to go. I'll see you around."

Before he can say anything, I turn around and find Olive before heading out.

She bumps my arm. "I'm proud of you."

I find myself smiling a little. "I am too."

"But," she adds, "I think Danny deserves to know what's going on. You've been avoiding him more than he's been avoiding you. It's not just on him. Somebody has to step up and start the conversation, Sky."

My lips twitch. "I know."

The text comes hours later.

Danny: We need to talk

I stare from the paper with a B- written in the top corner to the text waiting unanswered from me. I'd sent him a simple "hi" after Olive called me out at the library, then put my phone on silent for the duration of class so I didn't have to think about it.

Me: Ok
Danny: Bea's?

I nibble my bottom lip and glance at the time on my phone.

Me: Meet you there

Forty-five minutes later, I'm sitting across from Danny at our usual spot in Bea's Bakery. It's not as packed as usual, but the quiet atmosphere doesn't make me feel any less uneasy since I walked in.

"Is everything okay?" I finally ask.

When I walked in, he was already at the table. As soon as I came over, he pulled me into a hug and pressed a kiss against my temple that made me think my worries about us were all in my head.

Until the silence came.

The apology is at the tip of my tongue. For everything. For shutting him out. For our fight. For not giving him what he's wanted. Yet I swallow the words.

Danny picks up his pastrami sandwich and brings it to his mouth. "How's your salad? If you want something else, let me know. That doesn't look like much."

I frown at the chef salad Bea made for me. It's bigger than most salads I'd get on campus, but I don't tell him that. "This is fine, but thanks. Are you sure that you're—"

"Don't worry about it, Skylar." His tone has a cool edge to it, making me believe he's definitely *not* fine. Blowing out a breath once he sees me stare open-mouthed at him, he scrapes a palm down the side of his face. "It's nothing that you need to worry about. I want to spend time with you. To talk to you since we've been giving each other space. I want us to enjoy ourselves."

"I'd enjoy myself better if you told me what's bothering you. I know that's a lot to ask when I haven't been doing the same, but maybe we can change that. Is it me? Am I what's wrong?"

He curses under his breath, pushing his plate of half-eaten food away. "It isn't you. I swear. Caleb told me you saw him, and I...do you really think I'd end things through my friend?"

I hesitate. "I don't know."

His eyes narrow. "I wouldn't."

"What am I supposed to think, Danny? I don't know what this is. It seemed like you wanted to date when we were in Boston. Then we..." My eyes go to the few people at the tables around us. "Then we got into that fight. I felt awkward trying to make something work if it was doomed from the start."

"Doomed? That's what you think of us?"

"I..." I swallow.

"And we didn't fight, Skylar. We had a disagreement and

things got awkward for a while. But don't you think it's time to work that out? We gave each other space, and I didn't like that."

"You didn't?"

"Why would I? I opened up to you in Boston. I told you what I wanted from you—what I wanted to be. So no. I didn't like that you iced me out. And I definitely don't fucking like that you believe we're doomed."

"I don't really think that." Embarrassment heats my face. "It's just my head messing with me. You're...you. Everybody loves you. We both know what people think about me."

"Who the fuck cares about them?"

"I know I shouldn't, but..."

He's quiet for a second. "Look, some days are going to be better than others. But what people think of you shouldn't make you think any differently about yourself. It doesn't make me look at you any differently."

I blink at him in surprise.

"And the fact that you look shocked makes me feel like shit about myself. I won't lie. I haven't judged you once. If anything, I liked being with you because you were nothing like what your roommate spread around."

"So...?"

When he stares at his sandwich, it makes me antsy. "So I don't want to end things, Blondie. I never did. That was all in your head."

My relief doesn't last long.

"Now that's out of the way, I need to ask you something. Have you talked to Aliyah recently?"

The question throws me. "Ali? No, not since before the break. Why?"

Weariness washes over me as he shakes his head. The

only reason I can imagine him asking is because of the conversation we had not long ago, and that doesn't make the tension in my shoulders go away.

When he flicks his gaze upward at me, I bite my bottom lip.

"The guys told me that Wallace was brought in for questioning after a report was made, so I figured she must have gone to the campus police," he says.

My brows dart up. I passed along the suggestion to Ali, but she didn't seem that enthused about following through. She told me she'd think about it.

"She must have..." My voice breaks a little, so I clear my throat. I'll have to text her after we're done to ask her about it. "I don't know if she went or not, but if what she said is true, then it's not only her who knows about the stuff he does."

He makes a face. "True."

"What's going to happen to him?"

"Right now, they're just questioning him. It's up in the air. But keep an ear out. And if you know anything..." His words fade as he gives me a meaningful look. "Sky, when we were talking about your friend, I wasn't just saying that *she* needed to make a report. If there's anything you want to say about Wallace, you should too."

My body stills.

"Because what happened after..." His brows arch slightly. "What happened back in Boston tells me more than you have, and I'll give you time to come to terms with whatever that is, but I hope you'll tell me too. If it's something you need to tell somebody else though—"

"Stop," I tell him in a cracked tone.

"Skylar—"

"Danny, I know you're right. Having to think about that

night is one thing. Distracting myself from it…it was addicting to me. Because the more we did, the less credit I gave to what I'd already done. I got to choose who I let in my bed, who I let touch me. But talking about it is hard for me."

"Dammit, Sky." His abrupt words cause a couple of the other patrons to turn toward us in curiosity. "I know it's hard for you. I'll never understand on a personal level, but I'm trying. I've *been* trying. And you know what? These allegations against Wallace make this situation harder for more than just you. This isn't about you being honest with me anymore. It's about being honest with yourself."

"Danny, I—"

"Before you shut me down—"

I stand, grabbing my phone. "Maybe if you stopped cutting me off you'd know I'm trying to do the exact opposite. I like you, Danny. I like you so much and I'm terrified of it. Because we keep doing this—going around in circles. Picking little fights with each other. Making assumptions that hurt us."

He frowns but remains silent.

"What I remembered back in Boston ruined how perfect that moment was between us. All I could think about was how desperately I wanted to cling to what we'd done, but then that night, that *stupid* party, had to come and wreck everything."

His jaw ticks as he looks away.

"It's not *easy*. It's hard. Whatever is going on with Wallace is hard. Life is fucking hard, Daniel."

"Please sit back down," he says, voice softer than before. "I didn't mean to upset you or act like I knew better. I'm not trying to pick a fight. And I shouldn't have cut you off. I just want to understand so that I can help you move on. And if this is all related, then it's a step in the right direction."

I stare at the seat, not wanting to sit even though there are more than a few sets of eyes on me as I stand here. "Then take me to the house."

His face twists with confusion. "What?"

"The room..." I take a deep breath. "I remember which room it was. I told you that I'd show you."

If he wants to put this in motion, then he might as well take me back to where it all started. This is me opening up. Letting him help me.

Or try to anyway.

"Are you sure you really want to do that?" he asks, looking up at me with wariness crossing his features.

I shake my head. "No. I don't want anything to do with this, but I don't have much of a choice."

"You *always* have a choice—"

I cut him off before he tells me what I've been trying to convince myself of for months about that party without really saying it. Once those words are out, they become too real. I'll have to accept that I'd been... My throat thickens. "You're right, I do. And I'm choosing to let you in. I'm choosing not to let the past choices I made drown me. I want to move on. With my life. With you. I want this to work, Danny."

He stops talking, presses his lips together, and stands.

We're silent as I follow him to his Jeep parked out front. I can feel Bea's eyes on us as the door closes behind us, but I can't find it in me to care. How many people have chosen to stare at me all semester? Chosen to whisper? To believe the worst in me?

Maybe now, with Danny at my side, they'll have something new to talk about.

As we drive to the football house, a place where I've

taken up a lot of nights on the couch watching the guys play video games and in the kitchen eating whatever one of the players makes, I pull out my phone and text Aliyah.

Me: Did you go to the campus police about Ricky Wallace?

The message is marked Read within minutes.
But Aliyah never texts me back.

Chapter Thirty-Five

SKYLAR

I SEE JUSTIN FIRST when I walk in, noting the lack of crutches by his side. He's got a knee brace on with a subtle limp as he walks from the kitchen with something that looks about as bad as it smells in his hand.

"Hey, Blondie," he greets.

Ever since Danny started calling me that, his friends have begun doing the same. "Hi. How's your knee?"

"Physical therapy blows, but it'll get me to where I need to be," he responds.

We wave him off and near the stairs, me trailing a few steps behind Danny and gripping the wooden railing. I recall each floorboard creak like it's cemented into my memory from the morning after and wince at the sound.

Halfway up, I stop. The boy in front of me looks over his shoulder with a frown. "Skylar?"

I hold up my hand.

It'll be quieter up here.

Has anyone ever told you how beautiful you are?

We can stop if you want to.

The breath I release is choppy as I clench my teeth and walk the rest of the way up. My fingernails drag along the wood of the rail, and I wonder if they leave marks behind.

We can stop if you want to, he'd said.

I blink slowly and repeat those words in my head. *We can stop, we can stop, we can stop.* But he didn't stop at all. He'd gone too far.

He lied.

Danny watches as I pass by him silently and walk down the hall, throat thick and body tense. My eyes focus solely in front of me, on putting one foot in front of the other.

Three doors on the left.

My chest hurts from how hard my heart is pumping inside it.

I stop outside the door I'd crept out of, staring at the cracked wood as if something is about to happen. My fingertips drag along the wood design that's twisted with two different color finishes—almost as twisted as me.

Looking over my shoulder, I see Danny shaking his head slowly back and forth. He peers between me and the room my hand is reaching out to open the door to, his face pale.

"Skylar—" His voice is hoarse. "Are you positive it was this one?"

"I don't remember a lot," I tell him gravely, as if my emotions have been drained out of me slowly every single day leading up to this moment. "But I do remember this."

My hand turns the knob and pushes it open, not caring who or what is about to be revealed.

But the room is empty.

Lights off.

Bed unmade.

Clothes scattered haphazardly.

I blink.

Blink again.

There's a shirt that looks familiar thrown on the end of the bed, tangled in black sheets. The smell is vaguely familiar too...

"Skylar, that's...it can't..."

I turn to him.

"That's *my* room."

My lips part.

A door down the hall cracks open, and somebody says something, but I don't know what.

"What?" I breathe.

Danny steps forward.

I step back, hand raising on instinct.

Pain fills his eyes at my motion. "I was at the party, but you have to believe me when I say I didn't sleep in there that night." There's a desperation to his tone as he stares at me. Waiting. Expecting. Needing me to say something.

I can't though.

The words are lodged in my throat.

We can stop if you want to...

He didn't.

Blond hair. Or was it?

Was it darker?

His hands were big. Strong.

He smelled like alcohol.

His body was heavy.

Heavy on mine.

Danny has stopped *me* before. He'd stop if I asked him to. He would. I repeat that inside my head, but my lungs squeeze from the rising panic nestling into my rib cage.

Prickly sparks shoot from my heart and down my arms as I quickly dart around Danny and head for the stairs. I'm walking faster than the morning after, head clearer but still fuzzy for new reasons.

With confusion.

With unspoken feelings.

Unspoken truths.

Footsteps follow me, the heaviness of each step feeling like a chase that sparks adrenaline throughout my body and urges me to go faster. I'm out the door within seconds, Danny's voice yelling after me.

"Wait! *Skylar.*"

An arm hooks around my waist and I'm jerked to a halt before a bigger body is blocking my path, causing the panic to worsen as my arms swing around to try getting away from the limb attempting to hold me still.

"Hold up, baby." His eyes burn into my face and beg me to look at him, his grip loosening when he sees the fearful expression painted across my face. "You need to tell me what you're thinking," he pleads, swiping at my cheeks. Even the gentlest touch makes me flinch, causing his frown to deepen. "I know what you must think, but you know it wasn't me. It couldn't have been. I was there, but I slept downstairs in the basement. Please believe me."

My mouth opens, then closes a few seconds later. I want to tell him *I know*, but the words are jammed in my throat.

Danny shakes his head, his eyes going between me and the house. I hear people's voices behind us gathering at the front door of the house.

"I didn't know anyone used my room," he tries explaining. "We don't keep things locked up as well as we should. The guys…it could have been anyone. Wallace—"

"*Stop*," I finally force out, not wanting to hear that name in this conversation.

"I'm trying to explain—"

"I don't want you to! What does he have to do with this?"

"You know it wasn't me. Tell me you know that, Sky. We've been over this. We've talked about—"

"Just stop! *Stop*." I brush off his hands and back away, shaky hands going to my hair. "We've barely 'been over' anything. I need to think. You need to let me think."

"What is there to think about?" he demands, getting back in my way and forcing me to look at him. "Blondie, I'm right here. We need to talk this out. Don't shut me out again. Not this time. This is too important."

Too many thoughts circulate.

About hands.

Voices.

Scents.

Why can't I see the full picture? It's blurry. The face. The body it belongs to. It's there but it's not. At the tip of my tongue—the edge of my mind.

So close, but so far away.

Those hands reach out to me again, but I bat them away because I can't be touched right now. By him. By anyone.

Danny doesn't give up. "What do I need to do? Do you want me to get on my knees and beg?" He does just that, dropping to his knees and looking up at me with pleading eyes. He doesn't care about the audience watching my turmoil unravel before them. His blue eyes cloud with devastation as if my decision will determine just how much these past few months with him meant to me. If they were real or not.

Deep down, I *know* it couldn't have been him. I know it in my bones—in my soul. But I'm too flustered, too *angry* to let him know that.

"I'm doing it, Skylar." He throws his hands up. "I'm begging you. I beg you to trust me. I beg you to believe that I would never lie to you. I wouldn't hurt you. I'll do anything to prove it. Fucking *anything*."

The words that leave my mouth crack me wide open—heart and all. Exposing every vulnerable piece of me.

"It's too much right now," I tell him in a shattered tone. "You and I have been rocky from day one. This makes it…" I lick my lips and shake my head. "I don't know where we stand. You wouldn't even let me tell you what I wanted to earlier before jumping to conclusions. This? Showing you the room? It meant something. It still does. But it's *your* room and I don't know what to do with that."

"Baby." His voice is weak. "You know you can trust me. You know that."

"I told Olive," I whisper, every inch of me quaking from the reality sinking further and further down. "That's what I was trying to tell you at the bakery. I opened up to her like you told me to. I wanted you to be proud of me."

His eyes widen. "I am. That's…shit, Skylar. I'm so damn proud. Let's go back inside and figure this out."

I shake my head again. "No."

"Blondie—"

"Don't you see, Danny? I'm broken. Somebody *broke me* in that room. That's why I didn't want to tell you. Because the only thing I can be certain of is that what happened in there makes me weak. Messed up. What if I can't trust anymore?"

He reaches up and squeezes my hand. "I don't believe

that for a second. You've already trusted me. We wouldn't have done what we did in Boston otherwise. You know that. And I promise that I'll get to the bottom of this. That's why I was so busy. That's why I wasn't trying harder to see you. I gave you space, tried to use my time to figure out what Wallace was up to so I could—"

"*Why do you keep saying his name?*" My jaw quivers with irritation over how pushy he is about his teammate. I know he's a logical suspect from everything I've heard. But putting a name to a face, to the person guilty...

Danny stares at me. "Skylar..."

"Why?" I croak.

When I can't stand the way he watches me, I look away. His hand slips from mine. "Why do you get worked up when I say his name? If you know something—"

My fists clench at my sides. "Maybe you're trying to fit the wrong puzzle pieces together for your own reasons," I snap, stepping away from him.

"Do you hear how ridiculous that sounds? I'm trying to help you. That's all."

"If you want to help, then leave me alone to process this." I blink back the onslaught of tears that blur his image on the ground in front of me. "I just need you to leave me alone for now."

He pauses, the silence thick between us. "For how long?"

I don't answer.

"How long, Skylar?"

I simply shake my head and hear someone approach slowly from behind me. Ivy.

"I'll make sure she gets back okay," she tells Danny quietly. She doesn't touch me but shows me her hand, pointing toward Aiden's truck parked in the driveway.

I follow her over to it.
Eyes follow me. Burn into my back.
When we drive away, I feel empty inside.

Chapter Thirty-Six

DANNY

MY SURGERY IS SCHEDULED for December 22, and the only person I really care about telling isn't speaking to me. Not for my lack of trying either. Messages have gone unread and unanswered for over a week now, making me fucking crazy. If it hadn't been for Olive telling me Skylar was doing okay when I pulled her aside on my way to class, I would have stormed to her room and demanded she talk to me.

She hasn't been in film class.

She hasn't been at Huden.

Caleb and Aiden have held me back from seeking her out. If I hear "give her space" one more time, I'm going to slug them both in their faces even if it's a fight I know that I won't win.

> Ma: Doctor Siegel says your preop will be the day before the surgery, so you'll need to come home right after your last final

I glance at the screen again and grind my teeth. The surgery can't be held off any longer than I've let it go, which is the only reason I agreed to have it a few days before Christmas. But now I need to pack up my shit for the extended winter break even earlier than planned.

I only have a handful of days to try getting Skylar to talk to me—to tell her I'm not ready to give up on us. I don't want to believe that she thinks I have anything to do with the night of the party. Deep down, I'm sure she doesn't believe that at all.

Hell, as soon as I got my act together when Ivy drove her to campus, I stripped my bed, threw out my fucking sheets, and started sleeping on the couch in the den. A new mattress was delivered a week ago, but I still can't find it in myself to sleep in that room. The guys don't say a word even though my sleeping arrangement has spoiled their video game time.

Despite the hollow way Skylar watched me kneel in the cold grass that day, I recognized the trust she had in me. And that means more than anything else I could ask for.

So time is what I'll give her.

Me: Sounds good Ma

~

When Coach Pearce drops down into his creaky office chair, he leans back. "Surgery date?"

"End of December."

"Recovery time?"

I lift the shoulder in question. "At least six weeks plus physio."

It isn't like he didn't expect that, but he still grunts over the news. "We'll be sad to see you go. Not a great way to end the season."

No. No, it's not.

"I know I've been hard on you," he says, crossing his arms over his chest. "But it's only because I know you're capable of more than you let yourself think you are."

I don't believe that for a second. "All due respect, sir, but I call bullshit."

Both his graying brows arch.

"What's happening with Wallace?" I ask, wondering why he's out on the field with the others considering what's going on. I've read the handbook—had it thrown at me a few times with threats of consequences if I didn't get my shit straight in my first couple of years here. I know that what Ricky Wallace is being accused of is grounds for probation. He shouldn't be participating in any type of athletics.

The guys were all questioned one by one by the police lieutenant, giving statements and information about the parties we'd been to with Wallace. I have no idea what the others said, but I was honest. I never saw him do anything, but I heard a lot of talk from him about the girls he was with afterward. The problem with that is it's my word against his, and nobody at the station seemed inclined to do shit about hearsay.

"He shouldn't be out there," I tell Coach.

"Since when are you the coach?" he asks, offense thick in his words. "You'd better be careful about what you say."

"Or what? You'll bench me?" I gesture toward my shoulder. "I'm already out, Coach. Brady is out. Just because Wallace is a decent player doesn't mean he deserves to be out there playing. There are other guys who can replace him."

"None nearly as good as—"

"A possible rapist?" I spit.

His eyes narrow. "Watch your tone."

I lean forward in disbelief. "Do you fucking hear yourself? You care more about winning a game than you do about the reputation of the team."

"Right now, it's nothing but gossip."

My leg starts bouncing. "Are you going to be singing that same tune when the Dragons are talked about on ESPN and the nightly news because the team's coach chose to bury a scandal about its quarterback?" I cock my head as his fists clench under his arms. "It won't be our stats that they're highlighting if you sweep this under the rug. If it *is* true, which knowing Wallace wouldn't surprise me, then you're letting a real sketchy motherfucker get away with things nobody should get away with. And for what? Just so you can say you trained another NFL hopeful." I ignore the death glare he gives me because I'm on a roll. "Let's say he gets drafted and signs with a big team. There will be stories about him. Background checks done. He'll have a report on his file here unless you make that magically disappear too. And what if he decides to make more power plays out there because he thinks he got away with it already? Then it's not some small-town college news. It's national. And it'll link back to the *great* Coach Pearce who basically told him it was fine to do what he wanted because he knew how to catch a fucking football."

That is not what Coach wants to hear. He stands up, leaning forward until his hands are pressed against the top of the desk and his face is dangerously close to mine. "Do you know how many reports like this have been filed during my time here, son? Do you know how many times one of my players has been accused of this shit from girls who couldn't lock down the members of the team? They do it because they're jealous. They do it to get attention. It's no goddamn different than them claiming they're pregnant for their fifteen minutes of fame. You don't know what you're talking about here."

I click my tongue, not about to back down because he thinks he knows Wallace. "There's a big difference between those situations. Ask any of the other guys what they've heard your famed second string spewing since he got too big for his jersey, and you'd know that you're only saying these things to save your own ass. You think *I* don't know anything? I know a fuck ton more than you do based on this conversation." I stand up, mere inches away from his seething face. Unflinching, I lock eyes with him and say, "I'm glad my season is up. I wouldn't want to represent this team under its current leadership with an attitude like yours anyway. Not when there are going to be a lot more people stepping forward because of the quarterback."

"Like I always said," he spits as I walk toward the door. "Wasted talent."

My responding chuckle is dark, uncaring of his remark. Once, that used to sting. "Spew your bullshit to somebody who cares, because that's no longer me."

I walk out of his office, not bothering to close the door behind me. There are a few guys outside it gaping at me who obviously heard, newbies who are shocked anyone would have the balls to stand up to Coach like that. But what do I have to lose? I'm not going to sit around and watch him coddle Wallace and hold his hand through this. I'm not going to be holding the dustpan while he sweeps up Wallace's excuses into it. There's going to be talk one way or another, and I want nothing to do with it.

Caleb finds me sometime later, jogging out of the building with freshly washed hair and his sweats on after practice. "Is it true?"

"That depends on what you're referring to."

"Did you quit the team?"

He matches my steps as we walk toward the closest parking lot, where our vehicles are. "I plan on supporting you guys, but not him. I won't be on the sidelines so long as Wallace is playing out there. You know he shouldn't be. If it were any other player—"

"Hey, man. I'm with you." He looks over his shoulder at something. "Listen, a few of us were talking, and we'd be willing to walk."

I stop and stare at him.

He nods once. "None of us like Wallace. He's constantly acting like he's king shit. It's going to get him into serious trouble even if that time isn't now. But you know how he-said, she said situations work. We all do. It's a lot of back-and-forth unless there's hard evidence. It sucks, man, but that's how this is going to go. I think Coach is banking on that to keep Wallace on."

As much as I want to argue, I know Caleb's right. There can't be a lot done unless there's more than verbal accusations made against him.

"The team would really walk away?"

"We win together and lose together."

I look away for a second. "This whole thing is fucked," I murmur, moving hair out of my face.

"It'll get straightened out one way or another," he tells me earnestly.

My eyes narrow. "You say that like you know something I don't."

"Matt said Rachel was going to look into something for us," he says quietly. Matt Clearwater is another teammate, and Rachel Holloway is the athletic adviser for a lot of us. It's obvious there's something going on between them even though she's older and on staff. Last I knew, she was in grad school to become a professor. Even more reason for Matt to steer clear, not that he will.

"What is she looking into?" She has way more connections than we do in her back pocket since she works for the department. But that also means her job can be at risk. It's what's paying for her master's degree, so I don't want her getting into any trouble.

"Medical records. Wallace played while the others got benched after testing positive for STDs earlier in the year, remember? But knowing Coach…"

"He probably still let him play," I finish for him, feeling my eye twitch.

"It's a theory," Caleb tells me. "Nothing is proven."

But if it *is* proven, then that ties Wallace to Skylar and the night of the party.

"This whole thing is…"

"Yeah, man." He blows out a breath and shrugs. "You know, Capone wasn't arrested and convicted on murder charges."

I gape at him for a second, wondering what the hell that even means.

Then I watch him grin and walk away.

~

Commotion at the front door of the house after a long-ass day of exams has me walking down the stairs tiredly and witnessing Marks make a fool of himself.

"Damn. You taken?"

"Yes," the unfamiliar female says coldly.

"Got a sister?" Marks pries.

"Yes, I do. Skylar. Now tell me where the fuck Daniel Bridges is."

I quickly rush the rest of the way downstairs and step beside a stricken Marks to see a California Barbie standing at the other side of the door. Blond hair, blue eyes, and tan as hell, just like the pictures Skylar has of her in her room.

"Serenity?" I ask skeptically.

Her eyes turn to me, narrowed and icy like they are in most images I've seen over the past few months. "*You're* Daniel?"

Marks finds that funny, so I smack my palm against his chest and shove him away until he's stumbling back to whatever the hell he was doing before answering the door.

"I'm DJ, yeah."

She eyes me from head to toe, not looking very impressed with what she sees. "I'm in town to pick up Skylar."

My brows pinch. "She's not here. I—"

Her palm raises, stopping me. "I know she's not here. She's packing her things for our flight back to California." She flips her hand and points to the massive rock on her ring finger. "Do you see this?"

I blink. "Yes…?"

She deadpans as she moves the ring around her finger. "It can cut through anything. *Anything.*"

I hear a few of the guys snicker from the den where they're eavesdropping. "Got it."

Her head tips once. "I don't know what happened or who's to blame, but you better believe if I find out you did anything to hurt my little sister, I will find a way to hurt you."

My lips press together.

She steps into my space. "I know how to get criminals out of serious trouble, so don't think I don't know a thing or two about getting away with murder."

Popping my lips, I nod. "Now I know why Skylar loves watching true crime documentaries in her free time. For research."

Serenity hums. "Damn straight."

She moves her hair over her shoulder and steps back over the threshold. "I love my sister. I don't want to see her hurt."

I have approximately three seconds to debate on whether my next statement is a smart one to say out loud, but I decide it needs to be said no matter how much shit I'll get from the guys. "For the record, I'm pretty sure I love her too. Not as fiercely as you, but I do."

For once, the slightly intimidating woman standing in front of me is silent.

I hold up a finger. "Do you mind waiting there for a second? I have something for her. I wanted to give it to her in person, but…" I'm 99 percent positive she dropped out of film class because of me. "Just wait there."

I bolt upstairs, digging through the mess on my desk until I produce a red envelope. When I pass it over to Serenity downstairs, she stares at the messy scrawl of Skylar's name on the front before peering up at me with curious eyes.

I stuff my hands into the pocket of my hoodie and tip my chin toward the card. "If you could give that to her, I'd appreciate it. It's her Christmas present. And an early birth-day one."

I'm not sure what the blond woman in front of me is thinking, but she eventually nods after contemplating what's on her mind. "Fine, I'll pass it along."

"Thank you."

We're quiet for a few awkward seconds.

I ask, "Is she okay?"

Her head cocks as she studies me. "She's an Allen. She's strong."

I nod in agreement. "Where does she think you are right now? And how did you even get my address?"

"Like I said, Daniel, I have my ways."

That's all she leaves me with as she struts away to a fancy car parked in the driveway.

Marks comes back over to the door and leans against my good shoulder. "Fuck New York. I want whatever they're feeding women over there. Did you see the legs on—"

I smack him upside the head and close the door. "Shut up, Marks."

He sighs. "I'm just saying."

It's Justin who calls out, "Nobody cares what you have to say, dickwad."

Chapter Thirty-Seven

SKYLAR

SERENA KNOCKS ON MY childhood bedroom door and pokes her head in. I can hear Sienna and Serenity bickering behind her, making me sit up in bed. "I thought you were going out."

It's Sienna who pushes the door open and walks in without waiting for an invitation. The other two follow suit. "We decided it was better to stay here since you refused to go."

Serenity huffs and sits at the foot of my mattress. "Can you blame her? From what I hear, the movie has been getting bad reviews anyway."

Serena rolls her eyes and settles beside me in my bed. "Then why did you want Tony to bring you so badly a week ago when you realized it was coming out?"

Our oldest sister just scowls.

I smile a little, fiddling with the throw blanket draped over me.

"We need to talk," Sienna declares.

Three sets of nearly identical blue eyes focus on me, pinning me to my spot.

"Guys, I don't—"

Serenity stops me with a single look. "Skylar, you've been a mess for weeks. You've lost weight since starting at Lindon. You're pale. Your eyes…"

"They lost their light," Serena says sadly.

"And you're on, like, your second dose of antibiotics since you ignored us about going to the doctors when we first told you to."

I wince at the jab. I hadn't wanted to go back to the clinic in Bridgeport after the first time, so I went to the one on campus. All they told me was that it looked like I had a throat infection and needed proper medication, but they couldn't write me a prescription. Finals were kicking my ass and I didn't have a lot of free time to go anywhere in between studying and trying to get in some sleep. Olive was in the same boat as I was, so asking her to take more time out of her day for me wasn't fair to her.

And asking Danny wasn't an option, even if I briefly considered it when even drinking water hurt.

Serena takes my hand in hers. "I know you weren't telling me the whole story when you called me crying. Please tell us what's going on. We're getting really worried about you."

Even Sienna is showing a semblance of concern, which isn't common. She and Serenity are good at keeping their feelings hidden. It used to bother Mom growing up because she could never tell what was on their minds.

But the truth is, they probably have a right to be worried. I've lost two clothing sizes to the point very few pieces of my wardrobe fit me properly. My tan has been gone for a while now, and even though my skin is fair, I've looked peaked. Professor Albertson took me aside after I handed in my math final and asked if I was feeling all right.

"Mom doesn't think you should go back," Serenity informs me, making me gape. "She says she's watching her baby girl vanish in front of her eyes, and no college education is worth that."

The other two nod grimly.

"She...said that?"

More nodding.

I swallow.

Serena squeezes my hand. "It seems like whatever is going on there is more than just Becca and the other girls. What she said was horrible—"

"And I'm still salty I didn't find her little punk ass while I was there," Serenity grumbles.

Serena rolls her eyes. "We just want to know what you haven't told us. You know we're here for you."

"Always," Sienna vows.

Serenity dips her head once in confirmation, making the tears I'd managed to keep at bay reappear.

I stare down at my sister's hand before glancing at the other two waiting for me to reply. "I did something stupid..." I start with.

They sit.

They listen.

They stare.

And by the time I'm finished talking, I'm not the only one crying.

The oldest Allen sibling leans forward and takes my other hand. "Skylar, you need to make a formal report with the police."

My eyes widen in fear.

"And we need to tell Mom and Dad," Serena sniffles, wiping at her cheeks with the back of her hand.

I quickly start shaking my head, but Serenity doesn't let me speak. "I need you to listen to me, Sky. If you were drinking as much as you said you were, there was no way for you to properly consent to sex. Do you understand me?"

Hot tears pour down my cheeks. "I wasn't—" My jaw quivers. "That's not what happened to me, Serenity."

Sienna puts her hand over the one Serena has on me. "Sky Sister, Serenity is right. You may not remember telling him no, but that doesn't mean you didn't. If you were that drunk, he shouldn't have done anything with you at all."

The lawyer in our family sighs lightly. "I know you don't want to hear this," Serenity reasons, "but I've had to study a lot of cases like this, especially cases from college campuses. Sienna is right. You couldn't consent to anything. You were too inebriated to make a choice like that. What he did was wrong, and I do *not* want you to put that blame on yourself anymore."

"But *I* was the one drinking. *I* followed him upstairs—"

Serenity grips my shoulders, pinning my blurry, glazed eyes with hers. "You. Were. Drunk. And what little you do remember tells me he was sober enough to con you into doing things you shouldn't have agreed to. *If* you really agreed. Guys like that are pieces of shit because they do it for the power. They want to control every aspect of a situation by handing women drinks and encouraging them to do whatever they want. You have to talk to the campus police."

"I don't know who it was."

"Are you sure about that?" she asks, one of her plucked brows raised. "Because it seems to me like deep down, you do. I understand why you freaked out the day you showed Daniel the room. Anybody in your position would have because it's a lot to take in. But he may be onto something with this Ricky guy. You don't know."

391

"Exactly! *I don't know.*"

The room is quiet for a few beats.

A hand squeezes mine twice before Serena murmurs, "We love you. So, so much. And we know this isn't going to be easy, but don't you think it's important to tell people what you *do* know if it can help other people? Your friend Aliyah? Or...others?"

My throat thickens. "Do you think there are others like me?"

They all give me sad looks.

Serenity, always the realist, states, "In my experience, there are hundreds like you out there. Which is why this needs to be stopped. I can fly back with you and be there for you when you file a report. By speaking up, you may stop it from happening to others. Whether it's Ricky Wallace or another guy. Don't you want to make sure nobody feels like you do?"

"We can all go," Sienna offers.

I shake my head, rubbing my runny nose and blinking back tears. "You all have lives."

"We're a family," Serena reminds me.

It's Serenity who finishes for her. "And we always stick together."

I let out a shaky breath and blink back more tears. "I'm scared."

They all hold on to me.

~

Before she leaves my room with the others, Serenity passes something to me. I recognize the handwriting on the front of the red envelope instantly, looking up at my sister with shocked eyes as she shrugs. She simply walks to the door saying, "I had to be sure he wasn't out to hurt you before I passed it along."

My fingers toy with the card before I peel it out of the envelope. Lips wavering into a watery smile when I see penguins dressed in Santa hats on the front, I open the card and gape at what's inside.

Two tickets to a sold-out book signing hosted by my favorite author. "How did he...?" My thumb rubs over the information inked on the admission tickets, gaping at the dates.

It's been sold out for months. To my knowledge, there was no way to get these once they were sold out.

I let out a choppy breath and move my eyes over the generic MERRY CHRISTMAS FROM OUR FAMILY TO YOURS written in bold on the inside of the card. But when I move the tickets aside, I see what's written underneath in smudged ink.

Blondie—Giving you space hasn't been easy, but hopefully it'll be worth it. Especially if you decide to use this extra ticket on me. But if not, it's yours to do what you want with. I just want you to be happy. Text me. You know my number.

Short and sweet.

I wouldn't expect anything different from Danny.

I stare from the words written in my card to the tickets to my phone, resting on my nightstand. When I pick it up, I hesitate only a few seconds before typing out a reply.

Me: Merry Early Christmas

A few seconds after sending that, I thumb out another quick text.

Me: I'm sorry

When he doesn't reply, I worry I may already be too late.

Chapter Thirty-Eight

SKYLAR

My phone buzzes me awake way before I want to be up. I absentmindedly reach for it with my eyes cracked open and see an unknown Boston number flashing across my screen.

I sit up quickly, head spinning a little from the quick movement. "Danny?"

"It's Meadow," his grandmother says.

I blink past the grogginess of early morning brain fog. "Oh. Hi." Panic instantly settles in. "Is Danny okay? I texted him yesterday, but he never responded."

A million things swirl through my head. How did Meadow get my number? Did Danny get into a car accident? Is he okay? Is that why his grandmother is calling me and not him? Did something happen to his mother—

"His surgery was yesterday," she explains. "He's been a bit out of it since. Pain meds always hit that boy hard."

His surgery was yesterday? "I didn't know," I murmur sadly. He hadn't told me. Then again, when would he have been able to? Guilt cements itself into my stomach. "How is he doing? Did everything go all right?"

"That's why I'm calling."

I nibble on my thumbnail, drawing my warm blankets up my chest for comfort.

"He needs a pick-me-up," the older woman tells me. "Kept yammering on about you when he was off his rocker on the anesthesia. It's how I got your number. The boy insisted somebody call you to let you know what was going on, but my daughter and I felt it was best to wait. Now he's moping around like he used to when we'd tell him no as a kid."

"He was talking about *me*?"

She hums, amusement clear in her tone. "Wouldn't stop. The nurses in the recovery room said he just wanted to talk to his woman. They thought it was cute."

Heat blasts under my cheeks. "That's…" I clear my throat. "Sweet."

She chuckles. "If you think that's sweet, you should see the video his mother got of him yammering away on the car ride home. All he talked about was how he was going to wife you up, whatever the hell that means."

Oh my God.

"So what do you say? Do you want to come cheer him up after the holidays? He'll probably need a solid week to rest as much as possible, but after Christmas, he should be a little bit better."

I glance at the card on my nightstand, feeling the tension ease from my shoulders, knowing he's okay after I hadn't heard from him. That's…good. Better than good. "I need to talk to my family, but I think I can make that happen. Can you tell me what airport I'd need to fly into?"

~

I managed to pass math with a C-, and if I hadn't dropped from film, my GPA would be far lower than the 2.8 I scraped by with for my first semester. A far cry from the 4.0 I always held in high school.

It's a deflating feeling when my parents ask me how I did, seeing the disappointed frowns on their faces when I admit the average. Some of my old assignments are still hanging on the fridge with As and high remarks from old teachers, only making me feel worse when I meet two sets of sad eyes.

But it's nothing compared to the crushing feeling that consumes me when my sisters convince me to sit Mom and Dad down and tell them what I'd told them the night before.

Everything. From start to end.

And it goes about as I expect it to.

"You are *not* going back to that school," Mom informs me, swiping furiously at tears as she paces in the den.

"Mom—" Serena tries coaxing.

Our mother snaps her a look that has her quieting quickly.

Serenity speaks up. "If she doesn't go back, then he wins."

It's our dad, who's been eerily silent this whole time, who looks to his firstborn with surprise and says, "You didn't even want her going there in the first place."

"That's because she's better than *Lindon*. We all know she would have thrived at any Ivy League that accepted her, but that's not what she wanted. This is. And I'm telling you both that it would be a mistake to pull her away. It's not her who should leave."

I sit straighter, glad to have Serenity's fierceness backing me. Even though my time at Lindon U hasn't been great,

I don't think running away is the answer. "I won't lie, I considered dropping out a few times when things were… bad." A few eyes focus on me as I sink into the cushion I'm sitting on. I play with my hair. "But Serenity is right. I don't think it's fair if I'm the one who has to say goodbye to the few good things I have going for me there."

Dad swipes at his jaw. "Pumpkin, we don't want to see you get hurt any more than you already have been."

"Did you really…" Mom's soft words fade as she studies me carefully. "Did you really have to go through all that alone? You had to get treated for—" She winces.

Admitting to my family that I caught chlamydia was probably the most awkward part of this experience. But the anger and disappointment I expected to be met with didn't who on any of their faces.

They just looked…shocked.

Sympathetic.

Mom cried harder.

Dad's jaw clenched.

Serena and Sienna held hands.

Serenity patted my back in a much more maternal way that I ever would have expected from her.

"Yeah, I needed to go on antibiotics for it at the beginning of the semester. I was too embarrassed to tell anybody. I thought I'd get judged or get in trouble, so I…" I lick my lips and shrug defeatedly.

"Baby." Mom comes over and sits back down on the other side of me, taking my hand. "I know we don't always see eye to eye, but you could have told us. We would have *never* judged you for what happened. It wasn't your fault."

It wasn't your fault.

Olive told me that.

Danny.

All my sisters too.

And now my parents.

Maybe it's time I start believing it.

My throat bobs as I slowly begin nodding, trying to let those words absorb into me until they loosen my tense posture.

Mom brushes at my damp cheeks with her thumbs. "People like to pretend others are the bad people in life so they don't feel guilty about the things they've done to them. Do not for one second believe you're the villain. What that boy did, whoever he is, and what Becca has been making you feel like are not valid. So if staying at Lindon is going to make you feel safe, is going to make you feel like you have a fighting chance to prove to them they're wrong, then I'll support you. But your sister is right, sweetie. You need to file a formal report."

I find myself quietly agreeing.

It's Dad who says, "There have to be medical records of people treated for the same diseases."

"There would be," Serenity agrees. "But that isn't something that can be easily obtained. There'd have to be a targeted audience for investigators to even look into before collecting any information from them, and there are a lot of hoops to jump through to get it. Frankly, that's even *if* they take this kind of case seriously."

My shoulders drop.

Serenity squeezes one of them.

Dad growls, "What the fuck do I need to do to get my hands on a copy of the fucking reports?"

"Dad," Serenity warns. "We both know that would never happen. No amount of money will gain you access to that sort of thing. It'd be a major HIPAA violation to breach anybody's medical reports, even if they're a person of interest in a case under investigation."

His anger is palpable. "You've done it before. I know you have."

Mom hugs me into her side as Serenity glances at our red-faced father. "Yes, I have. But those instances were much more...serious than this one." She gives me an apologetic frown. "I know you don't want to hear this, but cases like this one would not garner any type of judicial approval for us. It's not even likely a thorough, formal investigation will happen without hard evidence."

The room is quiet. Deafeningly quiet.

It's me who decides to break it after the tension is too thick to bear. "When I go back, I'll talk to the campus police."

"One of us will go with you," Dad says.

Mom nods. "I think that's for the best."

I nibble the inside of my cheek. "I'm going to spend part of the break in Boston."

More silence.

Serena clears her throat. "Are you going to see Danny?"

I manage to nod despite the look Dad gives me, who doesn't seem thrilled over the idea of me leaving earlier than planned. "He had his shoulder surgery, and once he recovers, I'm going to spend time with him." I look to Dad, then Mom. "I'll spend Christmas and New Year's here and then go there for the rest of break."

Dad swipes a hand through his gray hair. "Do you think that's a good idea? Adding a boy into the mix after the semester you've had is—"

"A good thing," Serenity cuts him off, challenging him

with a deadpan look. "I think it'd be good for her. I met him. He's not bad."

I gape at her. I mean, obviously he had to give her the card to pass along to me somehow, but I've been too shocked over having the tickets to think about how the exchange even happened.

"And he didn't even flinch when I threatened to chop his dick off if he hurt her."

"You did *what?*" I shriek.

She shrugs casually. "It needed to be said. You were upset and I didn't know if he was the reason or not. But he seems like a good person, and it's obvious he cares about you." When we lock eyes, her lips lift slightly. "Deeply."

I blink a few times, taking that in.

Serena pipes in with, "I agree. I think Skylar should enjoy some time with him. She deserves to be with somebody who's on her side and makes her happy."

Sienna nods, looking to Mom as if her vote in this will sway Dad. And she's right. Even though most of us have him wrapped around his finger, it's Mom who's always been the decision-maker when it comes to them.

When Mom relents with a soft sigh, she pecks my cheek. "*Does* he make you happy?"

It doesn't take me long to respond. "Yes."

Her thumb dries what's left of my tears. "Please be careful. With him. With yourself. With your *heart.* You've always had such a big one, and I'd hate for anybody else to take advantage of it."

Dad's expression is grim as he drops whatever argument he has against me going back to the East Coast. "If anybody does *anything* to you—"

"I'll be okay," I assure him, offering a small smile to prove it.

Serena claps excitedly. "Let's book you a flight then!"

A dramatic sigh comes from Sienna. "Our little sis is growing up so fast."

Our mother laughs lightly and kisses my forehead before walking over to our father. He pulls her into her side, and it reminds me of what Danny always does with me.

It isn't until just this moment that I realize how badly I've missed him and his little touches and cheesy jokes and everything in between. I like when he holds my hand and plays with my hair and attempts to paint my nails even though he's really bad at it.

I've been unfair to him when he hasn't deserved it, so I know this trip is exactly what I need to prove to him that I'm willing to put in the effort. To show that I'm all in.

If he'll still have me.

Chapter Thirty-Nine

DANNY

"ARE YOU SURE ONE of us shouldn't check on Grandma?" I ask Ma for the umpteenth time from where I'm lounging on the living room couch. "I thought she'd be back by now."

The feisty woman left over an hour and a half ago to grab some things from the store. It never takes her this long.

"You know your grandmother," Ma tells me, kissing my head and passing me a cup of hot chocolate. "She probably saw somebody she knows and stayed to chat with them." She sits down beside me and watches the ESPN reels playing on the screen from a different college game. "Why do you do this to yourself?"

"What?"

Ma points toward the screen with a shake of her head. "I know how much you love football, Danny, and I know how much you're upset that it's over. I still think you're doing the right thing, but I'm worried because all you've wanted to watch is *SportsCenter*."

My leg starts bouncing, so to stop it, I drape my crossed

ankles onto the coffee table. I know I'll get away with it this time because I'm still recovering. But give it a week or two and Ma will be smacking me upside the head and telling me to take my feet off her furniture.

"I just want to stay up to date on things."

"Your friends will do that for you."

I scratch the side of my neck. "It wasn't supposed to be like this," I finally tell her with a heavy sigh. I cross my arms over my chest and sink into the couch. "I was supposed to finish the season. Help us *win*. I was supposed to finish college feeling like I was part of something big."

Shaking my head, I grind down on my teeth, thinking about how everything has changed. I'm not the same person I was when I first started at Lindon. I wanted to be the big man on campus. The one who everyone liked. The one who helped bring the football team to the top. Coach was going to love me for everything I contributed to our stats, and so were my teammates. I would have made a difference.

I don't care that Aiden became the guy I always thought I would be, especially considering Coach focuses a little too heavily on the people he wants to make big, consequences be damned. That's too much pressure, too much bullshit for me to handle.

"Coach Pearce cares about making a name for himself through others. There's a lot of shit going down with the team because of Wallace. The new QB. Remember how I was telling you about his little extracurricular activities?" My jaw ticks at the thought of him.

She makes a face. "And I told you that boy will get a taste of his medicine in time."

"He's hurting women," I tell her quietly.

Her eyes narrow. "How do you mean?"

I fill her in on the latest updates I know. Aiden says that the campus police and local sheriff's office aren't inclined to move forward with any type of investigation because there's nothing to go on. The only thing they've offered is restraining orders for the girls to make sure he doesn't get too close to them, but it's more restrictive to them than Wallace. From what the guys said when I spoke to them, he can still go anywhere he wants, whenever he wants.

"Please tell me you're not plotting anything" is her response. "I know that twinkle, mister. You're never up to any good when I spot it in your eyes."

I brush it off. "I'm not planning anything that isn't justified."

And technically, it's Matt that's doing the plotting. Not me.

"Daniel…"

"Ma," I return, knowing when the full name is out she's not playing around. "I need to do this. Guys like him shouldn't have the kind of freedom he does. I may not like Coach all that much, but the Dragons don't deserve to go down as an infamous team that *SportsCenter*"—I gesture toward the screen—"reports on because of one player and his bad reputation. It's not fair. I may not have football anymore, but those guys do. And a lot of them are working their asses off to make a name for themselves." Closing my eyes and pinching the bridge of my nose, I murmur, "I think he hurt Sky. Or tried to. I don't know. There's not enough evidence that points in his direction. Yet. But I have this feeling in my gut, Ma. A bad one."

She's so quiet I have to glance over at her.

When I see the deep frown set on her face, I'm not sure what she's going to say. But then understanding clouds over the disapproval. "You always did want to do anything it took to protect the people you love."

My eyes snap to hers.

She smiles. "You do love her, right?"

My heart starts hammering in my chest when the three-letter word leaves me. "Yes."

Her smile widens as the front door unlocks and pushes open. "That's good. Something tells me it's mutual."

I'm not so sure about that.

Before I can voice my doubt, Grandma Meadow calls out, "Boy, you better be looking decent because I have something for you."

My brows pinch as I turn my head to see Grandma M come into view with a dark-haired girl behind her. "*Skylar?*"

I've never stood so quickly in my life.

She gives me a sheepish wave, smiling between me and Ma. When her eyes lock on mine again, she says, "Surprise. Hopefully a good one."

"The best," I breathe, walking over and pulling her into a one-armed hug.

It's my grandmother who pats me on the back. "Next time you tell me I can't keep a secret, remember this moment." She walks over to where my mother stands. "Come on, Carrie. Let's leave these two be for a bit. Something tells me they have a lot to discuss."

I guide a timid-looking Skylar to the couch that I've been using as a temporary bed. There's less room to flop around on my shoulder, so Ma and I thought it was best.

"I can't believe you're here," I tell her, taking the seat Ma had occupied.

She drops her hands to her lap. "I wasn't sure if you'd want me to come. I texted you a couple times after I got your card, but you didn't reply. I figured you were upset."

"Ma took my phone away because I kept sending random

texts to people," I admit, flinching a little from some of the messages. Most of them were to the guys, who found them funny as hell. One was to Coach, who was less than amused. That was when Ma decided I shouldn't have phone privileges until I was less doped up.

Skylar turns to me, drawing one of her knees onto the couch. "Danny, I'm really sorry about what happened at your house. I freaked out on you, and you didn't deserve it. Having to take that all in was too much, and I lashed out at the wrong person."

While her apology sends instant relief to the piece of my heart that was worried she'd thought I was the bad guy in this situation, I don't want her to think I held it against her. "I appreciate it, Blondie, but you don't need to say you're sorry. That would have been a lot for anybody to deal with."

"I do though. I took my confusion and frustration out on you because you were there, and it wasn't right. I don't want to cast blame on people. Not the wrong ones anyway."

I stare at her carefully. "Does that mean...?"

Her eyes evade mine for a moment, her fingers fiddling in her lap. "I told my family. About everything. I promised them that I'd talk to somebody when I got to campus and let them know what happened. It's time. Overdue, really."

My hand quickly finds hers, threading our fingers together. "Are you okay?"

When she peeks up at me, there's something shadowed over her eyes. "Yes. No. I don't know. Serenity has been a huge help in getting me to see that I can't keep quiet about this. Bottling it up obviously only made me angrier." She winces, giving me another apologetic look. "I may not ever know what happened that night. Not all of it. I have to accept that. But I don't want to keep quiet about it when there could be other girls out there who went through what I did and may remember more than me and are just too afraid to speak up. You know?"

I nod. "I get that."

"So is it okay that I'm here? Really?"

I inch forward until our knees are touching. "Skylar, I've been wanting to see you since Ivy drove you away. Caleb had to physically restrain me from showing up at your dorm. But I knew that wasn't what you wanted from me. So yeah. This is more than okay. How long are you here for?"

"Your grandma told me I could stay until we have to go back. As long as that's—"

I stop her from asking if it's okay again by kissing her. The second my lips crash against hers, she melts into me. I taste her, breathe her in, touch her cheek, move that same hand backward to cup her skull, anything I can do to keep her close.

To prove to her I mean what I say.

When I pull back, she lets out a shuddering breath and a cute-ass giggle. "Okay. I'm convinced."

I peck her lips again and grin. "It was the tickets to Ocean Fest, wasn't it?"

Her hand comes up to cup my cheek, stroking the stubble I've let grow in. I plan to shave it before heading back to school, but I'd be lying if I said I didn't enjoy the way she paid it special attention. "That may have been part of it. How did you even get your hands on them?"

I'm never going to tell her the truth—that I messaged four different people attached to the book con, including the big-ticket author she's dying to see, to plead for their help in winning over a girl. It was the very person whose books she introduced me to who responded with the information to claim the tickets in hopes I win Skylar over.

Instead of admitting that, I say, "I have my ways, Blondie. Don't you know that my charm is my biggest ally by now?"

She snorts, not believing my bullshit answer for a second. Her lips press against mine lightly, exploring them before I open my mouth to let her in deeper. The little noise she makes the second our tongues meet has my dick growing instantly.

Our hot little make-out session only lasts a few minutes before a throat clears. "You better not be making babies on my brand-new couch," Ma says from the hallway.

Skylar breaks our kiss breathlessly, her cheeks turning the shade of pink I've missed for weeks now.

I lean in until my lips brush her ear and whisper, "She didn't say anything about not making babies on my ten-year-old mattress upstairs."

She slaps my chest and puts distance between us.

Probably smart.

I'm almost tempted to haul her over my good shoulder and carry her upstairs to see just how far she'll let me get.

~

The rest of break is spent hanging out around the house. Once a week, I join Skylar for FaceTime calls with her family so they can all interrogate me. Even after an intense grilling, I'm reassured by the scariest sister that I'm well liked for their sibling.

Skylar and I go out a few times, usually just to eat because I'm still beat as hell from all the medicine and appointments I've been going to before heading back to campus. I've been cleared to make the drive after a few scans, even though my ma, grandma, and girlfriend—I still have to make that official—insisted that Skylar drive for at least part of it to give my arm a break since it's still sensitive.

It's crazy to me that I'm in my last semester of college. It's even crazier that one little surgery is changing exactly how that semester is laid out. Usually there's a lot of gym time, training, and early practices with the guys. Now I have no idea what it's going to look like. The routine I'm used to is long gone, and I'd be lying if I said I wasn't grieving that a little.

This summer, I'll have my bachelor's degree and will be moving on with my life, along with the rest of the people I've grown close to over the past four years. Maybe having one last semester adjusting to that change is a good thing.

Even though Caleb plans on sticking in Lindon and running his family's hardware store, most of the other guys who are graduating are spreading out.

Aiden is officially done with school, and I only just learned that Ivy is dropping out. They'll be out of the house while Aiden trains for the combine that he was invited to. It's inevitable he'll get drafted, and obviously his girl will be following him for the ride.

Justin accepted his enrollment at Cornell University and already has a new place lined up for after graduation.

Marks has even less of a clue as to what he's going to do with his life than when he started college.

Then there's me.

"I have something to tell you," I say to the girl next to me on my bed, nudging her foot to gain her attention from the screen where a movie is playing. "I got into grad school."

Her eyes widen. "What? When? Where?"

"It happened a couple weeks ago. Got the email confirmation, then the packet in the mail a few days later."

She fiddles with the drawstring of the hoodie she stole from me the first night she arrived. It's gigantic on her but hot as hell. The only thing that'd be sexier is peeling it off her. "So you're leaving in a few months?"

The disappointment in her tone has me smiling like a fool. "I'm attending grad school at Lindon. Sorry, Blondie. Can't get rid of me for another couple of years."

Her teeth bite into her bottom lip before she releases it. "I'm happy to hear that. I don't think I'm ready to give you up quite yet."

"Yeah?"

She nods. "I was wondering if you'd help me with something before we go back."

"Anything. Name it."

That's how, two hours later, I'm crammed inside the upstairs bathroom one-handedly helping Skylar bleach and color her hair back to something close to the shade of blond she was born with.

When Grandma Meadow and Ma peek their heads in, they both smile. At me. At the girl with a towel draped around her shoulders as I help her brush and dry the newly dyed strands.

And I can't help but smile back, probably for the first time since break started.

I ask, "Doesn't my girlfriend look fine?"

Skylar doesn't correct me.

She simply beams.

Chapter Forty

SKYLAR

AFTER A LONG MEETING with my adviser to prepare for spring classes starting tomorrow, my stomach rumbles with an appetite that's been missing for too long. Spending the last couple of weeks in Boston has helped me gain a little bit of the weight I lost back—probably more than I would have liked, although Danny has definitely shown his appreciation over it.

He never shied away from feeling me up any chance he got, especially when the sun set and his family went to bed. We'd explore each other's bodies like we hadn't seen them in years, drawing out little moans from one another as our fingers and mouths reacquainted themselves with certain body parts. The thought of him groaning when I got on my knees and lowered his jeans and boxers to take him in my mouth for the first time still makes my heart do funny things in my chest. He carefully guided my movements after I urged him to show me how to make him come, and I still think about the noise he made when he emptied himself into my mouth.

It was only a couple hours after getting back from Boston and settling in when I told Danny I was ready to talk to the police. Not only did he go, but Olive and Aliyah did too. I'm not sure how Olive convinced Aliyah to talk, but the group of us went in together to share what we knew. About Wallace. About the parties we'd been to. Danny held my hand the entire time leading up to them passing me a piece of paper and asking me to write down a written statement in my own words.

It's the kind of progress I wasn't sure I was able to make. Telling someone. Letting people in to help me do it. But there's a pride woven deep inside me for being able to after so long of keeping quiet.

I'm halfway to the dining hall with my fingers touching my lips, lost in the memory, when a hand snakes around my arm and tugs me in between two of the brick academic buildings, slamming me against one of the hard, scratchy walls.

My breath catches when Ricky Wallace's face appears in front of me, jaw clenched and nostrils flaring with anger. "Did you really think changing your fucking hair color would help you disappear?"

"What?" I ask choppily as I quickly glance at the empty quad for help.

His grip tightens on my arm, making me wince at the sting of pain from it. "Take back your statement. I'm not going to have a blond bitch ruin my shot at a future for no real reason. It's bad enough your little guard dog fucked me over with the team."

I swallow. "Ricky—"

"I don't want to hear any excu—"

"What the fuck is going on?"

Wallace is ripped away from me, causing me to stumble sideways and drop my bag full of textbooks. The zipper busts open and the books scatter across the slushy ground.

Despite the amount of money that I spent on them, I couldn't care less about them when I see Caleb and Danny standing there, holding their teammate back.

"What do you think you're doing with my girlfriend?" Danny asks Wallace, jerking him back so there's distance between us. "I told you to stay the hell away from her."

His teammate scoffs. "Why don't you ask your girlfriend what she's done to me?" His bloodshot eyes snap in my direction, causing my stomach to tighten from the unwanted gaze. "Are you jealous? Is that it? Angry I didn't pay you more attention?"

My eyes widen at the question as Caleb holds him back and murmurs, "Stop while you're ahead."

But Wallace doesn't heed his warning. He shoves Caleb away from him and turns back to me with a pointed finger. "Couldn't handle it, could you, princess?"

Heart racing so fast it hurts, I shake my head and try to process what Wallace is talking about. I have to clench my hands into fists to stop them from shaking, but the feeling travels up my arms and into my limbs until it settles into my chest and squeezes my heart.

Danny doesn't like Wallace pointing at me almost as much as I don't. He steps in front of me, blocking his teammate's view of me with his broad body.

Which is good, because I can feel it happen. The panic. The way my lungs hurt. My heart hurts. Everything *hurts*.

"If you don't put that fucking finger down, I'm going to break it. Understand me?"

"You used to be fun. Remember that? All the guys said

you could get any girl you wanted. If this is what dating somebody does to a guy, I'm glad I have no interest in doing more than screwing them." Wallace's voice is cold as he looks over Danny's shoulder at me. "What the fuck do you even see in her? She's not that attractive."

The insult has me paling as Caleb cusses and Danny takes a step closer to the man sneering. I grab his forearm as his fists clench. "Your shoulder," I remind him quietly, knowing he'd make good on the whole breaking bones thing if he needed to. Grounding him will help ground me. I know it. If he gets hurt or in trouble because of me…I wouldn't forgive myself so easily.

Caleb gets between the two football players, holding them back from going at it with each other so neither of those things happens. "Do you think fighting will solve anything? It's going to make it worse."

"He fucked me over!" Wallace yells, trying to get past Caleb. "Ask him what he did. Ask him what he convinced his girl to do."

I turn to Danny in confusion.

Caleb shakes his head. "Whatever is happening to you is your own damn fault. Quit blaming everybody else and own up to your shit for once."

"They made me take a drug test," Wallace seethes, glaring at Danny and me.

This is about a drug test?

A few more people join the spectacle that Wallace is making, including Stephen and Justin. As soon as they see who's involved, they come over and help split everybody up before an actual fight breaks out.

"Come on," I tell Danny, pulling him toward me. I don't want to be here. The feeling in my gut when I'm around Wallace is bad—it's suffocating. I want to get as far away as possible from him and whatever this conversation could lead to.

Danny glances at me, then down at my ruined books on the ground. "Fuck." He kneels and helps me collect them, frowning at the water and muck dripping from a few.

"Don't worry about it."

"He ruined—"

"He's being taken care of." I gesture toward his team guiding a very angry Wallace away from the crowd that was probably hoping for something big to happen based on the cell phones pointed in our direction.

Danny blows out a breath, pausing as he rocks back on his heels. "Did he hurt you?"

I shake my head, picking up the last book and trying not to sigh at the dirty water-stained pages. I think to myself, *I think he may have once.* But I still don't know. The way my heart skips and stomach drops tells me all I need to though. Still, I say, "No. He was just angry. You guys came before he could do anything more."

His nostrils flare. "I'm going to—"

"Do nothing," I stop him, narrowing my eyes skeptically. "What was he talking about with the drug test?"

A small smirk lifts his lips, but it looks more devious than playful. "I'm making sure he's taken out one way or another. The asshole doesn't deserve to be on the field acting like he's untouchable."

"So you made him take a drug test?" My doubtful tone has him snickering as we stand. He takes a couple of the books out of my hands and carries them for me, nodding for us to walk away from the people lingering behind.

"No. I called in a tip to someone above Coach Pearce's

head who would actually give a shit if the Dragons were in the news for anything other than the games we win."

I blink in silence, not following.

"The day I went with you and your friends to the station—" He presses his lips together and shakes his head in exasperation. "It was obvious after you spoke to the cops that they weren't going to do anything."

I frown.

After all was said and done, nobody seemed that interested in pursuing anything. In fact, I got reprimanded for drinking underage and was told they'd let me off "with a warning" since I've never gotten into trouble before.

"It pissed me off," he tells me with a heavy sigh. "So I took it into my own hands without getting physically involved."

"Like you were about to be sixty seconds ago?" I prod, jabbing my finger behind us. "You could have gotten hurt, Danny. I don't want you to do that for me."

He stops walking and turns to me, a sad smile on his face. "Don't you get it by now, Blondie? I'm willing to do anything for you. Be your friend. Be your mentor. Be your bodyguard. What I want more than anything is to be your boyfriend, which means I'm going to keep being a mixture of all those things even if it means me almost punching somebody in the face. Especially someone as scummy as Wallace."

"And breaking their fingers?" I inquire.

"That too."

"You're a little crazy," I inform him, smiling. He's more than capable of breaking somebody's fingers, which is oddly...sweet. Sort of.

"But you love it."

I meet his eyes. "I…" Licking my lips, I take a deep breath and nod. "I do love that about you. I love *you*, Danny. And I know things haven't been very easy with us, but I do hope that we have time to smooth things over. Especially since you're staying here a little longer. If that's…if that's something you'd want too."

The vulnerability in my voice has his throat bobbing. Bending down, he captures my lips with his in a soft kiss before pulling back. "I love you too, Blondie. And I plan on proving that to you for as long as you'll let me."

We stare at each other.

Suddenly, the hunger I'd felt before is for something completely different.

I grab his hand and lead him away from Huden and toward the path leading to Ellis.

When we get to my room, he presses me against the door and whispers, "I want you to be sure. We don't have to do anything else."

"I'm positive I want this," I promise, kissing him again before leading him inside.

He wastes no time dropping my books onto my desk and returning to me. "I was really hoping you'd say that."

And then he kisses me.

Hard.

Chapter Forty-One

DANNY

THERE'S AN URGENCY IN our kiss. Her hands go to my jacket, pushing it off my shoulders. I do the same to hers. Our boots are left in a puddle by the locked door. Socks. Jeans. Shirts. All discarded in a trail leading to the bed.

My hands fumble with the clasp of her bra until I pop it open and let that join the rest of our discarded clothing. The second her breasts are exposed to the cool air, her nipples pebble.

Dipping my head, I suck one into my mouth, flattening my tongue against it, then do the same with the other until she arches her chest forward and claws at my hair. I chuckle against her, nipping playfully before moving back to her lips and kissing her harder.

"Climb on top of me," I tell her, hopping onto the bed and patting my stomach after lying flat on my back.

She's wary for a second, her bottom lip drawing into her mouth as she watches me palm myself. I'm hard as fuck and want nothing more than to see those tits bounce while she rides me.

I groan at the thought and squeeze my cock, feeling it grow in my hand. It's only then that she crawls over me, straddling my lap until she's pressed against where I want so badly to be buried inside her again. "I want you to ride me, baby." I cup her face and push up to kiss her. It'll take some of the pressure off my shoulder until I can get some strength back into it to really show off my skills in bed.

But we have time for that.

Plenty of it.

"I've never done that." Her nerves only make this moment that much hotter because I get to show her how it's done.

"You're in total control," I say against her lips, pecking them and moving down her jaw. When I press my mouth against the sensitive spot below her ear, she shivers. "It'll feel fucking great for the both of us. But we can stop at any point if you change your mind. The choice is yours. All the choices are yours."

She releases a shaky breath before nodding, drawing back to meet my eyes. Her fingers trail along the hem of my briefs, making my abdominal muscles tighten from the featherlight caress.

"Come here," I coax, gesturing toward my face as I settle into a better position for what I want from her.

Her brows pinch.

"Want you to ride my face first."

The flush on her cheeks makes me smirk. I've become a big fan of her pussy—feasted on it as many times as I could over break.

"I don't want to hurt y—"

I stop her by tugging her toward me as I lie back again. "Baby, the only way you'd hurt me is by *not* sitting on my face. You're killing me here."

"That seems a bit dramatic."

"If I wanted to be dramatic, I would have said I'd be honored to die of suffocation by pussy. Imagine that on a gravestone."

Her eyes grow comically large. "Danny!"

"Babe," I laugh. I knead her bare thighs, one of my favorite features of her. Her hips give me the perfect handful, especially for times like these. "I promise. This will feel good for you. I want to make sure you're ready for when it's my cock you're riding."

Her signature blush is back.

Thankfully, she doesn't keep fighting me on it as I help guide her to hover over my face. I move her panties aside and lean up enough to kiss her seam. She shudders above me and lowers down as I grip her hips and use my tongue to swipe along her and trace her tight entrance that's already wet as fuck for me.

"*God*," she rasps, hands pressed flat against the wall as she moves her hips. I let her grind on me as I suck her clit and move back down to her entrance. With every swipe, she becomes louder, needier for release. Her legs start to shake on either side of my head, telling me she's close.

I don't let up until the moment she detonates, eating her out like my life depends on it. Because right now? It just might.

Her head tosses back as she arches forward through her orgasm, clenching at the wall. When she looks down and meets my eyes, her breath catches. She moves down my body until we're kissing again, tongue twisting, breaths mixing, and we're helping each other take off the last layers of clothing between us.

"Condom," I tell her, pointing toward my jeans on the floor.

She climbs off me long enough to grab one from my pocket and repositions herself on top of me, her fingers helping guide the latex over my erect cock. The feeling of her hands on me has me grinding my teeth. It'd be embarrassing to come before anything begins, but I'm that close to losing my shit.

"Pick up your hips," I guide, watching her obey as I fist myself and position the head of my cock at her opening. "I can't tell you how many times I've jacked off thinking about this moment."

One hand on her hip, I squeeze the soft flesh as she lowers down slowly. Her lips part as we lock eyes, never looking away from each other as she takes me in inch by slow inch. She picks her hips back up and does it again, this time taking me in deeper than before.

No words can really describe the feeling of my dick being squeezed by her hot, wet warmth. I watch as she becomes more confident in her movements, setting a slow pace and resting her palms flat against my chest, careful not to put pressure on my shoulder.

I arch up with a low grunt the second I'm seated fully, causing a garbled noise to escape my lips from the tight feeling. Her lips crack into a tiny smile that quickly vanishes when I roll my hips into a circle to stretch her. The moan that crawls up her throat has me doing it again, helping her get used to me until I can't help but clench onto her hips.

"Need you to ride me fast, baby. I'm so fucking close. I need to come in you."

Her exhale is sharp as she lifts up and drops back down with a startled gasp. I help her set a faster pace, dropping her onto me harder until her tits start doing exactly what I hoped they would. When she gets used to the rhythm,

I palm her breasts in my hands, tweaking her nipples and kneading them until the noises she makes start becoming as desperate as the ones leaving me.

The sound of our skin slapping and her pussy sucking me in has my head dropping back onto the pillow. "Fuck, Skylar. So goddamn good."

Bed frame creaking loudly as she rocks into me faster, she slams down onto my dick and swivels her hips until her face goes red. "D-Danny, I—" Repeating the motion one more time, I feel her clench me so tightly, I go temporarily blind as I come harder than I have in a long fucking time.

My back arches, filling her deeper as we both orgasm at the same time. She pulses around me, milking me of every drop of come I have until our bodies collapse onto the bed, chest on sweaty chest.

One of my arms hooks around her waist as my other lifts to stroke her hair. We're quiet for a long time as we catch our breaths, staying like that until I soften inside her and have to pull out.

After taking care of the condom, I crawl back into the bed, tugging her into my side. Kissing the side of her head, I ask, "Are you okay?"

She looks up at me, a light in her eyes that I don't think I've really seen more than a few times since meeting her back in September. "I'm more than okay. That was..."

Half my lips pull up. "I know, Blondie. I don't think I have any words for that either."

Kissing her softly, I explore her mouth until a content sigh leaves her.

"Real glad we both wound up here," I tell her, pulling her closer into me. My cheek rests against the top of her head as I pull her comforter over top of both of us. A few minutes later, I hear her stomach start to rumble. I laugh, squeezing her to me before asking, "Want to go to Reavers for some pizza?"

I feel her body shake with quiet laughter as she murmurs, "Sorry for ruining the moment."

Swatting her ass, I sit up. "As far as I'm concerned, I'm helping fuel you up for round two. We're both going to need our energy for the rest of the night."

Skylar gapes. "The rest of the night?"

I nip at her bottom lip before passing her her clothes. "We're just getting started. There are at least three other positions I want to teach you tonight."

She swallows.

I grin.

And I make good on my word, because I know Skylar trusts me to keep it.

Epilogue

SKYLAR

I SHARE A SIDE hug with Caroline as Danny walks across the stage and waves at his teammates, dressed in the same red gown as him, who are hooting loudly. They've done it for every football player who's walked so far, and even though Danny insists he's not a Dragon since walking away after his injury, his friends don't count him out during his moment to shine.

Secretly, I think he's relieved.

After disciplinary actions were taken against Ricky Wallace that officially pulled him from the team, their season ended. The relief Danny probably feels is nothing compared to mine. Although a part of me is still unsure of who assaulted me that night at the party, there's a gut instinct that says it was the same boy in question. And while Wallace being punished for drug use is better than nothing, I know there's a lot more he probably got away with.

But I'd take it. Because at least he's gone and unable to hurt me or any other girl.

While most of the guys took Wallace's leave well, there were some who called Danny out for what he'd done to get him kicked off the Dragons. They blamed him for their early season as if they should ignore the things they knew he'd been doing.

But his closest friends stuck by his side, and after a few months, Wallace ended up getting into serious trouble that nobody really knows the details of and was expelled from Lindon. That had people singing a whole different tune about cutting ties with him before that point.

"Our Danny Boy did it," Meadow says from my right, wrapping one of her arms around mine. "Seems like just yesterday he was telling us he was going to drop out of elementary school to join the circus."

Caroline laughs. "Those were the days."

Now that Danny has his degree in marketing, he's spending the summer doing an internship with my father and using it as credit for an independent study toward his master's in business. He was excited when Dad offered him the opportunity during one of our many FaceTime calls. When my father asked Danny what came next for him, grad school had been his second response to the inquiry. His first response had been, "Skylar."

Caroline tightens her arm around my waist and lets out a long sigh. "My baby is growing up. I can't believe I'm here right now. Soon enough, he'll have his own babies."

I sputter on air. "Um…"

Meadow laughs. "Stop trying to scare the girl, Carrie. Let them live their lives before you curse them with that responsibility."

I blame Danny for even making it seem like children are in our near future. When we were at Ocean Fest back in March, he offered to hold an eight-month-old while her mother was getting books signed, and our pictures were taken by a lot of people who kept asking us if the baby was ours. Ever since, he's been convinced it was a sign. But something tells me he'd think differently if the baby hadn't been sleeping peacefully the entire time.

Did that stop me from saving a few photos of him cradling the little girl to my phone? No. I still sneak peeks at them every so often because seeing the way Danny looked down at her bundled up made me picture something similar for us in the very, *very* distant future.

"He always did want a big family," his mother says as we watch Danny hug a few people in line next to him and clap a couple other people's hands as the next row of students make their way to the stage.

I know that same tidbit about her son after a long talk about contraceptives in the hotel room after the book signing. We were tired from the amount of walking we'd done all day and giddy from the people we got to meet, so we lay down in bed and talked about everything.

Us.

School.

The future.

Our future.

We made a pact.

To be patient.

To get through school together.

And to never give up on each other. No matter the disagreements. No matter the arguments. We both know nothing about dating is easy. It's about getting through it.

Like my friendship with Olive and the blossoming one between Aliyah and I since she told off Becca at the beginning of the semester and cut ties with her and Dee, I have a feeling this relationship with Danny is for the long term. Especially when he came with me to the therapist's office in the student center after I booked an appointment to finally talk to someone.

Sighing at his supportive nature, my focus goes to the man himself, who instantly finds my eyes in the crowd like he knows I'm watching him.

I smile.

He smirks and shoots me a wink.

And his mother squeezes me again like she thinks the same thing I do about what the future holds for me and her son.

After the ceremony, Danny and I walk side by side to see Caleb and Raine surrounded by a group of friends and family.

Caleb sinks down onto a knee.

I clench onto Danny's hand, feeling my heart thunder in my chest at what we're about to witness. I've only ever seen this sort of thing in movies.

"Will you marry me?" Caleb asks his long-time girlfriend.

Raine looks at the crowd wide-eyed before glancing back down at her boyfriend kneeling in front of her.

Slowly, her head shakes. "I'm sorry. I'm so sorry, Caleb."

People start muttering around us.

Danny cusses under his breath.

My jaw drops.

Raine whispers, "I can't."

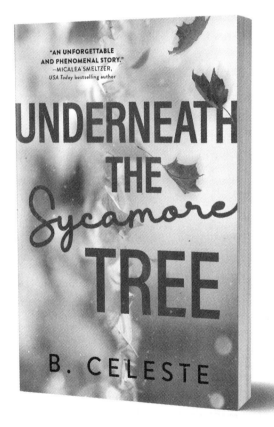

One

THERE'S A DEAD CLUMP of caramel hair resting in the palm of my porcelain hand. I run my chipped yellow nails over the once-silky strands and stare long and hard like I can somehow reattach them.

Two months ago, I tried dyeing it. The evidence of my failed attempt rests in my hand, a mixture of brown and blond undertones. It was a summertime project that Mama told me not to bother with. She insisted my hair was too brittle.

Like always, Mama was right.

Like always, I was too stubborn to listen.

Not only did my tender scalp burn from the dye, but my hair fell out minutes after applying the color. It left my blond strands in patches that Mama helped me rinse out.

Wrapping the evidence of my abnormality tight in my grasp, I stare at my reflection in the large mirror that hangs over the vanity. I see paleness. Baggy, glassy green-brown eyes. Narrowed cheekbones tinted pink but not from the expensive blush like Mama wore once upon a time. Mine is from my body's internal war on itself.

I've filled out since starting new medication last month. The doctor told me it should help regulate my system so I stop losing weight. My cheekbones aren't as prominent anymore, nowhere near as hollow and sickly. Instead of the three pills I was taking before leaving Bakersfield, I take nine. It's worth it, I suppose, to not look so skeletal.

Usually I keep my head down while I go about my morning routine. It's easier than seeing the way my collarbones stick out and my hair thinly frames my face. I hate seeing my reflection because I don't recognize the girl staring back.

Today I force myself to look. Dropping my fallen hair onto the granite countertop, I study what the mirror shows from the waist up. A sliver of my lean stomach peeks out from the blue tank top I sleep in. Travelling my gaze upward, I notice slim arms, narrow shoulders, all the way up to thin, chapped lips. Nothing about me is particularly beautiful, yet I still see Mama in my frailty.

For the longest time, she wouldn't look at me for more than a few seconds. Her eyes would find mine as she told me good morning or wished me a good day at school, but then they would quickly go anywhere else. Grandma would pat my hand and tell me not to let it get to me. It wasn't that easy though.

When Mama looked at me, she saw Logan and the possibility of another early funeral. I was always going to be a reminder that one of her daughters was dead, and for all she knew, I was mere steps behind.

So I called Dad.

Grandma told me I didn't have to move, but I knew it was for the best. I didn't want to know that Mama's eyes turned gold when she cried. They were always a shimmery, golden brown when I was around.

The mirror in front of me is bigger than the one in my old house. Unlike that old stained beige bathroom with chipped tiles, this one is light gray with hardwood floors and all new fixtures. Instead of a walk-in shower, I've got a large bathtub that could fit two sets of twins in it if necessary, and the amount of shelf space would have made Lo jealous.

A knock at my bedroom door pulls me away from my assessment. Brushing the loose hair into the white garbage can by the counter, I walk into the main room and hear Dad's voice on the other side of the door.

"Are you up, Emery?" His voice is gravelly and hesitant, a tone he's held since he helped unpack what little I brought with me from Mama's house to this one across the state.

Truthfully, I'm not sure why either he or Mama agreed. I only ever heard from him on my birthday and Christmas, and the conversation never lasted more than ten minutes if he could help it. He's remarried with a gorgeous wife who's the exact opposite of Mama in both looks and personality and a stepson who's broody and evasive no matter how hard I try getting to know him.

His life here was perfect.

Until me.

I open the door and give him a sleepy smile, which he returns easily. He tries to make me comfortable. His wife, Cam, has been nothing but sweet, and her son, Kaiden, despite his typical avoidance, could be worse. They've been welcoming since I arrived a month and a half ago, giving me anything I needed. A new doctor, a chance to decorate my room how I want, and space. Lots of space.

Dad works at a pharmaceutical company now. I don't remember much of him from when I was little, just the suits he wore and the way he would give Mama a chaste kiss if we were around or a simple nod if he thought we weren't looking. I never realized how unhappy they both were then.

This man doesn't look like the one I remember. His dark-brown hair is peppered with gray, especially around the ears, and his hairline is receding. The natural tan skin I've always been jealous of is slightly wrinkled, and his eyes have a dullness to them that I don't recall seeing in the past. Is that from age or circumstance?

"Cam has breakfast cooking." He rubs his arm, covered by a navy blazer, and gives me a weary look. "If you aren't up to going today..."

Today. The first day at a new school. It's my senior year even though I should have already graduated. After missing too many classes from hospital admissions, I was held back.

"I'll be fine." It's a weak reassurance that neither of us truly believes. It isn't a lie though. I won't be walking into a shark cage bleeding, so there are worse things to experience.

His gaze lingers, his eyes a light shade of brown with the same specks of emerald Mama told me I have. I don't see it when I look in the mirror though.

"Emery..."

I stand there, gripping the doorknob in my hand until my fingers hurt, waiting for him to say something.

He clears his throat. "Happy birthday."

Today. My nineteenth birthday.

The way Dad looks at me is like he's trying to see someone else. Maybe he wonders if Logan would have looked the same. It's been ten years since she passed, eleven since he left.

What does he remember of her?

Instead of asking, I swallow my inquiry and force a tight-lipped smile. "Thank you."

I told him I didn't want a party or even a special dinner. When I was younger, he and Mama would ask what we wanted for our birthdays—the meal was always our choice. Lo would always ask to go out, while I always asked to stay in. The cake was the same. Red velvet with white buttercream frosting.

Honestly, there was nothing I wanted from Dad now besides temporary shelter.

No home-cooked meal.

No red velvet cake.

Part of me feels like wanting anything from Dad is somehow cheating on Mama. Like forgiving him means I don't care that he left or hurt her or us. No matter what, he abandoned us when we needed him. When Lo needed him.

He tips his head, pauses, and then turns toward the downstairs. Kaiden's room is down the hall from mine, but he doesn't bother him. I wonder if he's already up and ready, an early riser. Sometimes I'll hear him leave his room late at night and watch him sneak out of the house.

I wonder where he goes. Or if Cam knows. Or if Dad does. It isn't my place to ask, so I leave it be.

It takes me fifteen minutes to throw on a pair of blue jeans with one of the knees ripped out and an oversize black sweater that falls off my shoulder. Running a brush through my tangled hair and leaving it loose, I note that it's finally passing my shoulders again. Mama would probably be happy to hear that; she always loved when Lo and I kept our hair long.

Slipping into a beige pair of Toms that have pineapples all over them, I grab my new black-and-white-checkered backpack and head downstairs. Dad is finishing up his breakfast because he has to leave for work, but Cam and Kaiden are both still working on theirs.

Cam greets me with a gentle smile, Kaiden doesn't look

at me at all, and Dad gives me a head bob before getting up and rinsing his plate off in the large stainless steel sink.

Their house is huge—two stories, plus a fully finished basement that's mostly used for storage. The outside is painted white, the windowsills on the bottom floor all have flowerpots attached with pink and purple plants, and the backyard stretches far enough to have a fire pit, garden, and grill area.

It isn't anything like the house I grew up in, especially inside. There's so much space to walk around in without tripping over furniture or people. Everything smells floral and fresh, and the modern matching style throughout every room differs from the rustic thrift store finds that litter Mama's house.

But I like Mama's house more.

It may have been small, but it made things more intimate. We could joke about tripping over the coffee table, which all of us had at some point. There was a bright green coat rack by the door that stuck out like a sore thumb against the pale yellow wallpaper that had little white and yellow stripes decorating the bottom half, and an orange bowl that keys, receipts, and other odds and ends always found their way into.

Mama's house is colorful, quaint.

Dad's house is…normal.

I never understood normal.

I'm playing with the scrambled eggs and bacon on my plate when Dad kisses Cam goodbye and tells Kaiden and me to have a good first day of school. We're both seniors.

Since I'm without a car, Kaiden is supposed to drive us and show me where the office is since Dad couldn't get time off to bring me to the school early and show me himself.

Cam tried getting Kaiden to take me last week to familiarize myself with the campus layout, but I didn't want him to feel obligated, so I lied and told her it was fine. Truth is, my heart is pounding so hard in my chest from nerves that I worry I'll die from a heart attack long before my disease does me in. If the room gets any quieter, they'd probably hear it drum an uneven tune.

I'm halfway done with my breakfast before I glance at the clock and then at Cam. She knows my worries and gives me a small smile before passing me a granola bar, money for lunch, and a signed piece of paper with Dad's name on the bottom.

For school records, she tells me.

Slipping everything into my bag, I ask Kaiden if he's ready. His response is nothing more than a grunt before he pushes away from the table, grabs his bag and car keys, and then gestures toward the front door.

He doesn't tell Cam goodbye.

She doesn't wish us a good day.

She just smiles sadly as we leave.

I want to ask Kaiden why he's so angry and won't talk. Cam seems like a nice woman, so I don't get why he acts so dismissive around her. I know better than to pry in other people's business. Then they'd have a right to pry in mine.

When we get to the school, I follow Kaiden inside from the student parking lot already packed with cars. He simply points in the direction of the office and shoots me a sarcastic "Good luck" over his shoulder before disappearing into a crowd of people who slap his back and greet him with big smiles while completely ignoring my existence.

Happy birthday to me.

ACKNOWLEDGMENTS

The biggest person I want to thank is the same person I dedicated this novel to. But first I want to tell you how this story came to be and why my real-life "Olive" means so much to me.

I wrote *Beg You to Trust Me* based on my own experiences at the first college I attended. My freshman year was not ideal. I got involved with the wrong kind of people who constantly tore me down with words and judgments. I was introverted and very, very shy, so I tried sticking to my roommate and some other girls who were a little more extroverted than me to attempt to come out of my shell.

Unfortunately, along the way, I lost myself. I realized too late that those girls I was trying to be like were not who I wanted to be. They made harsh comments about everything and judged people simply because they were different from them.

I spent my freshman year being bullied about my weight, my quiet personality, and everything in between. If guys showed me any attention, I was a whore. It didn't matter if I paid those guys any attention or not. If I kept to myself and tried to stay out of the drama, I was lame. Weird. Fake.

Like Skylar, I moved out of my very first dorm room and the environment that was making me stressed and sick. I thought it would be better for both myself and my roommate, but it only made things worse. And I'll take some responsibility for that. I hadn't been able to tell my roommate that I was leaving, and she walked in on me packing my things. Had I tried? Sure. Had I tried hard? No.

The truth is, there are a lot of conversations in this novel that happened in real life. Things that my former roommate said and things that were whispered about me behind my back. It got to the point where I didn't feel comfortable going out at all. Going to the dining hall made me feel like an anxious mess because I knew my roommate had been talking about me to anybody who would listen, and all I could feel were eyes on me.

If I'm being honest, this book changed drastically from the first draft to the one you read, because in the first version, Skylar was weak. She let everybody step on her. She never fought back. And the only reason I wrote her like that was because that was what I did. I sat down and took it until I chose to remove myself from that campus altogether. I transferred out and didn't look back.

Simply put, Skylar had no backbone, and nobody would have liked her. I needed to create somebody stronger than me. Somebody more people could relate to. And I needed to give her a support system.

I didn't have a Danny.

But I had an Olive—Olivia.

It wasn't until Olivia invited me to her wedding in the state I'd gone to college my freshman year that I realized how badly I needed to write this book. I needed to write my story in a way that would give me a sense of closure, especially before I went back to Vermont and saw some of the people I'd walked away from. Olivia included.

And I'm so glad I did because even though this story

was tough, it was necessary. I know there will be plenty of people who relate. People who can sense the deep emotions felt by Skylar and other characters.

So thank you, Olivia.

My Olive.

The person who made my freshman year a little less awful.

I don't think you realize just how much you saved me from self-destruction that year.

But hopefully you do now.

xx B

ABOUT THE AUTHOR

B. Celeste is a new adult and contemporary romance author who gives voices to raw, realistic characters with emotional storylines that tug on the heartstrings. She was born and raised in upstate New York, where she still resides with her four-legged feline sidekick, Oliver "Ollie" Queen. Her love for reading and writing began at an early age and only grew stronger after getting a BA in English and an MFA in English and creative writing. When she's not writing, she's working out, binge-watching reality game shows, and spending time with her friends and family.